NEW FROM LOVE SPELL

AN ANGEL'S TOUCH ROMANCES

The editors of *Love Spell* are proud to present An Angel's Touch Romances. Each heartwarming story will feature a beautiful heroine, a virile hero—and the heavenly being who brings them everlasting love.

Don't miss these unforgettable romances, which are sure to become time-cherished classics.

FOREVER ANGELS
Trana Mae Simmons
April 1995

DAEMON'S ANGEL
Sherrilyn Kenyon
May 1995

TIME HEALS
S

...and ma

Look

An Angel's Touch

Where angels go, love is sure to follow.

D1414799

THE BOOK SWAP
6618 GRAPEVINE HWY.
FT. WORTH, TX 76118
(817) 284-2513
AFTER YOU'VE READ IT
RETURN IT FOR CREDIT

An Angel's Touch ROMANCE

"Readers will remember Trana Mae Simmons's romances long after the last page has been read!"
—Michalann Perry

SOMEONE TO WATCH OVER ME

"Hurry, Michael. Use your powers. She's your assignment."

Michael glared directly at the bush, concentrating on making the roots hold. Tess swung her right leg back up to the trail, the heel of her hiking boot making firm contact with the packed earth.

Angela breathed a sigh of relief and glanced at him. "Michael! What's wrong?"

"I...ah...gadda...sn...ah...ah...Aahchoo!"

They both heard the bush roots give way and Tess's renewed scream as she tumbled over the edge of the trail.

Angela peered over the cloud, her total concentration on saving Tess from death. But Tess wasn't there!

"Oh, Michael, what have you done? You were supposed to keep her from getting killed!"

"Michael! Angela!" The voice boomed through the still air.

"Uh-oh." Michael's wings cringed against his shoulders.

Angela patted his sandy-gray head. "Come on. Let's stand up and face the music."

"Yeah," Michael grumbled. "What can Mr. G do? Kill us?"

Other *Leisure* and *Love Spell* Books by
Trana Mae Simmons:
BITTERSWEET PROMISES
MONTANA SURRENDER

Forever Angels

TRANA MAE SIMMONS

LOVE SPELL NEW YORK CITY

LOVE SPELL®

April 1995

Published by

Dorchester Publishing Co., Inc.
276 Fifth Avenue
New York, NY 10001

If you purchased this book without a cover you should be aware that this book is stolen property. It was reported as "unsold and destroyed" to the publisher and neither the author nor the publisher has received any payment for this "stripped book."

Copyright © 1995 by Trana Mae Simmons

All rights reserved. No part of this book may be reproduced or transmitted in any form or by any electronic or mechanical means, including photocopying, recording or by any information storage and retrieval system, without the written permission of the Publisher, except where permitted by law.

The name "Love Spell" and its logo are trademarks of Dorchester Publishing Co., Inc.

Printed in the United States of America.

To my sister, Ann Riddle. Angela wouldn't have been the same without you, Annie! And to my boys, Richard, David and Michael Riddle. All of you have a special place in my heart.

Forever Angels

Chapter One

New York City
July 30, 1994
9:00 p.m.

Angela watched Michael stare around the expensively decorated New York City office, a look of disgust on his face.

"I don't see how people can stand being cooped up inside four walls, reading books and papers all the time," he said. "Give me the open skies any day."

"Shhhh!" Angela whispered.

Michael glanced at her from across the cloud. "She can't see or hear us, unless we want her to."

Angela bristled slightly at the challenge in her pudgy, sandy gray-haired companion's voice, tensing her wings to keep them from fluttering in agitation.

"I know that. But you're supposed to be paying attention to your assignment, not complaining about where you have to perform it."

"Dash nab it!" Michael griped when he took a step forward and caught his toe on the hem of his white robe. He fluttered his wings frantically, barely righting himself before he tumbled straight into her and knocked them both off the cloud.

"I'm always tripping on this thing!" Michael growled, jerking on the skirt of his robe to raise it so he could stomp back from the edge of the cloud. "I'll never understand how women on earth walk in those danged long evening gowns."

"Please! Watch your language!"

"Now what'd I say?"

Angela sighed and shook her head. Probably she should look on it as a challenge, she supposed. After all, Michael had only decided he wanted a change in his angelic duties a week ago, while she had had eons of experience to pass on to him.

What in heaven had ever made Michael decide he wanted to be a *guardian* angel, she asked herself as she slipped a sideways look at him. She would just have to do the best she could to teach him what he needed to know, since tutoring him was her own assignment. And she was a bit grumpy herself, although she tried her best to suppress it by remembering that she'd had other slow-to-learn pupils over eternity.

Of course, part of her irritation lingered from the scene she and Michael had witnessed earlier in the day, Angela admitted. She looked down at the teary-eyed figure standing in front of the window in the office where she and Michael floated invisibly on their cloud. The darkness beyond the window mirrored the reflection in the glass pane.

Michael's first assignment wore a conservatively styled navy business suit, entirely proper attire for her position as an up-and-coming member of one of New York's oldest law firms. But she managed a touch here and there to confirm her femininity—a small ruffle of lace on her pale blue blouse and a fashionably short skirt that emphasized her long, slender legs.

During business hours she wore that glorious mass of auburn hair tightly cinched with a plain barrette, but she had pulled the barrette out over an hour ago to run her fingers through her hair and massage her scalp. Springy curls fell around her face and past her shoulders. Even in the vague window reflection Angela could see those lovely green eyes, misty now with unshed tears.

The woman stood in front of the window now—not the sharp-minded attorney who had clawed her way up from a poverty-stricken, male-dominated background to a career on the verge of culminating in a partnership in the firm. She would be the firm's only woman partner if she successfully litigated the case contained in the file folders spread over her desk. The founder of the firm himself had hinted strongly at what the reward would be in the staff meeting during which she had laid out her ideas for the defense of their client.

As a guardian angel, Angela had watched the long-overdue strides of women on earth with interest. She knew how much this career move meant to Tess Foster, the woman Michael was assigned to protect against harm.

But one thing hadn't seemed to change over the years: At times women still tried to pick their men with their minds instead of their hearts. Just look at how a bright woman like Tess Foster had become involved with that lout who was now her former fiancé.

Whoops; guardian angels weren't supposed to make judgments on the character of the people they observed in their assignments.

"Well, I can think of a word worse than lout to call that self-righteous fool," Michael responded when he read Angela's mind.

"Michael!" Angela shook her head and pursed her lips in disapproval.

"Uh-oh," Michael said, motioning her to silence. "I think she's had about enough of feeling sorry for herself. Look."

They crouched to peer over the edge of the cloud, their eyes wide with dismay as they watched Tess stride from the window and sweep the files from her desk. Papers flew around the room, but the heavy folders landed on the thick carpet without a sound. Tess clenched her jaws and aimed a kick at the nearest folder, smiling grimly when it skidded across the carpet and landed with a thump against the bookcases that lined one wall of her office.

"Boy, she's got a temper, hasn't she?" Michael whispered. "I'll bet she wishes that folder was her boyfriend's head."

"I can't say as I blame her," Angela admitted. "Oh dear, there she goes. Come on."

Grabbing Michael by the hand, Angela whisked them both through the door a second after Tess slammed it.

Adirondack Mountains
New York State
July 31, 1994
6:00 a.m.

She wasn't going to cry. Damn it, she was *not* going to cry again!

After an all-night drive, Tess steered her little station wagon into the Keene Valley parking lot just after daybreak and pulled into a marked space. She shut off the engine and leaned her head back against the seat, breathing deeply of the clear mountain air flowing through her open window.

After what had happened yesterday afternoon she needed this trip desperately. The tall buildings in the city had crowded in on her—the noxious exhaust fumes tainting the air she breathed deepening her depression. Trying to force herself to concentrate on reviewing the files in preparation for the imminent trial had proved useless. Only here, in the Adirondack wilderness area that reminded her so much of the West Virginia mountains, Granny, and home, could the healing start.

"Tess Foster. Haven't seen you up here in a while, Tess. Are you all right?"

She took a firm hold on her emotions and opened her eyes, reaching for the door handle. "I'm fine, Freddy," she told the red-haired ranger as she climbed out of the car. "I was just enjoying the cool air."

"I hear it's hot as blazes in the city," he said with a grin. "I feel sorry for you folks back there. Not sorry enough to come visit you, though. You ought to get out of that rat race more often."

"I will . . . from now on." She opened the wagon back and lifted out her backpack, slinging it over her shoulder as she started up the hiking trail.

"How are the trails?" she asked.

"Where you headed?"

"As far as I can go in a day."

"Figured that, knowing you. Well, we've closed some of the higher trails to less-experienced hikers. Had some slides after that rain last week. You'll probably be all right, though, as long as you're careful."

"Then I guess I'll head up the Range Trail—plan on spending the night on Mt. Marcy."

"Beautiful trail." Freddy nodded and made a notation on the clipboard in his hand. "Watch your step going down Saddleback. It can get rough there near some of the cliff faces."

"I will."

"See you tomorrow evening then. Have a good hike."

Several hours later Tess brushed away yet another tear and blinked angrily as she trudged up Saddleback Mountain's eastern slope. Pausing for a second, she leaned against a tree and gazed out over the scenic vista on her left, hoping some of the pristine beauty would work its magic and soothe her shattered spirit.

Far below, a tiny road snaked through the valley, barely visible from this height. The bright sun had long ago burned off any lingering mists, yet the breeze counteracted the heat. The wind whispered through the treetops for the most part, a faint accompaniment to the bird and squirrel chatter.

Maybe she should have stayed on the Johns Brook Trail, since she hadn't hiked in a while. She could already feel a slight strain in her calves from the climb. Johns Brook was definitely safer than the Range, but there she would have rubbed elbows with dozens of other backpackers. At least up here she had a measure of solitude.

And besides, the very safety of the Brook Trail negated any chance of a hiker having a view as beautiful as this, where huge pines and birch covered the slope below. Higher on the surrounding mountain peaks the trees thinned out, allowing a view of scenery so beautiful, it almost made the eyes ache.

Tess frowned, as though it were the view's fault that another tear trickled down her cheek.

Hell, it wasn't really a total surprise. Things had begun to fall apart almost as soon as Robert slipped the diamond on her finger.

She turned back up the trail and immediately stumbled on a jutting rock, wincing at the pain in her toe. This was stupid. She'd better watch out or she'd tumble down the mountainside. Freddy wouldn't let her back up here if he had to come rescue her.

She readjusted her backpack, which had slipped sideways when she stumbled. When she lowered her hand a sun streak shot into her eye, and she glared at the engagement ring. Now it seemed rather ostentatious, but she had been so proud of it at first. Proud of Robert too. And, yes, just a little bit proud of herself for making such a catch—a man who epitomized the dream of the perfect husband she had carried in her mind for so long.

Robert, so tall and blond, with blue eyes that gazed at her as though she were the only woman worth noticing in a room full of stunning women. Trouble was, he made any woman he spoke to feel the same way.

Robert, from old money and old blood lines traced all the way back to a ship arriving just years after the *Mayflower*—and, oh, so very proud of that too. No one mentioned that the first Stuyvesant might have been an indentured servant—or a convict sent to America as his punishment—since no trace of Robert's side of the family could be found in England. Instead, the family insisted that, at the very worst, Gerald Stuyvesant might have been the bastard son of a titled family.

Robert, whose usually unlined brow creased in puzzlement when Tess adamantly refused even to consider signing the prenuptial agreement that was handed to her in his attorney's office yesterday. After all . . .

She swiped at another stray tear trailing down her cheek. After all, Robert's somewhat high-pitched voice echoed in her head, she couldn't expect to have any claim to the money that had been in his family for so many generations if their marriage failed. And, though he loved her with every fiber of his being, who knew what the future might bring? Surely she didn't think that if for some silly reason he slipped and had a one-night stand, she would be able to make him pay by giving up half his trust fund. Not that it would ever happen, Robert had assured her.

"Why did I ever think it would work?" she muttered. "Hell, he's never been backpacking in his life, and I can't stand to go even a month without some time in the wilderness. I get seasick—he loves sailing. Okay, so we both love to ride. But I can't stand those damned English saddles, and I'll be double damned if I ever learn to *post* when my horse trots!"

She paused for breath when she realized she was gasping her words because of the exertion of her too-fast climb as her feet pounded in time to her angry words. She'd never make the peak without a long rest if she didn't start pacing herself.

Sweeping a lock of hair from the side of her face, she glared at a chattering squirrel sitting on an overhanging limb on the trail.

"That stupid agreement just brought all the doubts I'd been having about the entire engagement together," she told the squirrel. "He didn't even tell me ahead of time why he wanted me to meet him there! Funny thing is, I was tempted to sign it, just so I wouldn't have to face the fact that it was over. To try to prove to him that I wasn't interested in his damned money."

The squirrel swished its tail at her and scurried away through the treetops, leaping from limb to limb. A bright blue jay swooped from its perch, its loud squawks of "Thief! Thief!" signaling its displeasure at being disturbed by Tess and the squirrel.

"Oh, shoot," she mumbled as she hung her head. Glancing down at her hand, she quirked her lips wryly and slowly reached for the diamond. With a deep sigh she twisted the ring from her finger and stared at it for a moment, moving it back and forth in a ray of sunlight.

She finally slipped the ring into a pocket in her tight denims and bent slightly forward to resume her walk up the mountain trail.

Oklahoma Territory
July 31, 1893

"If you're here for the reason I think you are, Tillie Peterson, you can turn that damned buggy right back around and head for town!"

"You're well aware of why I'm here, Stone Chisum! You have to listen to reason. Those children will be better off with their own people."

"*Those children* are *my* children, legally adopted and mine to raise. Some misguided busybody's not going to interfere in my family!"

Mrs. Peterson tightened her fat fingers around the reins and huffed out an indignant puff of breath. "How dare you!"

"I'll dare whatever I have to in order to protect my kids," Stone said in a steely voice.

"Oh!" Mrs. Peterson's washed-out blue eyes crinkled malevolently. "And I suppose if I try to argue with you any more, you'll strap on that gun you used to wear and shoot me with it!"

"It's temptin'," Stone said with a malicious smile. "Mighty temptin'."

"You wouldn't dare!"

"I used to get paid for not backing down from dares when I wore that gun, lady. And you're pushin' it. Now, are you going to leave, or should I help you on your way?"

"That adoption is only legal under Indian law, for whatever good that will do you. You haven't petitioned the U.S. courts." Mrs. Peterson gave him back his malicious smile, which somehow fell short when it warred with her wobbling triple chins.

"When Oklahoma becomes a state I'll be one of the first ones in court. Right now, Indian law's good enough for me." Stone narrowed his eyes. "I'll bet that horse can run pretty good, even pulling a load like you. If it got spooked, that is."

"You . . . I refuse to let you intimidate me, Stone Chisum!"

Rain Shadow chuckled with amusement as he slipped away from the side of the cabin and headed toward the hill in back. He wasn't really afraid of that nosy old woman. His pa, Stone, would take care of her. After all, didn't his and Flower's Cherokee grandfather call Stone by the name Man Who Walks With Right?

Rain Shadow winked at Mountain Flower as he passed, and his sister shook her head as she dunked a sheet into rinse water.

"Are you done with your chores?" Flower asked.

"You better believe it," he replied. "You don't think I'd be going hunting if I wasn't, do you? Pa would skin me alive."

"No he wouldn't." Flower laughed. "But he might take away that gun you're so proud of, so you couldn't hunt for a while. He's not going to be in a very good mood after Mrs. Peterson leaves."

His face puckered into a sudden scowl. "Flower, you don't think there's any chance the stupid white man's court will try to take us away from Pa, do you?"

"I don't know, Rain." Flower shrugged. "I try not to worry about it. Pa always tells us that nothing is going to break up our family. But we're half white, as well as half Cherokee. I don't know if that makes us bound by white law too."

"Pa will handle it," he said in a positive voice. He shifted his rifle to his shoulder and headed toward the corral. "I'll be back in time for evening chores," he called to Flower over his shoulder.

Adirondack Mountains
July 31, 1994

"I wonder what's going to happen now?" Michael asked.

"You know as well as I do that neither one of us is allowed to know what will happen." Angela sighed. "All you need to know is that your job is to stay near Tess and watch over her—make sure she doesn't slip up and let something foolish happen to her body before it's time for her spirit to leave it."

Michael flapped his wings to follow Angela when she drifted toward another cloud. He shot straight through the fluffy mass and spread his wings wide to halt his plummeting descent. When he glanced up at the cloud he saw Angela peering down at him, shaking her head.

"I can't believe that all through eternity you haven't learned to have better control over your wings, Michael," she said in a scolding tone. "Surely you know that flying is more thinking than flapping."

"Flying's more thinking than flapping," Michael repeated in a mimicking voice. He restrained the urge to shoot back up to the cloud and whisk right by that blond head, scaring Angela into tumbling backwards. Instead, he gently waved his wings, making a perfect landing beside her. "Look, this end of the business is all new to me. I'm trying to keep an eye on my assignment down there, listen to you, and fly all at the same time! That makes me clumsy, because I've never had to concentrate on several things at once before!"

He caught the smirk of satisfaction Angela tried to hide at his indirect admission of her superior experience, deciding to ignore that unangel-like lapse on her part. Besides, he was feeling a bit peevish toward his companion right now, and peevishness could be called an undesirable trait too. They had to work together while he was in training for his new position, and he'd been assured Angela was a very capable teacher when he had finally decided which new assignment he was going to ask for.

"What were your duties before you decided you wanted a change?" Angela asked. "You never said."

"And you never asked," Michael growled, still grumpy. The slight hint of hauteur in her voice overrode his resolve to get along with his teacher. "All you've got on your mind is how much more experience you have than me at being a guardian angel—and how much fun it is to laugh at my clumsiness while you boss me around."

"Oh!" Angela said with an indignant sniff. "I'm not bossing you around." Michael glanced at her with a disbelieving look, and she continued, "Well, I'm not! I'm just trying to be helpful."

"You can be helpful without sounding so dad-blasted superior."

"Michael, *please* watch your language."

"Michael, watch your language," Michael mocked. "Michael, I can't believe you haven't learned to control your wings better. Michael, you're tripping on your gown. Gosh darn it, Angela, you've been at this business lots longer than me. Give me a break."

"I never said a word about you tripping on your gown," Angela defended herself. "And you're the one who decided you wanted to be a guardian angel. Would you rather go back and try something else?" she added somewhat hopefully.

"What? Lay around all day and think up creative ideas for the writers on earth to write about or pretty pictures for artists to paint? I don't have any feelings one way or the other about a Van Gogh over a Picasso. Maybe I ought to help cook up meals to tickle everyone's tongue? Grow pretty flowers? I looked at all those options and at some others when I got tired of what I was doing. But I didn't count on feeling like a newly arrived spirit who had to be led around by the nose and shown the ropes."

"Oh, Michael." Angela's laughter tinkled in the blue sky. "I'm sorry; really I am. I'll try to be more patient. Was introducing newly arrived spirits what you did before?"

Somewhat mollified, Michael nodded. "I guess that's what made me want to be a *guardian* angel. Those poor human spirits arrived pretty rattled and confused. I liked guiding them through their confusion, and I was always interested in the lives they'd lived. I figured it'd be even more interesting working more closely with people who were still living."

"Surely you had to help the human spirits learn to control their ability to fly. . . ."

Michael glared at her, and Angela quickly bit off her words. "Uh . . . well, I'm sure you'll come along with practice."

In the middle of carefully negotiating the rock-strewn trail halfway down the backside of Saddleback Mountain, Tess glanced skyward. Funny how the breeze sometimes soughed through the tall pines, almost sounding like human laughter.

Suddenly her left foot slid on a moss-covered rock and her ankle twisted cruelly in a rut beside the rock. She screamed in pain while she windmilled her arms and desperately tried to maintain her equilibrium. Overbalanced by the backpack, she stumbled nearer the edge of the trail.

Fear joined the pain in her mind. The injured ankle gave way and she fell, her legs hanging over the precipice. Grabbing a bush, she hung on for dear life and tried to swing her body back to the trail.

She didn't dare look down. That steep cliff face ran several hundred yards down the mountainside. The heavy pack dragged on her slender back, the pull of gravity making her sob in terror and cling to the bush until the rough bark cut into her palms.

The roots of the bush slowly began giving way and she screamed again in panic.

"Hurry, Michael. Use your powers. She's your assignment."

"Okay. Okay. Don't rush me. I'm trying to . . ."

"There's no time!"

He glared directly at the bush, concentrating on making the roots hold. For a second it looked as if he'd accomplished his task. Tess swung her right leg back up to the trail, the heel of her hiking boot making firm contact with the packed earth.

Angela breathed a sigh of relief and glanced at him. "Michael! What's wrong?"

"I . . . ah . . . gadda . . . sn . . . ah . . . ah . . . AAH-CHOO!"

They both heard the bush roots give way and Tess's renewed scream as she tumbled over the edge of the trail.

No matter what the rules, Angela had to interfere! She peered over the cloud, her total concentration on saving Tess.

But Tess wasn't there!

Angela blinked in surprise. The ledge on the side of the mountain that she had conjured up was there, close enough to the top of the trail for Tess not to have been too badly injured when she hit. And close enough to allow her to climb back onto the trail.

But no Tess!

"Oh, Michael, what have you done?"

"Me? You jumped in and used your powers! This was supposed to be my assignment."

"You were supposed to keep her from getting killed! You lost your concentration when you sneezed. No human body could have lived through that fall."

"MICHAEL! ANGELA!" The voice boomed through the still air.

"Uh-oh." Michael's wings cringed against his shoulders.

She gave his sandy-gray head a comforting pat. "Come on. Let's stand up and face the music."

"Yeah," Michael grumbled. "What can Mr. G do? Kill us?"

She giggled softly and stood, her toes clenched in the fluffiness beneath her the only sign of her timorousness. Michael sighed deeply and joined her.

Chapter Two

Oklahoma Territory
July 31, 1893

Rain squinted against the sun's glare and propped his rifle against a tree. Raising his arms, he rubbed the heels of his hands against his eyes, then cautiously peeked through his lashes.

She was still there. Now she was sitting up and rubbing the heels of her hands against her own eyes. She hadn't been there a second ago. Instead, he had been aiming at a wild turkey, visions of a toasty brown drumstick dancing in his mind. The turkey was long gone now, after emitting a confused gobble of surprise and disappearing over the hill.

And look at those clothes she was wearing. Once Flower had dared to wear a pair of his old pants, insisting to Pa that her long skirts got in the way when she did her chores. Pa had squashed that idea right off. And Rain's old pants on Flower were baggy, not skintight.

Suddenly a cloud materialized over the woman's head, then disappeared in a blink. Rain's eyes widened. He could have sworn the other lady—the one he'd had a brief glimpse of on that cloud—had seen him too.

No, he hadn't imagined it. But there were still almost two years to go before he would return to his grandfather and prepare to seek his vision—the vision that would lead him into complete manhood at age twelve. He didn't dare try to speak to a spirit on his own before then.

Rain studied the woman sitting on the trail again. That pack on her back looked awfully heavy. And what were those sticks the straps were wrapped around made of? Not wood, like the packs Indian women still used sometimes.

The woman shrugged out of the pack, then bent to rub at her leg.

Were those boots on her feet? None like Rain had ever seen. Bulky, they came to just above her ankles.

The cloud appeared again, but the woman on the trail didn't seem to notice. She started unlacing her left boot, her head bent nearly to her knee.

Rain looked at the cloud, and the blond-haired woman in the flowing white robe waved her wings and placed her index finger against her lips, winking at him. Rain nodded in return.

Maybe these were white men's spirits, rather than Indians'. But white or Indian, the spirits weren't to be discussed without the proper fasting beforehand and reverence for their spiritual state. His grandfather, Silver Eagle, had told Rain that more than once. Silver Eagle, a shaman, should know.

Angela wasn't surprised that the boy could see her. Lots of children could see angels. The boy still looked young enough—probably around ten. Usually by their teens, children had picked up enough stress to deal with in their lives to have lost their childish wonderment and closed their minds to things they couldn't explain.

She sat down on the cloud. No telling how long it would be until Michael joined her again. He hadn't had to use the time-travel abilities angels have in his former assignment, and in order for him to follow her now, someone else would have to show him how to enact that power. She had to follow a very direct order to keep an eye on Tess until Michael showed up.

A thought crossed Angela's mind, and she glanced overhead. She sure was glad Michael hadn't slipped and used that somewhat irreverent name during their attempts to explain how their lapse had allowed Tess to fall into that time warp. Mr. G, indeed!

Tess stared at her hiking boot, biting her lower lip against the pain and debating whether to loosen the laces or try to pull them more snug. The ankle felt broken, but maybe it was just a bad sprain. Either way, it would probably be less painful if she wrapped it in the elastic bandage in her pack.

Still, Freddy wouldn't look for her until tomorrow evening, and it would be easier to try to get back up to the trail with the support of her boot.

At least someone else might come by there. Other hikers might miss her down on this ledge if she happened to fall asleep, which seemed likely, given the fact that she hadn't slept last night.

"You should take off your boot before your foot swells. Otherwise the boot will have to be cut off, and you won't be able to wear it again. Boots cost a lot of money."

Tess's head had swung up at the first word. She blinked eyes misty with unshed tears of pain to try to clear her vision. The little boy crouched a few feet away, and her eyes swept over him, disbelieving.

What in the world was a child doing hunting on a hiking trail? An Indian child, wearing a plaid shirt—not the T-shirts children usually wore. His hair didn't look too out of the ordinary. A leather band held back the long, black locks from his face, but even young children these days set their own hairstyles.

No wonder she hadn't heard him approach. He wore moccasins on his feet. She slid a sideways glance at the rifle held upright in the boy's right hand. That definitely had no place on a hiking trail.

"Look," she began in a tentative voice, "I'm darned glad you're here, but there's no hunting on this mountain. Where are your parents?"

"Mountain?" the boy repeated in a puzzled voice. He turned his head to study the area around him. "You must be from pretty flat land if you think this is a mountain, instead of a hill."

She followed his gaze and her jaw dropped. Where the hell was she? Rocks and brush littered the hillside, intermingled with jack pine and spruce, not huge white pines, white ash, and red cedar. Suddenly she became aware of the stifling heat—not cool mountain air.

She swiveled her head to the left and fearfully glanced upwards, hoping against hope to see the hiking trail snaking down Saddleback Mountain. Instead she saw more brush and what could have been a tumbleweed, caught between two bushes.

A faint sound down the hillside drew her attention, and she gazed over the little boy's shoulder. Snuggled in the valley below sat a log cabin. A small figure struggled to drape what looked like a large white sheet over a clothesline in the backyard. An unpaved road led away from the front of the cabin, and Tess licked suddenly dry lips with a powdery tongue when she saw a horse trotting down the road, pulling a black buggy.

"The dirt roads around here are all jeep trails," she said, a corner of her mind still hoping to deny that she wasn't on the mountain, though her eyes refused to leave the incongruous vision of the horse and buggy. "Why is there a buggy on that road down there?"

"A jeep?" he questioned. "I don't know what that is, but that's Mrs. Peterson's buggy. And if you ever saw her, you'd know she has to drive a buggy 'cause she couldn't ever climb on a horse. Poor horse, if she did."

Tess took a determined breath. "All right. I don't know how it happened, but somehow I've stumbled onto a movie set. If you'll just go get someone from the crew to help me, I'll get out of the way and go to a hospital, so they can x-ray my ankle. Still," she continued in a musing voice, "what the hell did they do with the mountain? How far down that mountainside did I fall?"

"You didn't fall," the youngster said. "You just . . ." He shrugged his shoulders. "You just appeared."

"What!?" she jerked her head around and stared at the little boy in amazement. "What do you mean—I just *appeared?*"

"You scared the turkey away, too, and I was almost ready to shoot it. Good thing I saw you before I squeezed the trigger, or I might have shot you. And what's a movie?"

"Oh, good grief. You know darned well what movies are. Just like the one they're obviously shooting here. Where is everyone else?"

"You sure use funny words. There aren't even words in Cherokee like the ones you use. And there's no one else around here. Just my sister and my pa, down at our cabin. You saw Mrs. Peterson leaving. What kind of animal is a movie? Is it good to eat if I can shoot one?"

She gritted her teeth, both against the pain in her ankle and her fast-evaporating patience. "Let's start over again. My name is Tess. Tess Foster. And you are . . . ?"

"Rain Shadow. But after I seek my vision, my name will probably change."

"Your vision?"

"Uh-huh. When I'm twelve. Grandfather said his name was Running Cub while he grew up, but now it's Silver Eagle."

"Silver Eagle?"

"My grandfather," the boy repeated patiently. "He's a shaman."

"Okay. Look, Rain . . . uh . . . Rain Shadow . . ."

"It's just Rain, since you're a white woman. Whites only use one word of their name when they talk to each other. My sister is Mountain Flower, but Pa just calls her Flower."

"I see." She really didn't, but this conversation wasn't making a lick of sense. "And what's your father's name?"

"He doesn't ever use his Indian name, even though he's got one that my grandfather gave him. Pa's name is Stone Chisum. He used to be a gunfighter, but he gave that up when he adopted Flower and me. 'Course, he really wasn't a gunfighter. He was a sheriff, and then a marshal. People just called him a gunfighter sometimes, because he was faster than anyone else with his gun."

Tess shook her head, her curls swirling around her face. She blew back a stray strand from her forehead, then bent to lay her forehead on her knee. Her ankle throbbed, and she tentatively rubbed her fingers above the pain.

"Pa said it was time to give up guns, anyway," Rain continued. "He said the country was gettin' civ . . . civilized now. Even Geronimo agreed to live on a reservation. Why, Pa says that one of these days a lot of men won't even know how to shoot a gun. Those that do will just use them to hunt animals."

Her head snapped up. "What are you talking about?"

"Guns?" Rain asked.

"No. What did you say about G . . . Geronimo?"

"He's Apache, not Cherokee, but I know about him. He was the last Indian to go onto a reservation with his people. Pa says there's talk of him getting permission to go around the country with

Buffalo Bill's Wild West Show. He promised we'd go see that, if it ever came close enough."

"Rain, Geronimo's been dead for years!"

"Gee, you must be pretty dumb in history. Flower and me, we like history best when we study. Pa says that's good, because he doesn't want us to ever forget our Indian heri . . . history."

She sat in stunned silence. The little boy sounded like he meant it—like he believed every word. His brown eyes met her gaze without a trace of evasiveness.

She stared around her again. Where in the world had she landed when she fell? She darned sure wasn't on Saddleback Mountain. But she had to be. She couldn't have traveled through space.

"Rain." No, she couldn't ask that. It was outlandish even to allow such a crazy thought into her mind!

The little boy must be an actor, thoroughly immersed in his role. Hadn't she read somewhere that the really good actors—the ones who won Academy Awards—sometimes had trouble returning to reality after taking on a demanding movie role? Wasn't he awfully young to have learned that immersion technique, though? But then, what did she know about acting?

A blackout: She must have hit her head when she fell—had a blackout, as she'd heard alcoholics did at times—or amnesia? Somehow she had wandered away from the mountain afterwards.

She remembered falling, though, just as if it was a minute or so ago. She remembered who she was—and the only pain was in her ankle, not her head. Frowning in concentration, she played over the moments during her fall. The debilitating fear when she plunged over the mountainside—the gasp of relief when she grabbed the bush.

Her inability to swing her leg back up to the hiking trail—then . . . a sneeze? She definitely remembered a sneeze, and had thought that any second someone would hear her struggles and help her. But then the bush roots had given away and terror had crowded her mind as she fell.

She remembered . . . a tunnel? Yes, darn it, a tunnel of blackness. She'd swept through it as though floating on an air current. Then there had been more blackness until she realized she was sitting here on this hillside which, after the little Indian boy arrived, she'd confirmed was definitely not Saddleback Mountain.

She *had* to have blacked out—hopped a train—or a plane—nothing else made sense. During her blackout she had traveled to . . . Where the hell was she?

"Rain, what day is it?"

"Saturday," he said promptly. "Flower and I don't have to take classes from Pa on Saturday and Sunday, just during the week."

Good. Or was it? It had been Saturday morning when she started up the hiking trail. If it was still Saturday, and from the looks of the sun, still just early in the afternoon, how had she traveled this far? Had she been in the depths of the blackout for a week?

"What . . . what date is it, Rain?"

"July thirty-first. In white man's time. Flower and I tell time in Indian, too."

The same day!

"Uh . . . uh . . . what year is it?" she forced out around a gulp. "In . . . in white man's time?"

"Gee, you sure ask dumb questions."

"Please, Rain," she whispered.

"I'm sorry." Rain ducked his head. "Pa says we're never supposed to say something like that to our elders. Saying they're dumb, I mean. And I said it twice. You've got a right to be mad at me. Grandfather would punish me, too, if he heard me."

"Please, what year?" she repeated.

"It's 1893. In Cherokee, it's the year of . . ."

"Rain, say that again. Slowly. Please."

The boy frowned at her. "It's 1893," he said a little louder.

"Not . . . not 1994?"

"Heck, no. That's a hundred and one years from now. Flower and I are good in arithmetic, too."

"Where's your brother, Flower?" Stone asked as he walked up to the clothesline.

"Where do you suppose?" she smiled.

"Hunting, of course," Stone said, returning her smile. "You're not supposed to be working today, either. Just your regular chores. There's time enough for washing and cleaning during the week."

"I just did this one load. We didn't have any clean sheets."

"The beds don't need changing until Monday."

"Oh, you never know. What if company drops by?"

"About the only overnight company we have out here is someone from your tribe, Flower. And they bring their own bedding with them. Fact is, they even bring a tepee to sleep in, except for Silver Eagle. He leaves a tepee in our barn to sleep in when he comes. But they'd all be insulted if you offered them clean sheets."

"That's true," Flower said with an enigmatic smile.

"Honey, you're only twelve. You need a couple of days' rest each week, just like Rain. Why don't you go for a ride? Rain and I'll help you with the wash on Monday, like always."

"Come with me, Pa. Let's both go. We haven't been riding together all summer. Let's ride up the hill and see if Rain managed to get us any fresh meat for Sunday dinner."

Stone studied his daughter closely. That dress was a mile too short, and when had she started budding on top? Damn, had he been that busy all summer—too busy to notice Flower growing up right under his nose? He'd promised himself that he'd never let that happen—never let his son and daughter grow up neglected. It was definitely time to ride over to the Widow Brown's place and have her make Flower some new clothing.

"Rain'll have a fit if we ride up there and scare off his game."

"No, he won't. He'll be glad of an excuse to hunt some more. Anyway, we'll be careful."

"I suppose if Rain doesn't get anything, you're going to insist that I chop off the chicken's head again."

"Uh huh."

"All right, if you promise to make dumplings. But I think it would be a better idea for us to ride over to Widow Brown's. I brought a couple of bolts of material out from town that last trip—"

"We can go over there tomorrow," Flower interrupted, ignoring his frown at her lack of manners. "Let's ride up and look for Rain. Please, Pa? It's my free time, too, and I'd rather go up the hill."

"You act like there's something more up there than just maybe a dead deer for us to help Rain drag home."

"You never know, Pa. You never know."

Chapter Three

"Stop!" Tess said with a squeak.

"Shhhh." Rain laid a finger on his lips, then slowly brought the rifle to his shoulder.

The loud blast so close to her ear was the last sound she heard for several everlasting seconds. Finally the wall of silence receded, and she glared at Rain.

"What the hell do you think you're doing?"

"Pa says ladies shouldn't cuss. He threatened to wash Flower's mouth out with soap one day when he heard her use a bad word."

"Oh, and little boys are allowed to cuss, huh?"

"Nope," he denied. "At least, not until we get older."

"Where are you going?"

"I've gotta bleed the deer. If I don't, the meat will spoil. I'll be back in a few minutes."

"I keep telling you, it's not hunting season!"

"You didn't say that. You said that I shouldn't be hunting here, but I don't know why not. It's Pa's land. And there's no season on hunting. It's just whenever you run out of meat."

"Animals have young in the summer. What if that deer you shot had a baby somewhere?"

"It was a buck, not a doe."

She couldn't refute that, since she'd been too darned scared to look where Rain was aiming.

"I gotta get over there now, Miss Foster. Oh, you're probably thirsty, since it's so hot. There's a canteen in my pack." Rain removed the pack from around his waist and handed it to her. "Don't worry. I'll be right back."

"Rain, don't leave me, please! I can't walk. . . ."

But she found herself calling to Rain's retreating back as he scrambled across the hillside. Gritting her teeth, she shut her mouth and put down the boy's pack in order to concentrate on removing her boot.

She tugged the left leg of her denims up past her swollen ankle and groaned in dismay. Already her leg was discolored and swollen, protruding over the top of the boot. She should have removed the boot first thing, instead of sitting there talking to a boy who insisted it was a hundred and one years earlier than it actually was.

She glanced around her again. It darned sure wasn't Saddleback Mountain. But she would be just as crazy as that poor little boy appeared to be if she let herself even start to believe it could possibly be 1893, despite her lingering remembrance of that dark tunnel. It had to have been just a trick of her mind to shut out the pain and the realization that she was plummeting toward certain death.

She licked at a drop of sweat dribbling down her cheek. The salty taste lingered on her tongue, and she glanced at Rain's pack. A drink of water would taste awfully good right now. She didn't bother carrying water in her own pack, since there were water pumps at the various campsites in the Adirondacks.

Picking up the pack again, she untied the flap and spread the opening. There was the canteen. She pulled it out and unscrewed the top. After wiping the spout with her shirt cuff she drank several swallows of surprisingly cool water. The boy must have filled the canteen recently.

As she started to replace the canteen in the pack, she automatically scanned the other contents. Several extra shells—some rope—a tattered comic book. She lifted the comic out and read the title, *The Adventures of Wild Bill Hickock,* with a smile. Rain evidently liked to read as he whiled away the hours watching for game.

Her hand rustled against a newspaper when she stuck the comic back in the pack. Probably Rain carried it to clean game, she guessed, recalling that her own brothers had sometimes spent entire days out hunting. They would clean the game at times and roast it over a fire for meals.

A newspaper. No, damn it, she wasn't going to look at that paper, for the very same reason she had refused to open the comic and see when it had been printed.

She spread out the paper but closed her eyes

tightly. She couldn't seem to stop herself from crinkling a corner in her fingers and listening to the crisp crackle of fairly new paper.

Oh, shoot. She slit her eyes and stared down at the date on the paper: July 17, 1893. Before she could make an even bigger fool of herself she rapidly recreased the paper and shoved it back into the pack.

A movie set. It had to be a movie set. But they'd sure gone to a hell of a lot of trouble to make everything on it so authentic!

Angela blinked her eyes once, then again. The image beside her on the cloud wavered, became clearer, then disappeared again.

Well, she guessed Michael was learning to travel through time a lot faster than the other objectives she had tried to teach him. Or . . . she frowned slightly. Maybe he had a better teacher than her. Maybe that black-haired angel. What was her name?

Serena. All right, she had known the other angel's name all along. And jealousy was definitely not a guardian-angel trait. She quickly wiped the traitorous emotion from her mind.

Oh, who was coming now? She didn't understand at all why the people living on earth so enjoyed watching movies and television—especially those things they called soap operas. Real life was so much more interesting.

Hadn't Michael said something like that—about enjoying people? At least they had that in common.

* * *

Stone wrapped his fingers more tightly around the reins and pulled back the gelding's head against its chest.

"Settle down, darn it!"

"You should've brought Bay Boy instead of Silver Mane, Pa." Flower giggled. "You aren't enjoying this ride very much on him."

"Well, this one's got to be ridden if he's ever going to turn into a decent cow pony," he replied. "And you should have named him Hard Head, instead of Silver Mane. We can forget about not scaring off any of Rain's game while I'm riding this jughead."

"I heard a shot while we were saddling up. I'll bet Rain's already got something."

"Probably," he agreed. "He usually doesn't miss."

His horse rounded a bend in the trail, and Stone unconsciously jerked roughly on the reins. The gelding reared abruptly, then pounded its front feet back to earth and humped its back, lashing out with its hind legs.

Stone flew over Silver Mane's head, cursing his unresponsive muscles and carrying an inconceivable vision in his mind. Rolling his body to lessen the impact, he tumbled several feet, then sat up a bare yard from a pair of astonished emerald eyes in a face that jolted his senses with its beauty.

"Goddamn it to hell! Who the hell are you?"

Flower quickly slid from her saddle and ran to him. "Are you hurt, Pa?"

With a wrench he tore his eyes away from the green ones. "Just my dignity, honey."

But, despite the concern in Flower's voice, she wasn't looking at him. Her brown eyes rounded in wonder. Her mouth agape, she stared at the woman on the trail.

"Hello," his daughter said in a soft voice.

"H . . . hello," the woman replied. "Are you two part of the movie crew, too? Oh, please, tell me you're part of the movie crew."

Chapter Four

"What's a movie?" the young girl asked.

"Oh, no!" Tess groaned and bent her head, hiding her face from the too-near, craggy visaged man at her side. Against her will, her eyelids cracked open and she slid a look through her lashes.

She caught her bottom lip between her teeth to stifle an erupting giggle. Good heavens, he looked as astonished as she felt. And as helpless.

His arms hung loosely from his broad shoulders, his hands cradled in his lap. He'd landed in a sitting position beside her, his legs bent at the knees, crookedly cocked to either side of his slim hips. Oh! She had no business looking at that bulge in those tight denims!

She quickly glanced back at his face, willing her eyelids not to open fully as she tried to hide her perusal.

Lordy. Was this the Marlboro Man come to life?

He'd lost his hat in the tumble, and that rather longish brown hair waved in soft fullness around his head. Here and there she even caught a hint of a reddish tint, but it wasn't quite as prevalent as the shade in her own hair when the sun hit it. All he needed was a filter-tipped cigarette dangling from the corner of that full mouth to complete the picture. What color were that Marlboro Man's eyes . . . ?

"I asked you a damned question!" Those lips snarled now.

Her head flew up and she glared at him in return. "I'm hurt! I think my ankle's broken."

The brown eyes softened a little, lost just a hint of their glare.

"Well, I'm sorry to hear that. But I asked what you were doing here on my land."

"Boy, don't I wish like hell I knew," she breathed.

"Ladies shouldn't curse," the young girl said.

Tess looked over at her and smiled. "You must be Rain's sister. And I apologize for cursing. Rain already told me I shouldn't do that. He said your dad might wash my mouth out with soap."

"Where's my son?" the man demanded, drawing her attention back to him.

"He said something about going to bleed a deer—the one he shot."

"Guess you won't have to kill a chicken after all, Pa."

Stone scrambled to his feet and backed away from the woman, though he felt like he was struggling against invisible strands trying to hold him close to her. Damn, she was a beauty. Auburn hair and green eyes like Abigail's, but there the resemblance stopped. Her hair curled wildly, tumbling unrestrained down her back. His long-ago love, Abby, always kept her hair in a knot on her head—or at least tied back.

Abby had been little more than a girl at sixteen, though old enough to wed. Her breasts would have filled out more after she had children—indeed, they had been fuller when he had last visited her, not that he'd had any right to notice. They'd never gotten this full, though—and the woman's breasts weren't restrained, either. For God's sake, what had happened to her corset?

All at once he heard a chastisement of his irreverent language, though he could've sworn he hadn't spoken aloud. "Sorry, honey," he murmured distractedly in Flower's direction.

But when he followed his words with an apologetic glance at Flower, his daughter shrugged her shoulders and looked at the woman as though they both needed to tolerate some sort of strange behavior on his part. Neither of them appeared to understand why he'd felt the need to excuse himself, and his irritation flared. Just who the heck was in charge here?

"I hope you've got a dress in that pack! I don't allow my daughter to wear pants, and you won't either, if you expect us to help you out. What's that thing you've got wrapped around your foot?"

Tess clenched her fists, fighting against the confirmation of Rain's insistence that this was indeed the year 1893. Shoot, no, she didn't have a dress in her pack. Who on earth would carry a dress on a backpacking trip? At least, not one in 1994! Soon enough she'd have to tell him that, though.

For now, how the heck was she going to explain an elastic bandage to a man born years before vulcanization was even invented?

Suddenly it dawned on her that she believed it herself. Somehow—some way—somewhere—she had slipped through a time warp. That's what the tunnel had been—a hole in time. Frantically, she pushed this acceptance aside. She couldn't think about it right now. She had to get some medical attention for her throbbing ankle, and her only hope for assistance right now was this Marlboro Man and his daughter.

"Uh . . . uh . . . the bandage is just something to support the muscles in my ankle until I can get the foot x- . . . I mean, until I can determine if it's broken. Is . . . is there a doctor anywhere near-by?"

"Nope," he said. "Not near, anyway. You better let me look at it and see if I can tell if it's broken, instead of just sprained."

"No!" She gasped in pain when she jerked her foot away from his fingers. "I . . . I mean . . . don't you think it would be better for me to leave it wrapped until I get off this hill? It's not as painful with the bandage on it. "I can ride, if you'll help me on one of the horses."

"Where's your horse?"

"Mine?"

"You sure didn't get clear out here just walking," he said. "I've heard of you women having some newfangled ideas, but surely you've got sense enough not to travel around the country by yourself. Hell, even on horseback that's a stupid idea."

Holding back her fury took more gumption than Tess had left just then. "I suppose you're one of those chauvinistic pigs who think a woman's place is in the home! That we're just not as smart as men! That we shouldn't be paid as much, because we just don't do as much work as men!"

He grabbed his hat from the ground and slapped it against his leg to knock off the dust. Then he plopped it on his head and tipped it back an inch, staring at her from under the brim.

"Well, I don't guess I've ever been called a pig before, and I don't have any idea what breed of pig you're talking about anyway. But I'm darned well aware that Flower works just as hard as me at the ranch, so you can take that uncalled-for opinion of my character and stuff . . ."

He shook his head. "Look," he said in a more reasonable tone of voice, "all I want to do is help you. Neighbors out here do that for each other."

Tess's indignation diffused in a whoosh. Good grief, she was really going to have to watch what she said. But just how much was she going to have to say to explain how in the world she had shown up here?

She glanced at the Marlboro Man to see him studying the ground behind her. "What . . . ?" But she knew immediately what he was looking for. Her horse's hoofprints. He darned sure wasn't going to see them.

"What's your name?" she quickly amended.

"Rain told you his sister's name. Didn't he tell you mine?"

"Oh. Yes, yes, he did. It's Stone, right? Stone Chisum."

"What's yours?" Flower asked. She moved over and squatted beside Tess, holding out her hand in an offer of friendship.

"Tess." She gripped the girl's smaller hand and gave it a slight shake. "Tess Foster."

"That's pretty," Flower said. "Tess," she repeated.

"Before you ask, it's not short for anything." She laughed. "It's just plain old Tess."

"How old are you?" Flower asked.

"Thirty," she admitted wryly.

"Gee, you're almost as old as Pa, but you sure don't look that old. Are you married?"

"No. Not even engaged." *Anymore,* her mind added.

"You sure don't look like a spinster," the girl said as she rose to her feet. "One of the books I read said anyone who isn't married by the time she's twenty gets called a spinster. But I always imagined a spinster would be all dried up and ugly. You're awfully pretty, like your name."

Tess stared at her in dismay. How in the world could she respond to that comment?

Luckily, Stone intervened. "You'll have plenty of time to ask Miss Foster all the questions you want after we get her down to the cabin and make her more comfortable, Flower. Where did you say that horse of yours went, Miss Foster?"

"I . . . I've no idea," she replied. She wasn't lying; Sateen was back in a stall—somewhere back there.

"Hey, Pa! Am I glad you're here. You can give me a hand lifting the deer onto Smoky."

"Sure, son," Stone called toward Rain, who was trudging in their direction. "Just let me get Miss Foster taken care of first. It's mighty hot to just leave her sitting here."

"Her foot's hurt pretty bad, Pa," the boy said, glancing down at Tess with a smile of concern as he halted beside his father. "She must have hurt it before she got here."

"Before she got here? What the hell's that supposed to mean?" Stone frowned.

Tess took the only recourse she had when he glared at her. She screwed up her face in pain and even managed to squeeze out a tear that trickled down her cheek.

Rubbing her leg, she said with a sob, "Please. Can't we talk after we do something for my ankle? I've been lying here over half an hour, and I don't think I can stand the pain much longer."

When Stone dissolved into helpless confusion she bit back a stab of guilt, as well as a smirk of satisfaction at how well her ploy to divert his thoughts had worked. He reached toward her face, then jerked his hand back and grabbed his handkerchief from his back pocket instead. Thrusting the handkerchief into her free hand, he somewhat gruffly ordered Flower to bring her horse closer.

Stone bent and gently lifted her into his arms, carefully shifting her against his chest as she wrapped her arm around his neck.

"I'll try not to hurt you," he muttered distractedly. "Please, don't cry anymore. We'll get you down to the cabin. I think I've got some laudanum there. If not, there's some whiskey."

Tess closed her eyes against the pain, but she couldn't shut out the flare of sensation his holding her stirred up. Darn it, she'd been held by men before. Well, maybe nobody as blatantly masculine as this Marlboro Man, but she'd never chosen her men by whether they were hunks or not.

Her breasts were crushed against his chest, and she could tell he was looking down at her when she felt a feathery hint of breath on her face. With her eyes closed, her other senses were heightened, and she allowed them free rein.

He even smelled deliciously masculine. A faint hint of soap and sweat and—she took a deeper breath—a little horse odor. The size of the corded muscles in his arms beneath her knees and around her waist assured her that she was safe in his hold.

Why wasn't he carrying her on over to the horse, though? She slit her eyes just a little. Good lord, he was studying her face, and his lips were awfully close to her own. No wonder she could feel his breath.

"Pa, what about the deer?" Rain asked.

Tess felt him give a slight start as he jerked his head up.

"We'll get the damned deer in a little while, son," Stone said rather harshly.

"I'm sorry to be such a bother," Tess said in a soft voice, smiling at Rain. "I'll be out of the way just as soon as your father gets me on one of the horses."

The little boy's face lost its pout and he gave her a shy smile in return. "Aw, the deer's not gonna spoil that fast. It's more important to get your ankle fixed first."

"We need to get her off this hill first," Stone growled. "Where's . . . ?"

"Uh . . . Pa," Flower broke in, clearing her throat to get his attention. "Here's the horse. I've had it here since right after you asked for it."

Stone turned, and Flower stood right behind them, holding the horse's reins. Tess stifled a giggle as an actual flush of embarrassment flooded Stone's cheeks. How long had he stood with her in his arms without moving? The children probably thought their father had forgotten that he had called for the horse.

Had he been feeling a little of the sensations flowing through her as he held her? Had he wondered how well their lips would match?

"Think you could help me out here a bit, Miss Foster?" Stone asked in a gruff voice.

She jerked her head back, her neck popping with the strain. Tearing her eyes away from his face, she glanced at the horse standing beside them.

"Sure. S . . . sorry," she sputtered.

Bracing herself on his shoulder, she threw one leg over the saddle and reached for the saddlehorn. A very capable pair of broad hands cupped her rear and steadied her, pushing her upward. She almost went over the other side of the horse before she caught herself.

"Thought you said you could ride," he said as he rubbed his hands against his denim-clad legs.

"I can," she almost snarled at him. To prove her point, she neck-reined the horse around and started down the trail.

"Damn it! Wait for Flower!" he shouted.

Tess pulled the gelding up but refused to turn the horse around. Extremely aware of every movement Stone made, despite keeping her eyes faced resolutely forward, she waited until he hefted Flower up behind the saddle.

She lifted the reins, but Stone caught the horse's bridle before it could move.

"Wait for Rain and me, too. You'll need some help getting into the cabin," he said, his eyes sliding away from her brief downward glance.

"But, Pa! Like you said, it's awful hot," Rain said in a peevish voice. "I don't want that deer meat to spoil."

"Flower and I can make it alone," Tess assured Stone. "I've been riding all my life, and Flower can get me something to lean on so I can make it into your cabin."

"Well, if you're sure. Flower was counting on that meat for dinner tomorrow."

"We'll be fine. Really."

To emphasize her words, Tess picked up the reins again and quirked a questioning glance at Stone's hand on the bridle.

He held the bridle strap a moment longer. "Is there someone around here we ought to notify about you getting hurt? Your family will probably wonder where you are when you don't show up."

"No," she denied, then frantically tried to think how to explain that to him—or at least divert the new questions she saw forming on his craggy face. "I . . . oh, my ankle hurts." She blinked her eyes a time or two, as though fighting tears of pain, which wasn't too far from the truth. Her ankle was beginning to throb again as it hung down beside the stirrup.

Stone quickly dropped his hand and stepped back, and she kneed the horse forward. She paused at the bend in the trail where Stone had first appeared only long enough to give a nonchalant wave back, to indicate that she was having no problem at all with the horse. No, she told herself as the horse moved out again, she did not want to see if the Marlboro Man was watching her—seeing how well she handled the strange horse.

* * *

As soon as the horse carrying Tess and Stone's daughter disappeared, Angela watched him kneel in front of Rain and place his hands on the boy's shoulders.

"Now, what the heck is going on here, son?" she heard Stone say. "Where did Miss Foster come from? And what did you mean about her being hurt before she got here?"

Angela clapped her hands in approval. So Tess's attempt to divert Stone's questions hadn't worked. It had only delayed them. Not a dumb man, this one!

"What? You think we men can't see through all those wiles you women use, just because we let you get your way most of the time?"

"Michael! Welcome back," Angela said. "Shhhh. Let's listen. I really want to know what's going to happen next."

"Well, fill me in on what's happened so far. All I saw was that poor man getting flustered because Tess blinked those big green eyes at him like she was going to cry."

"Not now, Michael. You should have been watching all along, if you wanted to know the story. You'll have to wait for a commercial."

"A commercial! Dash nab it, Angela, we're not watching television!"

"Shhhh. Listen!"

" . . . and I really don't know where she came from, Pa," Rain said. "Like I told you, one minute there was a wild turkey there, and next thing I knew the turkey was hightailing it over the top of the hill, gobbling like I'd shot it in the rear with buckshot. Then there she was."

Stone could tell his son was holding something back, and the boy's evasiveness was a new trait he didn't care for much. Rain kept glancing beyond Stone with a look of wonder in his eyes. Yet when Stone turned he saw nothing but empty land and sky.

He felt Rain's forehead. "Did you bring a canteen with you? I've told you not to hunt in the summer heat without taking water with you."

"I'm not sick. Gee, you don't think I'm lying, do you? I've never told you a lie."

"No," he hastily assured his son. "But, Rain, sometimes we see things that aren't really there. Or maybe overlook things at first. You were concentrating on the turkey. You just didn't notice Miss Foster."

"Uh-uh, Pa. She wasn't there when I first aimed my gun. How could I have missed seeing someone that pretty lying right where the turkey was standing? Especially with that red shirt she's got on. And, look, you can see the turkey's tracks. It was standing right here—right beside where Miss Foster was."

Stone shook his head.

"And I was aiming my rifle, like I said! Do you think I would have pointed my rifle at a turkey that had a person laying right beside it? I know better than that. I'm a pretty good shot, but there's always a chance . . . I wouldn't ever try to make a shot like that unless I had to save someone's life."

"Rain, people can't just appear and disappear into thin air."

"They sure can't, can they? I don't know then, Pa." Rain shrugged. "Where did she come from? She's real, not a spirit."

"She's real, all right," Stone said, rubbing two fingers across the slight hump on his chest.

"She smells pretty, too, doesn't she? Kind of like the wildflowers in the spring."

Stone rose to his feet, nodding his head. He'd had ample time to contemplate that sensuous smell when he'd held her, caught up in some feeling he wasn't prepared to try to rationalize. Damn it, for a minute he'd thought of kissing her.

The pack near his feet caught his eye and diverted his thoughts. He didn't dare. That belonged to her, and he had no business invading her privacy—going through her things.

Besides, they'd better get that deer or it wouldn't be worth hauling home. He'd take her pack with him on the horse, after they loaded the deer. He'd give it back to her. Probably she had her extra clothing in there and all those feminine necessities women seemed to need.

He'd give it straight back to her.

"Come on, Rain. Let's get the deer."

"Boy, is he going to be surprised when he goes through that pack." Michael chuckled.

"He wouldn't," Angela denied. "You can read his thoughts as well as I can. He's decided he'll give it back to her without looking in it."

Michael grinned at her. "Those are just his surface thoughts. Humans have a vast amount of curiosity, remember? We'll have to see how long his sense of not violating Tess's privacy can hold that curiosity at bay."

Chapter Five

Gingerly, Tess shifted in the saddle and glanced at the ground as Flower dismounted. It had never looked that far away when she had two good legs with which to climb out of the saddle. Would Flower's horse prove as stoic as the mountain ponies she had learned to ride almost before she could walk? Those ponies allowed mounting or dismounting from either side, but most horses tolerated it only on the left—the side on which they had been trained. No way would her left ankle support her in the stirrup.

She tentatively leaned her weight into the right stirrup. The horse tossed its head and shied a step away from the hitching rail.

"Wait, Miss Foster. Let me hold him."

Flower grabbed the bridle and soothingly stroked the horse's muzzle. She nodded at Tess, and Tess eased her left leg over the horse's rump, then laid her stomach on the saddle and slid to the ground. Reaching for the hitching rail, she hopped a step, making sure her injured ankle didn't touch the ground.

"I'm going to need something to help support me in order to make it into the house," she reminded Flower.

The girl dropped the reins to ground tie the horse. "Do you think you could lean against me?"

"You probably couldn't hold me if I started to fall, honey. How about getting a kitchen chair?"

"We've only got benches around the table." Flower frowned. "I know; there's a stool I use when I churn."

The girl lightly ran up the steps, and Tess settled her bottom more comfortably on the hitching rail to wait. Taking a deep breath of the pure air, her eyes wandered over the yard.

It was really a beautiful place. The valley stretched out on either side of the small log cabin. The heat didn't seem quite as stifling down here, since a slight breeze wafted along the valley floor. She lifted her hair from the back of her neck and allowed the breeze to play across the dampness.

A small barn was off to the right, surrounded on three sides by a much larger corral. She had noticed a mare and a half-grown colt in the corral as they rode into the yard.

In the eastern end of the valley she thought she could make out some reddish shapes against the dark, velvet green. Probably some cattle, she realized.

She inhaled deeply again. How untainted and clean it smelled. Sometimes, even on the mountaintops where she backpacked, she could still smell the faint odor of civilization. And how many times had she found signs of other, less ecologically conscious hikers in the remote, pristine wilderness she loved? An empty candy wrapper skittering along the trail in a breeze—a crumpled aluminum can.

Once, with Freddy's assistance, she had even rescued a loon in a mountain lake. The poor thing had become entangled in a plastic six-pack holder someone had tossed negligently into the water. Probably the loon had been diving for food, Freddy had told her. Tess unconsciously rubbed the small scar on the back of her hand, the souvenir of how sharp a frightened bird's beak could be.

"Here we go, Miss Foster."

She murmured her thanks to Flower. Somewhat awkwardly, she managed the two steps up to the porch, silently blessing the fact that her jogging and hiking kept her legs in good shape. She hobbled into the cabin as the girl held open the door and gratefully sank onto one of the benches beside the wooden table.

"I took a minute and stoked up the stove, Miss Foster," Flower said as she reached for a tin basin on the sink. "Soon as the water in the teakettle gets hot, you can soak your ankle."

"Ice might be better, Flower—so we can get some of this swelling down and try to decide how bad my ankle's hurt."

"Oh, I don't think there's any left," Flower said in an apologetic voice. "Would you rather have some cold well water?"

How stupid, Tess told herself. Of course there wouldn't be any ice. She hadn't seen any power lines stretching across the valley.

"That'll be fine, Flower."

"Sometimes we have ice up into the spring," Flower started to explain. "If we have a real cold winter, Pa cuts the ice from one of the lakes and stores it in sawdust in our root cellar. But there was only a pile of sawdust there the other day. Our well's real deep, though, and the water's nice and cold."

"Can you manage by yourself?"

"Oh, sure. I carry water in all the time. I'll be right back."

After Flower left she stared around the kitchen. The cabin must be larger than it appeared from the outside; the kitchen was fairly spacious. Here and there she noted little touches that had to have come from Flower—a vase of almost wilted black-eyed Susans—a pair of curtains with wobbly seams hanging over the dry sink. She couldn't imagine either Stone or Rain caring much about curtains or flowers.

The table and stove were sparkling clean. But overhead in the rafters, where strings of peppers and corn—popcorn, maybe—hung, she saw a few dust-covered spiderwebs. And the corners of the pine flooring could stand a good scrubbing.

"Pa and Rain are coming," Flower said as she hurried into the kitchen and set the wooden bucket in the sink. She released the rope handle and rubbed at the small of her back.

"Heavens, Flower," Tess said. "How many times do you have to carry water in here every day?"

"Oh, dozens," Flower admitted. "But I'm used to it."

"Your back's never going to get used to it. You'll wreck it before you're twenty. Why doesn't your father at least install a hand pump in here for you?"

"Pa's busy. He said he'll do it someday."

Tess shook her head as Flower dipped water into the basin and carried it over to her.

Hesitating, Flower glanced at the door, then back at her. "Maybe you'd better move into my bedroom. Pa and Rain will need the table."

"Whatever for?" she asked.

"Well, they'll skin the deer outside, but they'll probably bring it in here to cut it up."

"They'll what!? Flower, they can just as easily butcher that deer outside and put it in . . . in your root cellar, or wherever you keep your meat."

"The smokehouse. But they always . . ."

"And who cleans up the mess after they're done?"

"I do. But . . ."

"And how many buckets of water do you have to carry to do that?"

Flower set the basin on the table and cocked her head to one side. "A bunch," she admitted. "Then the oilcloth has to be washed. And they usually manage to leave bits of tallow and hair all over the floor."

The girl picked up the basin again and knelt by Tess's foot. "Do you want me to help you take the bandage off?" She slipped Tess a wink. "You can have a good long soak while you sit here."

They joined each other in a conspiratorial giggle as Stone came through the door.

"Where's the oilcloth, Flower? Rain will need it in a minute."

Flower rose to her feet without answering Stone as Tess finished unwrapping the bandage and stuffed it into her back pocket. She sighed deeply and slid her foot into the cool water.

"Oh," she murmured, "I'm sure this will help the swelling, Flower. And I don't think I'd be able to move an inch right now."

Stone strode over and knelt on the floor. Frowning, he reached out a hand toward her ankle.

"Don't!" she said with a gasp, grabbing his hand. "Please don't touch it. The cold water's helping the pain."

Stone jerked his hand free and rubbed it against his thigh. She looked into his brown eyes a bare six inches from her own. His breath feathered over her face and she dropped her gaze to his temptingly parted lips. They moved, but she couldn't for the life of her understand what he said.

Michael drew his attention away from the scene below them when Angela clapped her hands and glanced at him.

"Oh, look, Michael," she said. "Isn't it wonderful? They're falling in love!"

"In love?" he responded with a snort. "They just met an hour ago!"

"Haven't you ever heard of love at first sight, Michael? Why, I could tell back on the hill that something was happening between them."

"Nonsense," he denied stoutly. "Love doesn't happen like that."

"How would you know? You've never had contact with live humans before. You've never watched them fall in love. I've seen it happen time and time again—sometimes after they've known each other for a while, I'll admit. But at times it happens almost at once, when two people first meet."

"There you go again," he said testily. "Flaunting the fact that you've been in this end of the business longer than me. Gosh darn it, we're never going to get along if you keep up that act!"

"I'm only trying to explain things to you," she said with a haughty sniff. "You really should listen to me."

"Look here, Angie, old girl, I *am* listening, but I can see, too. There might be something going on between Stone and Tess. Right now, though, it seems to me more like a physical pull of their bodies. You might think you know more about humans than me, but I'm well aware of how humans reproduce. And that urge always starts out with a sexual attraction."

"O . . . oh!" she sputtered. "You shouldn't be talking about things like that."

"What? Sex? It's a fact of life for humans, Angie. Without it we wouldn't have anyone to be guardian angels for, right?"

He thoroughly enjoyed watching Angela's flustered attempts to come up with a retort, though he admitted to himself that it might be a little unangel-like to feel that sort of satisfaction. But then, he was determined to get their relationship on a more even keel—more like a partnership than this teacher/pupil plane.

His companion finally managed to say, "My name is Angela, not Angie. Please try to remember that."

"Hummmm," he replied. "Prim and proper Miss Angela, huh? You need to lighten up a bit, Angie. How else are you going to pass on to me what I need to know about that end of humans' lives? After all, you've been around it for eons, and all I know about it is what I've heard from already departed spirits."

A guardian angel really wasn't supposed to stamp her foot or blush prettily, either, but Angela did both. And he fully enjoyed watching her.

"Pa, Rain's calling you."

"Huh?" Stone lurched to his feet. "Uh . . . go tell him to take care of the deer outside, Flower. I . . . we . . . where's your scissors?"

"In my sewing box, where they always are, Pa."

Flower headed for the door as Stone stared around the kitchen, frowning.

"Why do you want scissors?" Tess asked.

"Your pant leg," Stone murmured in a distracted voice. "It needs to be split up the side. Gotta be hurting you, that swelling."

"Most women keep their sewing boxes in a closet," Tess said.

"Closet. Yeah, probably in her bedroom." He hurried out of the kitchen, catching his toe on the doorjamb as he passed.

She shook her head at the muttered curses she heard echoing back from the bedroom. Good grief, he was awkward in the house. On the hill his movements had held a pantherlike grace for such a large man. Of course, the spaciousness of the kitchen had seemed to recede as soon as he walked through the door.

She heard a loud crash and ducked her head to hide the smile on her face when she heard his clumping footsteps returning to the kitchen.

"Hurts pretty bad, huh?" he asked as he stopped at her side. "It'll probably ease a little if we can get that tight pant leg split."

He knelt again and pointed the scissors at her leg. Carefully, he tried to work the scissors point under the taut material, where she had pulled up the denim.

"Uh . . ." he said when she gave a little gasp of pain. "Uh . . . maybe you ought to try to do this yourself."

"Maybe I should," she said, reaching for the scissors. She lifted her foot from the basin and laid her left calf across her right knee. Water dripped onto the floor, and she quickly shifted to hold her foot over the basin, her knee bumping Stone's chest.

"Sorry." She carefully worked the scissors point under the material and began cutting beside the seam in her jeans. The scissors were sharp and the material easily fell away beneath the blades. She cut well beyond the swollen flesh, up to her knee.

"That's far enough, damn it! What if Rain comes in?" Stone grabbed the scissors and threw them on the table, his eyes never leaving her exposed calf.

She rolled her eyes upward and huffed out an irritated breath. "Maybe you should get me a towel to cover my leg so I don't offend your Victorian sense of propriety!"

Stone rose and grabbed a linen towel from a hook beside the stove. He tossed it to her, then strode back to her side.

"Here. Don't cover up the ankle. Let me look at it."

She rolled the towel back and he bent over her ankle, which was swollen almost as large as her calf and covered with dark bruise splotches. She heard him grunt.

"You're going to need a doctor for this. It sure as hell looks broken to me."

"It feels like it, too," she admitted, wincing in pain when she attempted to move her foot. "But you said there wasn't a doctor nearby."

"Not near, as I told you. But there's one in Clover Valley, the closest town. It'll take me about four hours there and back. What happened? Did your horse throw you?"

"Uh . . . no. I . . . I fell."

"Fell off your horse?"

"Mr. Chisum . . ."

"Stone. Looks like you're gonna be here awhile. No sense standing on formality."

"Stone, then. You mentioned medicine for the pain?"

"Yeah. Let me see what I can find."

He walked over and opened a cupboard door, rummaging inside. He pulled out a box of medical supplies and held up a bottle to the light from the window.

"Laudanum's gone," he said. "I'll get some more from the doc." He tossed the bottle back into the box, where it landed with a clink, and reached into the cupboard again. Pulling out a brown jug, he set it on the countertop and picked up a tin cup from the drain board by the sink.

After pouring the cup half full Stone gave it to her. She sniffed it tentatively.

"If you want, I'll have Flower make a pot of coffee to mix with that," he said.

"No. This is fine." She sipped the whiskey and blinked her eyes at the burning fumes, then coughed at the fiery sensation when the whiskey hit her stomach. Taking a deep breath, she swallowed another large gulp before she set the cup on the table. A drop of liquid dribbled down the side of her mouth, and she flicked out her tongue to catch it, glancing up at Stone when she heard him give another grunt.

"Thank you. I . . ."

"I'll go get the damned doctor!" Stone left the kitchen in two strides, banging the door loudly behind him.

She stared after him in astonishment. "Oh, well." She shrugged. "At least he didn't keep after me about how I hurt my ankle."

Chapter Six

Tess lowered her ankle back into the basin, then stared around the silent kitchen, mentally refuting the evidence before her eyes. It just wasn't true. It couldn't be true.

Heck, Granny had cooked on a wood stove in West Virginia until the day she died fifteen years ago, turning out crispy fried chicken and flaky blackberry cobblers. But even Granny's log cabin had had pumped-in water. Cold water, and the pipes sometimes froze during an especially hard winter, but the water was clear and pure, bubbling from an artesian well on the mountainside.

Despite the hardships, spending summers and school breaks with Granny had been the only bright spots in Tess's childhood. Running barefoot through the wildflower-dotted mountain meadows; picking wild strawberries, blackberries, and grapes, which Granny preserved into jams and jellies that were lined up on a shelf in sparkling jars; even hoeing the garden rows until calluses formed on her palms and pulling weeds until her back ached hadn't seemed like hard work—especially the following winter, when Tess opened a jar of vegetables or jelly that Granny sent to the family each fall.

Evenings on the porch, rocking in her own chair beside Granny—watching the brilliant mountain sunsets and mists crawling up the hillsides, her hands automatically shelling peas or snapping beans. Those evenings were for dreams and discussions—heartfelt sharing with the elderly woman who seemed to be able to see straight into Tess's heart.

If not for Granny, Tess would probably still be back in the West Virginia mountains, the only break in a week of drudgery a bottle of beer at the nearest honky-tonk. Granny had given her the strength to stand up to her brothers and father, withstand the pull of her eager young body to succumb to the sexual stirrings of her teens—escape first to Boston on her scholarship, and then to New York City, the city where it seemed all dreams were possible.

Snooty. Thinks she's better than us. How many times had Tess heard those words whispered behind her back in school?

She shifted on the wooden bench and blinked her eyes, bringing the kitchen back into focus and frowning as the picture of the layout of the buildings beyond the cabin replaced the nostalgic vision of her New York apartment in her mind. She'd had no trouble identifying the purpose of the little shack with the half moon on the door between the house and the barn. Granny hadn't had inside facilities, either. And it was definitely becoming necessary for her to get to that outhouse.

The screen door opened and Flower entered, her arms full of clean sheets.

"I'm going to change my bed, Miss Foster. It'll be several hours before Pa gets back, and you need to lie down."

"Thanks, honey, but . . ."

Flower sped through the kitchen, leaving Tess's words hanging in the air. Lordy, that child had energy. If she only had enough to help Tess to the outhouse—or maybe there was a chamberpot somewhere, like Granny had kept under her bed.

A movement on the pine floor caught her attention and her eyes widened in horror. The monster on the floor picked up one hairy leg and waved it in her direction, then continued on its path, directly toward her. Her scream echoed in the kitchen.

Frantically, she scrambled onto the bench, splashing water from the basin, then levering herself onto the tabletop with her good leg. The monster ignored the spilled water, slowly lifting first one hairy leg and then another as it crawled toward the bench she had vacated.

She screamed again as Rain burst through the screen door and Flower also pounded back into the kitchen from the bedroom. The next thing she knew, Flower was perched beside her on the tabletop, her own squeak of dismay cut off as she clapped a hand over her mouth.

Rain stared at her and Flower, then followed her finger pointing to the floor. He set his rifle beside the door and his brown eyes twinkled as he grinned at them, curled up on the table.

"It's just a tarantula. Must have slipped in the door. It's too slow to bite you if you stay out of its way. Now, if it was a scorpion . . ."

"Get it out of here, Rain!" Flower shouted. "I hate those things!"

"Kill it! Right now," Tess demanded. She couldn't seem to tear her eyes away from the huge, dinner-plate-sized body creeping across the floor. One hairy leg and then another propelled it, almost in slow motion. It skirted the puddle of water and lifted one leg to caress the wooden leg on the bench.

"Rain!" Flower screamed.

"Better hush up." Rain laughed. "Those things can jump, you know."

"I know!" Flower shrieked, scooting closer to Tess. "Get it!"

She flung her arms around Flower, her eyes widening in horror as the tarantula placed yet another leg against the bench. "Can . . . can they really jump?" she asked through a dry mouth.

"Yep," Rain admitted. "This one looks like it might even be able to jump ten feet. I gotta be careful, if I want to get close enough to catch it."

"Rain! Do something!" Flower pleaded.

The tarantula started up the bench leg. She and Flower screamed in unison and skidded from the tabletop. Flower paused just long enough to grab her arm and pull it over her shoulder before leading her, furiously hopping, into the next room. She kicked the door shut behind her.

Tess flung herself onto the narrow bed, biting her lips against the pain in her ankle and trying to control her nearly overflowing bladder.

"Flower!" she gasped. "A chamberpot. Do you have . . . ?"

Flower reached beneath the bed and pulled out a ceramic bucket.

"You get that darned thing out of my kitchen, Rain!" Flower yelled at the closed door while she fumbled to help Tess unsnap her denims.

She pushed Flower's fingers away and pulled down her zipper. "Oh. Flower, I don't know if I can make it."

Bracing herself with her good leg, she lifted her rear and slid the denims down. With Flower's help she managed to scoot from the bed onto the chamberpot, closing her eyes in relief.

When she lifted her eyelids again she saw Flower opening the door a crack to peer through. Suddenly another yell sounded in the kitchen, and then a clatter.

Flower shut the door and turned back to Tess, a satisfied smirk on her face. "Guess he's not as brave as he thought he was. Serves him right."

"What happened?"

"It jumped, like he said it could." The girl giggled. "He was trying to catch it with the basin and it jumped right at him. It landed in the basin and he threw it against the screen door. Now he's trying to figure out how to get the door open with that spider sitting in front of it."

"Why doesn't he just kill it?"

"Rain doesn't believe in killing unless it's necessary," Flower explained. "Even when he kills animals for us to eat, he thanks the Cherokee spirits for the gift of their life."

"But that thing's dangerous, Flower!"

"Not really. I mean, it would hurt if one bit you, but it's not like a rattlesnake's bite; that could kill you. Rain'll probably go out the other door and prop the screen open, then try to get the spider to leave on its own."

Tess dropped her head to her chest and shook it. Tarantulas. Rattlesnakes. Scorpions. Where in the world was she?

Before she questioned Flower, though, she had to get up off this pot.

"Can you help me onto the bed, Flower?"

"Sure. Just let me finish with the sheets."

"Stop it, Michael! It's not funny!"

Michael grabbed his stomach and rolled back onto the cloud, his wings fluttering against his shaking shoulders, his laughter nearly drowning out her voice.

"Not . . . not funny?" he gasped. "Did you see them scoot off that table? I never saw two females move so fast in my life!"

She lifted a hand to her mouth. Still, a little giggle escaped. "I thought it was funnier when it jumped at Rain. Did you see the look on his face?"

"Yeah." Michael snorted. "If that thing hadn't hit the basin, it would have landed right in that boy's mouth!"

"Ugh." She shuddered, then giggled again, this time erupting in full-fledged laughter. Had she been with some of her other angel friends rather than Michael, she would never have broken down into such unrestrained emotion.

A moment later, she opened her eyes to find herself lying beside Michael on the cloud, her shoulders still shaking with abating laughter. Glancing at him was a mistake. He winked and guffawed, and she broke up again.

Finally she sat up and clutched at her aching sides. "Michael, we have to stop this. We're supposed to be keeping an eye on Tess."

"Okay, boss," he said agreeably. "What's next on the agenda? Is she off that pot yet? I'm not about to spy on a lady when she needs privacy."

"Hum, of course not. Let me see. Oh, she's getting undressed and into one of Stone's nightshirts. Why, it looks almost brand-new."

"He probably sleeps naked. Me, I don't understand why some humans get dressed all over again to go to bed."

"Michael!"

"Oh, come on, Angie. Don't tell me with all the eons you've watched humans, you never saw some of the women slip off their heavy nightgowns on hot nights. Wallow in some nice cool, fresh sheets."

"It gets awfully hot sometimes on earth in the summers."

Michael slipped her another wink.

The bedroom door opened and Tess stirred, slowly returning to wakefulness. A dream. Such a funny dream she had been having, and she had't even been reading before she fell asleep, had she? Sometimes her bedtime reading habit triggered weird, unexplainable dreams during the night. This one, though. The Marlboro Man had climbed right off that magazine page and. . . .

The door squeaked as it opened wider, and her eyes popped. A small, round man entered the room, carrying a black bag.

Oh, no! It wasn't a dream!

She stared around the room. Flower's room. She glanced down at her swollen ankle, pillowed at the foot of the bed. The angry, dark blotches confirmed the pain.

"Well, now, miss," the man said as he set his bag on a bedside table. "I'm Doc Calder. Stone tells me you've hurt your ankle. Let's get a little light in here, so I can see better."

The doctor lifted the glass chimney on a kerosene lantern sitting in a sconce on the wall and picked up a match from the tray on the table. He turned the wick up slightly, then scraped the match. After replacing the chimney he looked down at her, but she kept her eyes centered on the lantern.

"Wonderful thing, kerosene," he said. "And I heard there's some guy back east who can make light appear in a glass bulb. Ain't that gonna be something? Wonder what he'll call it?"

"Electricity," she murmured.

"See, you've heard of it, too. Funny name, that one, though. 'Lectricity." He slowly shook his head.

"Her ankle, Doc."

She peered past the doctor to see Stone standing in the doorway, his shoulder leaning against the doorjamb. Immediately she realized the too-large nightshirt had fallen from her shoulder, barely held in place by her breast. Good grief. She was covered a heck of a lot more than in her bikini, but for some reason a hot flush stole up her cheeks. Grabbing the collar of the nightshirt, she jerked it back into place.

She could have sworn that Stone's lower lip immediately shot out into a pout.

The doctor bent over her ankle, hiding Stone from her sight. He tsked and muttered almost to himself, gently prodding her swollen flesh with tender fingers.

"Can you move it?" Doc Calder asked.

"I can, but it hurts too much," she replied.

"Well, it looks broken to me. But sometimes a bad sprain will swell up and blacken just like this, too. I'm going to have to move it around and see if I can tell if there's a broken bone in there. I'd better put you out before I do that."

"No!"

"Now, miss, I've got some ether with me. You'll never know a thing."

"No," she repeated, unwilling to hurt the doctor's feelings by admitting to him that she was afraid of letting someone with far less training than an anesthesiologist in her time administer an anesthetic to her. "I . . . just give me something to relax me. Maybe some laudanum. I don't want to be put to sleep."

"If you say so. But I'm afraid you're going to wish you'd listened to me before this is over."

Stone watched Tess swallow the laudanum, grimacing at the bitter taste. While the doctor busied himself laying out what he would need from his black bag, she settled back against the pillows. She glanced at him, and he was once again drawn into those green depths.

Where in the world had such a pure, sea-green color come from? The fathomless depths remained clear, though—not darkening as the ocean did as it deepened. The whites reminded him of frothy wave crests, and thick, lush lashes surrounded them. The lashes blinked closed, and Stone tore his gaze away from her face.

His eyes wandering down her body caused a tightening in his groin. Auburn tresses curled around a smooth neck, tumbling in disarray over her breasts, and he could almost imagine that the second his eyes touched her breasts, her nipples puckered and pointed upwards—or had those tips been there all along?

He rolled his tongue inside his mouth. He could just about taste those nipples. Would she buck wildly under him if he ever got the chance to savor them? Would she throw that long, smooth neck back and toss those shiny curls in ecstasy?

She clutched the sheet over that flat stomach, but he could make out the mound of curls beneath the sheet and gown. Were they the same color as her hair? He could almost feel them brushing his mouth, and he swept his tongue around his lips. He shifted sideways in the doorway, cocking his leg out to hide his straining fly.

The doctor pulled the sheet and gown farther back from Tess's injured ankle, and Stone's gaze fell on her leg. There hadn't been anything left to the imagination in those tight pants she'd had on, and he already knew her legs were long and shapely. The doctor nonchalantly draped the sheet and gown on her upper thigh, well above her knee.

Good God! He'd better get the hell out of here!

"Stone, she's going to need something to hang on to while I do this," Doc Calder said over his shoulder. "Come over here."

Stone stopped in midturn and glared back into the room. "I'm not good at stuff like this, Doc. I'll send Flower in."

"That child's not strong enough. Get over here, man."

Hesitantly, he made his way over to the bed. Tess's lashes were still pillowed on her cheeks, her breathing light.

"She's asleep, Doc."

"No," Tess murmured. "Just drifting. The laudanum made the pain better." She opened her eyes partway and smiled lazily at Stone. "It works better than the whiskey."

He groaned under his breath and pulled a seat over to the bedside. Gingerly, he sat down, then reached out a hand. "Doc says you're going to need something to hang on to."

She nodded sleepily at him and trustingly placed her hand in his, threading her fingers through his larger ones.

"Hold on," Doc muttered.

Tess gasped and bit back a scream. Stone watched tears fill her eyes and felt her nails digging into his palm.

Doc moved the ankle again, and Tess whimpered and closed her eyes, biting her lower lip.

"It's broken," Doc said. "I can hear the bones scrape. I'm going to have to set them back into place. Sure you won't change your mind about that ether?"

Tess shook her head, and Stone realized that she was unable to speak because of the pain.

"Hold her, Stone."

He moved from the seat to the bed, opening his arms willingly. Damn, this was going to hurt her!

The doctor grasped her ankle again, and Tess screamed and buried her face against his chest to muffle the shriek. She flung her arms around his neck and clung tightly. The doctor gave a satisfied mutter, and Tess eased her hold on him.

Stone continued to hold her slender body close, reluctant to release her. He ran his hands up and down her back, caressing and soothing, as he had wanted to do on the hillside. When she tried to pull her head away he curled one hand in her silky tresses and laid his cheek against the top of her head.

"Shhhh, Tess," he whispered. "Doc's almost done."

"Michael, what's wrong with you? You look like you're going to faint."

"Is he done yet? Gad, I can't stand this."

"He still has to put on the cast. Michael, you better sit down. Heavens, it's not you he's hurting—it's Tess."

"I know. But I can't stand to see anyone in pain." He swayed and started to sit but missed the edge of the cloud. Frantically beating his wings, he realized he was falling.

"Easy, Michael," Angela called over the side. "Think flying; don't flap."

He landed with his rear on the edge of the cloud, then quickly tumbled backwards when he looked down at Tess. Clasping a hand over his eyes, he moaned. "Tell me when he's done, okay?"

Angela patted him on the shoulder. "There, there, Michael. Everything will be all right."

Chapter Seven

"Sorry you had to come all the way out here, Doc."

"Don't worry about it, Chisum. I get tired as hell of patching up drunks every Saturday night. Half the time they puke all over my surgery while I'm digging out bullets or stitching them up; then Mandy has to clean it up. Won't hurt them none to take care of themselves one night and let my wife have a good night's sleep. Maybe next week they'll think before they pull those damned guns or knives."

"Not much hope of that, unless the sheriff starts enforcing the law against weapons in the saloons. Whiskey does funny things to a man's mind."

"Yeah. Well, thanks for the bed last night. Glad I didn't have to drive back to town, though I suppose Perseus would've taken me right back to the stable if I'd've fallen asleep."

"Sure you won't stay for breakfast?"

"No, thanks. But you be sure Miss Foster eats right while that ankle heals. Lots of milk to help the bones, and meat and vegetables and fruit. She's too damned pretty to wind up with a limp. And from the looks of those legs of hers, she sure likes to walk. Say, Stone, you never did tell me how she ended up at your place."

He didn't know about the walking part, Stone mused to himself. He hadn't allowed himself to more than barely touch her injured ankle, even if his fingertips had tingled at the thought of seeing whether her thigh was as silky as it looked. Maybe some of the shapeliness of her legs was due to muscle tone, but it sure as hell would be a pity if those luscious legs were marred by a limp.

Milk they had a plenty, thanks to the cow. And the garden yielded a glut this time of year—tomatoes and cucumbers, beans and peas. He would check and see if the sweet corn was ready to pull. He wondered how soon the apples on the Widow Brown's trees would be ready.

"Chisum? Hey, Stone! Where'd you go?"

"Huh? What the hell are you talking about, Doc? I'm standing right here!"

Doc shook his head and lifted the reins. "I'll be back in a few days to check on Miss Foster. In the meantime, keep her off that foot. When I come back we'll see about maybe getting her up on crutches. I don't believe in letting my patients lie around too long. Seems they heal better if they're up and about as soon as possible."

"I'll take care of her, Doc."

"I'll bet you will," Doc murmured as he clucked at his horse and then trotted down the road.

Stone still stood with his fingers tucked into his back pockets, staring toward the garden. Suddenly he jerked his hands free and walked over to the edge of the plot. He bent down and picked some of the flowers and lifted the bouquet of sweet peas to his nose as he crossed the yard to the cabin. No wonder Flower liked to plant so many of them each spring and set jars of them around inside. He had never really noticed the clear scent before. A drop of dew clung to his nose when he lowered the bouquet, and he absently swiped it away.

"Oh, Pa," Flower said as he came into the kitchen. "Aren't they pretty? But you've never helped me pick my flowers before."

He thrust the sweet peas into Flower's hand. "Those flowers on the windowsill are gettin' wilted. Thought you might want some fresh ones."

"You've got enough sweet peas here for more than one bouquet. I'll take some in on Tess's breakfast tray." Flower dipped water from a bucket into a jar and a waterglass, then split the flowers and arranged them in the containers.

"Whatever," he muttered after a second. "How is she this morning?"

"Sort of grouchy," Flower admitted. "She couldn't believe we got up this early."

"Early? Hell, it's almost sunrise. What's she think we do—sleep 'til noon around here? It's hard enough to find time to get everything done as it is."

"She mumbled something about not even having to be at work until nine-thirty. She must have a job somewhere, but I've never heard of a store that opens that late. The stores in Clover Valley are always already open even when we get there at eight o'clock in the morning."

"Flower." Tess's voice floated through the open bedroom door. "I hate to bother you, but could you come here a minute?"

His daughter started to put down the knife she had picked up to slice the smoked ham, but he turned toward the bedroom.

"Go ahead with breakfast, Flower. I'll go see what she wants."

"Here. Take this with you, so it doesn't spill over on the tray."

Flower shoved the waterglass into his hand and turned back to the counter. For an instant he stood looking from the glass back to his daughter, then shrugged irritably and walked into the bedroom.

"I was wondering if you could help me . . ." Tess's words froze on her lips as she looked up at the tall figure standing in the doorway, a waterglass of flowers in his hand. She hurriedly jerked the sheet up over her shoulders. "You could at least knock first!"

"I'm not in the habit of knocking on doors in my own house!" Stone strode over and plopped the glass on the bedside table. "Flower sent these in," he growled.

"Thank her for me, will you?" she said. "They're beautiful. Sweet peas, aren't they? Granny grew sweet peas. And morning glories and four o'clocks—and . . . lots of other flowers."

"What did you need? Flower's cooking breakfast."

"Uh . . . I guess it could have waited. I'm sorry to be such a bother."

"Just tell me what the hell you wanted."

Tess stared up at the grim face above her. He had been so tender last night. Holding and stroking her—lending his rock-hard strength to cling to. Allowing her to curl her fingers in his own until she drifted off to sleep.

He must have made an attempt to tame his brown locks with water this morning. Too bad. The waves in his hair softened that planed countenance when they weren't slicked back. No touch of gray marred the temples, but she bet he would age well, even when it did.

His cheeks were freshly shaven. Good grief, how early did he get up each morning, if he bathed and shaved long before sunrise?

"What are you thinking about?" Stone asked quietly.

"How much better you look with your hair dry," she replied honestly. "And I was trying to decide if it was the sweet peas I smelled or your aftershave."

"It's Sunday." He shrugged. "Even if we don't get to church every Sunday, sometimes neighbors drop by to visit."

"Any special neighbor?" she asked, quirking her eyebrow.

"The Widow Brown drops by sometimes. There's not really anyone else too close. Once in a while one or two of Rain's and Flower's Cherokee relatives wander in."

Widow Brown, huh? "How old's the Widow Brown?" she asked before she could stop herself.

"How old? Hell, I don't know. About my age, I

guess. Her husband was a little older than me. Why?"

"No reason," she denied. "It just seems awfully rugged country for a woman to have to live alone."

"We help each other out when we can. Now, what did you need help with? I've got to get to my chores."

"Uh . . . oh, the pillow," she said. "It fell off the bottom of the bed, and my ankle feels better when it's propped on it. I couldn't reach it."

Stone moved to the foot of the bed and bent down for the pillow. Gently he lifted the cast and slid the goosedown-stuffed pillow beneath it. Five pink toes with rose-tinted nails wiggled before his eyes.

"That feels much better. Thanks so much," Tess said.

"This little piggy . . ." He reached out a finger toward her toes.

"Don't you dare!" She gasped. "I'm ticklish!"

He jerked his hand back. Good God, what was he doing? He hadn't even realized he had moved his arm—and he hadn't thought of that crazy little rhyme in years.

Glancing at Tess, he got caught in the sparkling depths of her green eyes as she gazed back at him.

"Ticklish, huh? Better behave yourself and follow all the doctor's orders then. And remember, I'm the boss around here."

"You're quite the tyrant, aren't you?" Tess giggled. "I can tell that Rain and Flower shake in their moccasins whenever you're around."

He laughed softly with her for a moment before

he draped the sheet over her tempting toes. "I've got to get busy or those animals will think I've forgotten them," he said as he turned to the door. "Flower will have your breakfast in a few minutes."

Whistling softly to himself, he strode through the kitchen and out the door, his step lighter than usual as he headed out into a day filled with work. In the yard, he paused for a moment to watch the sun creep over the distant hilltops. Usually it never crossed his mind to take a long enough break to watch the gray-tinged distance change to muted pink, then fiery red with golden streaks, announcing another day.

Hell, he had never taken time to bring a fresh bouquet to Flower, either. Now he glanced around the yard and noted the wild rose bushes Flower had dug up in the hills and transplanted here and there. A couple of them looked sort of wilted. Well, he guessed he could find a minute somewhere to haul water from the well for them. After all, Flower had enough to do.

"Michael, you aren't supposed to use your powers like that!" Angela chastised, though not too strongly.

"It was sort of cute, though, wasn't it, Angie? You know, I never realized that a woman's toes could be pretty. Most of the male human spirits I got to know were breast men."

"Michael!" She curled her own toes tight, burying them in the fluffy cloud. "I really wish you'd quit talking about things like that!"

"Angie," he said with an irritated sigh, "just because I've never been human doesn't mean I can't appreciate human beauty. And you're the one who said Tess and Stone were falling in love. All I did was give him a little push in the right direction, so he could show her with that little teasing that he was starting to loosen up with her. Men need a little push now and then."

"I thought you didn't agree with me on how they were starting to feel about each other," she said, miffed.

"Well, maybe I'm changing my mind. I could tell how much better Stone felt this morning than he usually does when he's facing a day's work. And I think it's because he knows there's a woman waiting in the house when he comes back. Someone to share a laugh with now and then. Someone to give a purpose to all that hard work."

"He has the children," she said, for some reason playing devil's advocate to Michael this time, though she didn't think that a proper term for their sparring match, given their angelic state. However, she admitted to herself that she enjoyed hearing Michael at last agreeing with her about something and wanted to prolong that pleasure, even if it meant taking the opposite side of the argument.

"That's a different sort of loving feeling. Why, you should feel the love flowing between two reunited human spirits meeting again, who'd had a special relationship when they lived."

He glanced at her with a condescending smile on his face, but she leaped from the cloud and headed for the barn.

"He's going to the pack, Michael! Come on!"

Stone propped his hands on his hips and stared at Tess's pack in the corner of the barn. Just as he started to kneel, the cow lowed loudly from its stall, and he frowned in her direction. What the heck was the matter with her? She usually waited peacefully until he got around to the milking.

The cow let out a loud bellow. He quickly headed across the straw-littered floor, almost tripping over three half-grown kittens that scampered from their hiding places, curling around his legs and mewing stridently.

"For pete's sake," he grumbled. "You act like I'm an hour late instead of just a few minutes."

He grabbed the three-legged stool and started to sit before realizing he'd forgotten to fetch a clean milk bucket from the root cellar. Dropping the stool again, he scooped up a can of grain from a barrel and emptied it into the cow's manger before he headed out of the barn.

The kittens quieted immediately, and one of them stood on its hind feet, batting overhead.

Angela drifted up out of the kitten's reach, a satisfied smile on her face as she looked over at the undisturbed backpack.

"He's gonna look in there sooner or later," Michael said with a grin.

"I've just got a feeling it should be later. I don't think he's quite ready yet."

"Okay, boss. Boy, it sure is dusty in here."

"Hay particles," she murmured. "There's always hay particles floating around in a barn."

Michael sniffed and waved a hand in front of his face. "Yeah, I can smell them. It's . . . ah . . . oh, no. *Aah* . . . "

"Michael, don't!"

"Aachoo!"

"Oh, good grief, Michael. The cow's gone!"

"I'll find her. Be right back."

"Michael, wait! Stone's coming back! Michael . . . !"

She quickly flew to the barn door and conjured up a breeze. The door swung on its well-oiled hinges and closed with a firm click.

Stone reached out and grabbed the handle, but the heavy door refused to budge. He shook the door, but it stayed shut. Frowning in frustration, he set down the milk bucket and used both hands to jerk on the handle.

Damn it, the door had swung easily enough in that sudden breeze. Now what the heck was wrong with it? It couldn't be locked from inside—the only lock was the bar on the outside of the door.

He gave a final jerk and landed on his butt. Then he glared at the swinging door for a full half minute before he stood up and brushed the dirt off his rear. Picking up the bucket, he stomped into the barn and stared around. He saw a few animal heads—a couple of horses and that darned cow—sticking out over the stall doors, but no sign of any human.

"Rain? Rain! Are you in here? That wasn't funny, Rain."

"What wasn't funny, Pa?" his son asked as he came into the barn.

Stone whirled around. "Have you been out there all along?"

"Well, yeah. I was greasing the axles on the wagon wheels, like you told me to do last night. I just came in here to get some more grease."

"While you're at it, grease those darned barn door hinges, too!"

"Sure, Pa."

Chapter Eight

Tess stared at the again laden tray and groaned. Three times a day for the past three days those trays had appeared, carried in by Flower for the most part, though Stone had brought in the supper tray this evening. He stood over her now in the familiar stance, his elbows cocked behind him, his fingers slipped into his back pockets. She bit her lip when she realized her groan hadn't stayed smothered under her breath and Stone's face was creased in a frown.

"What's wrong with it?" he demanded. "Don't you like pork chops? We had beef for dinner."

"Nothing. Nothing's wrong," she quickly denied. "It looks wonderful. Flower's really a good cook."

"Couldn't tell it by the way you eat. Hell, you haven't cleaned your plate since breakfast that first day."

She looked back at the tray. Two large, crispy

pork chops, a huge heap of mashed potatoes with gravy, and a mound of green beans with bacon bits for flavor lay on the plate, completely filling it with food. Beside it was a bowl of cucumber-and-tomato salad and two pieces of buttered bread.

She loved the fresh bread Flower made—and had made the mistake of voicing her liking. Now Flower even brought her a snack in midafternoon, when she usually baked bread for the evening meal. The afternoon snack, warm from the oven, was covered with melted butter and smeared with homemade jelly or jam.

And a huge glass of milk accompanied every food offering—cool and fresh from the well house, and unskimmed, Tess was sure. And then there were those pies and cakes to top off every meal. . . .

"You gonna eat or not?" he asked in an annoyed tone. "Flower worked too hard for you to let your food get cold."

"Of . . . of course. I . . . oh, damn it, Stone. I can't keep eating like this and lying around not getting any exercise. I'm not going to be able to get into any of my clothes when I get up."

"Then you ought to get some clothes big enough for you. Flower said you sewed up those denims, but they're too damned tight for you to wear around here. And please watch your language around the kids."

"Me? You sure don't!"

"That's different. Ladies don't swear."

She blew out an exasperated breath and lifted her eyes to the ceiling. Damn . . . uh . . . darn, she was bored. Oh, hell, listen to her. She couldn't even be herself in her own mind. She had been living inside her head for the past four days, trying to sort through her thoughts and get her bearings.

She didn't dare question Stone or the children too closely. She didn't even know exactly where she was—just that it was somewhere in the "Old West," the summer of 1893. Indians still roamed around, but she guessed they were pretty tame, since they visited Stone's ranch. If she could only find out what state she was in, maybe she could dredge up some buried knowledge from her high-school history classes. But then, history hadn't been her favorite subject—it ranked down there with geography and math.

"Look, if I go get my plate and come in here to keep you company, will you please eat?" Stone asked.

"No! I mean . . . I'll eat. You don't need to keep me company," she hurried to say. The few times she had glimpsed him looking into her room the past three days, she had read a million questions in his eyes. She wasn't prepared to answer them yet, since she hadn't figured out how to get her own answers in return.

And she *had* to get that backpack. Tomorrow marked the day to start her cycle of pills. She sure as hell didn't need them for birth control, but the doctor had told her that only regular cycles of the estrogen and progesterone would regulate those crazy periods of hers and help abate the crushing pain each month.

"You know, if I had my clothes," she began hesitantly, "I could join you at the table." At least there the conversation wouldn't be private. Flower's and Rain's presence would assure a flow of more innocuous patter.

"Doc should be back out tomorrow or the next day," he informed her. "He said you were supposed to stay off that ankle until he came back and looked at you again. Then he'd see about letting you up on crutches. And—he said for you to eat properly!"

She sighed and shifted to the side of the bed. When she winced in pain as her foot touched the floor Stone hastily grabbed the pillow from the bottom of the bed and knelt before her. She shot him a grateful smile when he tucked it under her foot.

She swiped at her cheek. "Stone, you're staring. Have I got a smudge on my face?"

"Huh? No, I was just noticing how even and white your teeth are."

"They should be," she said. "I suffered with braces for enough years."

"Braces? On your teeth?"

"It's . . . it's something new dentists are using . . . uh . . . back East." Good lord, when was she going to learn to watch what she said!

"Where are you from?"

She tensed. "I was raised in West Virginia. You know, I guess I am hungry." She grabbed her fork and speared several cucumbers. "I'll have to ask Flower to teach me how she makes this dressing. It's delicious," she mumbled around her full mouth.

"Dressing? Never heard it called that before. It's just vinegar sauce." He looked at her thoughtfully. "You've got a lot of strange names for different things."

She ignored him and picked up a pork chop with her fingers. Taking a huge bite, she chewed it slowly, her teeth crunching the crispy meat.

Stone rose to his feet. "All right, I get the hint, Tess. But we can only avoid this conversation for so long. We're going to have to sit down and talk pretty soon. If you're running from something, I need to know what it is. I don't want my kids put in any danger."

She swallowed the suddenly tasteless meat, still avoiding his eyes. She wiped her greasy fingers on the napkin, then picked up the fork and speared a green bean.

Cautiously she nibbled the bean and dared a look up through her lashes. Her eyes flew open. Stone had gone, and she hadn't even heard him leave. What on earth had ever made her think him awkward? That man could move as silently as a drifting cloud when he wanted to.

Stone walked out the kitchen door and found Flower and Rain talking together beside the rocking chair on the back porch.

"Pa," Flower said, "do you think it would be all right if I left the supper dishes for a while? It's so hot, and Rain and I were thinking about going swimming in the creek for just a bit."

"I don't see why not, honey," he replied. "It's still fairly light out. Just be sure you're both back before full dark."

"We will be," Flower promised. "Thanks, Pa. I'll go get us some towels and the bathing outfit Mrs. Brown made me this spring, Rain. I'll be right back."

Stone smiled as Flower hurried past him into the house, then glanced at Rain. "You know, son, we haven't had time to talk about what happened on the hill the other day. You been thinkin' about it?"

"Yeah, a bunch," his son admitted. "But I still can't figure out where Tess came from. Maybe Grandfather will have an idea when he comes."

"Why do you say that?"

"'Cause Grandfather's a shaman, Pa. He knows things regular people don't know. And he can speak to spir . . . I mean . . . uh . . ."

"Here are our towels, Rain."

Flower hurried out onto the porch and tossed a towel at Rain. He caught it easily and shot her a grateful look. They ran across the yard toward the creek in the trees beyond the barn.

Stone crossed the yard more slowly. He checked the prop against the barn door before he went in, assuring himself that it was snugly seated. He didn't want that darn door swinging shut again, locking him inside this time.

Tess's backpack was where he had left it, covered with dust and hay particles. He still couldn't figure out why she hadn't asked for it since she got here. Surely there were things in it she needed—but even when she'd mentioned getting her clothes so she could sit at the table with them, she hadn't followed it up by demanding that he bring the pack to her.

It went against every code he lived by to pry into that damned pack. A man just didn't go through another person's private belongings. He'd been tempted the other day, but he couldn't have gone through with it, could he? Hell, why didn't he just take the darned thing and give it to her. That was one way of getting rid of that hankering to see if anything in her pack would explain how that exciting piece of femininity had managed to drop into his life up on that hillside, with no signs of a horse or wagon having carried her there.

Shoot, he'd even gone back up there the next day to look for Tess's footprints and try to figure out which way she had come from. He'd found Rain's footprints—turkey tracks—deer prints and hoofprints from the three horses he and his children had ridden. No damned Tess footprints, though, except where she had sat down. And those darned soles on her funny boots would have left a real distinctive track.

Heaving a sigh of resignation, he reached down for the pack. He bumped it against his hip as he shifted the strap over his shoulder and immediately threw it back to the floor and jumped away.

A snake! He stared at the pack in horror. The hissing sound continued. A damned snake had crawled into one of the pockets on that pack!

Now what the hell could he do? He ran to the barn door and grabbed Flower's hoe from where it was leaning against the wall. Holding it at the ready, he started back toward the pack.

Still six feet away from the pack, he stopped and glanced at the mare staring out of the first stall. Horses hated snakes, and by all rights the mare ought to be trying to tear down the door and get out of the barn, away from that hissing sound. But the mare stood with ears pricked, totally unafraid. As he watched, the mare nonchalantly turned around to her feed box.

He cocked his head and listened to the sound. It was more of a crackle than a hiss. And no snake he'd ever heard could maintain a steady hiss like that. This sound had been continuous for at least a full minute.

Stepping up closer, he prodded the pack with the hoe. The sound continued. Hooking the hoe blade under one strap, he pulled the pack out into the yard.

"Oh, Michael, s . . . stop! Please!" Angela gasped. "I can't stand to laugh anymore."

Michael guffawed even louder. Dropping to his knees, he pointed at Stone, who stood staring at the backpack in consternation.

"M . . . maybe I oughta glue the zipper shut so he can't get in there and find that radio," he said through his hee-haws of glee.

"You shouldn't have turned it on in the first place!" She whooped again and clutched her sides.

"I didn't," Michael denied. "He hit the knob on his hip and turned it on."

"Oh, dear. Oh, my!"

"Look! Look, Angie!"

She dropped down beside Michael, her wings fluttering as her snickers continued. She gripped the rim of the cloud and watched Stone work the edge of the hoe into the leather thong threaded through the hole in the large zipper slide on the pack pocket. The slide moved smoothly, and Stone stepped back—waiting, Angela supposed, for the snake to crawl out.

When nothing happened except the constant hissing and crackle, Stone prodded the pack again. Then he stepped up and worked the hoe handle down into the pocket. The black radio flew out and landed at his feet.

Stone jumped at least six feet away and she and Michael howled with glee. Suddenly Stone whacked the black box with the hoe blade and silence descended—silence down there around Stone, anyway. Pure, unrestrained laughter reined on the cloud.

"Uh-oh," Michael finally managed to say. "He's headed in to confront Tess. We'd better warn her."

"How?"

Tess felt an uncontrollable urge to sit up and look out the bedroom window. She tucked the curtain back just in time to see Stone carrying her backpack into the barn. A second later he emerged with something in his hand.

Oh, no. That looked like her little radio. He'd been going through her things!

She wasn't ready to talk to him yet. What could she say? She jerked the curtain closed and stared wildly around the room. She sure couldn't hide—not in here. Besides, she couldn't even get out of bed and walk unaided.

Spying the laudanum bottle Doc Calder had left her for the pain, an idea formed. She hadn't taken any more doses of laudanum after the first pain-filled day, determined that she would endure without relying on the narcotic. Now she grabbed the bottle and reached under the bed for the chamberpot. She dumped part of the bottle in and hastily shoved the pot under the bed before she set the bottle back on the table and lay down on her pillow.

"You're not asleep, damn it! I saw you looking out the window."

She felt something fall on her stomach. She

flinched and her eyelids fluttered, but her eyes remained closed.

"I said, I know you're not asleep!" Stone shook her shoulder.

She slowly opened her eyes. "Hum? No, how could I sleep with you standing there shouting? But my medicine makes me sleepy." *There, that's not really a lie.* "Dr. Calder said I should rest as much as I could until he came back."

"Don't give me that. You're avoiding me again."

"Avoiding you? Stone, how could I avoid you when I can't even leave this room? You can come in here and talk to me anytime you want to. As you said, it's your house."

"That's not what I meant, and you damned well know it."

"Really, Stone. Do you have to swear at me?"

He gritted his teeth. "I want to know what that box is!"

"What? This?" She reached down and picked up her radio. "Oh, it's broken. Look. Did you drop it?"

"No. I hit it with the hoe. I thought it was a snake."

"A snake?" She turned the radio over in her hands, then back again. She raised her eyebrow and looked up at him. "A snake?"

He groaned in embarrassment and his face flamed. Turning on his heels, he stomped out of the room.

She heaved a sigh of relief and cradled the radio against her cheek. Lordy, lordy, was he mad. How was he going to act when he saw some of the other things she carried with her?

She dropped the radio on her lap and readjusted

the plastic piece covering the batteries. The batteries clicked back into place and a hissing sound filled the room. She twisted the tuning knob, but the static only continued. Radio stations were nonexistent in this time.

Chapter Nine

Rain leaned on his saddlehorn and studied the two spirits. It must be great to soar through the air—fly like the birds. Lots of times he stretched out on a hilltop to watch an eagle skim along the wind drafts or a falcon float lazily overhead, then drop like a stone to grab a field mouse or rabbit.

He wondered what their names were. The man spirit didn't look much different than other men on earth. He would have to ask Grandfather about that. The legends always seemed to indicate that warriors returned to their prime in the spirit world.

This spirit had a slight potbelly, and Rain could tell his age must be close to Grandfather's. He still had an almost full head of brown hair, with a few gray streaks, like the ones in Grandfather's black hair. And, like most older white men, Rain noticed a bald spot on the back of his head. He wondered why Indian men never seemed to lose their hair.

Of course, this spirit man wasn't Indian. Could there be two different spirit worlds for whites and Indians? He sure wished Grandfather would show up, so they could discuss how to talk to these spirits.

And that lady spirit! At first, when you looked at her, she seemed sort of plain. But there was something about her that quickly made a person realize just how beautiful she was. Once he and Grandfather had discussed how a person's true beauty came from within—from a person's unselfishness and caring about friends and family.

She was slender—almost skinny. She had the prettiest blond hair, which she tried to keep pinned on her head in a bun. But it kept slipping loose and falling over her shoulders, the curls tumbling around her face, softening her features. Those blue eyes were such a deep color—as clear as the sky above them.

Their gowns looked as frothy as Pa's shaving cream, and as light and airy. He guessed maybe the lightness helped them float freely. That gown looked sort of silly on the man, though, and Rain had seen the man stumble more than once on the hem. Heck, Rain knew how he felt. He wriggled out of his own nightshirt and tossed it on the floor after he crawled into bed each evening.

He guessed their being here had something to do with Tess. They never followed when he and Pa left to check on the cattle and, after all, they had arrived with her.

"Rain! Come on!" his father yelled from the edge of the yard, where he waited on his horse. "We've got to get that hole we found in the fence yesterday fixed!"

The lady spirit wiggled her fingers at him, and Rain raised his hand in return, then lifted Smoky's reins and urged him across the yard. When Stone still sat frowning after he stopped beside him, instead of turning and heading for the far range, Rain cast his father a quizzical look.

"Thought you were ready to go, Pa."

"Who were you waving at?"

"Sorry, Pa," he said. "I can't tell you that. Maybe after I talk to Grandfather I can, but not now."

"Is there something going on around here that I ought to know about, son? Other than how our mysterious Tess got here, I mean."

He shrugged his shoulders and glanced back at the cabin. The man spirit winked at him, shaking his head slightly.

"There's nothing *wrong*, really. I promise you, I'd let you know if I could. It's just that I have to talk to Grandfather first."

"All right, Rain. I'll trust you on this, since I never want to interfere with your Indian heritage. But I've got a feeling all the strange things happening around here have to do with Tess. When we get back this afternoon I think it's time I had a talk with her."

"I don't think she knows either, Pa."

"What's that supposed to mean?"

"We'll have to ask Grandfather."

This was stupid. Those were her belongings and she damned sure had a right to them.

"Flower," she called. "Have you got a minute?"

"Sure, Tess." Flower came into the room, wiping

her hands on a towel. "Do you need something?"

"Yes. Do you remember the pack I had with me?"

"It's in the barn, where Pa left it. Gee, I'm sorry. I should've thought to bring it in to you sooner. I'll go get it, if you need it."

"I do. Thanks, Flower. By the way, where did your father and Rain go? You usually have lessons in the mornings."

"They found a broken place in the fence late yesterday. Pa didn't have any extra wire with him, so they're going out this morning to fix it and round up any of the cattle that got out. We'll probably have lessons this afternoon. Pa doesn't usually let us miss a whole day."

Good; Stone would be gone for a while. She would have time to make use of a few of the other things in the pack, she thought, as Flower left the room.

Oh, for a good hot bath! That would be impossible, since she wasn't about to ask Flower to haul in that much water from that stupid well. Besides, the cast would make it too awkward.

She could at least request a teakettle of hot water and a slightly bigger basin, so she could wash a little more than just her hands and face. Then some skin lotion. Lordy, the dry air here made moisturizer a necessity.

And deodorant and perfume. Heavenly!

She didn't suppose she dared slap on even a speck of mascara, something she always carried with her, just in case she ran across a cute park ranger. Stone would probably notice and think her a harlot. Seemed like he noticed every little thing about her.

Something told her the confrontation between them loomed close. And she damned sure couldn't face that unless she looked the best she could—and had on some clothes.

"Can I stay and talk to you while you get cleaned up, Tess?" Flower asked as she reentered the room. "I can help you, if you need it."

"Uh . . . well, gee, Flower, I . . ."

Oh, what the hell. They were going to find out sooner or later. Maybe letting the young girl in on it just a little might make things go easier with Stone. Children were a lot more accepting than adults.

"I'd like that, Flower," she said in a firm voice. "First thing we'll need, though, is some bathwater. Do you have a bigger basin than the one we usually use in the mornings?"

"How about the dishpan? I'll scrub it out real good."

"That will be fine."

As soon as Flower left the room, Tess unsnapped the backpack and pulled out a few items. She closed it firmly again over the remaining things—things that would take a lot more explaining than she was prepared to give right now. She laid her plaid shirt over the pile on the bed, then quickly dry-swallowed a pill before she tucked the package back into an outside pocket on the backpack.

"Here we go, Tess." Flower set the dishpan on the bedside table and poured in steaming water from the teakettle. Pulling a towel and washcloth from beneath her arm, she handed them to Tess. "Just let me get a little cold water to cool this off. I'll be right back."

Tess leaned her face over the steam and felt

the tightness of her dry skin loosening. Recalling some of the pictures she had seen of prairie women in her history books, she gave a contented sigh. Thank goodness she had brought full bottles of both face and body lotion with her.

She frowned and straightened up. Even the full bottles wouldn't last forever. And forever stretched out before her like . . . well, like forever.

She couldn't stay here forever. Could she? All the bits and pieces of knowledge she had picked up over the years about research into time travel indicated that she had to return to the spot where she had initially passed through the time warp in order to get back to her own time. She had to admit, though, that all the thoughts on time travel were only theory. As far as she knew, no one had ever proven it possible. Yet theory was all she had to go on—along with her remembered flight through that dark tunnel, which appeared to support the reality of there actually being warps in time.

She couldn't get back to the hillside on her own right now—thanks to her broken ankle. As soon as she could, though, she had to go back up there and search for that opening.

The only other problem she faced was how fond she was becoming of these people taking care of her. Even though she'd only known them a short while, she would miss them after she left.

She hadn't seen much of Rain, but his tender concern for her on the hillside still touched her heart. Flower and she were becoming awfully close, since they shared not only the same gender but were with each other day in and out. The young girl would mature into a woman, and Tess felt an almost motherly pull to see her safely through the hazards of her teens, as Granny had done for her.

Stone . . . well, he really wasn't her type at all. Though she admitted to finding him ruggedly handsome and was truthful enough with herself about being attracted to him, her broken heart over Robert hadn't healed yet. She knew all about rebound romances. She'd be damned if she would get caught up in that, especially when she knew full well beforehand that nothing would keep her from returning to the nineties.

She had come too far. Sure, she had liked visiting Granny in her youth and hadn't minded the discomforts of mountain living for the short summer periods. But she had made darned sure her New York apartment had every snazzy new appliance. And a Jacuzzi, along with that wonderful, expensive stereo system, with all the latest compact discs.

Okay, so at least half of her collection was country music—and bluegrass, with the old mountain songs that Robert had scorned.

Not that she ever really got much time to listen to the stereo herself. She worked long hours at the law firm, determined that one day she would attain that partnership, dangled like a carrot beneath her nose.

That was another reason to get back to the hillside—even if she had to crawl on her hands and knees. She'd worked too darned hard to let that plum of a career-making case fall to another attorney, even if it was tempting to let Robert suffer the consequences of his foolish actions.

Robert, huh. The only reason her firm had become involved in handling his case was due to the chance meeting between herself and Robert on the bridle path. Robert's horse had carelessly pounded around a bend in the trail, spooking Sateen and causing Tess a frightening moment until she regained control of the mare. She'd thought it only just that Robert pay for breaking the rules of the path by buying her an expensive dinner, which he had offered.

The case must have been bothering Robert—as well it should have, Tess had agreed when he brought it up over dinner as soon as he found out she was a lawyer. And she had tentatively offered the services of her firm, since Robert was decidedly dissatisfied with the efforts of the firm his family had used for so many years.

Too, as well as giving her a plus in the eyes of the older firm attorneys for solving a seemingly unsolvable legal problem for a client, there was the possibility that Robert's family would move their legal business to Tess's firm. That hundreds-of-thousands-of-dollars-a-year account, along with her brilliant legal reasoning and research, would assure her future with the firm.

"Sorry, Tess," Flower apologized as she lugged the wooden water bucket through the door. "Pa forgot to let the cow out this morning, and I had to take care of her. He's getting awfully absentminded lately. Isn't he too young to start getting forgetful?"

"Much too young," she agreed solemnly. She'd forgotten how ancient anyone over twenty looked to a teenager—or near teen, as Flower was. But she well recalled how she had hated being laughed at in those tender years. "Maybe he's just got a lot on his mind."

"He's always so busy." Flower tipped some water into the basin. "The only time he ever sits down is when we have our lessons or meals. I worry about how hard he works."

"It's a man's way," Tess explained. "They all seem to want to build a legacy to leave behind someday. Sometimes they forget their family is their legacy, too. We women have to make them stop and think about that sometimes."

Women, too, she realized. Or at least most of the women she knew in New York, who seemed to have substituted clawing their way up in their careers for their yearnings for a family. She had buried her own desires, assuring herself that she had learned a lesson from her poor mother's lot in life. Yet she resolutely walked blocks out of her way to avoid encountering the park near her apartment, where young mothers or nannies lovingly kept watch on the babies and toddlers in their charge.

Flower thought for a second, then nodded. "Let's plan something for Sunday, Tess. You should be able to get around by then, after the doctor comes back. How about a picnic? There's a lake about an hour's ride from here that we can get to in the wagon. I'll fry chicken—and Pa loves to fish. It's far enough away that he can't come back here to check on things real easy. He'll have to relax and enjoy himself."

"Sounds great to me. But you have to agree to let me help cook. I'm so darned bored, I can't stand it. And I make a mean angel-food cake, even from scratch."

"From scratch? What's that?"

Tess took a deep breath. Now was as good a time as any.

"Where I come from," she said, "most women

just buy a packaged cake mix at a grocery store and dump in eggs and milk. Then they beat it up and stick it in the oven."

"Gee, that sounds like a flat cake."

"It isn't. It has all of the cake's ingredients already measured and mixed in. And there's even a special oven that can cook that cake in a flash, if you want to. I don't care much for those cakes myself, though. My grandmother and I always made our cakes like you do—all fresh ingredients and eggs straight from beneath the chickens."

Tess reached for the washcloth and dunked it into the water. "Do you understand what I'm trying to say, Flower?" She pulled a bar of scented soap from under her plaid shirt and opened the plastic wrapping.

"I guess. Pa says they have a lot of fancy stuff back East that we can only read about in books or newspapers here. I don't understand how an oven could cook any faster than mine, though. If it's too hot, everything burns. What's that clear stuff on your soap? And, gee, it smells good."

"The clear stuff's plastic. It hasn't even been invented yet."

"Oh, that's silly. How can you have it if it's not invented yet?"

Tess took a deep breath. "I came here from the future—from a time that hasn't even happened yet."

Flower's eyes rounded in awe. "Oh. Oh, Tess. You can't mean . . ."

"I'm afraid I do," she admitted. "Just a few days ago I was living in 1994."

"How? Rain said you talked about 1994 when you first appeared, and we've been trying to figure out . . . oh, you're over a hundred years old! You sure don't look that old."

"I'm not," she grumbled. "At least, I don't think so. Besides, I went backward in time, not forward."

"Then . . . then . . . you're not even born yet! How . . . ?"

"I can't really explain it. It should be impossible, but it happened. Damn . . . uh . . . darn, it sure did happen to me."

Flower dragged the ladderback chair closer and sat down.

"Tell me more," she said eagerly. "What else is there in the future? Golly, I probably won't even live long enough to see the things you've seen. I'd have to live a hundred and thirteen years!"

"Flower," she said tentatively, "you seem to believe me awfully easily. What makes you think I'm not just telling you a story?"

"Oh, I knew the first time I saw you there was something special about you. I even had a feeling you were coming, though I didn't know at first who you would be. Grandfather always told Rain and me to stay open to things around us. He says people miss lots by trying to explain everything. And, like I said, Rain and I've been talking. Rain swore you appeared in front of him out of nowhere. Please, Tess, tell me more."

"First, I want you to answer a few questions for me, all right?"

"All right. But hurry."

Tess finished her bath and moisturizing while Flower explained that Tess was in Oklahoma Territory, about a hundred miles north of the Texas border. Once the land had belonged to the Indians, Flower said—Cherokee, her own people, who mostly lived to the north and east—and the other tribes, now all on reservations.

"People have always come up here from Texas and settled," Flower said. "At least, that's what the history books say. Anyway, a few years ago the government started having what they called land rushes. They made deals with the different tribes to buy some of the land from them, then let the white settlers come in from Kansas and stake claims to the land. Pa got his land a little differently, though. When he took us to raise, Grandfather somehow gave Pa this land, so he'd have a home for us."

"It's a beautiful area," she said. "I'd always thought of Oklahoma as dry and windy."

"I think it is, farther west. But here we've got hills and lakes, and even the Ouachita Mountains over in the land the Five Nations owns. That's still all Indian land to the east of us."

"Oklahoma's not even a state yet, then."

"No, but Pa says it won't be long before it is. He says that someday all the land between the oceans will be different states that are part of the United States."

"Fifty of them eventually," Tess said, "including Alaska and Hawaii."

"Really? Oh, we have to tell Pa that he was right."

"Uh . . . not yet, Flower. Promise me you'll let me pick my own time to tell Stone about this. I have to approach it just right."

"But why? I believed you."

"It's a little different with adults, Flower. We sort of . . . well, I guess you could say we get sort of hardheaded about stuff as we get older. There are a few people who never seem to lose their belief in the wonders of the world, and this is what your grandfather wants you to do. However, most people limit any belief they have in the supernatural to a hope that there's life after death. Everything else, they look at skeptically."

"All right. But now it's your turn. You tell me some things."

"Hey, anybody home?"

"Darn," Flower grumbled. "It's the doctor to look at your ankle."

Tess quickly shoved her toilet articles under the sheet and raised a warning finger to her lips. "Not a word to him, agreed?"

"Agreed. In here, Doc," she called toward the open bedroom door.

"Knocked, but no one answered," Doc Calder said as he came into the bedroom. "How's my patient today? Itching to get up out of bed?"

"Itching at more than that." Tess laughed. "This darn cast feels like it's got ants crawling around under it."

"Can't be helped. If the swelling's down enough, have Stone fetch you a slender willow branch to use to dig down in there. Works wonders, so I hear."

"Thanks, I will, Doctor. And I sure hope you've come out here to release me from this bed. I'll be fat as a butterball if I keep eating Flower's cooking with no exercise."

"We'll see," the doctor said. "Oh, and here. Stone asked me the other night to bring these out the next time I came. He seemed to think you needed a couple of dresses. I think these will fit. I put them on Stone's bill at the general store."

Doc Calder handed her a brown-paper-wrapped package, tied in string.

"Thank you," she said with a grimace. She could just imagine what the package contained. Probably dresses to cover her from her chin to her toes, her shoulders to her fingertips. It was too darned hot to wear dresses like that, but she couldn't see any way around it. She hoped the dresses were made of cotton at least.

Chapter Ten

"Flower!"

Even inside the bedroom, they could hear Rain's frantic shout and Smoky's pounding hooves.

"Flower! Where are you? We need your help!"

Flower scrambled from the chair and ran through the door, with Doc Calder right behind her. Tess gathered the nightshirt around her and tried to rise, then glared at her ankle as she heard the kitchen door bang and Rain's voice.

"Something poisoned one of the waterholes! Pa needs our help to fence it off, Flower. He's keeping the cattle away until we can get there. Hurry! We've got to take some more fencing and posts out in the wagon."

The kitchen door slammed again and Doc Calder stuck his head back into the bedroom.

"Will you be all right here, Miss Foster? Stone could probably use my help, too."

"Did you bring me some crutches, Doctor?"

"Yeah. They're in the buggy. I'll fetch them while the kids load the wagon."

The doctor reappeared with the crutches and handed them to her. "Think you can figure out how to use those things on your own?"

"I know how to use them, Doctor. Go on and help the kids."

"Well, be careful. Crutches take a little getting used to. We don't want to add a broken arm to that broken ankle if you fall."

Doc Calder left the room, and she stared at the door with a worried frown on her face. A poisoned waterhole could probably mean a disaster for a ranch as small as Stone's. But then, Rain had said it was only one of the waterholes.

How many cattle would have already sickened, though, even died? Did the toxic waterhole have anything to do with the hole in the fence Flower had mentioned—or was it a natural phenomenon, caused by some defect in the aquifer?

She wouldn't be able to find out until Stone and the kids returned, and sitting here worrying about it wouldn't help them any. She unwrapped the package and lifted out one dress, her ears straining toward the barely audible sounds of voices in the yard.

By the time she had removed her nightshirt and pulled on the dress, she could hear the wagon leaving the yard. She drew back the curtains on the window beside the bed and saw Rain at the head of a small procession, astride a gray horse. Flower and Doc Calder sat in the wagon seat, the reins to the team in Flower's hands.

Flower slapped the reins on the broad backs

of two huge brown horses, and Doc grabbed the seat as the horses lurched into a run. Tess stifled a laugh when Doc released his hold and barely managed to save his hat from flying off his head.

Quickly she realized this was no laughing matter and dropped the curtains. She started to button the dress before remembering she hadn't even really looked at it.

Glancing down, she fingered the skirt. Why, it was really rather pretty. A soft mint green, sprigged with faint, violet flowers. She would have chosen the color for herself.

Thankfully, the dress had short sleeves, and the material felt like cotton. Creases marred the dress, but when she buttoned up the bodice the snugness smoothed out its wrinkles.

Good grief, it had a low neckline. Tugging on it didn't help a bit, and her breasts almost spilled from the top. At least it would be cool. She dug a pair of bikini panties from the pack, along with her right tennis shoe, and slipped them on.

Picking up the crutches, she tucked them under her arms and wobbled upright.

Whoops!

She frowned and glanced around. It had almost felt like someone had steadied her! Shaking her head, she took a few tentative steps until she felt she had the rhythm of the crutches. Then she carefully made her way into the kitchen and toward the door. After being cooped up in that room for almost four days, she needed to get outside for a while.

Maybe in a bit she could see what might be available to fix for a meal. Flower would probably be grateful for another woman's help in the kitchen. Wouldn't Stone be surprised that she knew how to use that wood stove?

Tess carefully lowered herself into a rocking chair on the porch, which reminded her of the one she had sat in at Granny's. No, she realized, Stone wouldn't be surprised at that. She kept forgetting that he didn't know she was from the future. Any man in this time period would expect a woman to know the tricks of a cantankerous wood stove.

She rocked slowly and stared at the hillside beyond the barn—the opposite way from where Rain and Flower had headed. It had taken her almost fifteen minutes to ride down from there on horseback. She could have hiked the distance in a little more than that, given two good feet—two good feet she didn't have.

She leaned her head back against the chair, turning her head slightly to take advantage of a shaft of sunlight. It was so peaceful here—like back in the West Virginia mountains. She could almost imagine Granny there beside her, the creaking of the two chairs harmonizing with each other.

Her eyes flew open. That wasn't another chair. Something was on the porch with her!

She gripped the chair arms tightly and stilled the rocking motion. Another porch board creaked loudly. Whatever it was had to be a heck of a lot bigger than even that huge tarantula, which had moved silently across the kitchen floor—or one of the chickens in the yard. She swiveled her eyes toward the sound, but a curtain of hair blocked her view, and her tense neck and shoulder muscles refused to budge when she tried to turn her head.

Scolding herself for acting like a ninny just because she was alone on the ranch for the first time, she willed herself to relax. Slowly she turned her head.

Her heart melted when a bedraggled, half-grown dog belly-crawled another inch forward, its tail wagging and its mournful eyes staring up at her.

"Oh, you poor thing! Where did you come from?"

The tail wagged a stronger beat, and the pup's head rose, its tongue hanging out.

"Here, boy."

She hung her hand over the side of the chair and clicked her fingers. The dog leaped to its feet and rushed forward, its entire body wriggling joyfully, a whine issuing from its throat. It plopped down beside the chair and leaned against it, while she patted its head and scratched that special place behind each ear.

"You look half-starved, pup," she murmured. "You sure can't be one of Stone's animals. I wonder how you ended up here?"

That question could wait. Right now this poor animal needed some care. She shoved herself out of the chair, and the dog cocked its head to watch her.

"Now," she warned, "don't get under my feet and trip me."

The animal got up and moved a few steps away, to the other side of the door. It sat and lifted a paw, waving it up and down.

"You silly thing." She laughed. "You act like you can actually understand me."

She studied the dog for a minute but couldn't even begin to imagine what breed it might be. Matted white fur covered most of its body and burrs caked the long tail hairs. The only other color was its brown face and head, along with a brown spot on its rump. Its ribs stood out starkly beneath the fur, rising and falling with each panting breath.

Tess struggled to the door and held it open. "Come on," she said. "It'll be easier for me to feed you inside. I can't carry food out here and handle these crutches at the same time."

The pup bounded in the door and stretched out by the table, its muzzle on its paws and its eyes going from her to the stove, and back again.

"Looks like you've at least got a few manners," she told it. "I hope they include house-breaking."

The dog wagged its tail and yipped.

Tess first dipped some water from a bucket Flower had sitting on the sink into a bowl and managed to bend down and place it on the floor. She clicked her fingers and the pup ran over, settling down to lap thirstily.

Under a linen towel, she found scraps from breakfast—three biscuits, one half-eaten, and some bacon strips. Three eggs had been on her own breakfast plate, and two of them were with the scraps. She set the entire plate down on the floor, and the dog turned its attention to it, gobbling hungrily. The food disappeared in a few gulps, and the dog looked up at her hopefully.

"I don't know if there is anything else, fella. Let me look."

Spying a loaf of bread, she cut off several slices, then hesitated. Oh, well. She pulled the butter dish over and smeared butter on the bread, then dropped it to the plate. It, too, disappeared quickly, but the pup must have at last been satisfied. He licked the plate a couple of times, then wandered back over to stretch out by the table.

"We need a name for you," she said after she braced herself on the countertop and leaned down to retrieve the plate. She left the water dish on the floor and poured another cup of water into it.

"Let's see. You've probably been out there a good while on your own, given the state of your ribs. How about Lonesome?"

The pup yipped, in agreement, she decided. At least that problem was settled. And it had a full belly. It was definitely time to do something about that matted coat.

After she went into the bedroom she awkwardly smoothed out the bed, then dug a plastic-bristled brush from her pack. It would wash easily after she used it on the dog. At home she even tossed it into the washing machine.

"Come on, Lonesome," she called as she swung back through the kitchen. The pup obediently followed her onto the porch and sat down in front of the rocking chair when she called it over.

"That was one thing she really missed in New York," Angela said. "Having a dog. She didn't think it was right to keep it cooped up in that apartment, what with the long hours she worked."

"Yeah. Hope Stone lets her keep this one."

"Why wouldn't he?"

"Well, ranchers have to be careful about what type dog they have," Michael explained. "If a dog takes a liking to killing any of the livestock, it has to be destroyed."

"Lonesome won't," she said firmly. "He didn't bother any of the chickens running loose in the yard."

"No, he didn't," Michael agreed. "Say, how are

things going out by the waterhole? Think we should go see?"

"Oh, not me. That cow we saw earlier suffered terribly before it died."

"Steer."

"What?"

"It was a steer, not a cow, Angie."

"What's the difference?"

She smothered her surprise as Michael fidgeted a little and avoided her eyes. Could there possibly be something he could get embarrassed about? Retaliation wasn't a desirable guardian angel trait, but what could be the harm in having a little fun at his expense?

"Michael, what's the difference?" she repeated.

"Uh . . . well . . . well, you see, Angie. Uh . . . well, you know cows are female and bulls are male."

"Even I know that. Oh, I see. That animal this morning didn't have a milk bag. But you called it a steer, not a bull."

"Uh . . . you have noticed that Stone keeps the cows and calves in a different pasture than the rest of his cattle, haven't you?"

"Yes, I did, now that you mention it. Why is that? And how do you know all this?"

"One of the human spirits I helped adjust was a rancher in life," he explained, still uneasily shifting from foot to foot. "And we talked about how ranchers made a living raising beef. Their cows are used for breeding, and when the calves are partly grown and ready to wean, the rancher culls out the males from the female calves. The males are put into a different pasture to be raised for beef. Ranchers keep a few of the better female calves for future breeding. It only takes one good bull to breed those cows every year—at the most two, depending on what bloodline a rancher's working on developing in his cattle."

"Okay. I can understand that part."

"Bulls can turn into pretty mean critters, Angie. A herd of a few hundred bulls would probably spend all their time fighting each other, instead of grazing and getting fat."

"So, how do they prevent that?"

"Uh . . . well, they castrate the male calves." Michael's face reddened. "It settles them down."

"Castrate them? Oh, doesn't that hurt them terribly?"

She continued to pretend a wide-eyed interest as Michael's blush deepened, and he groaned under his breath. How on earth he could openly tease her about human sexual habits and then get so flustered over talking about cows was beyond her. She could tell by his face, though, that this discussion was almost at an end.

"Michael?" she prodded. "For pete's sake, it must hurt those poor cows . . . er . . . bulls. Doesn't it?"

Michael flapped his wings and shot up several feet above the cloud. Hovering for a second, he called down, "I'm going out to the pond. Sure you don't want to go with me? Things will be fine here, what with Lonesome to watch out for Tess."

"You go ahead," she called back. "You need a break. You look like you need to fly around for a while and cool that flush on your face."

He didn't wait for further permission. He whisked out of sight before she could even bat her eyes, and she giggled softly to herself.

Well, now, it was a little different when the shoe was on the other foot. Evidently, there really *were* a few things Michael could get embarrassed about.

He sure was turning into a nice companion, though. She hadn't had so much fun in years. It had been nice sharing outright hysterical laughter at Stone's antics. She'd never been in such an amusing situation before—or, to be truthful, never let her guard down that much. She'd always felt it was such serious business, being a guardian angel. But Michael was showing her that they could have a little laughter mixed in with the soberness.

Yes, he was fast becoming more of a companion than a pupil, and she found herself enjoying their changed relationship.

Chapter Eleven

Tess groggily raised her head from her arm when Lonesome whined and rose to his feet. The kerosene lantern burned low, almost out of fuel, and the kitchen lay in deep shadows. It had to be close to midnight.

She had sent Rain and Flower to bed hours ago, then sat down at the table with a basket of mending she had found in Flower's room. One of Stone's shirts lay in her lap, and the shirt's owner walked through the kitchen door, pausing just inside to light another lantern on the wall.

"You shouldn't still be up," he said in a weary voice when he turned and saw her. "Doc wants you to take care of that ankle."

Lonesome growled low in his throat, and she quickly shushed him by laying a hand on his head.

"What in the world is that mangy thing?"

"He's not mangy!" she defended the dog. "He still

needs a bath, and Rain said he'd do that tomorrow. But he's got beautiful fur."

"Well," Stone drawled, "is he going to let me come into my own kitchen?"

"Probably," she said with a soft laugh, "if you let me introduce you to him first. He's sort of decided that it's his job to watch over the place, even if he did just arrive today."

"That's good. Long as he's got a job to do around here, I guess he can stay. There's no room on a working ranch for a lazybones. He is a he, isn't he?"

"Oh, yes. His name's Lonesome. Lonesome, meet Stone, the guy who's the boss around here—even over you."

Stone slowly crossed the kitchen and held a hand out toward the pup. "You try to remember that, will you, Lonesome? If you do, you'll be the first one."

Lonesome glanced up at her, and she nodded at him. "Say hello, Lonesome."

Lonesome sat on his haunches and lifted a paw.

"Aw, that's cute," Stone said as he grasped the paw and shook it up and down. "You've already been teaching him tricks, huh?"

"Not really. He just kind of does that on his own. At least with us older folks. He just jumped all over Rain and Flower. He and Rain had quite a tussle until Rain gave up and let Lonesome lick his face."

"And I'll bet he laid under the table and had scraps slipped to him all during supper," he said as he gave a final scratch behind one brown ear and straightened up.

"Well . . . Stone, you must be starving." She rose to her feet and reached for the crutches. "Sit down.

I've kept you some food warm in the oven. Gee, I hope it isn't all dried out."

"I can get it, Tess. . . ."

She shot him a stern look and leaned on one crutch to point a finger at the table. "Sit! You're exhausted and I've had a nap. I'll fix you a plate."

"See what I mean about nobody remembering that I'm boss around here, Lonesome?" Stone sat down, and the pup put its head on his knee and whined. "Yeah, it's kind of frustrating, isn't it, boy? I think you're already beginning to understand what us males have to go through."

Giggling under her breath, she swung over to the stove.

Stone absently scratched Lonesome's ears while he watched Tess. She handled herself pretty agilely on those crutches, even propping one against the countertop and using the other one while she worked.

Doc had picked out a nice dress for her, but then Stone had been clear on the colors he felt would look good on her. That darned dress was just as sexy as those tight denims, though. It outlined her upper body like a second skin, and the skirt draped enticingly over her hips, swaying with her movements and drawing a man's eyes down—only serving to tantalize his mind with what all that material covered. Probably wouldn't make any difference if she'd had on petticoats.

He frowned and blinked his eyes when Tess stretched along the countertop for the butter dish. Naw, he had to be mistaken. That dress skirt had appeared to outline a skimpy pair of underpants!

Lordy, he must be even more exhausted than

he'd thought. His imagination was running rampant. He closed his eyes and leaned back on the bench, against the table.

This was nice. He could hear Tess humming to herself, and his lips quirked. That was one little fault she had—that voice was just a hair off-key. He didn't recognize the song, but he had a pretty good ear for music, and that tune didn't sound right in that faintly minor key.

Still, it seemed to fit the mood. A quiet, late-night kitchen, with a woman bustling around almost silently, her skirts swishing softly. Some pretty-darned-good-smelling food odors. A man's dog lying at his feet. He wondered if he could teach Lonesome to fetch his slippers.

First he'd have to get a pair of slippers, he chuckled to himself. He didn't own any right now.

"What's so funny?" Tess asked quietly beside him.

"Hum?" He kept his eyes closed, breathing in the faint wildflower scent he had begun to associate with Tess. "Oh, nothing really. I was just wondering if you'd share Lonesome with me long enough for me to teach him a trick of my own."

He opened his eyes enough to study Tess, who stood over him, leaning on her crutches. The lantern light behind her glowed on that luxurious, silky hair.

"What sort of trick?" she asked in a teasing voice.

"To fetch my slippers," he admitted. "Soon as I get me a pair, that is."

"Right now, why don't you fetch your plate? I can't carry it."

He straightened and opened his eyes fully. "Will

you sit with me while I eat? Have something to eat, too?"

"Stone Chisum, I am *not* going to eat another bite today. But I did pour two cups of coffee."

"Good," he said as he rose. "I always hate it when I come in late and have to eat alone."

Tess settled on the bench and propped her crutches against the end of the table. Reaching behind her, she untied the strings of Flower's bib apron and pulled it over her head.

"What kept you out so late this evening?" she asked as he set a cup of coffee in front of her. "The kids said you'd rounded up all the cattle that had gotten out."

When he didn't answer she glanced up at him. But he managed to jerk his eyes away from the shadowed valleys in the gaping dress bodice before she caught him looking. What he didn't manage was to keep a splash of hot coffee from spilling out of his own cup when his hand relaxed, and he hastily set the cup down.

"I was following some tracks," he said as he sat down on the other edge of the bench, far enough away from Tess not to be tempted to peek again. "That fence was deliberately cut. Whoever it was even came back last night and pulled down the temporary poles Rain and I put up yesterday evening."

"Good lord! Then the waterhole was poisoned on purpose, too?"

"Looks that way."

"Do you have any idea who did it?"

"No, except that there were two of them. But they had sense enough to head for the road and mix their tracks in with others there. I don't want

Flower and Rain to know about this. They'd just worry needlessly."

"Shouldn't they at least be warned? After all, Rain roams around out there by himself all the time."

Stone shoved his plate away and propped his elbows on the table, leaning his head into his hands. "Aw, hell. I don't know." He shoved his fingers through his hair, then got to his feet and began pacing the kitchen.

"I really don't know. You're right. And trying to keep Rain caged up close to the house would drive him crazy. I've gotta protect those kids, though. But what if Rain and Smoky had stopped to drink out of that waterhole? We lost six steers before I got that water fenced off. They didn't die easy, either."

"Has anything like this ever happened before?"

"Nothing this bad. A line shack up at the far end of the range burned. I had a few tools stored there, and supplies. It could've just been someone traveling through—spending the night. Looked like the fire started around the fireplace, and maybe a log fell out of the grate while whoever it was slept."

"Do you have any enemies, Stone?"

"Lots," he admitted with a gruff laugh. "Any former lawman has enemies, and they don't forget their grudges just because the lawman hangs up his gun. By the way, can you shoot?"

"Shoot? You mean, like in shooting a gun? Definitely not. And I don't plan on learning."

"Yes, you will. A gun's a necessity out here. We'll start your lessons tomorrow."

"We will not! I don't agree that a gun's necessary. It just aggravates a situation when a gun's involved. And you can't recall a bullet after it's fired!"

He sat back down and pulled his plate closer. "If we lived in town, I'd agree completely with you, Tess. Hell, the first thing I did in every town I worked in was make sure the boys who rode in checked their guns with me—and picked them up when they left. But out here it's different. There's snakes—coyotes. We even had a mountain lion try to take one of the calves we were raising in the corral here after its mother died."

Tess set her lips stubbornly and picked up her coffee cup. He couldn't make her touch a gun if she didn't want to. There had been snakes in the mountains, too, but a person had to learn to be cautious. And any wild animal would run from a human, unless a person was stupid enough to corner it.

Even knowing in a corner of her mind that Stone was more worried about human rather than animal danger wasn't enough to convince her to pick up a gun. She practiced the self-protection techniques she had learned in the rape prevention seminar that first month in New York City religiously. Any woman who had a lick of sense these days—those days, she mentally corrected herself—at least knew enough to make an attempt to protect herself.

A kick in the groin—thumbs in the eyes. Mostly, though, she was always cautious about getting into a situation where it might be necessary to protect herself. And, okay, she did carry a can of Mace on her keyring.

But guns? Huh-uh. No way.

Chapter Twelve

"Damn it! Don't jerk the trigger—squeeze it gently."

Tess opened her eyes and glared at Stone. "What difference does it make, as long as that stupid little lever gets pulled back far enough to make the bullet come out?"

"The trigger doesn't make the bullet come out," he explained again. "It releases the hammer and the hammer shoves the firing pin against the primer on the shell casing, which explodes the powder inside the shell. *That* makes the bullet come out. And when you jerk the trigger your hand moves, which moves the gun, which screws up your aim!"

She stuck out her tongue at him in a completely childish reflex gesture. She settled her bottom more securely on the stool and raised the pistol again. Carefully she lined up the little ball on the end of the barrel with the slot at the rear, then in turn with the bottle on the stump.

She squinted her eyes, forcing herself not to close them completely this time, and barely tightened her index finger. Her eyes shot open in surprise when the bottle shattered.

"There," she said in satisfaction. "I hit it. Now can I have my crutches back, so I can go to the house?"

When Stone didn't answer she looked up to see his gaze centered on her mouth, an amused look on his face. She tore her eyes away from the laugh lines near his eyes and clamped her lips tight.

"How old did you tell Flower you were?" he asked in a teasing voice. "I haven't seen Flower stick out her tongue since she was nine."

"Harumph!" she replied. "Are you going to get my crutches, or what?"

"Or what," he said. "The *what* is that you still have to practice a little. You haven't shot the rifle yet."

"Stone, I don't want to shoot the rifle. Please?"

He chuckled. "Just once, Tess. The rifle works pretty much on the same principle as the pistol."

She slid a look at the rifle Stone held cocked over his arm. Maybe it worked the same, but it sure as heck was bigger. And she'd bet a month's pay the noise it made was a darn sight louder.

"My ears are already ringing," she said, pouting. "I'm not going to be able to hear clearly for the rest of the day."

"I'll help you out," he promised. "I'll put my hands over your ears this time. Now come on. Let me show you how to hold the rifle."

She sighed and handed him the pistol, which he

put on a shelf on the barn wall. When he held the rifle out she gingerly accepted it, then turned forward again on the stool.

"What am I going to shoot at? The bottle's gone."

"First thing you have to know is that a rifle shoots a lot farther than a pistol. Depending on the load in your shells, the bullet can travel four times or more the distance of a pistol bullet. See that tree with the dead branch, where lightning hit it?"

"That's too far away. I can't possibly aim this thing accurately at something that far off."

She started to hand him back the rifle, but he shook his head.

"You just have to know how to hold it, Tess. Here."

Stone stepped behind her and reached around for the rifle. Placing it against her shoulder, he first took her right hand and wrapped her fingers below the breech. Her left arm he stretched out partway down the barrel.

"Snug the stock tight against your shoulder," he said, his breath fanning her hair, "and tilt your head a little so you can see down the barrel."

"Hum?" she murmured. Instead of complying with his directions, her arms relaxed and she leaned into the support behind her.

"Tess?" he said with a catch in his voice.

He abruptly stepped away, thrusting out a hand to steady her when she wobbled on the stool.

"Darn it," she said. "I told you I didn't want to do this. The rifle's too heavy." It had seemed light as a piece of fluff a second ago, though, with those corded arms around her.

"Pick the rifle back up and hold it like I showed you," he ordered in a gruff voice.

"Okay, okay." She lifted the rifle to her shoulder and laid her cheek on the stock. She lined up the sights as she had done on the pistol, then carefully curled her finger around the trigger.

"You said you'd cover my ears for me," she reminded him.

Stone raised his arms and cupped his hands on the sides of her head.

The rifle wobbled, and she took a determined breath, lining up the sights once more. Just as her finger reached for the trigger again, she felt a callused index finger gently caress her cheek. She gasped—her finger jerked, and a loud boom split the air.

The stool toppled backwards and Stone grabbed her, her weight throwing him off balance and twisting his body to take the brunt of the fall on his back. Her skirts flying, she landed on top of him, whooshing the breath from his chest.

Stone's arms pulled her close as he drew in a ragged breath. "Tess," he demanded with his first exhalation. "Tess, honey, are you hurt? Your ankle. Tess!"

She levered herself up from his chest and glared down into his worried face. "You didn't tell me that damned thing would jump that hard!"

"Kick," he murmured. "A rifle kicks, it doesn't jump."

"Kick. Jump. Whatever. You should have warned me."

"I told you to keep it snug against your shoulder."

"Yeah. Then you touched me and broke my concentration!"

"I was already touching you, Tess." He raised

his arm and cupped his hand over her ear. "Was this the touch that bothered you, huh?" he asked softly.

"N . . . no," she admitted in a strangled voice.

"Maybe this one then." He gently rubbed his thumb over her hot cheek.

She barely bobbed her head in agreement, and his fingers closed more firmly around her head, gently tugging her towards him. Inch by inch she obeyed the slight pressure of his hand and lowered her head.

He only sipped her mouth at first, then each corner. His thumb traced a back and forth path on her cheek, and he curled his other hand into her hair.

"Tess," he breathed. "Oh, Tess."

Even with her eyes closed she found his mouth again—that beautiful mouth she had known all along would fit hers perfectly. Softly she tasted him once more, once again. His hands tightened, holding her firmly, as he growled deep in his throat, and she willingly gave in to his deep, soul shattering kiss.

Demanding, yet soft at the same time, the kiss spread waves of sensation downward, tingling across her breasts and stomach—curling her toes. Delicious came to mind—then sexy and precious, somehow mingled into the same feeling. In awe at the very intensity and depth of the physical and emotional impact of such a simple thing as a kiss, she quit analyzing and gave in to the wonder and delight her body was reveling in.

Stone's hands roamed her body, his fingers wrinkling her skirt and inching it upward, stroking as he pulled at the fabric.

Clenching her fingers on his shoulders, she raised her head a scant inch, sighing in pleasure when his mouth nibbled at her jaw, down her neck. He licked a slow, circular path on the mound of her breast, and her nipples contracted into a pebbled hardness. Her sigh caught on a strangled moan of ecstacy when his mouth found her nipple and his hand slid under her skirt to caress her thigh.

Honey. He had called her honey. She arched and, barely opening her eyes, she gazed down through her lashes, cupping her hand on the side of his head, curling her fingers in his rumpled hair. The look of utter rapture on Stone's face, half buried in her breast, sent a spiraling flame of near climax into her stomach.

"Stone," she gasped when his hand cradled the mound between her legs.

Glittering brown pools of passion centered on her face when he drew his head back and gulped in air. She leaned toward him, as though to give him breath from her own mouth, then caught her lower lip and smothered a moan when his fingers moved between her thighs.

"Tess," he whispered with a growl. "Beautiful, mysterious Tess. God, I want you, sweetheart."

He could have her. Nothing mattered right now except for him not to stop—for him to continue spreading this mind-shattering pleasure over her body.

"Yes," she whimpered. "Please."

Stone slowly pulled his hand from beneath her skirt and sat up, gathering her against his chest and burying his face in her neck.

"We can't," he murmured. "Not now." He nibbled her earlobe, then lapped gently around her ear with his tongue. "Sweetheart, we'll have to wait."

"No. I can't."

Stone groaned and kissed her again. Deeply, as though he would never stop—as though he couldn't stop.

But he had to stop. He had wanted her from the first second he'd glimpsed her, while tumbling over Silver Mane's damned head. The want had escalated into something more last night when they'd shared the quietness in the kitchen. She had seemed to fill a spot he hadn't even realized was vacant in the house. Or, if he had known, he kept the loneliness consigned to a corner of his mind.

Now more than just a cry for physical gratification crowded his mind. Joining with this woman could do more than just satisfy his lust. He would wake the next sunrise with his body sated, but that hollow spot deep inside him would long for a whispered, early-morning conversation, a kiss and a snuggle to start the day.

Stone gripped Tess's arms and pushed her away. Wrapping one arm around her back, he held her and lifted his thumb to her kiss-swollen mouth.

"Sweetheart," he murmured again. "It's broad daylight. We can't. The kids . . ."

Tess blinked misty eyes as his words penetrated. A flush of embarrassment started up her neck as she became aware of their sprawled positions, her skirt around her hips, the sun warming her bare legs.

"Don't, honey," he said, shaking his head. "Don't spoil it by getting mad or embarrassed. It's just as much my fault as yours—probably more. And I sure as hell can't bring myself to be sorry this happened."

She studied his face for a long moment as she sorted through her own emotions. Finally she gave a sigh of contentment and snuggled against his shoulder. Spoil it? No, she couldn't bring herself to do that either.

She had never even felt such ecstacy when her body throbbed with awakening sexuality in her teens. Never with Robert's grunting attempts to break through her reserve and consummate their relationship before their marriage vows. Where had Stone been all her life?

A hundred and one years in the past, her mind answered the question.

"Stone, we have to talk," she whispered.

"Yeah, I know," he agreed. "But whatever the hell it is you're running from you'd better get it through your head right now that we're going to work it out. Together."

"We . . . we might not be able to," she answered in a soft voice. "You see . . ."

A scream split the air, then rapid, sharp barks. Stone's head jerked up.

"Lonesome. Good God, he's attacking someone!" Stone scrambled to his feet and pulled her up beside him, then grabbed the stool and shoved it beneath her bottom. "Where'd the rifle go?"

"There." She pointed to the ground, where the rifle lay next to the dusty bed they had just shared.

Another shriek sounded as Stone grabbed the rifle and ran toward the cabin, Lonesome's high-pitched barks growing louder.

"Stay here," he threw over his shoulder.

She set her lips grimly and scooted off the stool. That was her dog out there, and she damned sure wanted to see what was going on. She lifted the stool and plopped it forward a foot, hopping up to meet it.

A coolness on her breast drew her eyes down, and Tess halted as she picked up the stool again. A small smile curved her lips as she set the stool back down and reached for her breast, still moist from Stone's mouth and hanging over the top of the low-cut dress. She shoved her breast back into the confines of the bodice and took a few more seconds to smooth her dress into place and shake the dirt from her skirt. After she ran her fingers through her tousled hair she grabbed the stool again.

Stone skidded to a stop when he rounded the corner of the house and found the source of the frantic din echoing in his ears. Mrs. Peterson's long skirt hung in shreds around her shoes, and Lonesome grabbed a scrap of material from the ground. The dog tossed the scrap aside, and Mrs. Peterson aimed a kick at his head.

Lonesome grabbed the woman's kid-clad ankle and growled fiercely. She lost her balance and fell against the buggy, and the horse neighed shrilly. Tossing its head, the horse surged forward, pulling the buggy with it. Mrs. Peterson landed in a heap of voluminous skirts and a cloud of dust, kicked up from her broad rear end.

"Lonesome!" Choking on his laughter, Stone somehow managed a shrill whistle to accompany his command as he set the rifle against the porch railing.

The dog gave a final shake of the ankle in its mouth and dropped it. He sat on his haunches, a low growl issuing from his throat and his eyes guarding the intruder.

"Get that brute away from me!" Mrs. Peterson yelled.

With an agile movement Stone would never have thought the hefty woman capable of, she pulled her legs under her and shoved herself to her feet. She lifted her leg for another kick, but Lonesome lurched with a snarl, and she hastily backed away from the dog, shrieking in anger.

"Get that vicious thing away from me, Stone!" she screamed again. "I'll have him killed! You just wait and see!"

Stone strode forward and stopped beside Lonesome, who turned adoring eyes up at him as he licked Stone's hand.

"Vicious? Why, Tillie, this dog's just a pup. Look how friendly he is." He scratched Lonesome's ear, and the dog leaned against his leg.

"You . . . you . . . liar!" Mrs. Peterson spat. "You just saw him attacking me!" She pointed a finger wavering in indignation at Lonesome. "I demand you shoot that dog before he tries to kill someone else!"

Lonesome growled again, and Mrs. Peterson clasped her hands over her huge breasts. "See?" she said with a gasp. "He's going to jump on me again!"

Stone reached to tip his hat up an inch, before remembering it was on the ground behind the barn. Running his fingers through his hair instead, he pulled out a piece of dry grass and stuck the stem in his mouth.

"Dog's just doing its job," he drawled with a shrug. "Protectin' my property. Keepin' unwanted visitors away. Can't blame him for that."

Mrs. Peterson dropped her arms, and her bosom wobbled with a wrathful gasp of breath. "I didn't come here to visit," she almost screamed. "I came here to tell you that the women in town will not tolerate you living out here in sin with that harlot!"

"Michael, don't you dare!" Angela made a leap for his arm and shoved it back to his side.

"Aw, come on, Angie. Just a couple of drops of rain. That dragon needs to get drenched—to drown some of that holier-than-thou priggishness out of her."

Angela glanced down at Mrs. Peterson and reluctantly shook her head. "I'd almost be tempted to agree with you if there was a cloud in the sky. But there's not."

"Let's make this one visible," he said eagerly. "Blacken it a little."

She stifled a giggle—one more of the frequent giggles Michael always seemed to draw from her. "We can't," she said. "It wouldn't be an appropriate use of our powers right now."

"Shoot," Michael grumbled.

Chapter Thirteen

Tess limped around the corner of the house in time to hear Mrs. Peterson's last sputtered comment clearly. She leaned on her crutches, which she had retrieved from the back porch, and glared at the bedraggled woman, standing with her hands on her extensive hips, a smirk of outright maliciousness on her face.

"Why, you old biddy," she muttered, though she could tell that, despite the woman's girth, she was probably the same age as Tess.

Spying the rifle leaning against the porch rail, she levered herself over and started to reach for it.

She jerked her hand back. Damn it, that was just what she had tried to get through Stone's head last night. A convenient gun only prodded a person into acting rashly. She shook her head and turned back to watch how Stone would handle the situation.

The front door of the cabin edged open. Rain and Flower slipped through and tiptoed across the porch to join her. The children sat down with their backs against the cabin wall, and Rain brushed a clump of soil from the board beside him. Quirking an eyebrow, he glanced up at Tess and silently patted the board.

She eased her crutches away from her and sat on the edge of the porch. Pulling her legs up, she ducked beneath the porch railing and settled back against the wall to watch the two combatants in the yard.

"You better listen to me this time, Stone Chisum," Mrs. Peterson said with an edge of self-satisfaction to her voice. "The Ladies' Guild will not tolerate this. One of the things we're striving for is a sin-free environment for the children of this territory."

"Well, now, Tillie," Stone responded. "You ought to know just what sins a person should avoid, I guess. Especially sins of the flesh."

"You bastard!" Mrs. Peterson's veneer of self-righteousness dissolved in a flash. "A gentleman wouldn't mention a lady's past! Besides, I'm not that same person anymore!"

"No," Stone agreed. "That other person was too puffed up with her own ego to notice if she had to step over a pair of copulating bodies right in her path. I think I liked you better that way, Tillie. At least you weren't always sticking your nose where it would cause trouble for somebody else."

"It's Mrs. Peterson to you, *Mister* Chisum. I've been married and widowed, and I'm due your respect now."

"Was a time you'd have been real happy for me to call you Tillie," Stone mused.

"You are not going to sidetrack me!" Mrs. Peterson emphasized her words by crossing her arms beneath her breasts. "Dr. Calder came out here and treated a woman living with you. He bought clothing for her in town and put it on your account at the store. One of the members of the Ladies' Guild checked with Pastor Jones and found out that he hadn't been out here to perform a wedding ceremony."

"That's true," Stone admitted. "You don't think I'd have left you off the invitation list for my wedding, do you, Tillie?"

"I'd sooner attend your funeral than your wedding!"

"Sorry. Can't accommodate you there."

"There's an empty room at the boardinghouse," she ground out. "I checked before I drove out here. I'm perfectly willing to do my Christian duty and take this woman into town and help her get moved into the boardinghouse. You can't keep her out here with you, around those innocent children."

Stone cocked his elbows behind him and slid his fingers into his back pockets. "Boardinghouse's rooms are all upstairs, and she's got a broken ankle. I'm sure you know that, since you seem to know everything else. It'd be too hard on her, climbing up and down for meals. My cabin's all on one floor."

"You can't keep that woman out here!" Mrs. Peterson yelled. Taking a few steps in his direction, she leaned forward and propped her hands on her ample hips. "There might not be anything we can do about you and that neighbor of yours, but the Guild will not tolerate you corrupting your children by moving a whore into your bed."

Stone laid a hand on Lonesome's head when the dog growled a warning. "You seem to have an awfully strong interest in my love life, Tillie," he said in a deceptively mild voice. "Don't suppose you're jealous, are you?"

When Mrs. Peterson gasped in indignation Stone leaned toward her and lowered his voice even further, though his words still carried to the porch. "And if I ever hear you mention the word 'whore' again in the same breath you use to talk about Tess, I'll sell tickets, then kick that fat ass of yours up and down Main Street for the show!"

Rain doubled his arms over his stomach and bit his lips, trying to hold back his laughter. Flower muffled a snort beside him, then gave up the struggle. Despite Tess's attempts to quiet them, both children howled with unrestrained glee, and Rain even rolled to the porch floor, clutching his stomach and drumming his heels against the boards.

"Oh, lord," Tess breathed when she looked up to see Mrs. Peterson's pale eyes glaring at them. Tess glanced at Stone and lifted her hand to wiggle her fingers at him. Shrugging her shoulders to indicate to Stone that she had absolutely no control over his children, she slid to the edge of the porch and picked up her crutches.

Stone was doing a good job on his own, but she wasn't about to hide behind a man's muscles.

Lonesome leapt to his feet and ran to meet Tess, his tail wagging and his tongue hanging out as he followed her back to Stone. He sat down between Stone and Tess, swiveling his head from one of them to the other.

Tess leaned on her crutches, refusing to make a

grab for her bodice when the top gaped open with her movement.

"Hello," she drawled in a syrupy voice. "I'm so glad to finally get to meet one of Stone's neighbors. Mrs. Peterson, isn't it? I'm Tess Foster."

Mrs. Peterson's face reddened, and she swung her head wildly. "I . . ." flustered, she nodded an acknowledgment of Tess's words.

"Matilda Peterson," she managed to say. "I drove out here to offer you a ride into town, Miss Foster. It is *miss,* isn't it?"

"Sure is," Tess returned with a false smile. "And I couldn't possibly take you up on your kind offer without checking with Stone first. He always makes it very clear to all of us here that he's in charge of the ranch."

Mrs. Peterson's sniff merged with Stone's muted snort.

"Well, my dear," Mrs. Peterson said, "sometimes we just have to stand up to our men and do what we know is right."

"Perhaps," Tess mused. "Does the boardinghouse take dogs?"

"Of course not," Mrs. Peterson replied.

Tess shrugged as well as she could with the crutches under her armpits. "Then I guess I'll have to turn down your so kind, Christian offer of charity, Matilda." She gave an insincere sigh. "I'm afraid Lonesome would pine away without me, and I couldn't bear that. He seems to have attached himself to me and might not eat if I'm not here to feed him."

"That vicious brute needs beating rather than feeding," Mrs. Peterson spat. "Just look what he did to my dress."

"I hope he didn't bite you, Matilda." Tess widened her eyes, feigning horror. "I haven't had him long enough to make sure he doesn't have any diseases—maybe rabies. I'd suggest you see Dr. Calder immediately."

"Rabies?" Mrs. Peterson screeched. She pulled up her ragged skirt hem, exposing a huge black-clad calf. "Oh, my God. Look. His teeth caught my stocking! There's a hole in it."

Dropping her skirt, Mrs. Peterson whirled and ran for the buggy as fast as her corpulent body would allow. The springs on the vehicle groaned in protest as she pulled herself into the seat and unwrapped the reins from the brake handle. Not looking back, she slapped the reins on the horse's rump. The buggy lurched forward with another squeal of protest and the horse galloped down the dirt road.

Michael wiggled one finger, his hands clasped behind his back. A gust of wind blew the buggy top open, and a crash of thunder split the air. Rain poured from a sky that had slowly been gathering dark clouds for the past few minutes, spattering more gently near the cabin, more fiercely along the buggy's path.

He rolled his eyes skyward and pursed his lips, whistling and rocking back and forth on the cloud.

"Gee," he mused in an innocent voice. "Think it looks like rain, Angie?"

She swatted him on the shoulder and collapsed on the cloud in laughter.

Chapter Fourteen

"MICHAEL. ANGELA."

Their laughter stopped immediately.

"Uh-oh." Angela stared overhead fearfully. The voice had only been mildly censuring, but she was filled with an overwhelming sense of guilt. She glanced at Michael and saw his apprehension, which mirrored her own feelings.

Michael sighed deeply and reached down to help her to stand. "It's okay, honey," he said. "Mr. G knows it was my fault."

"Not totally," she whispered frantically in return. "I knew you were going to do that when you started gathering the clouds."

A soft voice broke into their conversation, saying only a few words before it fell silent.

"Yes, Sir," Michael replied. "I know it was sort of a mean thing to do, but that woman is mean herself."

"Michael." She tugged on his sleeve. "Don't argue!"

He ignored her and continued, "And you've got to admit, Sir, that it got the point across without really hurting her. But I promise, I'll think before I act from now on. I know we're supposed to be forgiving, not vengeful."

He quirked an eyebrow at the sky. "Isn't that right, Sir? The forgiving part, I mean?"

A muted clap of thunder rolled across the sky, sounding almost like laughter dying away.

Stone set Tess on her feet beneath the porch overhang and handed her the crutches. Glancing at Rain and Flower, he said, "Aren't you two supposed to be working on your lessons?"

"Yes, Pa," they answered together. Stifling giggles, they scrambled to their feet and ran into the cabin.

Tess shook her head, one corner of her mouth lifting in a wry grin. "I'm afraid we weren't a very good example for them out there, but I just couldn't seem to stop myself from taking a few jibes at that beastly woman. Who does she think she is, anyway?"

"Aw, Tillie's not so bad," Stone said with a suppressed chuckle. "I kind of enjoy arguing with her. And, after all, Lonesome did attack her. Tillie's always been sort of above herself, though, thinkin' she knows what's best for everyone else. She's been ticked off at me ever since I let her know I was immune to her charms in that town back in Texas where her daddy owned the bank."

When Tess gazed toward the road the buggy had taken with a disbelieving look on her face, he laughed and continued, "She wasn't always that big. And she wasn't always so hoity-toity, especially when it came to matters of the flesh. I have to hand it to her, though. She stuck by her daddy after I sent him to jail. I hear she still gets letters from him."

"You sent Tillie's father to jail?"

"He was embezzling from his bank. Tillie married one of her beaux right after her daddy went to prison, and they moved to Oklahoma. Her husband got killed in a stagecoach wreck less than a year after they were married, but he left her pretty well off. I'll admit I was surprised to see how fat she'd gotten when I ran into her in Clover Valley. She must've let herself go after her husband died."

"I still don't like her. Did you hear what she called me?"

"Well, maybe she'll leave us alone for a while now—at least until she's sure she's not going to die of rabies."

"That was mean of me, wasn't it? Especially since we could see that the skin wasn't broken under that hole in her stocking."

"Yep," he agreed. "You're one mean lady, Tess Foster." Lifting her chin with his index finger, he murmured, "Maybe I ought to try to kiss a little of that meanness out of you."

"Maybe you should," she whispered.

He bent his head and kissed her tenderly. A long moment later he raised his head and nodded toward the swing on the other end of the porch.

"Let's sit a minute," he said quietly. "Before I fall completely and irrevocably in love with you, I'd like to know just who it is that's crawlin' into my heart."

She gasped and stumbled backward, shaking her head wildly. "No! You can't! We can't let this happen!"

As Tess wobbled on her crutches he grabbed for her. His hands on her shoulders to steady her, he stared down into her frightened green eyes, scowling in disbelief.

"You kissed me back like you were feeling the same damned way! You've wiggled yourself into my life—into my kids' lives—made us start caring for you! What the hell's your reason for backing off now?"

Tess wrenched her eyes from his and bit her lip. He'd never believe her. How could he? It was almost too outlandish for her to believe herself, and she was the one living it. Just about a week ago she had climbed down the back side of Saddleback Mountain and fallen a hundred and one years into the past. Found the man she hadn't even realized she had been searching for all her life—found two kids who were the smartest, most wonderful children who could have ever lived.

But that was just it. They *had* lived—had lived seventy years before she had even been born. And it was confusing as hell when she tried to reason it out. Was she actually living her future now, or was it in abeyance? How could she live her future in the past?

She admitted to feeling an ever stronger urge to push aside her former life and stay here with Stone and the kids. Yet she seesawed the other way each time that feeling surfaced. She'd worked so hard to overcome her impoverished background and get to the point in her profession where she appeared to be only a scant distance from the top of the mountain. If she won the case she was working on, her entire future would be assured—her future back in 1994. She knew she had the brains and guts to have a brilliant career, and at one time that had been her most fervent desire.

Yet she kept recalling the lonely, late-night hours in her office—her apartment gathering dust—the antacids she bought more frequently lately.

And there was another worry she couldn't seem to find an answer to: If she did find the time warp and reenter it, would she emerge in her own time period? Or, if time was passing back there, would she reenter her world with a lot of explaining to do about her absence—perhaps at a point where her career would be in ashes due to her absence?

Her main struggle right now, though, was whether she even gave a damn. The years ahead of her in her own time stretched forward in a lonely void. Here, in 1893, she had found the possibility of true love and a family. There, in 1994, she would have left them in the murky past—her only contact with them the genealogy section of the library.

"Damn it! Answer me, Tess!"

Stone shook her slightly, and she covered her face with her hands, her crutches dropping to the porch with a clatter. A small, miserable sob escaped her confining hands. She heard Stone give a muffled snort of annoyance as he swept her into his arms for the third time that day and carried her over to the swing.

"Stop that," he demanded after he sat her down in the swing seat. "You're not going to pull that on me again. You know I can't stand it when you cry. You're not playing fair."

"I . . ." She dropped her hands and sniffed. "I'm not playing. You just don't know. And I'm sorry; I don't usually cry at all. I . . ." A hiccup shook her shoulders, and she buried her face again.

The muted sounds of misery crept over Stone's skin on caresses as soft as angels' wings. He reached for her—jerked his hand back and grabbed his handkerchief from his back pocket. Thrusting the handkerchief into the bend of her elbow, he stomped to the edge of the porch, resolutely turning his back on her.

Rain cascaded over the porch eaves, silvery sheens like the tears from a woman's eyes.

"Aw, shit!" he muttered. Frowning in puzzlement, he glanced overhead. For just a second he'd thought he heard a voice whispering a reproof of his profane words. It couldn't have been Tess—she was sobbing much too hard to speak.

He closed his eyes and bowed his head, shutting out the sight of the pouring rain. But short of covering his ears with his hands like some sissified weakling, he couldn't shut out the sounds of Tess crying. His shoulders slumped and he turned back to the swing.

"Tess."

She took a final swipe at her eyes with the handkerchief and then balled it in her hands.

"I'm sorry," she said with a sniff. "It must be those stupid pills making me weepy. The doctor warned me it might take my body awhile to adjust to them."

"Doc Calder didn't say anything about leaving you any pills to take."

Tess straightened and lifted her gaze to his face. Though her hands continued to twist the handkerchief, she breathed deeply.

"It wasn't Dr. Calder. It was my doctor back where I live."

"In West Virginia?"

"No. New York City."

He walked over and lifted her skirt hem, exposing the tennis shoe on her right foot. "And do they wear funny-looking shoes like that in New York City these days? I noticed them when your skirts flew up out behind the barn. When I kissed you and when you kissed me back."

"It's . . . it's a Reebok. It's a very expensive running shoe. I've also got a pair I wear in my aerobics class."

"That's not what I asked you." He dropped her skirt and slipped his fingertips into his back pockets.

The handkerchief gave with a rip. "Oh, I'm sorry," she murmured. "I'll wash it and sew it up for you."

"You don't have to tell me you're sorry, Tess. Just answer my question."

"No," Tess barely whispered. "It's not what they're wearing in New York these days. But it's what women and men both are wearing in 1994."

He sat on the swing and tenderly placed an arm around her. "Honey, I'm the one who's sorry now. Look, I didn't mean to push you like this, and if you're not ready to talk right now, I can wait. Just . . ."

"Darn it, Stone!" Tess jerked away from his arm and turned to face him. "Listen to me! Rain wasn't lying to you up on the hill. Neither was I—not really. I did fall, but it wasn't from any horse. I fell off a mountain in upper New York State on July 31, 1994, and the next thing I knew I was sitting on a hillside in Oklahoma Territory on July 31, 1893!"

"Tess, honey . . ."

"Don't you *Tess honey* me in that patronizing voice! I don't have any more idea how I managed to fall into a time warp and end up here than you do. Things like this don't happen, except in books. Shoot, there's probably a Loch Ness Monster and a Bigfoot, too!"

"Let me take you in for a rest. I'll have Flower fix you something to eat, and then you can take a nap."

Tess threw the handkerchief at him, a look of exasperated fury on her face. "Flower believed me! Why can't you?"

"You've been telling the kids this stuff? Look, Tess, let me get Doc Calder back out here. He really didn't examine anything other than your ankle when he came out before."

"And I suppose you want him to examine my head this time, right?"

"Well, when people get injured sometimes things don't show up right away."

Tess nodded her head. "Okay. Hand me my crutches, so I can get into the bedroom."

"I can carry you. . . ."

"Hand me those darned crutches, Stone Chisum," she said through gritted teeth. "I'm perfectly capable of getting in there under my own power."

"All right. All right," he said as he rose. He picked up the crutches and held them out to her. "Or . . .

okay, which is what you're always saying. I assume it means the same thing as all right?"

"Yes." Tess grabbed the crutches and wobbled to her feet. "And there really are things like Jeeps and movies, too—in 1994!"

Tess levered herself over to the door and leaned on one crutch to pull it open. Halfway through the opening, she paused and looked back at Stone.

"Aren't you going to come with me? Keep an eye on me, so I don't fall?"

"Huh? Oh, sure, if you want me to."

"I do," she said under her breath. As she swung down the hallway, she passed two doorways on her left. "Are those yours and Rain's bedrooms?" she asked Stone.

"Uh . . . yeah. I guess you haven't seen the rest of the house, have you?"

"No, only the kitchen and Flower's bedroom."

When she entered the kitchen she saw Flower and Rain with their heads bent over their books at the table. She stopped for a second, glanced at Stone and then back at the children.

"What are you kids studying?" she asked when the children looked up.

"History," Rain answered. "We're making a list of the presidents and the most important thing that happened while they were in office."

"Who's president now?" Tess asked.

"Grover Cleveland," Rain said promptly. "He beat Benjamin Harrison and General Weaver last year."

Tess thought for a moment. Although history hadn't been one of her best subjects, she still had a good recall of the various dates and lists she'd had to memorize.

"Cleveland will get beat by William McKinley in 1896," Tess said in a decisive voice. "With Theodore Roosevelt as his vice president." No sense telling them that poor McKinley would be killed by an assassin's bullet in Buffalo, New York, shortly after he began his second term.

"Tess," Stone murmured in a warning voice.

"Look, kids," she said, ignoring Stone, "you about ready for a break here? There's some things in the bedroom I want to show you."

Flower immediately jumped to her feet. "Oh, have you told Pa? Are you going to show him the plastic and tell us about some of the other things in the future? Pa, Tess said there's an oven that can cook things in a flash. Wouldn't that be neat? I wouldn't have to spend half of every day just cooking meals."

A thunderous look spread over Stone's face. But before he could explode, she ushered the children into the bedroom.

"Are you coming, Stone?" she called through the door in that sticky-sweet voice she had used on Tillie Peterson.

"Damn right!" he muttered.

Tess had the pack on the bed beside her, and Flower and Rain sat on the floor. Nodding at the empty ladderback chair, she waited until Stone slumped into it, stretched out his legs, and tucked his fingers into his pockets before she began unbuckling the straps on the pack.

"I guess you and Rain have probably been discussing the things we talked about yesterday, haven't you, Flower?" she asked.

"Well, yes," Flower admitted. "You didn't say Rain and I couldn't talk about it. You just wanted me to wait and let you tell Pa yourself."

Stone snorted and slumped down even farther in the chair, but she disregarded his glowering face.

"That's right, honey," she told Flower. "And did you believe what Flower told you, Rain?"

"Sure," Rain replied. "It made sense to me. I'm the one who saw you appear out of thin air, remember?"

"I remember." She dug in the pack and laid out several items on the bed, then set the pack on the floor. Picking up her inexpensive instant camera, she flipped up the flash attachment and held the camera to her eye.

"Smile, you guys."

The flash exploded, and Stone surged upright in his chair. Tess pulled the picture from the bottom slot and aimed the camera at Stone, clicking the shutter again. She giggled softly when he bit off his growl of anger and blinked owlishly at her.

"Now," she said in a determined voice, "if my travel through time didn't hurt the film, we'll have pictures of all of you in less than a minute."

"Really?" Flower said in awe.

"Really." She picked up the two cardboards and handed one to each child. "Here. You can watch them develop. Hold them by the bottom here, on this white space. That way you won't get fingerprints on the picture."

Rain and Flower stared at the cardboards with rapt attention. Almost immediately, Rain gasped.

"Something's happening," he said. "It's . . . look, Flower! There's a picture appearing here. Look. It's you and me!"

"And this one's Pa," Flower said in an excited voice. "You ought to see the look on your face, Pa." She laughed. Then she scrambled to her feet and thrust the picture under Stone's nose. "And look—it's changing into color. I've never seen a camera picture come out in color. They're always just black and white."

"Bull," Stone said. But he reached for the picture, staring down into it. He glanced at Rain, and Rain passed his picture to his father.

"This doesn't prove a darned thing." Stone tossed the picture on the bed. "So there's a newfangled camera. The newspaper articles I read about the last World's Fair reported all kinds of new inventions these days. There's even something called a telephone, where people can call up other people miles away and talk to them."

"In my day," Tess said with a smirk, "you can even see the person you're talking to on the other end of some of the telephones. It doesn't matter if you're calling from New York and talking to someone in California."

"Bull," Stone repeated.

She sighed and picked up a plastic lighter from the bed. She flicked the roller and a flame spewed from the top.

"I'm not sure what that liquid is inside this," she said, "but I guess it's some kind of liquid gas. When it runs out you just throw it away and get a new one." She released the lever and the flame died. "See, I always bring at least two with me, in case the fuel runs out in one. I use them to light campfires."

She handed Flower and Rain each one of the plastic lighters and picked up a can of soup and her can opener. Fitting the opener to the rim, she squeezed it. It burred softly as the can circled under the opener and the lid fell free.

"The opener works on a battery," she explained. "I usually just bring freeze-dried food with me . . ." She showed Stone one of the packages of freeze-dried vegetables. "But the canned soup tastes better. It's a little heavier to carry, but it's worth it on a chilly evening."

Stone sniffed the soup tentatively. He dipped a finger in and licked the moisture. "Flower's chicken soup tastes a heck of a lot better than this."

"I agree." Tess smiled. "Granny's tasted lots better, too. But when I go backpacking sometimes I'm gone several days. I don't think it's practical for me to carry a live chicken with me and make soup from scratch, especially when there's all this other, lighter food available."

"You're not proving anything, Tess." Stone set the soup on the bedside table. "You haven't shown me one thing that couldn't just be stuff that's in use back East that hasn't made its way out here yet. There's all kinds of canned goods in the stores in town. And so what if someone's figured out an easy way to open the cans? Probably some guy got tired of his wife always griping about how hard it was to open them."

She shook her head and leaned down to the pack. "I was hoping I wouldn't have to show you these. Maybe Flower and Rain shouldn't . . ."

Before she could finish Flower reached for one of the objects in her hand. "New books! Great, Tess. I've read every book we have at least three times. Sometimes I get so desperate for something to read that I even read ahead in our lesson books."

Flower flicked open the step-back cover on the paperback book in her hand and her eyes widened. "Oh! Oh, isn't he handsome!"

Stone ripped the book from Flower's hand and threw it back at Tess. "What the hell are you doing carrying around filthy stuff like that? And how dare you show it to my daughter?"

"This is perfectly suitable reading material in my time!" she spat at him. "And it's not pornographic. It's a love story—a wonderful type of escapism. I read books like this when I'm overstressed and need to relax. And the picture is not erotic. It's meant to convey the deep love that the hero and heroine have for each other, which includes physical love."

"You get those damned books out of my house!"

"Oh, Pa, hush up." Flower reached for the book again, while Stone stared at her in amazement. "That's a beautiful picture—a lot prettier than the one over that bar in town where you drink sometimes. That lady in the bar is as naked as the day she was born, and she's got a look on her face that . . ."

"Mountain Flower Chisum, go to your room!" Stone roared. "You will not sass me!"

"I am in my room, Pa," Flower said in a mild voice as she flipped another page in the book. "Oh. I guess this is what you want us to see, huh, Tess?"

Flower held the book open and pointed at the copyright on the inside page. "It was printed in June of 1994."

Tess nodded, then cast a worried look at Stone.

"Let me see that!" Stone grabbed the book and stared at the page. An incredulous look replaced the anger on his face.

Chapter Fifteen

"Go on back to your lessons, kids," Stone said, his eyes never leaving the book. "And shut the door on your way out."

One glance at his face and his children rose to their feet. Rain started to hand the plastic lighter back to Tess.

"You can keep that if you like, Rain," she said. "And here." She handed Flower the pictures. "We'll take some more pictures later. I brought a couple of extra boxes of film with me."

"Thanks, Tess," Rain said, a huge grin splitting his face.

Flower's thanks were more hesitant. She accepted the pictures, glancing at Tess and then back at her father. "Uh . . . Pa, you aren't going to yell at Tess, are you? I mean, it's not her fault this happened to her. And I won't read the books, unless you say I can."

"Hum?" He turned another page in the book, his face creased into a mixture of grimness and interest. "No, I won't yell, honey. Go on now."

As soon as the door closed, Stone looked up at Tess. "Pretty good writing here, for a book like this. But I still don't think it's appropriate for Flower to read."

"That's your decision. You're her father. All I want right now is to know if you believe me—believe I traveled through time to get here. Or do you still think I'm crazy?"

Stone closed the book in his hands, then opened it again to what she could see was the copyright page. His lips thinned and she felt a sudden urge to kiss his mouth, soften it. He raised his head and she saw the confusion in those wonderfully deep brown pools.

"I guess I have to believe you," he said. "You've got an entire backpack full of proof there. What *I* need to know now is how soon you're planning on going back."

"I don't even know if I *can* go back," she admitted. "I'd have to find the time warp again, and I'm not real sure how it would work. I've tried to remember the area around me up there on the hillside, and I didn't notice anything strange. But then, I didn't see the warp I fell into last week, either. I only remember traveling through it."

"Do you want to go back that badly?"

"Why, of course." She knew as soon as the words left her lips they were only a half-truth. She hadn't really come to a decision one way or the other. However, as much as she was beginning to care for Stone, it wouldn't do to give him any false hope that they could build a lasting relationship.

She stumbled onward, justifying and rationalizing as she spoke. "I mean . . . I mean, that's where I *live.* My apartment's back there—my job. I'm a lawyer and in line for a partnership in the firm I work for. If I get it, it means a lot more money and a secure future for me."

"Women aren't lawyers," Stone scoffed. "At your age, you ought to be raising your own children and letting your husband take care of you!"

"Women are *too* lawyers! Just as good as men. And will you quit with the references to my age?" she demanded angrily. "In my time a woman's not considered a spinster at twenty! In fact, she doesn't even have to get married, if she doesn't want to! If she wants a child, she can have one on her own—raise it on her own!"

"Is that so?" He quirked an eyebrow. "And just what marvelous invention do they have in *your* time to take a man's place in getting a woman with child?"

Her anger dissolved into a giggle as she stared at him. "You . . ." She gasped back a laugh. "You'll definitely never believe me if I tell you the truth about that!"

"Try me."

Her green eyes sparkling, Tess gazed directly into his eyes. "It's called artificial insemination. For years veterinarians used it on cattle and horses. Then they discovered a man's sperm could be frozen and used later, too. Or, in some cases, the man comes to the doctor's office first, then the woman comes in a few minutes later and has the sperm implanted in her uterus."

"Bull crap!" he snorted. "And I suppose the doctor knows just what day a woman can conceive."

"Yep." She grabbed for her camera. "Oh, Stone. You should see the look on your face."

Before she could bring the camera to her eye he jerked it from her hand. With a quick motion he turned it on her and pushed the shutter button. The flash filled the room, and he pulled the cardboard from the bottom of the camera, as he had seen her do, hoping the image before him was captured accurately.

The wildly curling hair, backlit by the sunlight coming through the window. That beautiful mouth, open in a smile of gay laughter. Those emerald eyes sparkling in mischief and delight.

Handing the camera back to her but keeping the picture securely in his fingers, he said, "Sounds like a cold-blooded way of lovemaking to me."

"Tit for tat," Tess murmured. She took a picture of him and cocked her head when she lowered the camera. "It is," she agreed. "Cold-blooded, I mean." Tess held his picture behind her back when he tried to reach for it. "But sometimes a woman wants a child awfully bad—and she just can't seem to find the man she wants to share the rest of her life with."

"Must be a pretty poor crop of men back in your time."

She nodded absently.

"Especially if you're still unmarried," he continued. "Must be a bunch of fools back there. Or is there something else besides your job you want to get back to? Someone, maybe?"

"No, not anymore," Tess said.

"Then there was someone," he prodded.

"Well, yes, I was engaged for a while, but it didn't work out."

"What happened?"

"Stone, it would take me a long time to explain that to you. Let's just say I found out we had different values. I wasn't about to spend the rest of my life with a man who thought more of his purse strings than he did me."

"Rich, huh?"

"Oh, yes," she agreed. "Very, very rich. He had money so old, it had mold on it."

Despite the stab of jealousy and pain that went through him, he managed a short laugh. Money was something he couldn't offer Tess—every nickel he had was tied up in the ranch. Not that he and the kids ever lacked for anything they really needed, but he'd already borrowed against his herd this year. If that new bull panned out the way he hoped it would, he might at least find himself comfortable in a few more years. Until then, though, he had to squeeze each penny until it said ouch before he turned it loose.

He couldn't offer a woman a darned thing except a life of hard work day in and out, just to make sure they would have three meals a day on the table. He'd even been worried that the owner of the general store might refuse to put the dresses for Tess on his account, since he was sort of behind on paying it at the moment.

And that brought him face-to-face with the need to bring in some money pretty quick. Much as he hated to disrupt Rain's lessons and leave his herd unprotected after the attempt to poison it, he had to leave to look for the wild horse herd that roamed a day or two's ride away. The steers needed another couple of months' fattening before he could make a decent profit on them, but horses, even half broken, always found a ready market.

He tucked Tess's picture in his shirt pocket and rose to his feet. "I see what you meant a while ago, I guess."

"What I meant?"

"About my not letting myself feel anything for you," he replied. "And I won't forget it. But I'd appreciate it if you'd keep that in mind about the kids. They don't need to lose another person in their lives. They've already lost too much."

"Stone, I . . ."

"Don't worry. You'll have a home here as long as you need it. You've got no business trying to find that time warp with a broken ankle—let alone trying to go back through it. I want you to promise me something, though."

"What?" Tess asked hesitantly.

"That you won't try to go up there on your own—without me. It could be dangerous."

"I won't leave without telling you, Stone, if that's what you want."

"I do want that. I want your promise."

"I promise," she said sincerely.

"Thank you. I'll go along with whatever you decide after your ankle heals. But if you stay around too long, the kids will start caring for you too much—get too attached to you. Try to remember that, will you, while Rain and I are gone the next few days."

"Stone, you can't stop people from caring about each other. And where are you and Rain going?"

"After some wild horses," he said, ignoring her other comment. "We'll be back in four or five days—six at the most."

"But what about your cattle? And Flower has a picnic planned for Sunday."

"Can't be helped; work comes first. But I was going to ask you if you felt like riding. You seemed to be pretty good in the saddle the other day, even with your broken ankle, and there's a gentle mare you could mount from the fence. Maybe you and Flower could at least ride out each day and check the cattle, as long as you agree to take the rifle I'll leave here for you. If you find anything wrong, though, just go on into town and get the sheriff. He'll know where I'm at when you tell him I've gone after horses, and he'll send someone after me."

"I'll be glad to do anything I can to help. You've already done so much for me."

He strode to the door without another word. But he stopped with his hand on the doorknob and stood with his head bowed for a second. Then he opened the door and turned to look back at Tess.

"You're right, you know," he said in a quiet voice. "You can't stop people from caring about each other."

Tess's eyes filled with tears when Stone turned abruptly and almost ran through the kitchen. Darn those pills. If they were going to affect her like this, she'd have to quit taking them.

Gazing down at the picture in her hands through a mist of moisture, she admitted the truth. No, it wasn't the pills. It was Stone. Quiet, awkward, bossy, caring, wonderful Stone.

How she had wanted to admit her own love for him on the porch—scream it to the world and shake her fist at the decision she had to make.

Her fate lay in her own hands. She had found a wonderful man she could surely love, who had already told her that he cared for her in return. How hard it had been to lie to him about wanting to go back to her own time. But a commitment to Stone would have to be absolute. She would have to walk away from all she had fought and struggled for and accept totally being relegated to the past.

Would he and the kids want to come with her? Could they?

She tried to imagine Stone in New York City. Oh, Rain and Flower would probably love it at first, as they took in the sights, but it would be so dangerous for them there. Drugs. Gangs. Muggings and other crimes.

Well, they wouldn't have to stay in the city. One thing she had insisted to Robert was that they move to the country when they decided to have children. Yet she knew in her heart Stone would never adjust in her time. What could he do? He was a rancher and a proud man. He would never be able to build a career for himself there, and he would never live on her salary. Their love would suffer as surely as the seasons changed.

Pipe dreams were all any of her hopes could be until she came to a firm decision. If she decided to stay here, the same thing might happen to their love. She might grow to resent the loss of her hard-won career. Perhaps the best thing to do was for her to leave while she still had the strength to do so—before she fell any deeper in love with Stone.

She sniffed and looked out the window when she heard horses' hooves. It had stopped raining and she hadn't even realized it. It must have been only a brief shower.

She watched Rain and Stone ride out of the yard. Once Stone pulled his horse to a stop and sat without moving for several seconds, but he never looked over his shoulder. She heard the faint echo of Rain's voice calling to his father and shoved the window up.

Leaning out the opening, she kept her gaze fixed on the two riders until they disappeared from view. Even long afterwards she stared at the last spot where she had been able to see them. Finally, telling herself the watering in her eyes was from eye strain, she turned around and picked up the picture again.

Lonesome padded into the room and jumped up beside her. Curling her arms around the pup, she buried her face in his newly washed fur. Maybe she could at least take him back with her.

Angela swiped at a tear trickling down her cheek and choked back a sob.

"Angie, don't," Michael said, wrapping his arm around her smaller shoulders. "We don't know that things won't work out."

"That's just it," Angela said in an angry voice. "We don't know. We aren't allowed to know. How are we supposed to know what to do? They're in love with each other, and they'd make a perfect family—Tess, Stone, and the kids."

"But what if Tess decides to go back to her own time?" he asked. "Then we'd have four broken hearts."

"We're going to have four broken hearts anyway. They already love each other—all of them. And what's Tess got back there? An empty apartment—a father and two brothers she hasn't seen in years, because about the only use they have for Tess is to ask for a free handout when their paychecks run out before the next payday and they need a case of beer. Darn it, Michael, Tess doesn't really want to spend her life as a lawyer. It's just something for her to do, since she doesn't have a family of her own."

"We can't interfere with destiny, Angie. That's what you told me, even though I still haven't figured out how we can go *back* in time—know what happens in history but still not know what happens to Tess."

"It's because it's Tess's destiny. We're her guardian angels, and she's still living her life."

He screwed up his face in concentration, then shrugged. "Maybe I'll understand better after I've been at this a while. Anyway, you said we're just supposed to take care of Tess's body—not her emotions."

"Emotional health sometimes ties into physical health," she said in a determined voice.

"Angie," he warned, "I think we might already be on some sort of probation. Or at least I am. I'd sure hate to get whisked back and have Mr. G stick me in some other field of practice until I learned my lesson."

"Field of practice? Oh, Michael, you do have a way with words sometimes!"

Chapter Sixteen

Tess stared down into the colt's eyes as it stood inside the corral fence, lifting its little muzzle for her to scratch. It had such pretty brown eyes—liquid brown, the same color as Stone's. Well, not exactly like Stone's. His eyes could change—go from chocolate pools of passion to walnut hardness when he got frustrated with her. A few times she had even seen a flinty, near blackness of anger in his eyes, and could almost imagine him standing in a dirt street, his legs spread and his hand inching near his gun.

Probably more than once he had faced off against another gunslinger when he worked as a sheriff. The old westerns she had loved to watch on television had always sent a chill up her spine during the gunfight scene. The deadly glint in each man's eyes—the tenseness in their shoulders—the low-slung holsters, holding pistols that in another second would flash into the men's ands.

Mostly it bothered her, though, that one of the two men on the screen would be dead in a second. No matter that the bad guy had shown over and over again that he was corrupt and beyond redemption—sometimes the scene was so well done that Tess forgot for a moment that it was only a screen death. It always came as a jolt for the man to be so alive and living one second, then nothing but an empty body destined for a cold, dark hole in the ground the next.

How many times had Stone faced something like that? How could the man she knew now—that gentle, caring, loving man—have stood looking into another man's face, knowing that in another second he might send a small ball of lead into the man's chest and kill him?

How many times had it come close to being the opposite—the ball ending up in Stone's chest, snuffing out that beautiful, caring spirit of his?

Flower led two horses out of the barn, with Lonesome bounding beside her, and Tess gave a final pat to the colt. It scampered away, kicking up its heels, full of the joy of life. Its little nickers, so different from the more mature neigh when its mother called to it, brought a smile to Tess's face.

"Are you sure you don't want to take the wagon, Tess?" Flower asked. "We'll be riding farther today than we did yesterday and the day before."

She shook her head. "I'll be fine, Flower. It's not that I don't think you're perfectly capable of handling the wagon, but I'd really rather ride horseback. And we'll get there faster—have more time to spend at the lake. You've been looking forward to this picnic all week, and we're going to go and have a lazy day of indulgence all to ourselves."

"We've sure got plenty of food." Flower giggled. "Ham sandwiches, cheese, cucumbers, tomatoes, hard-boiled eggs, apple pie, angel food cake, sweet cider, and elderberry wine. We've even got egg sandwiches for Lonesome."

"That's all part of the day. Today we aren't going to worry about diets or cholesterol. We're going to eat anything and everything we want. And for some reason that crazy dog likes eggs better than ham."

"What's cholesterol?"

"I'll explain that on the way. Right now, let me get up on this corral fence so I can climb on the horse. Lead her over here, will you, honey?"

Propping her crutches beside her, Tess levered her bottom onto the top corral rail. The gentle mare Flower had brought in from one of the pastures stood quietly while Tess climbed into the saddle and settled herself. When Flower handed her the crutches she tucked them under her left leg and tied them to the saddle with the rawhide thongs normally used only for decoration.

"There. I'm ready, honey," she said. "But I guess you better go get the rifle."

"I already put it in my scabbard, Tess. Gee, it's too bad you had to split your denims again, after you sewed them up."

She glanced down at her leg. It was still a tight fit getting the jeans over the cast, but she'd be darned if she would struggle with those flapping skirts another day.

"They'll sew back up again."

Flower swung onto her horse and reined it over beside Tess. "Well, they sure are a lot more comfortable than riding in a dress. I'm glad you let me wear your extra pair, even if they don't fit me as well as they do you."

"Just don't wear them in front of your father," she said with a wink. "He'll banish both of us to your room."

Giggling conspiratorially, they rode out of the ranch yard. Lonesome bounded ahead, already familiar with the route they had taken the last two days. Tess watched him even ignore the jackrabbit that leaped from a clump of grass as they passed. Stomach still full from breakfast, he had no need to hunt for food these days.

Forever faithful to their assignment, Michael and Angela followed overhead. Angela smiled at Michael as they floated along. The past few days had been peaceful, with Michael only having to keep an eye on Tess when she navigated around with her crutches and rode the gentle mare.

Michael was becoming quite adept at handling his duties, and Angela felt a little prickle of pride at her student. Not pride in herself for doing such a good job teaching him, she assured herself. Pride in others was acceptable but unangel-like if it went beyond satisfaction at doing her own duties well.

It took a little more than an hour to ride to the lake, since they had to check the cattle first. Tess had to admit the ride was worth it. Flower had been right—it was a perfect spot for a picnic.

Huge pines, dogwood, and live oak lined the shores, but Flower led her to an opening, where lake waves had washed out a sandy beach. The breeze picked up the coolness of the sparkling blue water, and Tess sighed in contentment as she slid down from the mare.

Not that they needed it on such a hot day, but a picnic just didn't seem right without a fire. After they unsaddled the horses Tess spread one of the saddle blankets on the beach and sat down to scoop out a depression in the sand, while Flower gathered some wood.

An hour later they both lay back groaning on their blankets. Tess unsnapped her jeans and slid the zipper down an inch or two.

"I'm so full I think I'm gonna bust," she said with a moan. "Whatever made me eat so much?"

"Look," Flower said. "Even Lonesome's full." She held a piece of angel food cake under the dog's nose, but Lonesome shifted his head an inch on Flower's leg and turned away.

Tess laughed at the pup, then propped an arm under her head and gazed at the sky. Soft, white specks of fluff moved lazily across the brilliant blueness, and she watched them for several quiet minutes. Merging, then separating, they changed shape almost magically and without notice. One moment she would be eyeing a fire-breathing dragon—the next a knight on horseback.

For a while she and Flower amused themselves by pointing out the different figures each saw in the clouds. Flower would point an indolent finger at a cloud she said looked like a fairy-tale princess, with long, flowing hair. Tess saw an ogre, and had Flower giggling as she described the ogre's humped back and gnashing, pointed teeth.

Tess saw a buffalo, and Flower insisted it was a white stallion. They both agreed on one cloud, though, that reminded them of the muscled physique on the book from Tess's pack.

"Tess," Flower finally murmured, "do you think you'll just disappear someday, the same way you appeared?"

She rolled to her side and looked at Flower's worried face. "No, I don't think it will happen that way," she said. "I . . . honey, you've accepted the way I came here so well, I hope you can understand what I'm going to say now."

"Do you *want* to go back?" Flower asked.

No! Tess's mind screamed. But she managed to hold her head steady, instead of shaking it in denial.

"I don't know right now," she said instead. "There's thirty years of my life back in my own time—things I've worked awfully hard to accomplish. Try to put yourself in my place, honey. If you suddenly found yourself in another life, something completely different from what you've lived up until now, how do you think you'd feel?"

The young girl's brow creased, and she remained silent for several seconds. Then she shook her head. "I really can't imagine it. I mean, if I had Pa and Rain and Grandfather with me, I guess it might be sort of interesting for a while. But I'd miss the ranch and my other friends here." Her eyes were sympathetic as she continued, "Do you miss your family back there?"

"Not much," she said before she thought. When Flower's face creased in puzzlement she quickly amended her answer. "My family's not in New York, Flower. There's just my father and two brothers, and they live in West Virginia. They have their own lives there, and we don't have a lot in common anymore."

"Your mother's dead, too? How old were you when she died?"

"Ten. I went to live with my grandmother during the summers after Mom died. I'm the youngest—my brothers are lots older than me."

"I was seven when my mother died. I remember her real well," Flower said. "Most of my memories are good, but that last year was pretty awful. I felt sort of guilty after Pa showed up and took us with him, because mine and Rain's lives got so much better. But Grandfather's life is lots better now, too, when we go visit him."

"Would you like to tell me about it, Flower?"

"Uh-huh, if you'd like to listen."

She nodded silently and listened without interruption while Flower spoke.

What she remembered most about those years, Flower told her, was constantly being on the move. Sometimes they would just get settled somewhere and, almost the next day, her mother would be tearing down their tepee and loading it on a travois. As soon as she was old enough, Flower realized they were always moving out just ahead of a dreaded bluecoat patrol that was attempting to overtake her people and kill them.

Her mother tried to make light of each move, make it seem like an adventure instead of the flight for their lives that Flower now knew the moves had been. Even her mother couldn't protect her and Rain from seeing what happened during that last, horrible battle, though, the one that would forever be etched on Flower's mind.

The terrible cloud of gunsmoke hanging over the tepees when Flower looked back from the top of a hill after her mother grabbed her and Rain and made their escape as the bluecoats thundered down on the tribe. Her father and the other warriors fighting ferociously against what they had to have known were overwhelming odds. Her father falling, being trampled . . .

"There weren't very many of us who got away," Flower said. "Somehow Grandfather managed to escape, and he found us a couple of days later. He was the only man with us all that winter. It was just my mother, Rain and me, and two other women with their babies. Grandfather did the best he could, but we were always cold and hungry. Lots of times I remember my mother saying she really wasn't hungry and giving her food to Rain. He was so little—just five."

Tess reached over and squeezed Flower's hand. How terrible it must have been. As poor as her family had been back in West Virginia, they never went hungry. Neighbors helped each other—shared both food and clothing. And she had never had to worry about someone chasing her, wanting her dead.

Flower turned to her with a smile. "Even if I can't really forget that last year," she said, "I mostly try to remember the good times. You knew my mother was white, didn't you?"

"No! I didn't know."

"My father kidnapped her from a wagon train," Flower said with a sigh. "It was so romantic. He said he'd been watching her for days, and he just knew he had to have her for his wife. One night he just snuck into her wagon and took her—picked her up while she was sleeping beside her aunt and carried her back to his camp."

"And your mother just went right along with this?" she asked, quirking an eyebrow.

"Not at first." Flower giggled. "She woke up when my father was putting her on his horse and fought him like a wildcat. He showed Rain and me the scars my mother put on his neck and chest. He said they were worse scars than he ever got in any battle."

"But she eventually fell in love with him?"

"Uh-huh. And Pa was real mad at her when he showed up to rescue her. My mother told Pa that she was married and already carrying me. She said he was welcome to visit any time, but that she was staying with her husband."

"Your pa? Stone? Why was he the one to come after your mother?"

"Oh, Pa was madly in love with my mother, too," Flower explained. "Pa was the leader of the wagon train my mother was traveling on. That was before he started working as a sheriff. He couldn't come after my mother at first, since he had to make sure the wagon train got where it was headed safely.

"But he hunted for her after that, and rode right into the Indian camp when he found out where she was. My mother said the only reason the warriors didn't shoot Pa on sight was because they admired his bravery for riding straight into camp. Or maybe at first they thought Pa was touched in the head, and the Indians never bother a person they think is crazy."

"What . . . what was your mother's name, Flower?"

"Cherokees never speak the name of the dead, Tess. I can only call them my mother and father."

"Oh."

"You look sort of like my mother, you know. She had the same color hair and eyes. I guess that's why I liked you so much when I saw you the first time—you reminded me a little of her."

"Oh," she said again, unable to think of another comment.

"What did your mother die of?" Flower asked.

"Uh . . . pneumonia. Granny told me that people didn't usually die of that, but Mother had smoked most of her life and had damaged her lungs."

"Is pneumonia some kind of disease that gets into your lungs?"

"Yes. Well, I don't know if it's a disease so much as a virus."

"My mother must have died of that, too. She had so much trouble breathing, and she was so weak. Grandfather said he tried to drive the evil spirits out of her chest, but they were too strong. She didn't smoke, though. The only ones who smoked in our tribe were the warriors."

"I guess Stone must have come to visit you over the years?" she said, her inflection turning the comment into a question.

"Uh-huh. And just before my mother died she begged Grandfather to get word to Pa and ask him to take Rain and me. You should've seen Pa when he came, Tess. He acted like he was scared to death of me and Rain. He told me once that he really was scared, too, scareder than he'd ever been in his life. He said it was one thing to just come visit us, but something different when he looked at us and realized he was going to be responsible for raising us."

Flower shifted to her side and propped her head on her hand, her shining black hair spilling over her shoulder.

"Pa said we looked like a couple of ragamuffins. We had dirty faces and bare feet. It took Pa hours to get my hair clean and the tangles out of it, but he said he was bound and be darned he wasn't going to cut it. What I remember most about when Pa came that time was looking up and up at him, 'cause I was still pretty small, too. I wasn't scared, though. I just felt safe, and it was a good feeling after the awful winter we'd just been through."

"Stone's done a wonderful job with you kids."

"He's a real good pa," Flower agreed. "I'll never forget my real father, but I love Pa an awful lot."

Me, too, Tess agreed in her mind. But she couldn't help it when the thought continued, asking how much of Stone's love for her was due to her similarity to his old love.

Stone must have loved Flower's mother desperately to risk his life by riding into an Indian camp alone. And he would have been devastated when she told him that she loved another man.

Tess glanced at Flower to see her head pillowed on her arms and her eyes closed. Flower's even breathing told her the child was asleep, and she studied Flower's face.

Under a few traces of baby fat yet, the promise of a heartrending beauty came through. Stone would have his hands full beating off suitors when Flower was ready for dating. Tess could only guess how much of Flower's beauty came from her mother.

Grimacing in distaste at her jealousy for a dead woman, which she couldn't quite wipe from her mind, she leaned back and closed her eyes. And hadn't that horrid Tillie Peterson said something about Stone and one of the neighbor women? Maybe she had been referring to that Widow Brown.

Well, what the heck did she expect? A wonderful man like Stone would have no trouble finding a woman with whom to share his life. The strange thing was that he was still unmarried. If she left, he probably wouldn't have any problem finding a willing female to console him.

Maybe Stone wouldn't need consoling. After all, he'd as much as told her that he wasn't going to let himself fall in love with her. Care for her—yes—but love had to be out of the question—for both of them.

She closed her eyes. An ember popped in the dying fire and a faint whiff of smoke curled around her nose. An infinitesimal niggle of homesickness tugged at her as she recalled the many nights she had spent camping on one of her backpacking trips. After analyzing the feeling for a moment she realized it wasn't nostalgia for home. Instead, she found herself storing up the memory of this day to brush off later in her mind.

The soft sound of lake waves lapping the shore—the smell of fresh air, mingled with a hint of smoke. She could even smell the grass near her nose, and she imagined she could hear the trees growing. A twig snapped as though stretching its bark.

Lonesome leapt to his feet, a warning growl in his throat, and her eyes flew open. She stared directly into the wrinkled face of a man squatting a few feet from Flower.

A scream built in her throat.

Chapter Seventeen

The Indian man raised a finger to his lips and shook his head. Lonesome's tail started wagging, and Tess glanced at the dog, cutting off the scream in midwhoosh. Lonesome sat on his haunches and raised a paw, and immediately her fear left her. She sat up and glared at the Indian.

"You shouldn't sneak up on people," she whispered, loath to disturb Flower's nap. "I might have shot you."

The man grinned at her, his face creasing into a thousand more wrinkles. "She is my granddaughter." He nodded his head at Flower. "And you should not leave your gun on your saddle if you plan to shoot at someone."

He rose to his feet and moved to the other side of the fire. Lonesome followed him and repeated his gesture of friendship. The man solemnly shook the proffered paw, then sat down and motioned for Tess to join him.

She saw him eyeing her jeans as she got to her feet with the help of her crutches and swung over beside him. One of the crutch tips sank into the soft sand, and she wobbled slightly, but the man made no move to get to his feet and help steady her. Instead, surprisingly, she caught her balance at once, almost as though she could feel his hands on her.

She sank down beside him and saw him staring overhead. She twisted her neck to follow his gaze, but only an eagle drifting on the wind drafts in the clear sky with its scattered clouds caught her eye.

"What are you looking at?" she asked. "The eagle?"

"No," he replied. Instead of offering any further explanation he looked back at her and said, "You have come far—from a time far away."

He knows. The thought flashed through her mind almost as though the Indian had spoken it to her.

"You're Silver Eagle," she said eagerly. "Rain told me you're a shaman. Shamans are supposed to have magical powers and be able to communicate with the supernatural. Please tell me what's happening to me—what I should decide."

"Do you truly believe that a shaman can do this?"

"Well, no," she admitted. "But . . ."

"Then you must work on your belief before we can talk," Silver Eagle said with a wry smile. "The true belief is part of what you think is the magic."

"Darn it! How can I work on believing in something if I don't know what it is I'm supposed to believe in?"

"That is part of what you must learn, too."

"Now just a blasted minute. You're sitting there telling me that I have to learn to believe in something that you're not prepared to discuss with me until I believe in it? Just how the heck is that supposed to work?"

Silver Eagle threw back his head and laughed, a sound like dry leaves rustling in the fall. When he looked back at her he said, "You have begun to learn when you start asking the questions. When the answers start coming to you it will be the time for us to talk."

"That makes about as much sense as a riddle in a fairy tale!"

"I have heard of these fairy tales from Mountain Flower. She reads them and tells them to the other children when she comes to visit us. Does not the meaning of the riddle always make itself known at the end of the tale?"

"Well, yes. But that doesn't make it any easier to understand right now—or the decision I have to make any easier."

"Grandfather!" Flower scrambled to her feet and ran to the old man. Throwing herself into his arms, she hugged him tightly and then kissed his cheek. When she stepped back Silver Eagle quirked his eyebrow at her attire, and Flower giggled at him.

"When I visit I'm going to tell all the Indian women how much more comfortable pants are, Grandfather," she warned. "You men have kept that a secret from us for too long."

"If you want, Granddaughter," he said with a nonchalant shrug. "But I remember how I used to like seeing a glimpse of your grandmother's leg now and then when she danced at the feasts. I would think young men now would enjoy this, too. I saw Wolf Hunter watching Sunflower last month, when we celebrated the marriage of Leaping Horse and Soaring Bird. Sunflower's dress had many long fringes, which sounded pleasant when they swished around her legs."

"You old rascal," Tess whispered under her breath when Flower glanced down at her jeans, a worried frown on her face.

"Wolf Hunter," Flower said in a tentative voice. "Has he . . . is he going to offer a lot of horses for Sunflower?"

"I don't think so," Silver Eagle said. "Once two summers ago Wolf Hunter told me that he might wait as long as ten more years before he took a wife. But I suppose he could change his mind."

"The last time I visited," Flower said in a quiet voice, "Wolf Hunter told me he was thinking of going to one of the white man's schools back East. He said he thought maybe he could help our people when he came back."

"Yes, he has spoken of that, too," Silver Eagle agreed. "Now, are you going to offer me something to eat? I have traveled far to see you, Granddaughter, with thoughts of the sweets you make riding with me."

"Oh, of course, Grandfather!"

Flower hurried over to the remains of their meal, and soon Silver Eagle had finished two ham sandwiches and the rest of the angel food cake. He started on the last half of the apple pie as Flower poured two glasses of elderberry wine and handed one to him and the other to Tess.

Tess sipped at her wine, studying the old Indian as he finished the pie and held out his glass for a refill. Even at the Indian's advanced age she could see a trace of Rain's features. The eyes, surrounded by deep sun wrinkles, reminded her of Rain's brown-eyed gaze when she'd first met him on the hill. They shared the same chin and high cheekbones, but Silver Eagle's nose was a little wider. Rain and Flower both must have inherited either their mother's or grandmother's nose.

Silver Eagle wore a combination of white man's and Indian clothing—a cotton shirt, buckskin trousers, and moccasins. A leather headband held back his graying hair, and the beaded belt at his waist carried two pouches, holding a tomahawk and a knife, and a holstered pistol.

"Do you want some more wine, Tess?" Flower asked.

She looked down, surprised to find her glass empty. "No, I don't think so, Flower. We'd better get started back, so we can do the evening chores. If you're finished, that is, Silver Eagle."

"You're coming back with us, aren't you, Grandfather?" Flower asked. "Rain and Pa should be back in a couple of days, and they'll want to see you."

Silver Eagle nodded and gave a huge belch.

"Excuse you," Tess murmured automatically.

"Oh, Tess," Flower said with a laugh, "Grandfather's just showing us how much he enjoyed the food. It's not bad manners in Indian society to belch, as it is in white."

Tess flushed with embarrassment, but Silver Eagle smiled serenely at her and gave another burp.

"Dashnab it, Angie," Michael shouted. "If they don't get moving, I'm going down there and give them a push! Stone needs their help right now!"

"Rain's scared to death," Angela agreed frantically. "What should we do?"

Michael stared overhead and raised his arm. Loud claps of thunder immediately filled the air.

"It's working," Angela said with relief in her voice. "Look."

Michael glanced down and smiled grimly when he saw Tess and Flower hastily gathering up their picnic items. Silver Eagle hurried over to catch the horses, pausing once to glance up at the sky. Michael waved his arm again, and the gray clouds darkened.

"Move it!" Michael ordered. "I just hope you're not too late."

Tess grabbed her crutches and hobbled toward Silver Eagle as he swung the saddle onto her mare. As soon as the cinch was tight, he cupped his hands to help her into her saddle and then mounted his pinto. Flower was already on her way, and when another rumble of thunder sounded, Tess urged her mount into a gallop, hoping they could reach the shelter of the ranch before the rain hit.

It still took them over half an hour to make the ride, and the horses were blowing through their foam-flecked nostrils when they galloped into the ranch yard. The kitchen screen door flew open and Rain yelled frantically.

"Where've you been? Hurry! Pa's been snake bit and I think he's dying!"

"Oh, my God! Please, no!" Tess slid from her saddle without assistance and jerked frantically at the knots on the thongs holding her crutches. The rawhide pulled tighter, and she shot Silver Eagle a grateful glance when he reached over her shoulders and untied the crutches. Jamming them under her arms, she levered herself toward the house, where Rain and Flower had already disappeared inside.

"Please, my darling. Please don't let me be too late," she whispered in a terror-laced voice as she climbed the steps and opened the door. She swung through the kitchen and down the hallway, figuring that Stone would be in his own bedroom.

At the open bedroom door she came to a dead halt. Stone lay on the bed, his leg swollen and ugly and his face as gray as death. Flower and Rain turned tear-streaked faces up to her.

"It happened yesterday," Rain sobbed. "We rode all night to get back here, but I think it's too late. Pa just now stopped breathing, Tess!"

Chapter Eighteen

Face is pale, raise the tail.

The axiom flashed across Tess's mind, and she flew into action. Almost throwing herself across the room, she landed on her knees on the bed, ordering Flower to pile pillows under Stone's legs to raise them.

Pressing the heel of her hand on his breastbone without even checking to see if he really wasn't breathing, she began CPR. After five sharp thrusts she leaned over him and filled his lungs with her breath. She repeated the sequence three times before her panic receded and she could think more clearly. Pausing for a second, her hand ready to thrust again on his breastbone, she forced herself to focus on his face.

Beneath her hand, she felt a slight movement—very slight, but she leaned down and a soft, bare hint of air feathered on her cheek. Then he took a stronger breath, and moaned in her ear.

She drew back, elated to see a touch of color returning to his gray cheeks, although his eyes remained closed.

Shock. Frantically she searched the recesses of her mind for everything she had learned in the first-aid/CPR class she had taken so long ago.

Blankets. Warmth.

"Rain, go get some more blankets," she ordered. "Flower, run get my backpack. Hurry, kids!"

The children almost bowled over Silver Eagle as they ran out the door. She watched the Indian cross the room and stare down at the purplish-black mass surrounding the two puncture marks on Stone's calf muscle. The wounds were criss-crossed with deep slashes, where Stone had evidently cut with his knife to try to suck out the poison. Silver Eagle pulled his hunting knife from its sheath and slit the leg of Stone's denims nearly to the crotch.

"Rattler," he said in a worried voice. "A big one."

Tess smoothed back Stone's matted hair, resisting the urge to cover him with her own body to combat the clammy coldness her palm encountered.

"How can you tell?" she asked.

"Coral snake—he would be dead now. Cotton-mouth and copperhead do not get big enough to leave so big a bite. A big diamondback."

"I hope like hell you're right," she said grimly. "It makes a difference what kind of antivenin you use to treat different snakebites."

"I am sure," Silver Eagle said.

As soon as Flower and Rain raced back into the room, Tess grabbed her backpack.

"Get the blankets on him, kids, and lower his legs now, so the poison doesn't seep upward with the blood," she said. "Rain, did you see the snake?"

"No," Rain said in a strangled voice. He took a deep breath when Silver Eagle laid a hand on his shoulder. "Pa . . . Pa was getting some wood for the fire when I heard him yell. On the way home he told me it must've been a rattler, 'cause the brush pile was beside some rocks where they like to lay. But it got away before he saw it, and he didn't hear it rattle."

"That's an old wives' tale," Tess murmured distractedly as she pulled the syringe from her snakebite kit. "Rattlesnakes don't always rattle in warning, especially if the snake was half asleep and Stone startled it."

After scanning the directions in the kit she grabbed a Styrofoam package from it and opened the lid to reveal a dozen glass vials, each filled with a powdery substance.

"You have brought this medicine with you?" Silver Eagle asked.

"Yes," she answered. "I took a class—got certified. I had to have a doctor write me a prescription so I could carry this with me when I went backpacking."

She glanced worriedly at the shaman. "I'm . . . I'm supposed to make sure he's not allergic to this first, because the antivenin could hurt him worse than the snakebite if he is. But it's been so long since he was bitten, I'm afraid to wait any longer."

Silver Eagle looked at Rain, and Rain turned his gaze heavenward. As soon as his grandson's eyes met his again, Silver Eagle spoke to Tess.

"He is not what you said—allergic. Give him the medicine."

Tess hesitated, turning her face toward him, a plea in her eyes. "How can you be sure? I could kill him."

"I will do it, if you don't. You brought the medicine here when he needed it. It wouldn't be so if it were wrong."

"But I'm not sure how much to use," Tess said with a sob. "It's meant to be used immediately. After a person's been affected for a while it takes a larger dose."

Silver Eagle gave an exasperated sigh and reached for the package. Almost as though something guided his hand, he picked out several vials and scooped them to one side. His hand hesitated a second, then he added two more vials, until eight of them lay loose on the bed.

"These," he said, waving his hand over the vials.

Something in the shaman's voice and steady gaze gave Tess back her confidence. "Take his pants off."

While Silver Eagle removed Stone's denims, she grabbed the bottle of sterile water and drew a syringe full to mix with the powdered antivenin, handing each vial to Rain and murmuring for him to shake it. She then drew the vials of the mixture back into the syringe and pushed the plunger until a small stream of liquid spurted out, displacing the air in the needle.

With a fairly steady hand, she inserted the needle into Stone's upper thigh and slowly depressed the plunger. After the last drop disappeared into his body she removed the needle and grabbed a cotton ball from her kit to press over the small drop of blood that welled up on his leg.

She knew it was her imagination, but a deep sense that she had done the right thing immediately engulfed her. She replaced the still usable items into the medicine kit before she settled beside Stone on the bed and pulled the blankets up around his neck.

"It'll be a while before we know if it worked," she said, smoothing a stray curl from Stone's forehead. "I'll stay with him tonight."

Rain and Flower hesitantly approached her, and she opened her arms to them. Gathering them close, she rocked them gently for a moment, making a wordless attempt at comfort.

Her own terror and fear threatened to overwhelm her again, but she forced herself to think of the children. They had lost their parents within months of each other, and now the man around whom their world centered lay near death. Stone's words of a few days ago whispered in her mind: The children had lost so much already—she had to do everything in her power to bring Stone through this crisis.

For the children's sake—and for her own. She loved Stone so terribly much.

Flower pushed away first and put a hand on Rain's shaking shoulder. "We should get our chores done, Rain," she said quietly. "Pa won't like it if he wakes up and finds out we haven't done them."

Rain gave a sniff, then hugged Tess's neck one last time. He glanced, embarrassed, at Silver Eagle when he stood. But the shaman smiled at Rain and nodded.

"It is good to show you care, Rain Shadow. But

your sister is right, and the time will pass faster if we do the work that needs to be done. I'll help you both in a minute."

Rain and Flower slowly walked out of the bedroom, pausing at the door to look back at their father. The pain on their faces, mixed with their childish attempts at bravery, tore at Tess's heart. She forced a nod at them, hoping the gesture would ease just a little of their worry, although she was far from sure herself that Stone would live.

So many things could still happen, she thought to herself as soon as the children disappeared and she turned back to Stone. Shock had weakened that wonderfully strong body. Infection could set in. He could still have convulsions. . . .

"We will need the plants for the fever and the swelling in his leg," Silver Eagle said. "Rain and I will gather them and prepare them. And we will do a ceremony to drive out the evil spirit left behind by the snake."

"Please," she said softly. "Do everything you can. We can't let him die. The children need him so much."

"He will fight," Silver Eagle said. "He has many good reasons to live—the children's love—and yours."

"Yes," she agreed without reservation. "If love can pull him through, he'll make it."

Long after midnight, Tess still sat in the rocking chair Rain had brought in from the back porch for her. Stone's breathing was deep and steady now, as though he slept a healing sleep, rather than tortured unconsciousness. His thready pulse had evened out shortly after she had given him the injection, but he still hadn't opened his eyes.

Rain slipped into the room, as quiet as a shadow.

"You should be asleep, Rain," she murmured. "I promised I'd call you kids if your father got worse."

"I can't sleep. Please, Tess. I want to stay, too."

"Okay. Come here."

Though he was a little large for her lap, she lifted the blanket she had tossed over herself when the evening cooled, and Rain sat down on her knee. She pulled him close and wrapped the blanket around them both, settling her chin on Rain's silky black hair when he snuggled into her neck.

"Tess?" Rain asked in a hesitant voice. "Is . . . is Pa gonna live?"

"I'm pretty sure he's going to make it now, Rain," she murmured soothingly, stroking his small arm. "He's a lot better than he was when you got him back here."

"Then why hasn't he woken up?"

"He's resting now, getting his strength back and fighting the snake's poison."

"Oh."

Rain snuggled just a hair closer to her and stifled a yawn. She touched a toe to the floor, and the chair rocked slightly. Long, quiet moments passed as she cuddled Rain close, breathing in his faint little-boy scent and enjoying holding him in her arms. Her eyes never left the bed, though, where Stone lay unmoving.

"Tess?"

Rain's voice was groggy, and she kept the chair rocking, hoping he would drop off into much-needed sleep.

"What, Rain?" she whispered.

"I was awfully scared. Men aren't supposed to be scared, are they?"

"Rain, honey, I don't think men or women ever get over being scared at times. Especially when someone they love is in danger. But you should be very proud of yourself. You kept your head and got your pa back here, where we could help him. He might not have made it without you."

"It seemed like it took us forever to get home."

"I'm sure it did. It's funny, isn't it, how sometimes time flies by and you feel like you have to run to catch up to it. Other times, you almost want to push it to make it go faster."

"Uh-huh. Did it go fast or slow when you came here to us, Tess?"

"To tell the truth, I don't know, Rain. But I guess it must have been pretty fast, since it was about the same time in the day that I fell when I woke up here."

"You must have been pretty surprised, huh?" Rain said with a slight chuckle.

"You better believe it," she admitted. "And I was pretty scared, too. I'm just glad I landed here with you and your family, instead of someplace where I might have been in real danger."

"The spirits probably brought you," Rain said with another yawn.

"You mean, so I'd be here when your pa needed the snakebite medicine?" She shook her head slowly, Rain's hair stroking her cheek with the movement. "I'm not sure if I believe in your grandfather's Indian spirits, Rain, but a couple of weeks ago I didn't believe a person could travel through time, either. So your grandfather's right about one thing—there are lots of wonders in the world we don't understand."

"Ummmm." Rain's eyelashes brushed her neck, and he relaxed in her hold. "But your spirits are white, Tess," he murmured just before he dropped into a deep sleep.

She adjusted Rain to a more comfortable position in her arms and smiled down at him. That was a new idea—she had never read anywhere that any Indian religion believed in a division of spirits, white for white people and Indian for Indians.

Sensing something different in the room, she glanced at the bed to see Stone's eyes open and centered on her. She gave a soft gasp of joy, and only the burden in her arms kept her from flinging herself onto the bed.

"Stone, darling," she breathed. "Oh, God, we've been so frightened."

"Is he too heavy for you to lift him over here beside me?" Stone asked softly. "I don't think I can help you."

"Please don't even try. I think I can do it."

Bracing her uninjured leg under her, she scooted to the edge of the rocking chair and managed to lay Rain on the bed without waking him. Stone stifled a groan and moved over on the bed, drawing Rain with him and slipping an arm under the boy's head.

"Now you," he said to her. "There's room, and you've probably been sitting there all night."

She hesitated, eyeing the space on the bed longingly. It didn't beckon her for sleep, though, as much as the thought of being so close to Stone.

"Do you want something to eat or drink?" she asked. "Flower left some soup on the stove."

"I just want you beside me, Tess," he murmured. "Please."

She slipped into the bed without further protest and took Stone's hand when he held it out and laid her cheek against it. Their eyes met and clung, and she wrapped her fingers in his, drawing his hand to her mouth to kiss it.

His thumb gently stroking her lip, Stone asked, "Is Flower all right?"

"Uh-huh. And Silver Eagle's here. He came while Flower and I were having a picnic at the lake."

"Sorry I missed the picnic." Stone slipped his thumb between her lips, and she gently nibbled at it. "Have you been eating right and drinking your milk?"

"Um-hum." She watched Stone's eyes darken with emotion when she flicked her tongue around his callused thumb.

Stone pulled his hand free and buried it in her hair. "I need you to kiss me, Tess," he whispered. "If you don't kiss me within the next few seconds, I feel like I'll never get well."

"We can't have that, can we?" she whispered.

Carefully, she leaned across Rain and covered Stone's mouth with her own. His lips parted in answer to hers, and she closed her eyes, glorying in the softness of his mouth and the certainty that he was out of danger. When their lips parted for breath they murmured each other's name in unison, then sought each other's mouth again.

"Wanta go for a stroll, Angie?" Michael asked. "Looks like things are fine here for a while."

"Oh, that would be nice. It's a pretty night out under the stars."

"Sure is. And I'm ready for some fresh air." He gave a brief bow, then motioned for her to precede him. When they both hovered over the cabin roof they spread their wings wide and stretched to their full size.

"Michael," she said, "you did a wonderful job in that crisis."

"Aw, thanks, Angie. It's real nice of you to say that." He cocked his elbow and offered her his arm. "Shall we go?"

She slipped her hand onto his arm, and Michael took a step. The next second he tumbled down the roof end over end, and she swooped beneath him just before he reached the ground. Righting him, she drifted the last few feet with him.

"Oh, dear," she murmured. "Are you all right?"

"Danged robes!" he growled. A contemplative look came over his face, and he rubbed at his chin. "You know, we've got pretty much freedom as to what corporal form we take on."

"What do you mean?"

He blinked his eyes, then stared down at his legs with a smile of satisfaction. He now wore a feathery white pair of pants, cuffed at his ankles.

"Why, that looks very comfortable," she said.

"Why don't you try it?"

"Uh . . . no, that's all right. I like my robe."

"Suit yourself."

He held out his arm again, and she grasped it. He strolled up a set of invisible stairs, toward the star-strewn sky, and she willingly walked at his side.

Chapter Nineteen

"Get your butt back in that chair, Stone!" Tess called through the kitchen window.

Stone glanced at the door behind him, half expecting to see Tess standing outlined behind the screen. When he realized her voice had come through the window—she must be standing at the dry sink, where she couldn't possibly see him—he frowned at Lonesome.

"I've heard that women have eyes in the back of their head, boy," he said in a low voice. "But I sure as heck never knew they could see through walls."

Lonesome pricked his ears when Rain and Silver Eagle emerged from the barn, Rain on Smoky and the shaman riding his pinto. After what Stone took as an apologetic look, the dog leaped to its feet and raced across the yard. Lonesome circled the horses and riders once, then loped ahead of them as Rain waved at Stone and kneed Smoky forward.

Cursing the weakness that still lingered in his body, Stone sat back in the rocking chair. He should be the one riding out to check on the cattle and fences. As a matter of fact, there were a thousand and one other things he should be doing—not the least of which was getting back out there and making another try for some of those wild horses. Now he even owed Doc Calder for his visit out here yesterday to check on the snakebite.

He glanced at the garden, where Flower moved up a row of pole beans as she picked them and dropped them into the peck basket on her arm. He still hadn't been over to the Widow Brown's, either, and Flower's dress hung several inches above her ankles. Grudgingly, he admitted that the denims Tess now wore every day—ignoring any look of censure he gave her—would probably be a lot more comfortable for Flower to work in.

Tess placed her hands on his shoulders, her thumbs massaging his tight muscles. "You're not used to sitting here and letting everyone else do the work, huh?" she asked.

"I thought you could only see through walls," he said in a gruff voice. "I didn't know you could walk through them, too."

"What's that mean?" She laughed.

"It means I didn't even hear you come out onto the porch," he told her as he leaned back into the kneading strokes. "Um, that feels good."

"You're supposed to be resting, not sitting here all tensed up because you can't get out there and work yourself to a frazzle."

"Yeah. Well, the work won't go away. It'll just pile up, and there'll be more of it to do when I'm able to get back to it."

He felt her fingers dig deeper into his shoulders.

"Ouch! That hurts," he grumbled.

"Then for heaven's sake, relax. Lean your head forward."

He dropped his head onto his chest. After a second he closed his eyes and sighed deeply. Magic; she had magic in her fingers—magic to soothe his tense muscles, and magic that made him long for her beside him in his empty bed at night, so he could show her some sorcery of his own.

But sorcery had a dark, unexplainable side, too—as unexplainable as a hole in time, through which the woman he loved had found her way to him. She could also leave him that way, at any time she chose. He tensed again at the thought, and Tess murmured her annoyance as she kneaded harder.

After another moment or so her fingers left his neck, and Tess adjusted her crutches under her arms. She swung over to the other rocking chair and sat down, reaching over and laying a hand on his arm.

"The doctor said you could start walking around tomorrow, Stone. You have to let your body heal itself. If you do, by next week you'll be back to full strength."

"Yeah, yeah, yeah," he grumbled. He rested his head against the back of the chair and loosened his grip on the arm to turn his hand over. Twining his fingers around hers, he held her palm against his.

"And there will be another week's work piled up," he said with a sigh. "You and the kids can't do it all, not even with Silver Eagle's help."

"You've got that right, Pa," Flower said as she set her basket on the porch and plopped down on one of the steps.

Tess started to draw her hand away, but he tightened his grip.

"You should have seen Grandfather yesterday," Flower continued, slipping a sly look at their intertwined hands. "I thought maybe there might be enough pretty days left to grow some more radishes and lettuce this summer. So I asked Grandfather if he would help me plow up a small corner of the garden again."

Tess laughed gaily and Flower looked up at her. "Did you see what happened, Tess?"

"Uh-huh," Tess admitted. "I was watching on the porch. But for pity's sake, don't tell Silver Eagle. I got back inside before he saw me."

"Well, what happened?" Stone asked.

"The plow hit a rock, Pa," Flower said with a giggle. "The jerk scared the horse, and Grandfather forgot to let loose of the plow when the horse took off. Plus . . ."

Flower broke into laughter and couldn't speak. She looked up at Tess.

"He . . ." Tess controlled herself with an effort. "He had the reins wrapped around his neck," she said with a snort of laughter. "He finally had to let go of the plow, because the reins were choking him. The . . . the horse had stopped by then, thank goodness, and . . . and Silver Eagle got up and . . ."

Stone's laughter rumbled in his chest and his shoulders convulsed as the picture Silver Eagle must have made flashed in his mind. He dropped Tess's hand and clutched at his stomach while he waited for either Tess or Flower to continue.

Flower found her breath first. "Grandfather got up and said that a man was meant to ride on a horse's back—not follow behind its ass," Flower said around her laughter. "And he stomped off, so I had to finish the plowing myself."

"Watch your language, Flower." Stone tried to make his voice stern but failed.

His daughter tossed him a wide-eyed look from her twinkling brown eyes. "But Grandfather's the one who said it, Pa."

Stone chuckled softly under his breath and shook his head. "I guess you're right, honey. Look, why don't you give me those beans so I can clean and snap them for you."

"You?" Flower's amazement stilled her laughter. He saw Tess nudge Flower's knee with her toe. The girl glanced up and Tess winked at her. Hastily Flower rose to her feet.

"Uh . . . all right, Pa. I'll go get you a bowl to put them in."

Flower hurried into the house as Tess smiled over at Stone.

"It's something I can do while I sit here on my behind," Stone said. "And maybe it'll prove to you that I don't devalue the worth of the work women do, as you accused me on the hillside. But don't think for a minute that you're going to get an apron on me. There's still some things that are strictly women's work in my mind."

"Heaven forbid that I ask you to help cook," she teased.

"Just who do you think taught Flower how to use that stove in there, huh? She'd never cooked on anything but a campfire until she came to live with me."

The reminder of Flower's past sent a jolt of remembrance through Tess.

"Stone," she said quietly, "what was Flower's mother's name?"

"What makes you ask that?"

"She . . . Flower told me about her mother and father when we had our picnic. But she said she wasn't allowed to speak their names."

Stone gazed out into the yard, and she saw his fingers grip the arm of the rocking chair. Wishing she could take back the question, she opened her mouth to speak.

"Here's the bowl, Pa." Flower came through the door and set the bowl on Stone's lap, then reached down and handed him the basket of beans. "I'm going out to water my lettuce seeds now."

Stone sat for another silent moment after Flower left, and Tess sighed as she started to rise from the rocking chair.

"Abby," Stone finally said, and Tess dropped back into the chair. "Abigail O'Reilly, but I always called her Abby. The kids' father was Silver Eagle's son—Gray Wolf. I tried like blue blazes to hate that son of a bitch, but he came to be one of my best friends. I cried like a baby when I heard they were dead—and the tears were for both of them, not just Abby."

Tess rocked quietly for a while, not wanting to intrude on Stone's remembered grief. But she had to know.

"Flower said you were in love with Abby, Stone," she said after a moment. "But she said her mother chose Gray Wolf over you."

"She sure did," Stone agreed in a soft voice. "Stood there and stuck her stomach out at me; told me she loved her child's father and wasn't about to leave him. Gray Wolf just gave me this half-assed grin and said he'd fight me, if I wanted him to. Hell, wasn't any use in that. I might've beat Gray Wolf, but Abby made it plain it wouldn't have done any good."

"I'm sorry, Stone."

He leaned back in his chair and looked at her. "For what? Because Abby chose to stay with the man she loved? Because I got my young heart broken?"

She shrugged and dropped her eyes.

Stone reached over and lifted her chin. "I guess sometimes it takes a broken heart or two to realize what love really is, Tess. It's more than just wanting a nice-looking woman to sleep with at night—one you've got an urge to make love to. As I watched Abby with Gray Wolf and the kids over the years, I realized part of what I felt for her were those randy urgings of my youth. I hadn't thought about the fights we had almost every time we opened our mouths at each other."

He stroked her cheek, and she leaned into his hand.

"Might I hope there's a little bit of jealousy on those pouting lips, Tess, honey?" he said with a smile.

"A whole bunch. Even though Abby's dead now. But, Stone, we can't fall in love. We can't. I might . . ."

"And I might be dead right now, too, from that snakebite," he interrupted her. "We can't live our lives on mights, Tess. Yeah, you might decide to leave and break Flower and Rain's hearts. And mine, too, because I already love you more than I thought it possible to love a woman. There's not a darned thing I can do about it. My head keeps telling me there might not be a future for us, but my heart keeps saying it doesn't give a damn—that it wants what we can have today and the hell with tomorrow."

"But you just . . . Flower said I look like Abby. It's just . . ."

"No, Tess. There's a little resemblance there, but you're not Abby. You're Tess—the woman I love."

"I love you, too, Stone Chisum," she murmured. "And that love will last forever—forever in time, whether I'm alive or dead—whether it's 1893 or 1994."

"Even past 'til death do us part,' huh?"

"Yes. Even beyond that."

"So what do you think?" Rain asked. "Do you suppose there are white spirits who take care of white people?"

"It's a new thing to think about, Grandson," Silver Eagle said. "We will have to study it carefully. The white men call themselves ministers come among our people. They try to tell us that only belief in their religion will get us to their Heaven. I never listened much to them myself, because their place sounded too much like one of the reservations we live on now."

"These spirits seem awfully friendly, Grandfather. But I haven't tried to speak to them yet."

"Have they tried to speak to you?"

"No. They've waved and . . . well, done some other things so I could tell that they knew I could see them—like when the man spirit told me it was all right for Tess to give Pa that medicine. Nobody else can, though, not even Flower. She says sometimes she can tell they're around, but I'm pretty sure Tess and Pa don't have any idea the spirits are living with us."

Rain leaned back on his arms and glanced at Silver Eagle. "They're always with Tess, Grandfather, even inside the house. Then they're smaller—so they can fit inside on their cloud, I guess. Outside, they're just a little bit smaller than live people. And they look like live people, too, 'cept for those wings on their backs."

"Then they will come with Tess when Man Who Walks With Right and she come to bring you and Mountain Flower home. It's time for you to visit your people again, Rain Shadow. We will go after your father heals from the snakebite and does not need our help. The day before they come to get you, we will fast and prepare for them. Perhaps then we can speak to these spirits."

"Have you really talked to spirits before?" Rain asked in a hushed voice.

"Many times—in my mind and in the healing ceremonies. But only one time face-to-face, when I sought my vision. That does not mean I did not know they were always there when I spoke to them. My belief in them made it so."

"Well, I don't have any trouble believing in these two spirits, Grandfather. I can see them just as well as I can see you right now."

Chapter Twenty

"But Stone, I won't be able to dance. And I don't have a thing to wear." Tess dropped the ear of corn she'd been shucking to her lap.

"That's all taken care of," he answered with a superior smirk as he leaned against the porch railing. "I knew you'd bring up not having a dress, so Widow Brown's coming over this afternoon to fit you and Flower for the dresses she's making for you two to wear to the social. When Flower rode out with Rain and Silver Eagle the day before yesterday, they took her over there."

"But . . . but . . ."

"And Doc Calder said you've healed so well that we can stop by his office and get that cast off your foot the day of the social. He thinks if you just wrap your ankle snugly for another week or so and be careful, it'll be fine. Must be all that good food we fed you."

Stone looked so pleased with himself that Tess couldn't bring herself to tell him the real reason she was hesitant to attend the gathering that Doc Calder had told Stone about a few days ago. It was one thing to stand up to Tillie Peterson when Tillie was alone; Tess could just imagine the sniffs of disapproval she would face from a cordon of Tillie's cronies. Tillie had probably gossiped with them every day, decrying the scandalous situation of Tess living on the ranch with Stone.

No one in New York would blink an eye at her arrangement, whether or not she was sleeping with the man she lived with. Some of the women she knew even shared apartments with male roommates, partly for safety and partly because it just didn't matter—as long as the bills got paid.

"I guess it would be nice for Rain and Flower," she murmured. "They'll enjoy it."

"So will you, Tess," Stone said firmly. "But we won't be able to stay too late, because Flower and Rain will be leaving pretty early the next morning."

"Leaving?" She sat up in the rocking chair and the ear of corn fell from her lap. "Leaving for where? How long?"

"I told you about that, didn't I?" he said, frowning. "They always go with Silver Eagle a couple of times a year to visit the Cherokee. That's why Silver Eagle came by. He only hung around this long because he wanted to help out, but they're leaving on Sunday."

Her mouth went dry and she leaned down to grab the corn in order to avoid Stone's eyes. "How . . . how long will they be gone?" she repeated.

"Two weeks. We'll go out and visit a day or so

ourselves when they're ready to come home—bring them back with us."

Two weeks. Two entire weeks of no one else in the house to provide a barrier between the two bedroom doors. Two entire weeks of no Flower beside her in the bed to remind her that she had to control her desire for Stone.

There wouldn't be anyone around to interrupt a surreptitious kiss before it got out of hand. No one to stop her from running her hands through his hair any time he got near—slipping up on him when he chopped wood in the yard, resting her face on his shirtless back and flicking her tongue over a drop of sweat. Curling her arms around his waist and running her palms over that flat stomach—even lower, if she wanted to.

As though reading her thoughts, Stone said, "Do you want to get a room at the boardinghouse for those two weeks, Tess?"

"Not unless they take credit cards," she replied wryly. "I didn't stop at the ATM machine to withdraw any cash before I went backpacking. . . . Maybe I could get a job in town," she mused. "Stone, do you know if anyone in town is looking for a . . ."

"No!" he snarled. "You're not going to work! There's plenty for you to do around here, and you've been earning your keep, even on crutches. I took on the responsibility of caring for you and I'll do it."

"Good grief," she said in amazement. "I'm perfectly capable of holding down a job. I had a dozen of them during the years I went to school. I've been earning my own spending money since I was old enough to baby-sit."

"I said no!"

"Oh!" she said, her temper flaring. "And who died and made you dictator? For your information, I wasn't asking your permission. I was just asking if you knew of any job openings in town. I'll make my own decision about whether I live on your charity or get a job to pay my own way."

"It's not charity! If you sat around all day and made us wait on you hand and foot, now that might be charity. Besides, I'll need your help while Flower's gone. You can do the cooking and washing—keep the house clean."

"Women's work, huh?" she sneered.

"Yeah. And at least you'll be here where I can spend some time with you. Soon as Doc takes that cast off, you'll be free to try to find your time warp—decide whether you want to go back through it or not."

"Darn it, Stone, I could've ridden up to that hillside at any time when you left Flower and me alone while you chased your wild horses and ended up getting snakebit. But I promised you I'd let you know my decision before I went. Do you think so little of me that you believe I'd break my promise?"

Not answering her, he stomped down the steps and headed for his horse. "I said no job, and that's final!" He swept up his reins and swung into the saddle.

The well-trained horse responded instantly, spinning around and galloping across the yard. Stone set his lips grimly and resisted the pull he felt to look back at Tess.

He couldn't decide whether he believed her

promise or not. Maybe she'd end up thinking that a quick break—without the sadness of good-byes—would be best. Though she paid lip service to his status as head of the household, she had an independent streak and clearly made her own decisions.

Darn it, he'd only ridden back in from the field where he and Rain were cutting hay for the winter to remind Flower that Widow Brown was coming today. He'd had a faint hope that Rose Brown might show up a little early—then he could see Tess's face when Rose gave her the dress. Then she'd gotten him all riled up with that job business—made him feel the lack of ready cash, which always hacked his pride.

The heck with it. At least the darned dresses were paid for. He'd done some work for Rose—plowed her gardens and broke that new colt for her—in anticipation of Flower needing new clothing. There was plenty of room here at the house for Tess while Flower and Rain were gone. She didn't need to move to town and go to work.

He suddenly pulled Silver Mane to a halt. Hell, it wasn't because Tess was afraid of what people would say, though that might be part of it, he realized. The house would be empty, except for him and Tess, at night.

He'd kept that thought at bay ever since Silver Eagle had arrived. He'd known all along that the shaman planned to take his grandchildren for at least two weeks. That while he could still have his quiet talks with Tess in the evenings after Rain and Flower went to bed, there would be no Rain and Flower in their beds those two weeks. He and Tess had managed to keep the flames banked as long as the children were there. It sure hadn't been easy—heck, just last night Silver Eagle had given a false yawn and winked at Stone as he headed for his tepee.

And if that darned swing hadn't given a loud squeak when it started swinging wildly, he might have made love to Tess right there on the front porch. He recalled taking a firm hold of himself and wishing fervently that the kids were already gone.

Stone nudged Silver Mane forward. He was going to have to oil that damned swing.

The ear of corn snapped in her hands and Tess tossed it into the basin beside her and hurriedly shucked the rest of the ears. Balancing the basin on her hip, she went back into the kitchen and set the corn on the counter. Darn, she'd be glad to get this cast off.

For a second she stared at the broken ear of corn, almost wishing it was Stone's neck. He made her so blasted mad sometimes. Well, short of gagging her, he couldn't keep her from making her own inquiries about jobs while she was at the social.

Flower came out of the bedroom and headed for the door. "Here comes Mrs. Brown, Tess. I saw her from the window. Did Pa tell you she was making us some new dresses?"

"He told me, Flower."

Suddenly Lonesome's high-pitched barks split the air.

"Uh-oh." Flower ran out of the door.

By the time Tess got onto the porch Flower had Lonesome by the scruff of the neck and was gently scolding him. The woman on the sorrel mare reined her mount over to the porch and dismounted. She wore a loose white blouse and split riding skirt above her high-top boots, and Tess could almost feel the woman studying her in return while she fumbled to unhook the catch on her saddlebag.

The woman finally approached her, holding a package in both hands.

"I'm Rose Brown," she said with a nod. "You must be Miss Foster."

"Tess, please," she murmured. "Stone said you'd be coming over."

"I passed him on the way a minute ago."

"Mrs. Brown, are those our dresses?" Flower danced up to Rose Brown, her eyes alight with excitement. "Let's go inside so we can see them."

"I'm sorry to keep you standing there," Tess apologized. "Please, do come in."

She turned and led the way back into the kitchen, somehow knowing that Rose's eyes were now scanning her tight denims. Stiffening her shoulders, she forced herself to remember the manners Granny had drilled into her.

"Would you like some coffee?" she asked.

Rose handed Flower the package and removed her flat-brimmed hat, hanging it on a hook beside the kitchen door. A long braid of golden hair fell down her back. "Please don't trouble yourself," she answered. "You and Flower go ahead and look at the dresses, and I'll get us some coffee. I know where everything is."

"I wouldn't think of allowing a *guest* to wait on herself," she responded in a grim voice as she intercepted Rose at the stove. Tess had a couple of inches of height on the other woman and used it to her advantage as she stared down at Rose. "Please. Go ahead and have a seat."

Up close, she could see that Rose's face contained a few signs of aging—crow's feet beginning beside her blue eyes, just a hint of slackness at her jawline. A silent message passed between them, and Rose's full lips tightened almost imperceptibly. She dropped her eyes and moved toward the table, but Tess had the feeling this was only the first skirmish.

"Your father's looking very well, Flower," Tess heard Rose say while she poured the coffee. "A lot better than the first day I saw him after he was able to get back to work. You should have let me know Stone had been bitten by a snake. I would have come right over to help out."

"Oh, we managed, Mrs. Brown," Flower said. "But thank you for the offer."

Tess gritted her teeth and mopped up a coffee spill. Just when had that woman seen Stone? He sure as heck hadn't mentioned it to her.

The paper rustled, and Tess heard Flower's indrawn breath.

"They're beautiful, Mrs. Brown," Flower said. "Which one is mine?"

Tess carefully carried a cup of coffee over to the table as she watched Rose pick up a dark pink dress and smooth it over Flower's shoulders.

"This one, Flower," Rose said. "I thought it would look nice with your pretty hair and skin. I made you two other dresses," she continued, ignoring Tess, who set the coffee cup down in front of her and returned to the stove. "They're everyday dresses, but I don't quite have them finished yet. I'll either bring them over later, or Stone can pick them up."

"I'm going into the bedroom to try on my dress." Flower scampered from the room, leaving a tense silence behind.

After a moment Rose cleared her throat. "Uh . . . would you like to try on your dress? I may need to make some alterations, since I didn't have your exact measurements."

"I can probably handle any alterations myself," Tess replied. "My grandmother taught me to sew at a fairly young age." She could almost have sworn the glance Rose threw at her was an attempt to measure just how old she was. She took a sip of her coffee and leaned against the counter.

"If you want." Rose shrugged. "But one of the reasons Stone has me make Flower's clothing is because I have a sewing machine. This winter, when we're not so busy with other things, Stone's supposed to bring Flower over so I can teach her to use it."

Somehow Tess controlled her impulse to tell Rose Brown that her sewing lessons wouldn't be necessary—that she would teach Flower herself. But she had no earthly idea if she would even be here this winter. She could be, if she wanted to. All she had to do was make the decision to stay and avoid that darned time warp.

When Tess remained silent Rose picked up her coffee cup and took a sip. "How is your ankle?" she asked after she set the cup down. "Stone said you'd probably get your cast off in time for the social. There's going to be a dance afterwards, you know, and Stone truly does like to dance."

Stone said this; Stone said that. Tess mentally gritted her teeth. Didn't this woman have anything to say except what she parroted of someone else's words?

"My ankle's almost healed," she confirmed flatly. "But thank you for asking. I'm sure it will be in shape for at least some dancing by Saturday night." And more than just some dancing, she thought, because she knew exactly who would fill in as Stone's partner for any dance she was forced to sit out.

"Well, you really shouldn't overdo it at first," Rose said. "And I'm sure you're going to be glad to have your injury healed, so you can contact your family and let them know you're all right. Stone never did say how you happened to be so far out here all by yourself."

"You seemed to have had several conversations about me with Stone."

Rose slipped her a sideways look, making her realize the blonde had avoided her eyes during the entire conversation.

"Stone and I are the closest neighbors out here," Rose said with a shrug. "We've always done what we can to help each other out."

"Tillie Peterson mentioned that," she replied.

"That witch!" Rose spat. "You'd think she'd have the grace to at least be halfway embarrassed about that convict father of hers planning to come here to live after he gets out of prison. Instead, she acts like she's glad about it."

"Tillie's father's moving here?"

"Hasn't Stone told you?" Rose asked. "We were talking about it the other day. Oh, Stone's so stingy sometimes with words. Haven't you noticed that about him?"

"Not really," she denied, unable to suppress a

smirk of satisfaction when Rose's lips tightened in annoyance. "I guess we've just had more important things to talk about than gossip."

"I see," Rose said thoughtfully. "However, your not being able to visit in town because of your injury probably has kept you from knowing that you and Stone are the major topic of *gossip* now. I do keep up on things, what with the customers I have coming out to my place to have special dresses made. I really hope Flower doesn't hear any of it at the social. Children can be so cruel to one another when they repeat things they've heard from their parents."

"Flower's hardly a child."

"No, she's not, is she?" Rose sipped her coffee. "And it is so important for a young girl to have proper influences in her life. Women's reputations are so fragile. Men don't understand that sometimes, and I'm sure Stone will be devastated if Flower is shunned at the dance because her father is allowing you to stay out here with him."

A flush crawled up Tess's cheeks. "Spiteful gossips really are bitches, aren't they?" she said in a deadly voice. "I'm sure you wouldn't foster the kind of talk that would cause any harm to Stone's family, since you obviously want me to believe you're such a close friend of his."

Flower danced back into the room and swirled around. "Look, Tess. Isn't it pretty?" The pink skirt billowed around Flower's ankles, then settled against the floor, the hem just barely touching the pine boards.

"Very pretty," she had to admit. "And it fits you perfectly."

"Go try on your dress, Tess."

"In a little while," she murmured.

Rose stood up, seeming a little flustered to Tess. "I really must be getting back," she said. "There's so much to do this time of year, and I've got a couple of other dresses to finish for ladies before the social."

"Aren't you going to stay for supper?" Flower asked.

"Not this time," Rose said as she walked over to retrieve her hat. "Besides, I promised your father I'd fill his canteen from the well and drop it off on my way home. He said he forgot to do that when he rode in a while ago."

"You really don't have to trouble yourself," Tess said. "I was going to ride out myself in a few minutes and take Stone and Rain some sandwiches. I can drop off the water, too."

"Oh, it's no trouble at all." Rose settled her hat on her head and went out the door, calling over her shoulder, "It was nice to meet you, Miss Foster. I guess I'll see you Saturday afternoon."

By the time Tess managed to limp to the door Rose had gathered up her reins and was leading her horse toward the well. Tess watched her drop the wooden bucket into the well and crank it back to the top, brimming with cold water. She dipped the canteen in, then draped it over her saddlehorn and mounted the sorrel.

"I wish she wasn't riding in to the social with us," Flower murmured beside her.

"What do you mean?"

"Oh, Mrs. Brown said her buggy horse was lame and asked me to tell Pa she'd appreciate a ride in with us. 'Course Pa said sure. We have to help out our neighbors, you know."

"Doesn't look like there's a thing wrong with that horse to me," she said. She could almost feel her eyes shooting green sparks in the direction of the woman riding out of the ranch yard.

"That's her riding horse," Flower explained. "It's not trained to pull a buggy."

"Why don't you want her going in with us?"

Flower blushed and pulled at her skirt. "I didn't mean to say that I don't like Mrs. Brown," she said, ducking her head. "I mean, she made this pretty dress for me and all. It's just . . . well, it would have been nice for just the four of us to go in together."

"Yes, it would have," she murmured. It would be nicer yet if they could go as a family to lots more Saturday socials—and to church together every Sunday.

As Flower walked back into the house, Tess gripped her hands into fists until her nails bit into her palms. No wonder Stone had stormed away from her a while ago. Because he cared for her he battled this day-to-day uncertainty, too, and her indecisiveness kept their emotions stirred up. He was obviously getting tired of discussing the situation with her—"beating a dead horse," as her granny would've said.

But how could she walk away from her other life without giving it a lot of deep thought? All her training in law school had been geared to weighing the pros and cons of each and every decision. She was almost at the height of her career, almost able to walk into a roomful of stuffy lawyers in nearly identical, pin-striped suits and be accepted for her worth as an attorney. Her name was already near the top of the list for the most client billable hours in the firm—a necessity for her to be considered in line for a coveted partnership.

And what about the case she was working on? And did she really care, since her ex-fiancé probably deserved whatever happened to him?

Robert had made his own problems by trying to circumvent the law, even though the case law research she had turned up mitigated him somewhat. However, there were other, fully capable attorneys in the firm who could take her research and mediate the case to conclusion. Shoot, they could probably take the brief she had slaved over for two weeks and win a judgment.

She was damned proud of her abilities in the legal field—and justifiably so, she told herself. She'd worked her fanny off, and it would leave a large hole in her life to give up all she had accomplished.

Tess frowned as she recalled Stone's dictatorial attitude when he informed her flatly that she wouldn't be allowed to look for a job. Not be allowed, hah! Well, she'd see about that. Granny had seemed satisfied canning and cooking all her life. But Granny had never left the West Virginia mountains in her life—never felt the gratification of proving her mind could match any man's when it came to logical deductions and detailed thinking.

Where would her mind grow here? she wondered. Granted, she thoroughly enjoyed helping Flower keep house and feed Stone and Rain after a hard day's work, even though the lack of conveniences made cooking a time-consuming chore. And she enjoyed teaching the children, which freed Stone to have more time for the ranch work.

Would that be enough for her? Or would she

soon find her mind stagnating, yearning for a challenge?

She'd bet Rose Brown never worried about having an intelligent conversation with another adult. Rose seemed perfectly happy echoing thoughts planted in her mind by a man.

Trouble was, that man was Stone.

"Gosh darn it, Angie," Michael grumbled. "How are we supposed to know what to do if we don't know what's going to happen? Huh? I mean, if Tess decides to go back to her own time, maybe Stone would be better off with Rose."

"Bite your tongue! That shallow-minded woman would bore Stone to death in a month. There's a darn sight more to a relationship between a man and a woman than a man having a woman around to keep his stomach full and his clothes clean."

"I know that, blast it. But at least having someone to do that would be a help. And Rose seems to like the kids."

"Oh for pity's sake. Now you're sounding like some of the human males on earth. Show them a halfway pretty face and they can't see beneath the surface. Rose is kind to Flower because she wants to get to Stone through her. She's been working on Stone ever since her husband died."

"Well, they've both been alone out here. What would make more sense than them teaming up together? If Tess hadn't come into the picture . . ."

"She *did* come into the picture," Angela interrupted with a stamp of her foot. "And you're the one who put her here, with your lack of concentration and that sneeze. She slipped through that time warp before I could act. Now you just stick to your assignment and protect Tess from danger. Don't you dare try to interfere in her love life."

He glared at Angela. "If someone had interfered a year ago, she wouldn't have gotten mixed up with that idiot who broke her heart. And I'm getting mighty sick of you ordering me around."

"It was Tess's own decision to get involved with Robert, and she grew from the experience," Angela yelled, plopping her fists on her hips and jutting out her chin. "It made her able to appreciate a man like Stone. And I wouldn't have to order you around if you'd remember what the rules are!"

"Rules, schmules! I know what the rules are and I'm not about to break any of them. But that doesn't mean I don't have my own opinions about things. I reckon I've got an interest in this, too, since, as you so superior-than-thou-ly keep throwing up to me, it's my fault Tess is even here. You'll probably be reminding me a thousand years from now that I was the one responsible for Stone's heartache if Tess decides to go back to 1994."

"So you figure it might ease your guilty conscience if Stone at least has Rose to step into Tess's place, huh?"

"Maybe," he shot back. "But let me tell you this, Angie, baby. I'm not convinced that I'm entirely at fault for Tess's tumble through time. You're my backup while I learn this business, and you didn't jump in fast enough on that mountain!"

"Me? You're the one who messed up!"

"Did not!" he snapped.

"Did, too!" Angela stomped to the edge of the cloud and turned her back on him, crossing her arms over her chest, her wings fluttering in agitation.

* * *

Tess gave up looking for the two birds she could have sworn she heard chittering overhead as they fought to drive one another from the space each considered its own territory. She had watched those aerial sparring matches many times on her backpacking trips. Always before, though, she'd had no trouble locating the feathered combatants. Good grief! Surely all those long hours poring over fine-printed legal contracts couldn't have already strained her eyes to the point where she needed glasses at age thirty!

Chapter Twenty-one

Tess's fingers flew, and she blessed Granny with every stitch. The hours she'd spent learning to sew when she would rather have been roaming the mountain meadows now seemed well worth the effort.

She should have tried on that darned dress before this morning, but it had given her a distasteful feeling in her mouth each time she looked at it. She had to wear it today, but she'd be damned if she was going to look like the prune-faced spinster Rose had evidently had in mind when she designed that high-necked, tight-bodiced piece of trash.

Luckily, Rose hadn't bothered to trim off the excess material on the blouse seams. Probably she hadn't anticipated in her mislaid plan that Tess would be handy with a needle.

She snugged a final stitch and anchored the thread before she bit it off with her teeth. Then she stuck the needle in the pincushion beside her on the bed, held up the dress, and studied it thoughtfully.

The color was fine—a pale ivory that would set off the tan she had acquired on her frequent rides around the ranch. But she had almost choked when she tried to fasten the top button, and forget about flattening her breasts enough to pull the bodice together. She wasn't about to put up with those long, tight sleeves, either.

She shook the dress, and the lace-edged red ruffle settled back into place around the altered scoop neckline. Her spare teddy lay beside the pincushion, denuded of its beige lace and elastic, and only scraps remained of the red blouse she had worn the morning she arrived in Keene Valley. She had even covered her leather belt in red to match the ruffle. It would highlight her slender waist, especially since she had taken a nip and tuck or two in the waist gathers.

Capped sleeves now poofed out from the wide neckline, and she had only to press out the crease where she had let down the too-short hem. She thought longingly of the gold and red sandals in the closet of her apartment, but at least the long dress would hide her Reeboks—the only footwear she owned now, except for her hiking boots.

"Oh, let me see what you've done, Tess," Flower said from the doorway.

Tess smiled at her and shifted the dress around so Flower could see the front. "Do you think it looks all right, honey?"

"It's gorgeous," Flower replied. "And I'll tell you

a secret, if you promise not to let on to Pa that you already know. I talked him into it, but it wasn't very hard."

"And what could that be?"

"I'm going to run over to the general store while Dr. Calder takes your cast off and find you a pair of dancing slippers. I just need to measure your other shoes to see what size to get."

"That's not necessary, Flower. No one will see my shoes under this dress."

"Sure they will. Why, ladies get swung around a lot, especially later on in the evening, after the men have slipped outside a few times."

"Slipped outside? To get a drink, I guess."

"Uh-huh. But we always pretend we don't know. It's kind of hard sometimes not to wrinkle up our noses when we smell their breath, though."

"I better practice then, huh?" Tess turned her head sideways and pursed her lips, aiming her nose up an inch.

Flower giggled and imitated Tess for a second, until they both broke into laughter.

"You might as well drop Rose off at the picnic grounds, Stone," Tess said several hours later as the wagon entered the small town. "I'm sure she would rather visit with people instead of waiting around for us at the doctor's office."

"Oh, I don't mind a bit," Rose demurred. "I can keep Stone company."

"That's not necessary," Tess replied, shifting a half inch closer to Stone on the wagon seat and cupping her hand beneath his elbow. "I'm sure the doctor won't mind if Stone comes in and holds my hand."

She smirked at Rose, who had sat on the far edge of the wagon seat on the ride to town. Tess had plopped herself in the middle, assuring that Stone would be on one side or the other of her, separated from Rose. She hadn't missed the look of consternation on Rose's face when Stone escorted her from her small cabin an hour or so earlier.

Nor had she missed the look of surprise on Rose's face when she saw Tess's altered dress, though Rose had at least had the grace to blush slightly and murmur a compliment on Tess's handiwork.

Rose had obviously designed her own pale blue gown to enhance her more petite figure. A hint of rounded breast showed over the low-cut neckline, edged with a white lace ruffle to give an impression of more fullness than she possessed. Tess thought the ruffled skirt a little overdone for a woman of Rose's age, but she managed to swallow any catty remark.

With a jangle of reins and a "whoa," Stone pulled up the wagon beside a small, whitewashed church. Already Flower and Rain were calling greetings to several youngsters their own ages, and they both scrambled from the wagon bed.

"I'll see you over at the doctor's office in a few minutes, Pa," Flower said as she turned to wave. "I just want to say hello to Sally and Missy first."

Rain had already joined a group of boys, and Stone nodded at Flower as he climbed down from the wagon. He came around and reached up to assist Rose to the ground, giving her only a small smile when she thanked him.

"I'll keep an eye on Flower and Rain for you," Rose said as Stone started back around the wagon.

"They'll be fine," Stone said over his shoulder. "You just enjoy yourself with the other women folk."

A few minutes later Stone pulled up in front of Doc Calder's office, and soon Tess had the freedom to move her ankle for the first time in a month. She wiggled the ankle back and forth and gave a sigh.

"It feels wonderful, Doctor. You did a fine job."

"You did your part, too, young lady," Doc Calder replied. "And seems like you had good nursing care." He winked at Stone, and Tess saw him tear his eyes away from her lower leg, which Doc had uncovered to remove the cast.

"Now," Doc continued, "you be careful for a little while yet, until your muscles adjust to not having the support of that cast. Don't try to dance every dance tonight, or your foot will be swollen in the morning."

"Well, I expect to at least have one dance with my doctor," Tess said in a flirtatious voice. "I don't want to end up a wallflower."

"Harumph," Doc Calder said. "I don't think you're going to have to worry about that. I'll probably have to wade through every eligible male in town to claim a dance with you."

They heard the front door of the office open, and Stone turned away abruptly. "That's probably Flower," he said as he strode out of the room.

Tess glanced away from the door in time to see a worried look on Doc Calder's face as he stared after Stone.

"Is something wrong, Doctor?" she asked. "Stone seems fully recovered from the snakebite. Isn't he?"

"It's not that, Tess. He's fine. It's . . . look, Tess, Stone hasn't been in town for a while, and there's been some changes he ought to be aware of. I brought him a newspaper one day, but I don't think he took time to read it. He left it on the porch while I looked at his leg, and I saw that darned dog carrying it off later."

"So that's how that paper got scattered all over the barn," Tess said. "Flower gathered it up and we put it in the kindling box. It was pretty well chewed up."

"Well, I should have talked to him about it. But he was in such a damned surly mood . . ."

Flower came through the door with Stone behind her. She hurried over to the examining table where Tess lay, her eyes twinkling with delight.

"Is your cast off?" she asked. "Oh, it is. Good. Pa's got a present for you."

Stone handed her the brown-paper-wrapped package and tucked his hands into his pockets. "Flower picked them out," he said with a shrug. "Hope you like them."

She untied the string and laid the paper back to reveal a pair of ivory slippers, almost the same shade as her dress. "They're beautiful," she said, smiling at Stone. "Thank you so much."

The door of the outer office was flung open and a voice called, "Doc! Doc Calder! You here? Harry's gone and broke his arm!"

"Dang it," Doc grumbled. "You'd think they could behave themselves for one day and let me enjoy the social, too." Muttering under his breath, Doc left the room.

"We'd better get out of the way," she said as she swung her legs from the table.

"Try on your slippers first," Stone demanded. He picked up one and knelt to put it on her foot. The dainty slipper fit perfectly, and he leaned back on his heels, a satisfied smile on his face.

"It feels nice, Stone. But I'd better wear my tennies until the dancing starts. I brought my other one with me."

She handed him the Reebok she hadn't worn since she'd landed in Oklahoma, and Stone sighed in compliance as he removed the slipper. His thumb slid across her instep and she giggled.

"Don't," she said. "You know I'm ticklish."

Doc Calder appeared at the door. "Sorry, folks, but I need the table for Harry."

Stone held out the Reebok and she wiggled her foot into it, allowing him to tie the laces. She slid from the table and took a tentative step or two.

"Hum. I think it's going to be fine," she murmured. "Come on. We'd better get out of Doc's way."

Outside the doctor's office she paused as Stone took her elbow to lead her to the wagon. "Would you mind if I looked around town for an hour or so, Stone? I can walk out to the church in a while."

"I guess Flower could stay with you. I should get out there and see if they need some help setting up tables or something."

"Flower wants to visit with her friends. I'll be perfectly all right, for pity's sake. I just want to do a little window shopping."

"Well, don't go around the saloons," he ordered. "Stay at this end of town."

"Yes, sir, boss." She snapped him a perky salute, and he grinned.

"Yeah, sure," he muttered. "Boss. Huh." He turned to Flower and gallantly took her arm. "I guess I'll just escort this pretty miss to the picnic instead."

Flower dropped him a slight curtsy before she took his extended arm and moved toward the wagon. "Just until Tess comes, Pa," she agreed. "And you better not bid on my picnic dinner. It's the one with the pink ribbon that matches my dress."

"And just who do you have in mind to share that supper with?" Stone asked, frowning after he lifted Flower onto the wagon seat.

Tess waved to Flower and hurried down the walkway toward the general store, which they had passed on their drive to the doctor's office. She hoped whichever young man Flower had in mind had the courage to stand up to the glower on Stone's face as he bid on Flower's picnic dinner. She bit back a laugh. And she bet Stone and Rain would share her own basket within a few feet of whoever that lucky young man turned out to be.

Inside the store, she subdued her curiosity at the jumble of goods lining the shelves and floor. Only small paths led between the multitude of objects, which included everything from new saddles and harnesses to a shelf of bonnets and even a rod filled with dresses in one corner. She made her way to the counter where a huge cash register sat and peered through the glass top protecting a few of the more expensive items the store proprietor stocked.

"Can I help you, miss?"

She glanced up to see a tall, lanky man come out

from the rear of the store, wiping his hands on a stained apron.

"I don't know." She glanced down again through the dusty counter glass. "I see you stock some jewelry. I was wondering if you also buy pieces that women no longer have a use for."

"Sometimes," the storekeeper told her. "Depends on what you have you want to get rid of. By the way, I'm Sid. Don't remember seeing you around here before."

"Tess Foster." She held out her hand. The storekeeper took it in a firm grasp, and she liked the honest look in his eyes, and the fact that he dropped her hand as soon as he squeezed it once. His red hair reminded her of Freddy, and for a second she found herself wondering if he had gotten into trouble when he found she was missing from the mountain.

She shook the thought aside and pulled the diamond ring from the reticule Flower had lent her. She'd already made up her mind not to feel guilty about selling the ring Robert had given her. After all, it wasn't a family heirloom or anything. Robert had commissioned it from Tiffany's.

The storekeeper picked up a jewelry glass to study the ring stones and whistled under his breath. "Well, now, Miss Foster, I'm afraid I don't do a large enough business here to offer you what this is worth. I could give you a little something on it and take it on consignment. Then, if someone buys it, we could settle up."

"How much would you ask for it?"

"It's gotta be worth at least a thousand," he said. "Them small stones're emeralds, you know. Not worth as much as that diamond. Ain't never seen one that big—even the one the banker's wife's so proud of. I'll bet she might buy this, but she's gone to Oklahoma City to visit her sister for a few days. Soon as she gets back and sets her eyes on this, though, her husband won't have no rest until she gets it."

She didn't know exactly how much Robert had paid for the ring, but she had seen a similar one at Tiffany's for over fifteen thousand dollars. She had to remember, though, that money was worth a lot more in this time. It probably took the storekeeper several years to earn a thousand dollars.

"I could go a hundred on it now," the storekeeper mused. "Not today, though. Have to wait until the bank's open again on Monday and transfer it to your account. You got one set up at the bank?"

"No. Could you take care of that for me, too? I'm staying with Mr. Chisum, and we'll be going back to the ranch after the dance. In fact, why don't you just deposit the money in Stone's account? That way I'll be able to get it if I need it. I would like to have a few dollars today, though, if it's convenient."

The storekeeper pushed a button on the cash register, and the bottom drawer flew open with a clang. He studied the drawer for a moment, then looked up at her. "Probably could let you have thirty dollars. You want it in cash or credit?"

"How about ten in credit and twenty cash?" She smiled.

Sid nodded his agreement and she picked out a bonnet for Flower that cost two dollars and a new hunting knife for Rain that was slightly less. It took her longer to decide on Stone's gift, but she finally chose a turquoise-studded bolo tie, which

Sid informed her had been handmade by an old Indian man who sold his creations through the store. It seemed a bargain at five dollars, and she loved the intricate silver design that held the turquoise in place.

She expended the remainder of her credit on a small bottle of perfume for herself and dabbed a drop behind each ear before Sid tied up her purchases and handed them to her, along with a twenty-dollar gold piece.

"Thank you so much," she murmured.

"Now you come see me the next time you come into town," Sid said. "I'm almost sure that ring will be sold by then."

"If it is, just put the money in Stone's account," she answered.

She left the store, holding her purchases by the string Sid had wrapped around them, and headed across the street. She hoped the newspaper office hadn't closed on Saturday. Surely not; they would want someone to cover the social and write it up.

She glanced at the next window beside the newspaper office as she climbed the two steps to the walkway on the other side of the street and stopped to study the gilt letters on the pane. A law office; hum. The shade was drawn, though—the attorney was probably at the social.

A second later she pushed open the door to the newspaper office and a small, gray-haired woman looked up from the desk at which she sat.

"May I help you?" the woman asked.

"I'd like to look at some of your back issues, if I could," she explained.

"Of course. Come on back and I'll show you where they are."

Chapter Twenty-two

Tess collapsed on one of the benches lining the wall and waved off the friendly young cowboy's offer to fetch her a glass of punch after their dance. Instead, she'd been thinking of sneaking out to the wagon and snitching a piece of leftover chicken from the picnic basket. Though she had been so stuffed after the midafternoon feast that she'd had to loosen her remodeled belt a notch, she now felt as if she could eat twice as much all over again.

Must be the unaccustomed exercise, she guessed, though she'd enjoyed every dance—especially the old-fashioned hill dances she had loved back in West Virginia. A time or two she had stumbled and disorganized a square of eight. However, her partners good-naturedly had reformed their square and set off together. Soon her ears harkened once again to the square dance caller's cadence, and she flipped her skirt and doe-see-doe'd with the best of the women.

Tess glanced across the room and saw several men setting up a row of tables. Good; the people were finally preparing for the evening meal to which Flower had told her their leftovers would contribute. Her stomach had evidently adjusted to the three full meals a day she and Flower prepared, since for the last hour it had been grumbling off and on, reminding her it was well past the usual supper hour.

Oh, no! she groaned under her breath.

Tillie Peterson was making her way through the crowd, her corseted bosom preceding the rest of her, parting the sea of bodies like the prow of a battleship. Indeed, she looked something like a battleship in her gray silk gown. No mistaking her objective—those pale eyes gazing out from the folds of flesh in her face were centered on Tess.

She straightened in her chair and forced a smile to her lips. She'd be darned if she'd give in to the impulse to pull her ivory gown up an inch over her breasts.

"Hello, Tillie," she greeted her. "I understand your Ladies' Guild planned this social. I've been wanting to tell you how much I'm enjoying it."

"Why, thank you, Tess. I'll be sure and pass your kind words on to the other ladies. I'm glad to see that your ankle's healed. You haven't seemed to miss a dance this evening."

For just a second she thought she caught a hint of hurt in Tillie's voice, and the surge of sympathy she felt for the chubby woman surprised her. She had noticed that Tillie stood with the same group of women against the wall during most of the dances. Once she had seen Tillie dancing with an elderly man, though. And wonder of wonders, after the first dance of the evening—the only one Tess had shared with Stone—Stone had crossed the room after he left her and led Tillie onto the floor.

"I . . . um . . . I hope you truly are enjoying yourself, Tess," Tillie said as Tess fumbled in her mind for something else to say. "Uh . . . no one has . . . uh . . ."

"To be truthful," she admitted, "a couple of the women sort of sniffed and pulled their skirts aside when I came too near. I assume they're part of the group scandalized because I'm staying out at Stone's, instead of agreeing to move into the boardinghouse here in town."

Tillie's reaction surprised her further. She wrung her pudgy hands and murmured a quiet "Oh, dear," in a soft voice, then said, "That is a very lovely gown. Did you make it?"

"No. Well, sort of," Tess replied. "Rose Brown made the initial dress. I altered it a tad."

"Oh, then you sew!" Tillie said eagerly. "I was wondering when I saw your dress. I never learned. When I was growing up in Texas there was always plenty of money for dressmakers. Now, though—out here . . . well, Rose is the only person those of us who can't sew for ourselves have to make our clothing."

"Surely you can order through a catalog or something. And I saw some dresses on a rack at the general store."

"Nothing ever fits right," Tillie said with a sigh. "Rose made this gown for me. I did have something a little more feminine in mind, but Rose convinced me that I'd only be emphasizing my larger figure. I haven't always had that worry, you know. My dressmaker in Texas always said that I was a delight to fit."

Tess eyed the gray gown critically. "There are a few things you could do, Tillie. For one thing, that color does absolutely nothing for you. Have you thought about a soft violet? Your eyes have a touch of violet in the blue, and a gown that color would bring it out."

"I used to love wearing violet," Tillie said. "But surely at my age . . ."

"And what's that? Thirty?"

"Thirty-two. And I've been married and widowed. After all, propriety says I should dress according to my status."

"Propriety be damned," she said, feeling a stirring of liking for Tillie when the other woman giggled, then quickly glanced around to see if anyone had heard Tess's language.

"And," she continued, "those sleeves look awfully tight under your arms. I would think a looser fit in the bodice would be much more comfortable. A V-neckline, too, would be more . . . well, enticing. Different contours in a gown de-emphasize things we women aren't completely satisfied with in our figures."

"I read once in a fashion magazine that horizontal stripes sometimes flatter larger figures."

"They do—not loud stripes, though."

"I wouldn't have to worry about trying to look good if I could just lose this extra weight," Tillie said in a forlorn voice. "I wish I knew what to do about it. I guess it comes with age."

"Have you tried strictly limiting yourself to your

three meals a day—no snacks and no desserts? And exercising? Walking's best at first, until you build up your stamina. Eventually you can work up to jogging. I always ran at least five miles every morning before I hurt my ankle."

"Ran? Oh, my. What would people in town say if they saw me? Oh, I couldn't."

"Seems to me it's none of their business, Tillie. And when they see the beautiful woman emerging who's been hidden beneath your extra weight I'll bet you'll have a horde of women asking for your secret."

"Do you really think so?" Tillie asked in a voice filled with wonder.

"It won't happen overnight," she responded with a laugh. "Remember, it took you several years to put on that weight. It might take as long as a year for you to lose it. But think how much better you'll feel about yourself then."

"I'll try it." Tillie's eyes took on a determined glint. "Would it be all right if I asked your advice from time to time on how I'm doing, Tess?"

"Of course."

Tillie started to turn away, then stopped.

"Thank you, Tess. I . . . I want to say one more thing: I'm president of the Ladies' Guild this year, but it's just because we rotate among ourselves. Being president doesn't mean you're the one who makes decisions in the Guild. It just means you're the one elected to carry out the decisions voted on, whether you agree with them or not. Propriety . . . at times, yes, propriety should be damned."

With a rustle of yards of gray silk, Tillie swept away through the crowd, leaving Tess to stare after her in consternation. Her final words could mean several things, and Tess wasn't about to let down her guard completely against Tillie Peterson. The other woman might show a spurt of independence now, but once back in the folds of the Guild she would be expected to follow the rest of the sheep of the membership.

She did miss the companionship of other women, though, she admitted to herself. A shared cup of coffee while they hashed over the past weekend's activities . . . a women-only night now and then at someone's apartment, complete with mud treatments for their faces and giggling sessions in front of the mirror as they tried out various hairstyles. A good gossip over a bottle or two of wine—who was seeing who, and how on earth were they ever going to find a decent man among the bunch of losers who asked them out.

She'd missed that after she became engaged to Robert. Every free moment she could spare from her busy work schedule was spent with her fiancé, attending social functions with the New York elite—and a lot of moments she really couldn't spare, too.

But despite Tillie's tentative thrust of friendship, she couldn't bring herself to believe that she would find much in common with Clover Valley's women. They had already labeled her Stone's mistress.

Her eyes searched the room for Stone until she saw him come through the schoolhouse door with Rose clinging to his arm. The picnic basket he carried belonged to Rose—the same one Rose had brought with her from her cabin. Tess narrowed her eyes when the blonde pretended to stumble on an uneven spot on the pine floor. She clung even tighter to Stone's arm as she giggled and looked up at him with fluttering eyelashes.

"Since I haven't been able to get close enough to claim that dance, maybe I can escort you out to get your supper basket, Miss Foster."

Tess rose to her feet and took Doc Calder's proffered arm. "I'd be delighted, Doctor," she said with a smile. "But I wouldn't want your wife to scratch my eyes out when she finds me with her handsome husband."

Doc Calder chuckled and patted her hand. "Mandy's helping the women set things up. And she knows I've been wanting to talk to you. In fact, she's the one who saw you going into the newspaper office and mentioned it to me. We have our living quarters above my office. Let's stop a second so you can meet her."

Doc Calder steered her to the far end of the tables now lining one wall and toward a petite gray-haired woman. The moment the woman turned at her husband's greeting, Tess could feel the love flowing between the two people. Mandy Calder had no reason to doubt her husband's fidelity, and Tess immediately regretted her flirtatious remark to the doctor.

"I'm so glad to finally get to meet you, Miss Foster," Mandy said as she took Tess's hand. "Ed's told me so much about you, and we think the world of Stone and the children. Maybe now that your ankle's healed you can ride in for a visit once in a while. I don't get out much while Ed's off here and there tending his patients. Someone has to keep the office open."

"I'd really enjoy that." She felt an instant liking for the doctor's wife. "And please call me Tess."

"Of course. Now you two better go get your basket in here. The men need to put something in their stomachs to counteract that whiskey they've been sneaking outside to sample."

Doc Calder took Tess's arm again and led her toward the doorway. Though she caught a flash of pale blue at the edge of her vision and saw Rose unloading her picnic basket onto the already fast-filling table, she gratefully realized Stone was no longer at Rose's side. She and the doctor threaded their way through wagons and buggies until they reached Stone's wagon, but she didn't see Stone anywhere. Maybe he was visiting that hidden whiskey keg, she mused.

She hadn't caught any hint of whiskey on his breath during the one dance they had managed to steal for themselves, though. As always, there was a tang of mint intermingled with the smell of his aftershave. She had noticed that his evening beard already shadowed his face, but it only made him that much more handsome.

Too bad the dance had been a fast-paced square dance. The only time she could properly touch those broad shoulders in that perfectly tailored black coat was during the swing-your-partner calls. She really needed to remember to tell him how wonderful he looked in that white shirt and string tie. Of course he looked just as good without any shirt at all. And she preferred him in the snug-fitting denims he wore at the ranch to the looser dress pants he wore with his jacket.

"Uh . . ."

Doc Calder cleared his throat, and she shook herself back to the present when she realized they had been standing by the wagon for at least a minute. She started to reach for the picnic basket, but Doc Calder spoke again.

"As I mentioned, Tess, Mandy saw you go into the newspaper office. I guess maybe you were checking out that little matter we started to discuss in my office."

"I was. And I intend to talk to Stone about it just as soon as I can."

"Let me explain to you what it means. . . ."

"I'm perfectly capable of understanding that report from the territorial legislature," she interrupted. "A first-year law student could read that legal mess."

"But most women couldn't."

"This woman can," she replied with a grim set to her lips. "The bottom line is that all the previous homesteads have to be proved up before the new land rush next month if they're in the last year of their five-year period. And they've slapped a new tax on the lands that has to be paid on prove up."

"That's right," Doc said admiringly. "And the prove up is . . ."

"Stone doesn't have any problem complying with that. He has a home built and a barn. He even has most of his acreage fenced, though I can't recall if that was one of the old prove-up clauses."

"Old?" Doc mused with a quirked eyebrow.

"And he certainly has enough stock on the homestead," she hurried to say in an attempt to distract Doc from her slip of the tongue. "All he has to do is pay that tax assessment."

"That's where the problem might be," Doc explained. "Not only to Stone, but to some others in the territory. You see, a lot of the settlers are land rich and cash poor. Most of them, though, have had a chance to be forewarned of the new laws and the plan for the tax. Since Stone doesn't even know about it yet, and since the deadline's coming up pretty fast . . ."

"If you two are done discussing my private business, I think we'd better get back in there and eat before we start home, Tess. Flower and Rain have to be up early."

Her eyes flew to the shadowy figure she now saw standing beneath a nearby cottonwood. Stone stepped out into the moonlight, and she stifled a gasp as she caught the deadly glint in his eyes and the strained line of his normally full lips.

"Stone, we . . ." She lifted a hand toward him, but he turned away abruptly.

"I'll see you inside," he tossed over his shoulder.

"Darn his pride," she muttered. "He could at least discuss things with me."

"Men's business," Doc Calder said to her. "We don't like to worry pretty heads with financial matters."

"Yeah." She turned her eyes back on the doctor. "Women in this time are just supposed to be pretty ornaments that drop a baby for their men at least once a year. Well, let me tell you, Doctor, one of these days women are going to vote and hold down a hell of a lot of jobs you men seem to think they're not smart enough to do now. They'll run some of the biggest companies in the United States!"

"Mandy and I never could have any children," Doc said in a soft voice. "Even with all I learned about healing to become a doctor, I never could give her that."

The fire died inside Tess, and her anger was defused. "I'm sorry. I apologize. I didn't know."

"No reason you should." Doc Calder gave a shrug and picked up the picnic basket. "And, unlike most men in *this* time, I make sure Mandy knows all about my finances. She keeps the books for my practice and knows to a penny how much we owe and who owes us what—not that much of it will ever be collected. However . . ." He patted his pudgy stomach. "We never worry about food. Even if a lot of people are short of cash to pay for their doctorin', they make it up by sharin' their gardens with us— and meat at butcherin' time."

Somewhat abashed, she slipped her hand beneath Doc's elbow and walked with him back toward the schoolhouse. "It's different with you, though, Doc. You and Mandy are man and wife. I guess Stone had a right to be angry about my discussing his private affairs, but surely he'll accept some help from me if it becomes necessary."

"Don't count on it. A man like Stone's got too much pride to let a woman bail him out of a jam."

"That's not pride—that's muleheadedness." She snorted. "But . . . maybe there's a better way."

Doc gazed down at her with a questioning look, but she only winked at him and urged him on through the door. She took the picnic basket from him and headed for the end of the table where Mandy stood. While she shoved aside dishes to make room for her own food, she whispered to Mandy and received the elderly woman's agreement to slip away for a private talk as soon as the men were fed.

"I'll take Pa's plate to him, if you want, Tess."

She turned at Flower's voice to find the young girl standing at her elbow. "I thought you might be planning on eating with that young man who bought your dinner, Flower," she teased. "What was his name? Jess? Jeff?"

"Johnny," Flower said with a laugh. "And I am,

but I thought it might mellow Pa a little if I took him his plate like a dutiful daughter first. Then maybe he wouldn't glower at Johnny and me while we ate."

"Well, I've got a little making up to do to your pa myself. So I hate to disappoint you, but I really wanted to be the one to wait on him."

"All right. Johnny and I'll just pretend we don't see Pa glaring. By the way . . ." She leaned forward. "Pa likes the white meat best."

"Gotcha."

A few minutes later Tess carried a brimming plate in both hands as she skittered between the other diners in search of Stone. When she passed the end of the line at the table she turned to look behind her and saw Rose picking up a heavily laden plate. As well as she knew her own name, Tess was convinced that Rose intended to be the one to get to Stone first. Whirling around, she ran into an unyielding chest and barely managed to keep the food on the plate from sliding to the floor.

"Whoops!" she said with a gay laugh when she looked up into Stone's face. "I'd sure have hated to offer you your meal off the floor!"

Stone's lips curved into a smile as he stared down into her eyes. "I'm glad you remembered your place," he told her in a semi-stern voice. "The boss always gets fed first."

She managed a slight curtsy and offered him the plate. "Your meal, my lord," she said, simpering.

Stone laughed and shook his head as he accepted the plate. "You don't fit the pattern of an obedient servant, Tess, honey." He slipped his free hand around her waist. "Come on. I'll explain the rules to you a little better while we eat."

"But I should be helping the women feed the men," she said, saucily tilting her head. "Isn't that one of the rules—the men eat first? I should be standing in the serving line. Besides, I didn't bring a plate for myself."

"We'll share this one. And you need to rest your ankle before the last round of dancing."

Stone led her to a corner of the room and settled her on a vacant bench. She instinctively looked around for Rose and saw her glowering at them from near the serving tables. As soon as she noticed Tess's glance, Rose turned a brilliant smile on the nearest man and walked toward him, the plate in her hands extended.

"Maybe we should check on the kids first," Stone said as he set the food down between them.

"They're fine. I just saw Flower, and Rain's over there with that bunch of boys his own age, waiting to go through the serving line."

"Who's Flower eating with?" he asked, frowning.

"Johnny, of course. Stone, you've got to realize she's growing up. There are going to be a lot of young men paying attention to her."

"Johnny's all right, I guess," he grumbled. "At least his family's not bigoted about anyone with Indian blood. But I'm gonna be damned careful who I let come courtin' Flower. There's still a lot of whites who think an Indian woman is only good for one thing."

She gasped as a flash of anger stole through her. "That's ridiculous! Why, if I hear anyone talk like that, I'll . . . I'll . . ."

"You'll hear it," he promised. "And probably a lot worse. Hell, we fought the Indians for two hundred years. I was in a few skirmishes myself when I was leading wagon trains. You don't think that kind of enmity is going to just disappear, do you? Just because the slaves were freed in the South didn't assure them a comparable standing with the whites. And we've stuck the Indians on reservations, kept them separate from us. How can we ever hope to integrate the two cultures that way?"

"In my time we've got laws against prejudice."

He raised an eyebrow. "And can your laws legislate a person's mind and emotions? I suppose everyone stops and pages through his nonprejudice handbook before he makes a crude remark to someone of another race."

"No," she admitted. "We've still got a lot of disparity among the races, and even hate groups. I don't know if it will ever get wiped out. Oh, Stone, I don't want Flower to have to go through that."

"Sometimes I wonder if I did the right thing, taking Flower and Rain to raise," he mused. "But the alternative wasn't much better. There's prejudice among the Indians, too, that the kids' white blood would bring out, and Silver Eagle's getting up there in years. He couldn't protect them forever. And I sure as heck wouldn't want my kids in one of the schools springing up for the reservation kids. They cut the kids' hair—stick them in white men's clothes—insist they speak English, and pound every bit of their Indian beliefs out of their heads. The damned fools in Washington think the only way to blend the Indians in with us is to make them as white as they can."

"There's a way to fight things like that—by sending people to Washington." She leaned forward. "You'd make a good advocate for the Indians,

Stone, especially since you're familiar with the Indian culture. You could make a difference."

"And who'd run the ranch while I was gone—the ranch that supports me and the kids? The ranch that . . ."

Stone abruptly shoved the plate of food toward her and stood. "I'm not really hungry. I'm gonna get some air before the dancing starts again."

He started to turn away, then glanced down at her with a wry grin. "Sorry. I didn't mean to spoil our meal. Save me at least one dance, will you?"

She nodded dejectedly and watched him walk away, his hands thrust into his pockets and his shoulders slumped. She yearned to follow him and share his worry over losing the ranch. That must be what he was thinking about as he paced out under the stars. But she had her own plan. Hopefully, it would be a much more sensible solution to the unfair law threatening Stone's ranch than just stewing about it.

Picking up a chicken breast, she ate it, then stood and carried the still-full plate over to set it with the growing pile of dirty dishes the men were leaving for the women to wash. She caught Mandy's eye and nodded toward the back door of the schoolhouse. The elderly woman immediately rose and followed as Tess walked out the opposite door from where Stone had gone.

An hour later, Angela gazed down at the scene below her. Sleeping babies lay on blankets spread near the walls. A few of the older children still clung drowsily to wakefulness, determined to take advantage of their parents' tolerance for their delayed bedtime on this one night. More children were already curled up in wagon beds outside. Worn out from their active day, they would wake in their own beds in the morning, never even remembering being carried into their homes.

A few of the lanterns had been doused so the babies could sleep in the shadows, and Angela watched Tess float around the floor in Stone's arms, a dreamy expression on her face. The square dance caller's voice was silent now. Instead of the energetic, foot-stomping music played earlier in the evening, the fiddler gently plied his bow, accompanied by two guitarists, strumming quiet chords.

One more dance, probably, Angela thought. *A good-night dance to finish an evening everyone hates to see end.*

Dancing looked like so much fun. She'd attended many dances over the millennia of her existence. Every culture had its own style—sometimes purely for fun, and sometimes as part of their worship. The closest she'd ever come to participation, though, had been to tap her foot in time to the beat of an especially lively tune, or sway back and forth in rhythm with a slow, achy ballad.

"I suppose you're still too danged mad at me to dance with me," Michael said in a gruff voice.

She glanced at him, where he stood as far away from her as he could on the other edge of the cloud. A mixture of a pout and a little hope filled his face.

"I don't know if guardian angels are supposed to dance," she said softly.

"Well, if you don't know for sure, you can't know if there's a rule against it," he said, the pout giving way to the hope. "Listen, they're starting to play the last dance."

Somewhat shyly, Michael held out his arms, and she glided across the cloud. "I guess just one dance wouldn't hurt," she said as he drew her into the first waltz steps.

A second later she looked up at him in wonder. "Why, this is nice. You must be an awfully good dancer for me to follow you so easily."

"Lots of the human spirits I worked with loved to dance, and it sort of caught my fancy, too. I kept up on what the latest dances on earth were by practicing with them every once in a while. You can bet your boots I can cotton-eye-Joe and two-step with the best of them, but I've always loved a waltz."

"Me, too—or at least I always enjoyed listening to them. The slow dances always seem to survive, don't they? I mean, I've watched the teenagers come up with all sorts of different new dance gyrations over the years. Some of them scandalize their parents, but they always manage to keep the slow dances, too."

"Uh-huh. There's just something about a nice, slow dance between two people that lets them show their feelings for each other in public in an acceptable way. Look at Tess and Stone. Why, they're almost making love to each other with their eyes."

"Michael!"

She twisted out of his arms with a wrench, then clasped a hand over her mouth in horror when Michael teetered on the edge of the cloud. She quickly made a grab for him, but her hand fell an inch short. The pudgy little angel tumbled down among the dancers, and she knelt with her hand still extended, her eyes wide.

Of course, no one on the floor noticed. The waft of breeze through the room stirred a few curls on the women's heads, but they attributed it to air coming through the open doors of the schoolroom. As soon as he gained control of his wings, Michael zipped back above the dancers and hovered against the ceiling, his arms crossed as he silently glared at her.

Angela rose to her feet. "Uh . . . I . . . I'm sorry. I didn't mean . . ." She dropped her eyes and shrugged her shoulders. "Th . . . thank you for the dance, Michael," she murmured, her eyes filling with tears.

Michael's defiant stance wilted and slowly he drifted down to the cloud and settled beside her. "Oh, shoot. It's okay. Look, it was an accident. Let's finish our dance. Please?"

Tess lazily opened her eyes and glanced over Stone's shoulder. She saw Rain sitting in one of the chairs against the wall, but he wasn't watching the dancers. Instead he gazed up at the ceiling, not a hint there of the sleepiness she had seen earlier on his face.

Suddenly a grin split Rain's face and he lifted a hand, almost as though signaling a gesture of concurrence to someone overhead. She started to draw back in Stone's arms to try to follow Rain's gaze, but he murmured softly to her and lifted his hand from her back to draw her head onto his shoulder again. With a contented sigh, she complied.

Chapter Twenty-three

"I'm damned sure *not* going to stay here," Tess ground out the next morning after Silver Eagle and the children had ridden off. "What if something happens to you out there alone—like that snakebite? You could lay there and die!"

"You'll do what the hell I tell you to do!" Stone fired back. "I've told you over and over that my rules go around here!"

"Well, Mr. Boss Man, that might work on the kids, but I'm a grown woman. Just how do you think you're going to make sure I stay behind? Tie me to the bedpost? Or maybe you'll tie me and Lonesome out beside the privy and leave us each a pan of water and a bowl of food."

"Don't tempt me. Only thing is, I'd have to explain to Jasper why he had two extra animals to take care of."

"Animals! Why, you overbearing louse! You . . . you chauvinistic pig!"

"Oink, oink," he muttered.

She quickly clenched her bottom lip between her teeth and bit down hard. She wasn't going to laugh. No, darn it . . .

She balled her hands into fists and plopped them on her hips, glaring at him. He glared back. She had to retort—it was her turn. But she couldn't yell at him with her lip caught like that.

"You . . ." Big mistake. The giggles penned in her chest erupted. She snorted, and he wrinkled his nose at her.

"Here, piggy," he called softly, then burst into laughter when she fell onto the bench by the kitchen table, clutching her stomach.

Stone sat down beside her and took her hand. "Look, honey, I have to do this. The army post at Fort Sill will buy even half-broken horses at a pretty good price. And I promised Jasper Smith he could have his pick of the mares in the herd I'm bringing in if he'd stay here and care for my stock."

"And how are you going to drive a herd of horses to an army post all by yourself—even if you do manage to get some this time?" Tess tugged at her hand, trying to ignore the warmth spreading up her arm as Stone's thumb stroked her palm. "For that matter, how are you going to pen them up by yourself? Stone, let go of me. I can't think."

"Then don't think," he whispered. "Just feel." He shifted closer to her on the bench and dropped her hand. But he slipped his arm around her waist and bent to nuzzle her ear, his warm breath sending a cascade of shivers down her body and a throb of desire curling through her veins. He kissed a path down her cheek and nibbled at the corner of her mouth.

"That's not going to work," she said in as firm a voice as she could manage. "I'm still going with you."

Stone moved his nibbling to her lips, barely brushing them with cloud-soft caresses. One hand moved to cup the bottom of her breast, while the other stroked her back. Without ever kissing her fully he moved his mouth to her jawline and down to her neck. Nudging aside the collar of her blouse, he very gently nipped at the sensitive spot just above her collarbone, then circled the area with his tongue.

"So soft," he murmured. "So silky. So beautiful."

She moaned in surrender. The hands she kept ordering to shove him away curled into his hair instead. White hot yearning swept away any chance of conscious thought, and she gave no resistance when he cupped her hips and stood, kicking aside the bench to get to the table.

Wrapping her legs around his trim waist, she whimpered in longing and frustration at the denim material covering both their bodies. She instinctively moved against the bulge in his jeans, tightening her legs around him when he gasped and lay her onto the table.

He grabbed her mouth with his own, and she sparred with his tongue, her thrusts and his imitating the movements of their lower bodies. She unbuttoned her blouse and started on his shirt, fumbling uselessly almost at once when his mouth found her bare breast.

"God, I want you," he growled as he claimed her other breast.

"Please. Please, yes."

Lonesome's barks rang through the door as he surged to his feet on the porch. His frenzied yaps penetrated her drugged senses, and she clutched at Stone when he buried his face against her neck and whispered a vile expletive.

"S . . . someone's coming," she said in a shaky voice.

"Jasper," he muttered. He braced his hands on the table and gazed down at her. "Lonesome could probably hold Jasper off for a while," he said in a soft voice. "But when I make love to you, darlin', it's not going to be a hurry-up deal. It's gonna be soft and slow, then wicked and wild. By the time we reach the clouds we're gonna know every inch of each other's bodies. All right?"

She gulped and nodded her head. He stepped back, then grasped her hands to pull her up. His eyes still smoldered behind his slit lids, and he ran them over her face and down her upper body, branding her as his own. Twining his fingers in her hair, he bent and kissed her.

"I love you, Tess," he said after he released her. "Remember that while I'm gone, will you?" Without waiting for her answer, he turned away and strode across the floor.

She flinched when he let the screen door bang behind him. She lifted trembling fingers and caressed her swollen lips, her body still tingling with frustrated desire. Slowly she took a deep breath, trying to calm her racing heart and bring a semblance of sanity to her tumbling thoughts.

While I'm gone. The gravelly words echoed in her mind. Maybe while he was gone would be the time for her to make her final decision. It was the perfect opportunity, of course. She could ride up to the hillside undisturbed and search for the time warp—at least find out if it was still there.

For a second she concentrated once again on recalling the sequence of events during the few minutes before she found herself in Oklahoma in 1893. She remembered looking up at the sky, her attention drawn by what she imagined was the sound of human voices. But it couldn't have been—she'd been alone on the mountainside. She frowned as a more recent recollection came to mind. The imagined voices she'd thought she heard on the mountainside had sounded sort of like the squabbling birds she hadn't been able to see in the sky the other day.

Unable to make any sense of that portion of her memory, she recalled the stabbing pain in her twisting ankle—her fall over the cliff. She had definitely heard a sneeze—she hadn't imagined that, because the recollection was much too vivid. Then those bush roots had torn free of the soil.

She shook her head in puzzlement. If anyone had been up on the trail—possibly the person who had sneezed—that person wouldn't have had time to rescue her, because she had entered the time tunnel immediately. She hadn't recalled it at first, while she sat on the hillside talking to Rain. But after he left to bleed the deer, the memory of her abject terror when she felt herself falling, then the whooshing flight through blackness, came back.

If the time warp was still there—did those things close up?—if she could find it . . . What if she accidentally stumbled onto it—into it? She'd leave without saying good-bye to Stone and the two children she cared so deeply about. Stone's last memory of her would be her broken promise to him about saying good-bye before she left.

The decision she had to make continued to wobble in her mind. For one thing, she'd been happier here with Stone in this primitive log cabin than in her apartment, filled with gadgets she had no time to enjoy. However, thirty years of her life kept pulling at her.

Well, one sure way to assure herself that she didn't have to make her decision right away was to go with Stone. She set her lips into a determined slant and slid off the table, buttoning her blouse as she headed for the bedroom she shared with Flower. Once she made her decision, she knew it would have to be irrevocable. And until she had a clear, unalterable path set in her own mind, she was going to stay away from that darned hillside. That was all there was to it.

Grabbing the backpack at the foot of the bed, she turned around and retraced her steps. He hadn't left yet; his saddlebags, packed with provisions for his trip, still lay on the countertop. She swung them over her other shoulder and pushed open the screen door.

Michael grabbed Angela's arm and swerved their flight path into a turn. "Hang on, Angie," he called. "We can go back now. They're done necking, and she's headed for the barn. I think there's gonna be a different kind of fireworks this time."

Angela tried to pull her arm free and grabbed at a curl whipping around her face. "Michael! Oh, do slow down. We can think ourselves back to the ranch. We don't have to fly this fast."

"Come on, Angie. This is much more fun—and great exercise. Shoot, we don't even have to worry about running into any airplanes in this sky. Isn't it great?"

"Guardian angels don't need exercise." But she ceased trying to pull free and tipped her face up to let the wind caress her cheeks. It *was* fun, zipping through the sky and dodging clouds they could easily have flown through. And after all, there wasn't any rule against guardian angels having fun, was there?

Tess ignored the two men standing beside the barn door and dropped her backpack and Stone's saddlebags before she walked inside. She probably should have at least said a polite hello to the wiry man beside Stone, but she would introduce herself after she had her horse safely saddled. She wouldn't put it past Stone to order Jasper to keep her away from the horses and tack while he was gone.

"What the hell do you think you're doing?" Stone grabbed her arm before she could enter the tack room.

"Obviously I'm going after some tack for one of the horses," she said in a fairly reasonable voice. "What else do you go into a tack room for?"

"You don't need any tack. You're not going anywhere."

"Oh, but I am. I told you that in the kitchen."

"Damn it, I said you weren't!"

She stared up at his furious face and pried his fingers off her arm one by one. She shrugged her shoulder and tilted her chin up, then walked into the tack room. After lifting a bridle from a peg she started toward one of the smaller saddles draped over a cross bar.

The tack-room door slammed, plunging the room into dimness. She stiffened her back, not deigning to turn around to see if Stone had locked her in or whether he was still in the small room with her. The instant her fingers touched the saddle, she heard his indrawn hiss of breath.

"I said—you're staying here!"

"No. I'm not."

She tossed the bridle over her arm and hefted the saddle. Turning, she walked toward the door, where he stood blocking her path.

"Do you realize what almost happened a few minutes ago?" Stone demanded, refusing to budge from the door. "What the hell do you think there is to stop us from makin' love when we're spending nights alone out there chasin' that wild horse herd?"

"Why, nothing except our own rational minds, I guess," she murmured. "After all, we're adults."

"Rational? I lose any sense of rationality when I touch you. And you don't have any better control than I do!"

She stared up into his scowling face and quirked her lips when he jammed his hands into his pockets—probably to keep from either pulling her into his arms or strangling her, she figured. She shifted the saddle in her arms and pushed a straggling curl from her forehead.

"This thing's starting to get heavy. Are you going to move?"

"No!"

"You're going to have a heck of a time going after those horses and standing here guarding me at the same time. Which horse should I take?"

"None of them. Those horses belong to me, and I refuse to give you permission to ride any of them."

"What are you going to do? Have me arrested for horse theft? Golly gee, do they still hang people for stealing horses these days?"

Stone mumbled a curse and threw open the door. Muttering something about damned fool women who didn't know their place, he stomped toward the barn entrance. Shrugging, she crossed the dirt floor to one of the stalls, where a horse stood with its brown head thrust out.

"Not that damned mare!" he said angrily. "She's in foal. Take the gelding in the next stall."

"Whatever you say," she called back in a sweet voice.

"*Now* you follow orders," he growled loud enough for her to hear. "Just as long as what I say agrees with what you want to do." He raised his voice a notch. "I'm leavin' in thirty seconds, with or without you. You'd better know how to saddle your own horse, because you're not gonna get a damned bit of help from me."

She heaved the saddle over the stall door, then opened it and led the gray gelding through. She expertly slipped his halter off and the bridle on, then looped the reins through a round ring beside the stall. Sliding the saddle blanket from beneath the saddle, she swung it over the gelding's back and smoothed it carefully. The saddle followed, and as she reached beneath the gelding's stomach for the other end of the cinch, she glanced at the barn door.

"Are my thirty seconds up yet?" she called.

Stone snorted and disappeared from sight.

Chapter Twenty-four

Shooting stars flared periodically across the ebony sky, and Tess mentally counted them instead of sheep in her mind. She gave up when she realized she'd been counting Stone's breaths instead, timing her own intakes to match his. He lay on the other side of the fire, evidently not having her problem of sleeplessness.

Darn it anyway, she just couldn't figure him out. He'd never been at a loss for words to tell her exactly how she was irritating him, but today, he had communicated with her in grunts and hand motions—and then only when absolutely necessary. Otherwise he totally ignored her.

Supper had been a deadly quiet affair. She seethed again as she recalled Stone fixing his own meal of fried bacon and beans, then piling it onto his plate and walking over to a nearby rock to eat. He hadn't even left her one slice of bacon or a measly bean. He had, however, left a portion of his food on the plate and set it down for Lonesome, who had sat with cocked ears, watching Stone eat.

It was a darned good thing she had her own backpack with her. A nearby stream furnished water, and she had boiled a freeze-dried dinner of noodles and sauce. She smiled a satisfied smirk as she remembered catching Stone gazing at her food as she twirled the noodles around her camp-kit fork and ate them with gusto. She'd bet a week's pay her noodles had tasted better than that cold can of beans! Lonesome had gobbled his own share of that meal, too, and now lay curled at her side on her sleeping bag.

She reached down and scratched a brown ear. "Guess you know who packs tastier provisions, don't you, boy?"

Lonesome shifted to his back and one hind leg up in the air, hiccuping back and forth in time to her scratches. She giggled softly at the picture he made, sprawled with his belly unprotected, and teasingly shifted the cadence of her fingers on his ear. Two short scratches. A pause. Three scratches this time. Lonesome's leg followed suit.

At least she never had to second-guess the dog's attitude toward her. Ever faithful and loving, Lonesome always came when she called—bounding energetically up to her and forever grateful for a pat or a kind word. He never pouted over the few reprimands she gave him if he loped too close to her horse's heels and made the gelding skittish. When he stuck his nose into her backpack he immediately withdrew it at her command, sitting down and lifting a paw apologetically.

Pouting! Good grief, was Stone pouting because she had defied him and refused to stay at the ranch? Surely not. A grown man of his age should have enough maturity not to . . . pout?

Suddenly she remembered the first time Granny had appeared on the doorstep of their house in town after Tess's mother's death. Seldom did Granny leave the mountain. In fact, the only time Tess had seen her in town prior to that day was at her mother's funeral, six months before.

But Granny showed up the first day after school let out for the summer, informing Tess's father in no-nonsense tones that she'd come to fetch Tess to spend the summer with her. No, Granny had said, she wasn't going to leave Tess with her father to tend house for him. She didn't much give a darn that Tess's absence meant her father had to prepare his own meals and wash his own clothes. He had two older sons, who could just learn to use that darned washing machine themselves. If they couldn't figure out how to use the stove, there was always the barbecue pit in the backyard; men were always so proud to show their skills on that.

Tess, Granny said, was going back to the mountain with her grandmother—her only other female relative. She needed a woman in her life to talk to, share things with, learn a woman's ways with. Tess would return in the fall in time for school, when Granny would spend a day or so with her, helping her get some school clothes together.

And . . . Tess grinned to herself. And Granny better not find the house a mess when she got back or she'd have all their hides. She didn't expect her kin to live in squalor just because they figured it was beneath them as males to do housework.

The house had been clean, too, when she returned. Well, not immaculate, but at least livable. But each time summer approached her father and brothers had turned grumpy and noncommunicative toward Tess—not that they were much better the rest of the year. Their resentment had niggled at her until one summer she had discussed it with Granny.

Granny's voice seemed to float on the night air. "Why, honey, they ain't mad 'cause you're takin' off and leavin' them with all that extra work. They're bent out of shape 'cause they think you oughta be grateful you've got three big men in your life to protect you and tell you what to think and do. So you oughta work your little tail off makin' them comfortable in 'preciation of that. Heck, Tess baby, I'm the one they take offense to. I told them just how the cow was gonna eat the cabbage and they don't take kindly to bein' bossed around by a female."

Recalling Granny's tiny stature and the great, hulking bodies of her father and growing brothers, Tess laughed into the night. No, Granny never took any guff from the men in her family, especially her own son and grandsons.

"If you're gonna lay there and laugh and play with that animal all night, I'm gonna move my bedroll where I can get some sleep."

She turned on her side and cupped her hand under her head. "I thought you were already asleep."

"Do I sound like I'm asleep?"

"No. In fact, you sound more awake than you have all day. At least now you're talking instead of grunting. I thought maybe you'd gone mute."

"Ain't had nothin' to say."

"I noticed."

"Look, I didn't plan to have company on this trip, so don't expect me to act like we're having a polite conversation at an all-day tea party. I've got things on my mind."

"Why won't you discuss them with me? Don't you think it would be easier if you share your worries?"

"Talkin' about things doesn't solve problems. A man's gotta get out and take some action—use his own brains and muscles to find a solution."

"*His,*" she emphasized. "I don't suppose it ever occurred to you that a woman might have something to add that might help you find a way out of a problem. Especially a woman you claim to love."

"Claim to!" He rose to a sitting position and glared across the fire. "You listen to me, Tess Foster! I'm not about to play games with you. If you doubt my feelings just because I want to protect you and take care of you . . ."

"And just what do you call the way you've been acting all day, if not a game? You've treated me like a naughty child you'd really like to take over your knee and spank. You've been trying to get me angry enough with you that I'll turn around and go home."

"Which is where you should've stayed," he gritted. "Hell." He lay back down and clasped his fingers behind his head as he stared up at the sky. "Maybe a spankin' would've been easier."

"Wanna try to do it now?" she drawled.

"No. You know damned well what would happen if I came over there and laid a hand on you right now."

A shiver of desire crawled over her when Stone turned his head and looked at her. Reflected flames from the firelight danced in his hooded eyes, mirroring the banked passion she'd been fighting ever since this morning.

"If there's been any game-playin' on my part, darlin'," he murmured, "it's been a game of self-preservation. You know darned well I want to make love to you—strip you down until there's not an inch of you I can't touch or kiss. Fill myself with you and fill you with me. But that's one step I'm not prepared to take."

"Why not?" she whispered.

"Damn it, you know why."

"Because I still haven't decided whether to stay here or return to my own time," she responded, the desire his words stirred up giving her voice a throaty tone.

"Yes," he gritted. "It'll be hard enough for me to let you go loving you as I do now—having the memories I do of you now. If those memories included making love to you . . . you're not some woman I can just take my ease with and leave a five-dollar gold piece on the dresser for, Tess."

"Can't we at least talk about it?"

"No!" His voice softened as he pointed at the sky. "Look. That star there."

She glanced up, where another shooting star cascaded across the sky. This one streaked across the black, moonless night in a curve, instead of plummeting to the earth and winking out. She smiled and closed her eyes to make a wish. When she opened her eyes again the star was gone.

The next morning, Tess stood and stared around in the dim, pre-dawn light. So he'd left her; figured she would give up and go back to the ranch. She should have anticipated that. Good grief. Had he taken her horse?

Her eyes found a darker gray shape in the morning mist rising from the ground, and she sighed with relief when the gelding raised its head and nickered to her. Lonesome stood up and stretched, then sat down and cocked a leg to scratch his neck.

"Uh-oh," she said to the dog. "You missed your bath this week, didn't you, and now you've picked up fleas. Well, you'll just have to put up with them today. I'll give you a bath this evening, after we camp again. Right now you've got a job to do in a little while."

She leisurely stretched the kinks from her muscles, then squatted to dig in her backpack. She stuck a granola bar in her shirt pocket and made a necessary trip into the bushes. Ten minutes later she urged the gray gelding after Lonesome's wagging tail as he snuffled at the ground and followed the tracks left by Stone's horse.

"Traitor," Stone grumbled from his vantage point at the top of a ridge. Darn that dog.

He gave a sigh of resignation and urged his horse out from the stand of cottonwoods. Waiting until Tess glanced up and shaded her eyes against the rising sun so she could see him, he nudged his heels on the horse's flanks and turned it around.

Tess loosened her reins and the gray gelding leapt into a frisky canter. She shook her head, auburn tresses swirling behind her as she passed Lonesome and took the lead. As soon as she caught up to Stone, she pulled the gelding down into a sedate walk and reached into her shirt pocket.

"Want half?" she asked as she tore the wrapping off the granola bar and broke it in two.

"What is it?"

"A breakfast bar. The fire was cold, so I don't guess you fixed yourself anything to eat this morning."

"I've got some jerky in my saddlebags."

"Okay." Tess bit the bar. "Ummmm," she murmured. "This one's got raisins and chocolate drops."

He swallowed against the moisture in his mouth and stared ahead resolutely. Feeling something nudge his arm, he glanced down to see Tess's palm extended, the other half of her breakfast bar in her hand.

He gave in and reached for the raisin-studded bar, fully expecting her to make a snide comment. Instead, she brushed her hand against her denim-clad leg and leaned back in the saddle to tilt her face up to the sun.

"It's going to be a beautiful day," she said. "I hope it's a little cooler than yesterday, though. I've got a sunburn on my nose."

"Don't you have a hat?"

"Oh. Yeah, I do." Tess turned in the saddle and zipped open one of the outside pockets on the backpack tied behind her saddle. She pulled out a blue cap and plopped it on her head. Turning to him, she peered out from beneath the bill of the cap.

"Thanks. I forgot I had this with me."

"Who're the Cowboys?" he asked, reading the inscription on the hat.

"Who're the Cowboys? Why, they're a football team," she said in a saucy voice. "I had one of my old friends from law school send me this cap all the way from Texas. Just because I live in New York doesn't mean I don't know a good football team when I see one. 'Course you can't tell New Yorkers that. I almost got thrown out of the bar during the Super Bowl game this year against Buffalo."

"What the heck's football?"

For the next hour Tess explained the finer points of the only sports game she had ever had an interest in to Stone. Baseball, she informed him, was about as exciting as watching grass grow. But now football . . .

In the middle of explaining a Hail Mary pass, she suddenly swallowed her words and gasped in astonishment when they rode onto the top of a ridge. Down below them, spread out in a multitude of roan, palomino, black and white and various shades of brown, grazed a herd of horses. Several colts frolicked among the herd, but for the most part the horses grazed on a carpet of knee-high grass.

Stone and Tess both immediately reined their horses around and disappeared beneath the ridge top.

"Do you think they saw us?" she whispered as she slid to the ground.

"The wind was in our favor," he said as he joined her. "You did pretty good. You got out of there in a hurry before they spotted us."

"Thank you, kind sir."

Chapter Twenty-five

After tethering their horses Stone and Tess crept back up to the ridge. Lonesome, seeming to understand the necessity for caution, crawled up beside Tess and watched the herd below with pricked ears. While she scratched behind the dog's ear, she studied the horses spread out on the valley floor.

"Look how beautiful they are," she whispered. "Doesn't it seem a shame to capture them?"

"A wild horse doesn't have nearly as romantic a life as you'd think," Stone answered in a quiet voice. "The ones we manage to send to the army post will be well cared for."

"*We?* Can I take that to mean you're actually going to let me help?"

"Since you're sticking around like a burr on my horse's tail, I might as well make use of you. But this is one time you'd better do just like I tell you. That stallion's not gonna give up his mares easy."

"Oh, look how beautiful he is!" She breathed a sigh as the snow-white stallion reared and pawed the air. He dropped back to earth, then began a sweeping circle around his herd.

"He's getting ready to move them out," Stone said.

"Shouldn't we do something about catching them?" Tess asked.

When she started to scoot back down the hill, Stone stopped her with a stern look.

"Stay quiet, darn it! What do you think we could do right now? Ride down there shouting and screaming and scatter them all over creation? How many horses do you think we'd get that way?"

"But . . . but they're leaving!" She glanced up to see Stone shaking his head, a look of barely concealed intolerance on his face. "Well then, what *are* we going to do?"

"You, Miss Greenhorn, are going to do—like I said—exactly what I tell you to. Wild horse herds travel in a circle, even most of the time when they're being chased. But I don't think this herd will move far from that valley. This late in the summer a lot of range is dried up. There's good grass here and that stream down there has plenty of water."

"I see," she mused. "They'll probably come back here tomorrow to graze."

"Early tomorrow. Probably even before dawn. Then they'll leave again about this time, so they can keep on the move. We'll have to be ready for them. We won't get two chances at this herd, because I know that stallion. He's been on this range for years, and he's damned smart. That's how he's managed to hold onto a herd that large."

"Look! Oh, Stone, look!"

She pointed at the herd, which was now strung out along the valley floor as it followed a lead, paint mare. The white stallion, not satisfied yet with the speed of his herd, swept back and forth in the rear, nipping and snorting at the slower mares with colts.

"Yeah, they're pretty," he said.

"No. I mean, sure they are. But look at that black horse on the edge of the herd."

"That mare's not from wild stock," he said. "The stallion must have stolen her from someone's ranch."

"She looks like Sateen." She sighed.

"Who the heck's Sateen?"

"My mare back at the stable. She probably wonders what's happened to me, although I hadn't been able to take her out as much as I wanted to this past summer."

"Too busy with your social life, huh?" he said, frowning.

"That and my career," she admitted. "That case I was handling had me working sixty or more hours a week, and even most weekends, since I had to keep up with the other cases I couldn't foist off on one of the younger attorneys."

"I've been meaning to talk to you about that. Women shouldn't be attorneys. They've got no business tryin' to get killers or robbers off—standing up in court defendin' slime."

The white stallion disappeared over a far ridge as she turned to him. "For your information, *Mr. Chisum,* if it weren't for attorneys, there'd be a heck of a lot more injustice than there already is in this world! How many people do you know who are smart enough to defend themselves in court? To read the laws and make sure their rights aren't being violated? And I'm not a criminal attorney—I'm a corporate lawyer!"

"Maybe they ought to simplify the laws, then," he growled. "And I don't see what the difference is—a damned lawyer is a damned lawyer! Why didn't you tell me before that day in the bedroom what you did for a living?"

"You never asked!" Try as she might, she couldn't come up with anything stronger than that inane comment. Her anger blazed higher. Good grief, was her mind already stagnating? She'd always been good at thinking on her feet—giving as good as she got when another attorney played devil's advocate with her while they discussed a case.

"Just what exactly have you got against lawyers?" she spat, her eyes narrowed.

"I saw men I knew were guilty walk out of a courtroom more than once while I was sheriff down in Texas—men I'd arrested myself and knew had done the crime. All I could do was wait until they pulled something else and haul their asses back to jail again. The next time I got them, it was usually for a hell of a lot worse crime than they'd committed the first time. Once . . ."

Stone bit off his words and turned away. "Come on. We've got work to do before those horses come back."

She grabbed his arm when he started to stand. "Stone, wait. Finish what you were going to say." She studied his hooded eyes, catching a glimmer of pain in the brown depths. "Please," she added in a softer voice.

He took a deep breath and stared past her, his gaze unfocused. "She was just a whore. That's what they said, just a whore. Her name was Polly, and she worked one of the saloons. One of her . . . her . . ."

"Tricks," she supplied.

"Tricks?"

"Uh . . . that's what they're called back where I come from. The men who pay for a prostitute's service. Tricks or johns."

"One of her *customers,*" he continued, "decided an hour wasn't enough for him. He snuck out down the back stairway with Polly and took her out to the bunkhouse on the ranch where he worked. The guy who owned the saloon was pissed off as hell when he found her gone, since he didn't figure he'd ever get paid for that time. So he came into my office hollering that one of his girls had been kidnapped.

"By the time I got out there, almost every one of those six cowboys had had a turn. Polly was half out of her mind with pain, and bleeding all over the place."

"Oh, my God." She covered her mouth, fighting the rising gorge in her stomach.

"After I got Polly to the doc I took a couple of deputies back out there and hauled them all in. 'Course, at their trial they all claimed she'd been willing. Their fancy-pants lawyer convinced the jury that a whore couldn't be raped, and they all walked."

"And P . . . Polly?"

"Hell, her mind was gone. She sat up on the witness stand like a zombie, and they finally sent her to some institution. Later on the ringleader of the bunch made a try for a rancher's daughter he ran across out riding the range one day. But the rancher was just over the hill and he heard her scream. He killed the son of a bitch—gut-shot him and watched him die before he looped his rope around the man's feet and dragged him into town to my office."

Stone focused on her face at last. "You know what the hell happened then?"

"The rancher probably had to stand trial," she forced herself to say.

"Damned right. And he spent a year in prison for manslaughter. Another damned lawyer convinced that jury the rancher didn't have to kill the rapist—he could have just wounded him and still saved his daughter!"

"But Stone, for every case like that, there are thousands of cases where criminals get what's coming to them. Didn't a lot of the men you arrested end up paying for their crimes?"

"Most of them," he admitted grudgingly. "And even the rest of those cowboys got what was coming to them."

"What happened?"

"Turned out they were running a rustling ring on the side. They got caught. One of them let enough slip in a drunken binge for us to figure it out. We were waiting for them when they made their next raid and caught them with the running iron, rebranding the cattle."

He chuckled wryly. "They swung for that—every one of them. Funny, isn't it? Who'd ever think stealing cattle was a worse crime than rape?"

"Now, you listen here, Stone." She found herself warring with her emotions. Her legal mind saw the problem with his argument, though her total sympathy was with the two women attacked and traumatized. But loyalty to her profession meant she had to at least try to make him see the other side.

"You didn't have any witnesses—any proof—at that first trial for those cowboys. At the other one I imagine you had a whole posse of witnesses. That doesn't make the law wrong. It just means we have to be careful we follow the rules of the law. In the end, that protects all of us."

"Oh, I see. You're saying it's my fault. I should've known enough to take a couple of witnesses with me when I went out after Polly. We could've sat outside the window and listened to her scream for a while, then been able to back her up in court!"

"No! Darn it . . . I mean . . ."

"I know what you mean," he finally admitted. "It just chaps my ass to no end when a criminal walks free. Come on, honey. Let's see if that legal mind of yours can help me figure out how to trick those mares into heading into a trap."

"Oh, dear," Angela sighed. "I don't think we're ever going to get his language cleaned up."

"Probably not," Michael agreed. "But Stone's not our assignment, remember?"

"You're right, of course. I just don't understand why men don't think they're men unless they curse once in a while."

"He probably doesn't even realize he's doing it. It's a habit. Tess drops one of those four-letter words herself now and then."

"Usually when she's angry," Angela answered. "But that doesn't make it acceptable, either."

"Well, we'll see what we can do about that, too, Angie. Right now I'm more interested in how long it's going to take Tess to realize that's really her horse we brought here for her, if they manage to get Sateen into that horse trap. And I want to see what sort of a trap Stone has in mind."

"I haven't figured out myself how they're going to manage to corral that many horses."

"I talked with an old cow poke who came under my guidance once," he said. "There're different ways to build traps for horses, and this will be the first time Stone and Tess have had to work together on something. What you want to bet they've both got their own idea about how to do this?"

"I don't think I'll take that bet." She laughed.

A few minutes later Tess propped her hands on her hips and shot an exasperated look at Stone.

"What do you mean, we have to build it here? The canyon's a lot narrower up there. We'd only have to build a fence half as big if we did it up there."

"We're not going to fence it. We're gonna start a rock slide down each side of the canyon, and that will start the wall. Then you can pile more rocks up to make the walls higher while I build a gate and hide it with brush."

"Do you have any idea how high those walls will have to be so the horses can't jump them?"

"Yep," Stone said.

"I still think it makes more sense to do it farther up, where the canyon's narrower."

"For pete's sake, Tess, we have to have a big enough opening for the horses to run through. They'll turn right back on us if the opening's too narrow."

"Oh."

"Yeah, *oh*. You wanted to help—so let's get busy."

* * *

Several hours later Tess looked down at her chipped and broken nails with a grimace. Even the gloves she carried in her backpack hadn't protected her hands completely. In fact, she thought as she pulled the stained and torn gloves back on, she even had a blister or two. And it was going to take more than lotion to soften the calluses that were forming.

She bent and picked up another small rock, trying to ignore the pain in her back. One more row, Stone had insisted. Well, one more row he would get, if her arms held out. Seemed like he had the easier job, fashioning the gate. He almost had it finished. She paused for a moment, watching him test the gate by swinging it to and fro.

His shirt hung over the top rail, and he picked it up to wipe his forehead. Sweat glistened on his back, and the smooth muscles rippled under his tan. Wet curls clung to the back of his neck, a deep mahogany satin in contrast to the lighter, sun-streaked brown, lit by reddish highlights in the sun. She'd never seen a man's hair take on so many different hues.

He arched and massaged the small of his back and her mouth went dry. Lord, he was beautiful. His sleek power reminded her of the snow-white stallion's muscle-packed body, every part flowing into the other in a fluid picture of grace. She sighed with desire.

"Ouch!"

She grabbed her foot, then tumbled onto her rear. Staring at the offending rock, which had nicked her big toe when her fingers loosened and dropped it, she fought the urge to kick it with her heel.

"You all right?"

Stone started toward her, but she waved him off.

"I'm okay. It didn't really hurt—just surprised me and made me think it was going to hurt bad."

"If you're so tired you're dropping things, maybe we better take a break."

"Tired? You're darned right I'm tired! Why shouldn't I be tired? I've been hauling these stupid rocks around for hours and hours. And now the dumb rocks aren't even cooperating!"

"What do you think they should do? Grow legs and let you direct them where you want them to go?"

"Shut up. Just shut up and let me get back to work."

"I'm not stopping you," he told her in a mild voice.

Grunting, she lurched to her feet. Pressing her lips shut, she grabbed the rock and dropped it sharply in place. The rock crumbled, and pieces of it fell on both sides of her fence.

Chapter Twenty-six

Tess cautiously stretched her aching muscles as she watched Stone silently slip away from the spot where he had hidden her and the gray gelding. He disappeared almost instantly, since it was still pitch dark.

He wouldn't even let her make coffee this morning, insisting the fire smoke would settle in the valley and spook the horses away. And she wasn't worth a darn in the morning until after at least two cups of caffeine. She hoped her groggy mind could remember everything he had told her.

Wait for him to ride out and block the path the horses took yesterday morning when they left the valley, he'd whispered. Then ride out herself—fast—and try to head the herd into the trap. Don't worry about any single horses that managed to break out of the herd—let them go and concentrate on the main group. Whatever she did, stay the hell away from that white stallion.

She could hear the horses out there—now and then a soft whicker, even the grass pulling out of the soil as the horses grazed—though she couldn't even see a shadow in the pitch blackness. Her gray gelding was silent, making no attempt to communicate with the wild horses. Stone must have trained him well.

She contented herself with scratching Lonesome's ears while she waited. Stone had ordered her not to climb into the saddle until after she saw him ride out into the valley—the creak of leather as she mounted might carry to the herds' ears.

She blinked her eyes when she saw a movement. She'd been concentrating so hard, she hadn't even realized the darkness was fading. She glanced at the ridge top and was able to make out the jagged outline. Looking out across the valley floor, she found she could see the shape of a horse here and there.

Her muscles tensed in anticipation, and Lonesome whined slightly.

"Hush," she whispered. "Oh, hush, Lonesome. If we scare that herd away, Stone will probably spank us both."

Lonesome dropped down and propped his head on his front paws, silently watching the horses.

"Good boy," she breathed.

It seemed like forever as she waited. Where in the world was Stone? She saw the white stallion come alert, then rear, a bugling challenge splitting the valley air.

She swung into the saddle and the gelding leapt into an almost immediate gallop. Remembering Stone's instructions, she grabbed the rope coiled on her saddlehorn and swept it back and forth over her head, yelling at the top of her lungs as she sped toward the horses.

The stallion whirled to face the new threat, screaming defiance as he reared and pawed the air again. She saw Stone bent low over his own horse, galloping at the herd from the opposite side. Confused, the mares swirled in panic, neighing wildly to their colts as they waited for the stallion to head them in the direction he wanted.

A rifle shot split the air, then two more. Chancing another glance at Stone from the back of her smoothly running gelding, she watched him rein his horse to a skidding halt and aim at the stallion. A puff of dirt by the stallion's feet sent the white horse plunging away from his herd.

A half dozen mares split off from the herd and followed the stallion, but Stone's well-trained horse leapt back into action and cut off escape for the remainder. The bunched-up mares milled in disorder; then, catching sight of even their tentative escape route blocked by Lonesome's racing figure, they turned and galloped for the gate hidden at the canyon entrance.

The mares streamed between the two rock walls and headed deeper into the canyon. She knew they couldn't go far—the canyon ended in a steep cliff face, and both sides were way too rocky for the horses to climb. She reached the gate a few seconds after Stone had dismounted and watched him fling the last bush aside and swing the logs closed.

The white stallion reappeared, racing toward the gate, his body almost flat out against the ground. His lips were drawn back, baring his yellow teeth.

She kicked her gelding in the sides and the gray horse responded, leaping into a gallop.

"Damn it, Tess! Don't!"

She swung the rope over her head as she raced toward the stallion. "Get out of here! Get!"

"Tess!"

"Get! I said get out of here!" Suddenly she realized the stallion wasn't going to turn. Her eyes widened as the distance between the two wildly galloping horses narrowed. Frantically, she threw the rope away and sawed on her reins.

The stallion lowered its head and charged the gray gelding. Her horse neighed in terror and swerved, trying to avoid the attack. The stallion's shoulder hit her horse's hind haunch and it stumbled. She flew through the air in an arc, closing her eyes as she waited for the sickening crunch when she hit the ground.

Almost at once her eyes flew open again. How far away was that darned ground? The creek rushed up at her and she landed with a splash, the cold water shocking her almost senseless.

Sputtering and spitting out water, she scrambled to her feet and stared downward in surprise. The creek didn't look that deep, but she hadn't even felt the rocks lining the bed when she hit.

Swiping at the water streaming down her face, she turned when she heard Stone's shouts and Lonesome's frantic barks. She saw the white stallion racing away, with Lonesome nipping at its heels. Stone slid his horse to a halt and swung from the saddle, advancing on her with a deadly glint in his walnut-hued eyes.

"What the hell did you think you were doing?"

he snarled. "Didn't I order you to keep the hell away from that stallion?"

She backed up a step, almost tripping on a rock in the stream. "I . . . I . . . thought . . . he . . . he was c . . . coming after the mares."

"He was coming after *us!*" he shouted. "He could've had those mares back with no trouble if he killed us first!"

"Oh."

She took another step backwards. He advanced a step.

"Didn't I make it clear that you were supposed to do exactly what I said? And didn't I tell you under no circumstances to get near that stallion?"

"Yes."

He waved his arms and bent toward her. "Then why the hell did you gallop out there on a collision course with that white devil?"

She shrugged. "To try to keep him from getting our mares?"

Stone closed his eyes and stood breathing deeply for several long seconds. "To try to keep him from getting our mares," he finally muttered through clenched teeth. He slit his eyes. "I ought to tan your fanny until you can't walk!"

"Yeah. I told Lonesome you might do that to us both, if we screwed things up."

When Stone continued to glare at her, his jaws working as though he wanted to still shout at her but couldn't think of anything terrible enough to say, she shivered and crossed her arms over her chest.

"You're wet," he finally said.

"Yes. I landed in the creek, you know."

He glanced down almost in surprise to find himself standing in the creek with her. The water cascaded over his boots, well below the tops.

"This water's not deep enough to break a fall that hard." Suddenly he grabbed her by the shoulders. "Are you hurt? Damn it, Tess, don't try to put on a front. Tell me where you're hurt."

Not waiting for an answer, he swept her into his arms and splashed out of the creek bed. "We have to get you dry."

"Stone, really, I'm not hurt. I hardly felt it when I landed."

When he only grunted in disbelief she snuggled her head against his shoulder while he bypassed the two horses and continued carrying her toward the gate across the canyon. At least he wasn't yelling at her any longer.

Lonesome padded up to Stone's side and paced with them, his tongue hanging out in exhaustion, but a look of as much satisfaction as a dog could manage on his face.

"Oh, dear, Michael. I don't know if it was such a good idea, getting her wet like that."

"Now just a dad-blamed minute, Angie," he replied. "I thought it was a right fine idea. I had to fly her through the air just a little farther than she normally would've gone, but that water made the perfect landing spot. What would Stone have thought if she landed on that hard ground and didn't get hurt? We're not supposed to let them guess that we're around, you know."

"I didn't mean that. I meant . . . well, she's awfully wet."

"That's what usually happens when people get in water—they get wet."

"But look. Her clothing's clinging to her. She looks awfully . . . desirable. And they've been trying to keep their hands off each other while they're alone out here."

"Yeah, I see what you're talking about. I think Stone sees it, too."

Stone backed away from where he had sat Tess down on one of the larger boulders beside the fence. She lifted her hands to push back her sopping hair, and the movement thrust her breasts against her wet shirt. The soaking material clearly outlined the pebbled tips.

Darn it, he really wished she'd wear some sort of restraint on those beautiful breasts. He could even make out the dark pink centers through that pale blue shirt.

"I'll build a fire." He ordered his legs to move, but they remained as immobile as the rocks penning in the horses.

"It's already getting hot." She ran her fingers through her wet hair, working out the tangles. "My clothes will dry pretty fast."

"Not fast enough!"

Tess glanced up, pushing aside a soggy curl that fell over her eyes. "May . . . maybe . . . a fire would help," she said.

He turned his back on her abruptly. "Lonesome," he forced himself to say almost normally, "think you could go fetch those horses?"

He waved an arm in the direction of the spot where the two horses grazed, and Lonesome jumped to his feet and raced away. He watched the dog for several seconds, trying to concentrate on his amazement that Lonesome seemed to understand his order. The dog circled behind the horses, then began herding them back toward Stone. He could feel Tess's eyes on him.

"Quit staring at me!"

"Hm?" she murmured. "Are you growing eyes in the back of your head?"

He grunted and reached for the reins of his horse, which Lonesome had herded near. After a brief pat on its muzzle he moved around and untied his bedroll. He tossed it behind him in Tess's direction, resolutely refusing to turn and see if it fell close enough for her to reach.

"You can sit on that while I get the fire going."

"Okay."

He stiffened when her voice came from right beside him.

"But first I'm going to get some clothes from my backpack," she said as she walked past him toward the gray gelding. "Then I can hang these by the fire to dry."

"There's nowhere for you to change down here!" he snarled. "If that's what you want to do, the least you can do is ride back up to where we camped last night!"

"Oh, for pity's sake." Tess pulled her backpack from behind the saddle and set it on the ground. "You can turn your back, you know. I'm sure the horses won't get all hot and bothered if they watch me change clothes."

He groaned and laid his head against his horse's broad rump. The horse turned its head and looked at him for a second, then dropped its muzzle to resume grazing as Stone fumbled with the ties holding his saddlebags.

"Damned thing's in a knot," he grumbled.

"Can I help?"

"No! You stay over there!"

Finally wrenching the saddlebags free, he slung them down beside his bedroll and began gathering up pieces of dry wood. A deadfall that would furnish at least a cord of wood lay just on the other side of Tess—but that was the problem. He grimly set his lips and broke one of the larger pieces of wood over his knee.

Without thinking, he turned to carry the wood back closer to the saddlebags. He froze, and the wood tumbled from his suddenly nerveless arms.

The gray gelding stood sideways, and it had six legs. The two shapely female legs in the middle lifted one after another, while a hand tugged at first one, then the other wet denim cuff and pulled the jeans free. The jeans were tossed over the horse's saddle, on top of the pale blue shirt. Then a tiny scrap of rose-colored material shimmied down her legs, pooling around the ankles for a second until she stepped out of it. A pink-tipped toe caught the scrap and flicked it upward. Her hand draped it on the saddlehorn.

"Move, horse," he growled. But when the horse seemed to obey and stepped forward, those very beautiful legs moved with it.

Tess grabbed the towel from on top of her dry clothes on the gelding's rump and closed her eyes as she scrubbed it over her hair, then patted it over her body. The towel joined the wet denims, and she picked up her white, bikini underpants, laying on top of her dry jeans and shirt. Bending, she slipped them over her feet, tugging and swiveling her hips when the panties dragged on her still-damp skin.

The tight jeans gave her even more of a problem than the bikinis, but Tess finally managed to pull them over her hips. Sucking in her stomach and promising herself that she wouldn't eat any of Flower's desserts after the young girl returned, she yanked the zipper up and reached for her shirt.

As the gelding moved toward a tuft of grass just beyond its reach, she looked up to see where Stone was. She gave a squeak of dismay when the gelding switched its tail and swiped the shirt from her ineffective grasp.

Time nearly stopped as Tess stood wrapped in the cocoon of Stone's desire-laden gaze. Her knees threatened to give way and her breasts grew heavy with desire. Her eyes—the only thing that seemed capable of movement—slowly left his face and crawled down his chest. She tried desperately to stay focused on that first button below the open V of his shirt but gave up and fixed her eyes on the lower one. Sliding downward, her gaze bypassed the last button above his belt buckle—and the buckle.

How in the world did he fit all that masculinity behind those straining snaps? Surely it must be hurting him. She took a step forward and noticed those smooth thigh muscles flex as he began walking toward her.

"Michael?" Angela turned around and tugged on his sleeve to get his attention. "Michael, I think it's time for us to leave for a while."

He glanced over his shoulder. "Is Tess dressed yet? You said you'd let me know when she was so I could turn back around."

"Uh . . . well, she's partly dressed. But I don't think she's going to stay that way."

He cocked his eyebrow. "You mean . . . ?" He glanced down and saw Stone unrolling the bedroll and Tess almost floating across the ground as she walked toward him.

"Well, it's about time." He chuckled.

"Let's give them some privacy," Angela insisted.

"Right. Where would you like to go?"

"How about I surprise you? Close your eyes and let me lead this time."

She lifted an inquiring eyebrow, and he nodded, shutting his eyes. He felt her grasp his hand and then, her wing tip brushed his nose.

"AAH . . . AAH . . . Angie, I'm gonna . . . AACH . . ."

Angie whipped around and clapped a hand over his nose and mouth. "Don't you dare, Michael!" She kept a firm grip on him until he nodded his head and reached for her hand. Watching him closely, she released her hold.

"Are you sure you're not going to sneeze?" she asked.

"Aachoo." He ducked his head to avoid Angela's hand and danced away from her.

"Just teasing." He chortled gleefully. "Just teasing."

"Oh, you!"

Chapter Twenty-seven

Tess extended her arms and Stone rose to his feet, taking her hands in his own. She tilted her head back to look at him. His eyes smoldered a deep mahogany as he returned her gaze, and her lips parted, her breath escaping in a quick tempo. Sensation crept up her arms when he slowly caressed the back of her hands with his thumbs, and the tips of her bare breasts pebbled in response.

"I want you," he murmured in a voice laced with desire. "I've wanted you to be totally mine since the first moment I saw you."

"Yes," she replied in a barely audible whisper. She tried to pull her hands free to wrap them around his neck, but he held them tightly.

"If we make this commitment," he growled, "it's a forever thing. For today, tomorrow, and the rest of our lives."

She drew her bottom lip between her teeth and

worried it. She had no doubt he meant what he said, despite the strong waves of need she could sense he kept dammed behind his rock-hard countenance. His face remained stoic as she searched it, his eyes centered on her, his lips set grimly. Everything about him told her this was entirely her decision yet warned her what the result would be should she take that next important step.

With him so near, his lips so close, his presence sending the heat of desire through her body, her thoughts jumbled until all she could feel was the deep emptiness not having him would leave her. She yearned for him with an intense, physical need but knew satisfying their lust would never be enough—for her or for him, either.

They had so much more together—or could have, if she wanted it. Stone offered her not only his body but also his love. And not just love for today—a forever love.

"I love you," she said. "I want you, too, but it's more than that. I want to be part of your life—always have you near. I want to be totally yours, Stone. Forever."

He dropped her hands and gathered her fiercely into his embrace. With a deep growl he claimed her lips. She was crushed against his chest, held against him so tightly, she could hardly breathe. She gloried in the closeness, the hardness of his body, and parted her mouth willingly to the thrusts of his tongue. She clung to his neck, aching to be even closer, though their bodies touched completely.

Still plundering her mouth, he cupped her hips and pulled her feet from the ground. Her whimper grew into a moan when he thrust against her, and she wrapped her legs around his waist, straining and rubbing herself against him, creating stronger cascades of pleasure through her.

He wrenched his lips free with a gasp and stared down at her. His hands clenched in rhythm with her movements, and she threw her head back, unable to stop, lost in her need. She felt his lips sip at her breast, his tongue barely graze the nipple. Then, with a moan he sucked her breast into his warm, wet mouth, and nothing mattered except this incredible crescendo of pleasure. She cried his name, over and over.

Too sated to maintain her grip on his waist, she felt herself sliding down his body as her senses slowly returned. She opened her eyes as her feet touched the ground and reached up to caress his face.

"I love you," she murmured. "I want to make you feel as wonderful as I just did."

"That's only the start of it, darlin'. There's going to be lots, lots more."

She gently dragged her fingernail down his cheek and neck until it caught in his bandanna. Raising her other arm, she untied the knot and tossed it aside.

"Promises, promises," she murmured as she started unbuttoning his shirt.

"That's not a promise—it's a guarantee."

In one quick movement he unbuttoned and unzipped her jeans, shoving them partway down her legs, then bending down to kiss her while his fingers worked on his own jeans. Her fingers fumbled with his shirt buttons, and he pushed her hands away. He jerked the fabric and the final button tore free. With a shrug, he shook off the shirt and let it fall behind him.

She broke the kiss herself this time, pushing against his chest and stepping back just far enough to see him. She sucked in a gasp of heated desire as her eyes wandered over his broad shoulders and muscular chest. When her gaze touched the jutting evidence of his need he groaned loudly and sat down on the bedroll.

Two brisk jerks and his boots were off, followed instantly by his jeans. He held his hand up to her, trapping her gaze in the hungry depths of his own. She took his hand and knelt beside him.

"You're magnificent," she breathed. "It should be a sin for you to be so gorgeous."

"I'm glad I please you, sweetheart, but I'd be willing to bet you please me even more. Let me show you how much you please me."

He pulled her to him and kissed her again. Slowly he lowered her to the bedroll and covered her body with his. He traced a path with his tongue down her neck, then lower to her breasts. He kneaded one while he suckled the other, and she whimpered and tossed her head as the heat of need surged inside her. She buried her hands in his hair but lost her hold when he moved lower.

He rose briefly and tugged her jeans free from her legs.

"I wanted to take this slowly," he growled, "but I've been wanting you for so long."

"Not any longer than I've wanted you, my darling," she murmured. "Please. Make me yours."

When he bent again he curled his tongue into her navel, swirling it, then licking back and forth down the lower part of her stomach. Ever so gently he pushed her legs wide, then opened her with his thumbs. A low, keening moan escaped her when his tongue began swirling again against the hard button it found.

She arched and her stomach tightened as the glorious spiral toward culmination began again. Somehow she managed to cry out. "Stone, please, be with me!"

He covered her and thrust against her. Her legs went around his waist. Suddenly he stiffened and stared down at her in surprise, but she gripped him tighter, bucking upward. With a deep groan he covered her lips with his and drove into her, capturing her gasp of pain in his mouth.

"Mine," he murmured in awe a second later, his breath mingling with her own as he held himself still. "Only mine."

"Yes, yours. Only yours, Stone."

The pain receded almost at once, leaving her with only the pleasure of him filling her emptiness so precisely. She tightened her legs and nudged upward, stroking herself against him. His hiss of indrawn breath sent a deluge of sensation over her as he slowly withdrew, then entered her again.

She dug her nails into his back, her hold sure enough to allow her to urge him into an ever-increasing rhythm. She wanted it to last, but she wanted it to peak.

"Oh, my God!" he groaned, giving one final, powerful thrust, and she reached her own fulfillment. She could only gasp his name in echo to his guttural mutters of hers while wave after wave of unbelievable pleasure carried her ever higher until it shattered her very consciousness.

Always, though, she was aware that Stone rode with her, his gratification intensifying her own.

Chapter Twenty-eight

Stone nuzzled Tess's ear and whispered, "Why didn't you tell me?"

"What?" She stretched and slid her leg up and down his thigh. "That I'd never made love to a man before? That I was saving myself for that one special man, like Granny warned me to do? She was right, you know. Every minute of the wait was worth it."

"God, I hope so," he groaned. "I hope it was half as wonderful for you as it was for me. I never realized what a difference being in love with the woman I was with would make."

She leaned back and frowned at him. "And just how many . . . ?"

"Shhhh." He gently laid a finger on her lips. "As far as I'm concerned, this is the first time I've ever made love, too. This time it was really making love."

"I love you," she whispered. "With everything in me and then some. I love you so much, I ache with it, and it scares me to death. Nothing could ever mean as much to me as my loving you does, unless it's knowing you feel the same way about me."

"I love you," he replied. "You've captured a part of me I didn't even know existed until I saw you. You're the most beautiful woman I've ever seen."

"Ummmm." She brushed her breast tips against his chest. "Then it's just my body you love, not my mind, huh?"

He propped his head on his hand and ran his eyes over her nude body. "Well, I might have to think about that for a minute." He feathered a finger over her eyelashes. "I love those green eyes that remind me of new leaves on the trees after a spring rain. But they wouldn't be half as beautiful if they weren't yours."

He skimmed his finger down her nose and caressed her lips. "I love those wine-tasting lips, but I love them more because of the way they kiss me."

His fingertip ran down her neck and traced her collarbone. "Your skin's so soft—I can't believe it doesn't melt on my tongue, like cotton candy at the fair."

"S . . . Stone," she said with a muffled groan.

"I'm not done thinking yet," he murmured. "I love this." He gently lapped her breast. "And this one, too." He suckled her other nipple, then released it.

Running his hand over her flat stomach, he continued, "But none of those would mean a thing if they weren't all part of you. Of Tess, the woman I love. And every time I hear you say you love me, too, I can't believe how lucky I am."

"I love you, Stone, my darling."

Another hour passed before they fell into an exhausted slumber, their minds too tired to continue the delightful game of I-love-you-more-no-I-love-you-more.

Lying on his stomach, Stone woke first, frowning at the sun climbing up the sky and the pink tinge on Tess's skin. He gently shook her shoulder.

"Tess, darlin', you'd better get on some clothes. You're getting sunburned."

"Hum?" She lazily opened her eyes, then glanced down his back and giggled. "You are, too."

"I don't burn," he denied.

She ran a fingernail over his hip and he flinched.

"You probably don't usually lay out in the sun with that part of you bare, either," she said. "You've usually got it covered up with your pants. But it's awful pink right now."

He craned his neck to glance at his rear, then flopped over onto his back. "Maybe I'd better bake this side for a while to even things out, then."

"I don't know," she mused. "You don't really want to get a sunburn down there, do you? I know I'd rather you didn't."

He roared with laughter and got to his feet. Reaching down, he pulled her up into his arms. "What have I unleashed?" he asked. "An insatiable wench who's not going to be able to keep her hands off me?"

"You wish," she said, standing on tiptoe to flick her tongue over his bottom lip. "Remember, I've got a lot of years to make up for."

"Nope," he said, shaking his head. "You can't ever make up for opportunities lost. You just have to make the new ones count that much more."

"And when will another one of those new opportunities come around?"

"Maybe after we get a bath," he said. "And that cold water will stop this sunburn from getting any worse."

"Okay." Tess wriggled out of his arms. "I've got some lotion for sunburn, too." She walked to her backpack and bent over to dig in it.

Stone stood with his hands on his hips, his eyes glued to her rear end, which was sticking up in the breeze. Tess glanced back over her shoulder, and a flush crawled up her face. She grabbed a towel out of her pack.

"Uh . . ." She wrapped the towel around her. "I'll get the lotion after we bathe."

"I'll help you put on the lotion if you'll put it on the places I can't reach," he said, leering.

"You've got a deal." Tess turned and started for the creek.

The next morning, long after sunrise, Tess stood at the log gate, her arms resting beneath her chin as she watched the mares and colts. They stayed well down the canyon, shying away even farther when they caught sight of her.

Except for that black mare. She pricked her ears and took a half dozen steps toward Tess, a faint, inquiring nicker sounding on the morning air.

"It can't be," she muttered. "There's no way."

Unable to resist the temptation, she held out her hand and snapped her fingers. "Here, Sateen," she called. "Come on, girl."

The mare cantered up to the fence and nudged Tess's hand. She instinctively rubbed the mare's muzzle, then scratched that spot under the chin that her horse always enjoyed her paying attention to. The mare tossed her head briefly before she stretched her neck to allow Tess access again to the spot.

"What's going on here?" Stone asked as he led his saddled horse up to the gate. "Did you already tame one of those mares?"

She turned excitedly to him. "Stone, I think this is Sateen. It has to be! Somehow she came through that time warp, too, and now she's here with me!"

"Tess, darlin', calm down. This mare might look like yours, but she probably belonged to some rancher who had trained her already. She couldn't possibly be your mare."

"I know my horse!" She stamped her foot. "And I didn't see a brand on either one of her hips when she came up to the fence. If I could travel through time, why couldn't my horse come, too?" Without waiting for him to answer, she continued, "You just watch this!"

She slipped through the gate. The black mare stood quietly, and she wrapped her arms around its neck, rubbing her cheek against the soft muzzle.

"It is you, Sateen," she whispered. "I just know it is."

She stepped back and raised her hand. The mare reared, pawing at the air.

"Get the hell out of there, Tess!"

"Oh, shut up."

She dropped her hand, and the mare's hooves fell back to earth; then the horse lowered her head and arched her neck, pawing at the ground.

Tess lifted her hand three times in succession, and the mare's front hoof pawed the ground in time to her movements. When she stopped moving her hand the mare stopped pawing the ground.

"Now watch this." She tossed him a smirk before she looked back at the mare. "Sateen, how much is two plus two?"

Tess lifted her hand four times in succession and the mare pawed out the answer.

"See?" she said in a delighted voice. "It is her." She threw her arms around the sleek, satin neck and buried her face in the mare's mane.

"I'll be damned," Stone breathed.

"Let her out, Stone," she said after she raised her head. "She'll stay with me—we won't have to tie her."

"All right. She'll be company for you and the dog while I'm gone."

Stone opened the gate and Tess walked through, with the mare following, her nose near Tess's shoulder. After swinging the gate back and looping the rawhide thong over the post, Stone turned to her.

"I wish I didn't have to leave you here alone, but I think this is the best way. You sure you aren't afraid to stay here by yourself?"

"Of course not. Someone has to make sure that stallion doesn't come back and steal our mares while you're gone. And I've already promised you that I'd scare him off with the rifle if he's dumb enough to come back."

"That horse isn't dumb, Tess; you remember that. I didn't have any idea we'd be able to get this many horses away from that stud, or I'd have made other arrangements. The best thing for me to do now is ride into the Cherokee camp and hire some men to deliver them to Fort Sill for me. Silver Eagle will pick out men I can trust—and they'll get a cut of the money for the horses they deliver."

"And we'll be free to go visit the kids, instead of having to spend a week taking these horses halfway across the state."

"Oh, yes," he said, "we'll visit the Cherokee camp."

"Well, you'd better get going," she said with a final pat on Sateen's nose.

Stone swung into the saddle. "Where's the rifle?"

"Right here." She walked over and picked up the rifle that was leaning against a gate rail. "I'll keep it with me all day; I promise."

"I'll be back by nightfall. Soon as the Indians get going with the herd in the morning, we'll ride out for the camp."

She stood on tiptoe and offered him her mouth. He leaned down and brushed her lips, then grabbed her around the waist and pulled her up for a harder kiss. Setting her back on the ground, he frowned down at her.

"You be here when I get back, you hear?"

"I hear you, darling. And you be careful. I love you."

"Love you, too."

After Stone rode out she puttered around the campsite for a while, washing their breakfast dishes and rolling up her sleeping bag and Stone's bedroll, which they had spread out and shared the previous night. When the camp was tidy she saddled Sateen with the tack she had used on the gray gelding and rode her around the valley for a while, keeping a sharp lookout for the white stallion.

The stallion never appeared, and Tess finally turned Sateen loose to graze, sure the mare wouldn't go too far from her side. As the sun rose higher and hotter, she changed into the bikini in her backpack and slathered sunscreen on her skin. Grabbing one of the novels from her pack, she spread out a towel and settled down to work on her tan and read, with the rifle by her side.

She couldn't concentrate and gave up halfway through the first chapter. She threw the book aside and stared at Sateen. Stone had seemed to accept the fact that the mare had shown up in this time period without too much skepticism. Yet the mare's presence bothered the heck out of Tess.

She knew how *she'd* gotten here—her fall into a time warp. But she'd been at the right place at the right time. Her horse had been two hundred miles away, stabled on the outskirts of the city, an hour's subway ride from her apartment. How the heck had Sateen traveled through time? Did she come through the same warp? It was beyond any stretch of the imagination to believe that a similar warp had opened up at the exact, opportune spot for Sateen to be brought to her.

Something else—perhaps somebody else—had to be involved, yet even her logical mind, used to dealing with all the intricacies of the law, couldn't figure this one out.

She sat up and wrapped her arms around her knees. One thing she did know for sure was that she had made her decision. She was committed to Stone now and forever. She had made that commitment yesterday afternoon when she made love with him. Along with her virginity, she had given him her soul—placed her future in his hands. She would avoid the hillside beside the cabin and share Stone's life from now on. She would never return to the New York law firm.

Suddenly she clapped a hand over her mouth, then leapt up and ran over to her backpack. She dug in and pulled out the little laptop computer from its nest in the side pocket, unzipped the leather case, and opened the disk slot. Oh, dear. There it was—the disk that contained her brief—the brief that had all the information in it to clear Robert of the charges of violating his noncompete agreement with the new owners of the company he had sold.

The brief was so sensitive and confidential that the senior partner of the firm had ordered her to delete it from her office computer and only work on it at home. She had shredded all the hard-copy drafts after making revisions and only kept a backup disk each time. She reached into the pocket on the leather laptop case and pulled out her backup copy.

Possibly the senior partner could reconstruct the brief from the scanty case law Tess had given him in the staff meeting, but she really didn't think so. The case cites were on yet another disk, filed there in the leather case with her backup disk. Besides, it had been years since a senior partner had had to do legal research. They always depended on the associates to do that boring work.

Tess usually thoroughly enjoyed legal research, sometimes to the point that she had to pull herself away from a superfluous tangent she had become interested in when it didn't really bear on her case. While working on Robert's problem, though, she'd uncharacteristically had to force herself to call up the law firm's research program on her computer.

She knew why. Robert's former company, located in upper New York State, had manufactured and sold industrial chemicals. The chemical formulas were so proprietary, the company would not even apply for a patent, which would mean disclosing the formulas in public records. With her love of the wilderness, she had detested the thought of those offensive compounds being used and the residues disposed of in hazardous waste dumps.

Robert had sought to avoid complying with the noncompete clause in the company's sales contract by starting up another, similar company in a different state—Texas. His choice of states, not even a knowing decision on his part, would save his hide. Her hours of research had led her through New York, Texas, and even Florida laws, cross-referencing her notes until she was certain of her defense. Texas law would govern, and the noncompete clause for the New York sale did not contain an essential clause—geographical limitations—as required under Texas statutes. The icing on the defense cake was the New York company's refusal to disclose publicly their customer list, thus leaving them without proof Robert had solicited sales from his former customers.

Her research and the resulting brief had taken her weeks to complete. The law firm might be able to get a continuance now, given her disappearance. However, the New York courts were clogged with cases, and the judge assigned to this case was not known to have much sympathy for continuances.

She shook her head, then laughed. There weren't even any phone lines here, where she could hook up her little modem and transmit the information to New York—the information she alone had. Even if there was a phone line, how could she key in modem commands that would transmit a hundred years to the future?

Too bad. Maybe Robert would just have to live with the consequences of his actions. Maybe some of his old, moldy money would have to be used to pay off his contract violation, as well as any other civil fines. Golly gee, was there a prison term connected with that sort of white-collar crime? She couldn't really remember—she'd had a meeting set up with another branch of the firm to discuss that the Monday following the day she had stormed out of her office.

She'd had good intentions. Even as angry as she'd been when she went home and loaded her backpack, she'd remembered to pack the little laptop. She had planned to work on the brief a little more—refining it and correcting the grammar—at the campsite Saturday evening. It was to have been filed in court two weeks later.

Two weeks were past now in 1893. They were past back in her other life, weren't they? She wondered what had happened. Without that brief, the new owners had a good chance of winning a summary judgment.

She realized she didn't really give a diddly squat. Granny had always said what goes around, comes around. She had no idea how much money Robert controlled, but she bet a $50-million-dollar noncompete contract violation might just put a hole in it. And the resulting publicity in the business section of the newspaper would definitely hurt Robert's business reputation.

Nothing she could do about it, though. She zipped the little computer back into its case and shoved it in the backpack. Rising, she grabbed the towel she had hung over a bush to dry, picked up the rifle, and headed for the creek to wash off her sunscreen. She'd better change out of her bikini and see what she could scrounge up for supper. Stone had said something about there being trout in the creek, and he'd left her a hand line, in case she wanted to go fishing.

Stone returned just before sundown, with six Cherokee and a smoked venison haunch to supplement the trout Tess had caught. She sighed a little in disappointment after they ate and she unrolled the sleeping bag and bedroll, placing them side by side instead of arranging them together. She crawled into her sleeping bag fully clothed, then watched the men sitting around the fire to discuss their plans to move the herd the next morning. Her eyes drifted shut, but sometime later she stirred briefly when she felt an arm drape around her waist and pull her close.

"We won't have to sleep apart much longer, darlin'," Stone whispered.

She murmured a muffled "Love you" and sank back into slumber before she could ask him what he meant.

Tess woke to the smell of coffee and frying bacon. Opening her eyes, she saw Stone watching her from where he squatted by the fire. He winked and mouthed his morning "Love you" before he turned his attention to the skillet of bacon.

How wonderful it felt to wake up with Stone near. Her lips curved into a contented smile and she stretched herself, then climbed out of the sleeping bag. She frowned for just a second as she recalled Stone whispering something to her after he lay down beside her last night, but the words seemed to have escaped her memory. Oh, well. She could ask him later.

By the time the men checked the area to make sure the stallion wasn't lying in wait to cause them trouble with the herd, several hours had passed. Stone and the Indians worked the mares for a while in the valley after they opened the gate, until they became accustomed to being herded. After that they cut out the mares with small colts, leaving them to find their way back to the stallion. Still Stone had over three dozen mares to send to the Army post—some suitable for saddle mounts for the soldiers and others for the army scouts. He picked out one sorrel mare for Jasper and, following a brief tussle, tied her to the gate.

He found three mares with ranchers' brands on their haunches and made a list for the men to give the army commander. The commander would notify the ranchers by telegraph, and they could pick up their horses at the post.

At last the herd moved out, and he slipped his arms around Tess and nuzzled her ear.

"Now, where's my morning kiss?"

"Right here."

Her arms went around his neck, and he kissed her deeply. Then again and once again.

But then he pulled back and shook his head slightly. "Huh-uh," he murmured. "The next time I make love to you, you're going to be my wife."

"Your . . . what?"

Chapter Twenty-nine

Stone tipped his hat up an inch, then stuck his fingertips in his back pockets.

"My wife. You didn't think we were just going on like this, did you? Even a hundred and one years from now I reckon women know what can happen when a man and woman make love. I won't have a child of mine born a bastard—whether it's in nine months or a hundred and one years."

"But I won't . . . won't get pregnant, Stone."

"Sure," he said, almost sneering. "Look, I know there's a couple of ways to make sure I don't plant a baby in a woman, but we didn't do that. My child could be growing in you right now."

"No, it couldn't," she denied as she glanced at her backpack.

"I suppose you're gonna tell me you've got some magic pill in there that will keep you from getting with child."

She reluctantly nodded her head. When she saw a thunderous scowl crawl over his face she quickly backed away.

"It's not what you think," she gasped as she tried to defuse his anger. "I started taking those pills for a . . . a female problem. I have a lot of pain every month, and it was getting worse. The doctor said . . ."

"I suppose those are the damned pills you were talking about at the cabin! Are you telling me that we could've been making love all this time, instead of me havin' to go out to that well and pour a bucket of cold water over me every night?"

She plopped her hands on her hips and leaned toward him, until her nose was a bare inch from his.

"You just hold your damned wild horses, Stone Chisum! I told you—I wasn't taking those pills to keep from getting pregnant. I don't sleep around. To me, making love is a commitment, not a sexual release. I was saving my virginity for the man I wanted to spend the rest of my life with!"

"Exactly," he said, smirking. "And that's why we're going to get married."

"You said you wanted to get married because you were afraid I was pregnant!" she fumed.

"Did I say that? I seem to recall sayin' we weren't going on like this—that the next time we made love, you were gonna be my wife. If that's not a commitment, I don't know what the hell else you can call it."

"You haven't even asked me yet!"

"Oh. Is that what you're waiting for?"

"No! I mean . . . darn it, Stone, marriage should be a mutual decision. We should discuss it. You can't just tell me that we're going to get married without asking me how I feel about it."

"So tell me."

"Tell you what?"

"How you feel about it. How you feel about becoming my wife."

Stone ducked his head and stared at the ground. Her jaw dropped when he stuck out a boot toe and started shoving a small rock around, refusing to look at her. She wished she could see his eyes, but he kept his head turned a little, just enough for his hat brim to shadow his face. But she could see his lower lip, barely protruding.

Suddenly she realized that he wasn't nearly as confident as he tried to appear. He couldn't force her to say "I do," and she also realized at the same moment that she wanted to say those words just as much as she wanted to say "I love you."

She really ought to make him sweat a little bit more, though. After all, she wanted her marriage to be a partnership, not a dictatorship, with her on the receiving end of his orders.

"Well," she mused, and his head jerked up. She tilted her head sideways and chewed her bottom lip for a second.

"Well," she repeated, "I did promise Granny that I'd only make love with my husband. And I've broken that promise, unless I do marry you."

"Is that the only reason, darlin'?" he whispered.

"No. I love you. That's the real reason."

He reached for her and pulled her against his chest. "Then—will you marry me, Tess Foster? Be my wife in every way and share everything with me?"

"Yes," she murmured. "Oh, yes."

He kissed her until she was breathless—until she pulled away, gasping for air.

"You . . . you'd better stop now," she said with a small laugh. "Unless you want me to do my darndest to make you break that promise not to make love to me again until I'm your wife."

"Insatiable," he groaned. "I knew it."

"And who made me that way?" she teased.

He stepped back and frowned at her. "What about the guy with all that moldy money?"

"I told you that was over. I hope you're not going to be one of those men who think what's past has any bearing on the life two people plan to have together. Do you want me to start questioning you again about how many women . . . ?"

"Hush." He clapped his hand over her mouth. "I'm sorry. I won't bring it up again. But you have to realize, honey, that I don't have much right now. I've got plans for the ranch, but . . . and there's Rain and Flower. You'll be their mother." He dropped his hand from her mouth.

She smiled. "I already love them, Stone. You know that."

"And . . ." He glanced at her pack. "And I want children of my own. How long do you have to take those damned pills?"

She laid a finger beside her mouth and pretended to think. "Oh," she finally said, "the doctor did say that my first pregnancy would probably take care of my problem. He said he'd seen it happen with other women. After their first child the monthly pain subsided."

He swept her up into his arms. Whirling her around, he threw back his head and shouted, "I'm gonna be a father. Hear that, everybody? Tess and

I are going to have babies together—lots of them."

She giggled and pushed at his shoulders until he set her down again.

"That *lots* will be something else we'll discuss together," she said. "And I thought you wanted to get married first."

"I do," he agreed. "Come on; let's get moving. We can be married by tomorrow evening."

"But you said we were going to the Cherokee camp."

"We are. That's where we'll get married. I've already talked to Silver Eagle, and he'll do the ceremony."

"Silver Eagle? Silver Eagle's going to marry us?"

"It's legal, if that's what's worrying your lawyer mind. Oklahoma's still a territory, and Indian marriages are recognized. Hell, that and just living together were all a lot of people had for years out here, what with traveling preachers only showing up now and then. I suppose we could wait until we get back to Clover Valley, if you want a minister to marry us. But Flower and Rain are already pretty excited about the whole idea, and we'd have to wait until they got done with their visit and could be there. If you want, though . . ."

"I think an Indian ceremony will be perfect," she broke into his babbling. "Absolutely, utterly perfect."

And it would be, she thought to herself as she helped Stone break camp. What else could fit in so perfectly with this entire, fantastic episode in her life?

In an unguarded moment, she started to unzip the pocket in her pack where she kept her pills, then hesitated. In the flurry of packing at her apartment that night, she hadn't taken time to separate the things in the drawer where she kept her extra backpacking supplies—deodorant, toothpaste, Band-Aids, vitamins, and so forth. She'd tossed the year's supply of birth-control pills she had picked up the previous week at the pharmacy in that drawer, since there wasn't room in the medicine cabinet. In a hurry to be on her way, she'd dumped the entire drawer into a case and shoved the case into her pack, not stopping to consider that she wouldn't need the pills until she returned.

In the deepest part of her heart she wanted to scatter those pills here in the valley—the valley where she had truly become a woman in every sense of the word—Stone's woman. To start trying to get pregnant tomorrow night. Her hand fluttered to her stomach, imagining Stone's child growing there.

"Stone? Could you come help me here?"

Stone walked over to her. "Sure. What do you need?"

She handed him a package of pills. "This." She started punching pills through the foil covering, flicking her wrist to scatter the pills as they fell.

"Your turn," she said when her package was empty. "We've got ten more packages to get rid of."

He stared at her for a second, then whispered, "I love you, Tess. But are you sure you want this right away? Maybe we should wait awhile."

She lifted her face to his, and the breeze feathered through her hair. "No," she said in a determined voice. "I want our commitment to each other to start out on a forever basis."

Stone took a deep breath and started punching out pills.

"A church pew. How nice, Michael," Angela said the next evening after Michael rearranged their cloud.

"It's a holy occasion, Angie. And I'm feeling awfully spiritual right now, even for the state I'm in. After all, I had a little something to do with this wedding that's getting ready to take place down there."

"A little something? I'd say you had quite a bit to do with it. They wouldn't even have met if not for you."

"Yeah," Michael said with a satisfied smile.

"Now, Michael," she cautioned. "Too much pride is a sin, you know."

"How about just a smattering of pride then, huh? Part of doing a job well is the pride you take in doing it so well."

"I guess that makes sense," she said, smiling tolerantly at him. "And they are so right for each other. Although . . ."

"What?" he asked.

"Well, I guess their relationship is like the old adage that says opposites attract. I mean, Stone's an old-fashioned, laid-back . . ."

". . . my-wife-belongs-in-the-kitchen-barefoot-and-pregnant sort of guy," he broke in. "And Tess believes a woman has a right to a life of her own, as well as being a wife and mother."

"Well, they will have to make some adjustments. But that has to happen in any marriage. Stone's going to have to realize that Tess hasn't given up her own identity just because she's taken his name."

"I agree," he said.

"But I've dealt with humans longer than you have, Michael. Sometimes people get married and forget they fell in love because of the way that person was while they were courting. They set out to change the other person, or things that they think won't bother them about one another grow from molehills to mountains over time."

She paused and tried to smile reassuringly at Michael. "Surely Stone and Tess won't be like that. You heard Tess saying that they had to discuss things with each other."

"She didn't discuss that deal she and Mandy Calder cooked up back with those other Clover Valley women with Stone."

"How could she? He made it clear he didn't want her poking her nose into his problems."

"See what I mean?"

"Oh, dear," Angela said.

"Like you've said before, Angie, we'll just have to wait and see what happens. When are those Indian women going to get done with Tess?"

"Don't get impatient. A woman wants to look her best on her wedding day."

"Stone's the one who's impatient. Look at him."

Angela peered over the side of the pew and giggled. "He's trying to look so solemn. But he can't keep his feet still, and he's clenching and unclenching those fists like his hands are trying to go to sleep."

"He's scared to death," Michael said. "Look, here comes Tess—over on the edge of the camp. Boy, is she beautiful. She's gonna scare him even more."

"That's the dress Silver Eagle's wife wore when they got married," Angela informed him. "He kept it all these years. While Tess was going through the

Indian purification ceremony before her marriage, Flower told Tess that her grandfather would be honored if she would wear it."

"I missed that part, 'cause I wasn't gonna watch them wash and dress Tess, but that sounds nice," Michael mused. "I wish we had some music. Doesn't seem right not to have music at a wedding."

"The Indian drums fit the ceremony down there better," she said. "But we could have our own music up here, since they won't be able to hear it."

She waved her hand, and a chorus of voices filled the air. Smiling, she settled back against the pew. Michael lifted his hand and the pew tilted slightly forward, so they could see the scene below them better.

The whole camp had turned out for the ceremony, all wearing the finest clothing they owned. As Tess moved through the throng of people, they quieted and watched her pass. Even the children left their games and joined their parents, the smaller ones hiding behind the various buckskin and cotton skirts of their mothers, peeking out in awe at the pretty woman walking by.

Michael sniffed at the aromas rising from the camp. "They've been cooking down there all day, getting ready for the wedding feast," he murmured. "Almost makes me wish we could join them to eat."

"We don't have to eat."

"Who said anything about *having* to? We can if we want to. I used to thoroughly enjoy wandering over to our heavenly kitchen and sampling some of the dishes when I wasn't busy." He patted his paunch and winked at her. "How do you think the cooks on earth come up with new, divine dishes?

Why, they're tried out first to see if they're worth the trouble of inspiration."

"Now, Michael. Don't give in to temptation."

"All right." He sighed. "Sometimes it's a drag always being on the edge of everything."

"Oh, watch!"

Angela leaned forward even farther as Tess walked up to Stone and he took her hand in his.

They turned to face Silver Eagle, and the shaman's strong voice rose, blessing both of them and wishing them a life filled with joy as they shared it together. And—with a little smirk—a fruitful union, with many children to care for them when they grew old.

Angela sighed as she watched Stone and Tess gaze into each other's eyes, seemingly unaware of anything but themselves, their love, and the voice of the shaman, whose words were making them man and wife. Just before Silver Eagle said the final words of the Indian ceremony he paused and spoke to the gathering, explaining that Stone and Tess also wished to pledge themselves to each other in their own words.

Both Angela and Michael listened raptly as Stone placed one hand on Tess's waist and cupped her cheek with the other.

"I, Stone," he said in a husky voice, "take you, Tess, for my wife. What I have is yours to share, now and forever. You are the light in my life, the part of me that makes me whole. I pledge you my fidelity and love forever, throughout all time."

Angela and Michael saw Tess blinking back tears as she kept her gaze on Stone's face. "I, Tess," she said, "take you, Stone, for my husband. With you I've found the true meaning of love, and I shall cherish that always. I give you my trust, my heart, and my faith in the rightness of our love. I pledge myself to you, my darling, now and for all time."

Stone bent and tenderly kissed Tess, then turned and motioned to Rain and Flower to join them. Rain held out a slightly grubby hand as soon as he approached, and Stone took the ring he had traded one of the Indian craftsmen for in his fingers.

"This ring is for you to wear as a symbol to the world that I love you," he said. "But it's also from Flower and Rain, as a symbol that we're a family now—that you're part of us and we're part of you. Now and always."

A tear slipped down Tess's cheek as Stone placed the ring on her finger and kissed it. He dropped her hand, and Flower and Rain each grasped one of Tess's hands as Stone completed the circle by taking each child's hand.

"The circle of the ring will always remind me of the circle of love in our family," Tess promised.

She smiled into Stone's eyes, then hugged the children. Flower moved to Tess's side, while Rain stepped to the other side of Stone. Clasping hands again, Stone and Tess faced Silver Eagle.

"You are one now," the shaman said. "For now and forever, you will walk this earth as two, but you shall be as one."

Stone swept Tess into his arms and kissed her soundly as Rain let out a whoop that was quickly echoed by several of his young friends. The crowd began to break up and head for the cooking pots, but Stone held Tess close after he broke the kiss.

"Hello, Mrs. Chisum," he said.

"Hello, husband," Tess said dreamily.

Michael propped his elbow on the side of the pew and settled his chin on his palm. "Seems a shame we can't go down there and wish them happiness—maybe kiss the bride."

"And sample all that food." Angela laughed. "I can tell what you're thinking about. You know, I haven't seen Rain or Silver Eagle eat all day. They camped out up in the hills together last night and just came back in time for the ceremony this evening. And now Rain's not eating with his friends. You don't think he's getting sick, do you? He's always had a huge appetite."

"He's probably just too excited about Tess becoming his mother to eat," Michael said. "But you wouldn't think even that could hurt a growing boy's appetite, would you?"

Rain and Silver Eagle began walking away from the camp, and suddenly the wind rose. The church pew started moving as though following Rain and his grandfather, but when Angela glanced down she didn't see a stir of wind on the ground.

"Michael, stop that," she said. "We're supposed to stay with Tess. And I want to watch the rest of the celebration."

"I'm not doing anything," he replied. "Come on. Let's get off this thing."

"I can't," she gasped. "I can't get up. And my wings won't unfold."

"Neither will mine. What the danged blazes is going on here?"

Chapter Thirty

The church pew floated to the ground on one side of the dead campfire, and on the other side sat Silver Eagle and Rain.

"You figured out what's going on here yet, Angie?" Michael whispered.

"Not entirely," she replied quietly. "But I'd guess that Silver Eagle's powers are pretty strong. I'm sure we could break the spell if we really wanted to, but he's gone to an awful lot of trouble to try to talk to us. That must be what he and Rain were doing up here on this hill last night—preparing themselves spiritually to speak to us. Let's see what he wants."

"All right," Michael agreed. "Guess Mr. G probably wants us to talk to them, or He wouldn't have let Silver Eagle's powers bring us here, instead of us staying with Tess."

"It's their wedding night, Michael. We weren't going to stay there all night anyway."

"Yeah, I know that. And this seems like it might be a lot more interesting than watching the Indian dances." Michael laid an arm across the back of the pew and propped his ankle on his knee. "Think Silver Eagle can see us yet?"

Silver Eagle took a pipe from the pouch hanging on his belt and placed the stem to his lips. Rain reached up and flicked the lighter Tess had given him, and his grandfather drew on the pipe until the tobacco in the bowl caught. He glanced at the lighter.

"That is a good thing to have," he said. "Even better than the white men's matches."

Rain placed the lighter back in his pocket and stared at the spirits again. "When can we speak to them, Grandfather?"

Silver Eagle puffed on the pipe. He blew smoke in all four directions, then took another puff and handed the pipe to Rain.

"It is time you learned to smoke with me, Grandson."

Rain took a deep drag from the pipe and quickly blew the smoke out. His eyes watered and his chest heaved, but he managed to control himself and not cough like a child. He started to hand the pipe back to Silver Eagle, but the shaman nodded across the ashes.

"Oh, Michael, you can't!" the woman spirit cried.

"It's part of the ceremony," the man spirit said with a grin as he reached for the pipe. He took it from Rain and inhaled deeply. "Ahhhh," he breathed as he quirked an eyebrow and offered the pipe to the woman.

"No, thank you," she said primly.

The man shrugged and handed the pipe to Silver Eagle. "Women don't smoke in your ceremonies anyway, do they?"

"Not unless they wish to," Silver Eagle replied. "We have never been able to find a ceremony that will let us control a woman's mind."

"You never will, either," the golden-haired woman said with a huff. "And I'll thank you to remember that just because I'm outnumbered by the males in this group, I'm not going to be overlooked."

"We would never try to do that." Silver Eagle smiled.

"Well, let's get cracking here," the man said. "What did you want to talk about, Silver Eagle?"

Rain jumped to his feet. "What are your names? Where have you come from? Why can't anyone see you except me—and now Grandfather? How does it feel to fly? Can I . . . can I touch you?"

Rain saw his grandfather shake his head and winked at the man. "Grandson," he said in a slightly exasperated voice, "we have time. You need not ask it all in one breath."

He sank back to the ground, embarrassed. "I'm sorry, Grandfather. I forgot. I didn't mean to act like a . . . a child."

"It's all right, Rain," the woman soothed. "You've been watching us for weeks now, and I'd be surprised if you didn't have a whole lot of questions to ask."

His grandfather placed an arm around his shoulder and pulled him closer. "You have done well, Grandson. You followed our customs and acted with reverence toward the spirits. You prepared yourself, and I am sure they know you are respectful. We will ask them if they are permitted to answer your questions."

"I'm Michael," the man said when Silver Eagle looked at him. "This is Angie."

"Angela," the woman corrected.

"Okay, Angela." The man shrugged. "Angie and I are Tess's guardian angels. We're here to keep an eye on her and make sure she doesn't get hurt."

"But she broke her ankle," Rain said.

"Yeah. Well . . . a . . ."

The woman nudged the man in the ribs. "Go ahead, Michael. Explain that to Rain."

"You think I can't, don't you? Well, I've been thinking about it. I think it was meant to be. You see, Rain—" Michael shifted and recrossed his legs. "—You see, if Tess hadn't broken her ankle and started to fall off that mountain, and if I hadn't sneezed just then, she wouldn't be here with you all right now. She wouldn't have met your pa, and you wouldn't be a family."

Angela gently clapped her hands. "Good going, Michael. And I really think you're right."

"Thank you." Michael turned to her and nodded his head regally.

"My grandson has told me that your Tess is from the future," Silver Eagle said. "I would know how this happened."

"Like I said, with a sneeze," Michael replied, laughing. "I lost my concentration, and the roots of the bush Tess was holding on to pulled free. She fell through a time warp that neither Angie nor I knew was there until we looked over the cliff to see what had happened to Tess."

Suddenly Michael snapped his fingers and held

out a cigar to Silver Eagle. "Say, would you like one of these? It's a real Havana. Some of the human spirits that come to live with us tell me it's better than a pipe, and they splurged on them when they were alive."

Alive?" Rain whispered as his grandfather accepted the cigar. "They . . . have to die to be with you? Then, you . . . you're dead, too?"

"Yeah, well, Rain, you just haven't thought about that end of it, have you?" Michael asked. "'Course we're dead. Well, sort of. I mean . . ."

Michael gave the woman a helpless glance, but she calmly folded her arms and sat back on the pew. Silver Eagle was busy reaching into Rain's pocket for the lighter when Michael looked at him. The shaman pulled out the lighter and studied the mechanism. He flicked the wheel and lit the cigar. Then he blew out a long stream of smoke and lifted his brows inquiringly at Michael.

"Well, it's like this, Rain," Michael began. He cleared his throat, shifted his crossed legs again, and said, "Angie and I aren't really *dead,* as you think of the word. See, to be dead we'd have had to have been alive at one time, like the human spirits who lived on earth at one time, then come to stay with us. But Angie and I have always . . . well, always *been,* ever since the beginning."

"Beginning of what?" he asked in a confused voice.

"The beginning of time," Michael explained. "You see, that's the difference between angels, like Angie and me, and the human spirits who live with us."

For the next half hour Michael tried to explain to him the intricacies of life and death—human spirits and guardian angels. He started with creation, when the angels originated, and told of the war, which resulted in a split between the powers and the angels. He told of the different hierarchies and explained his previous duties before he decided to become a guardian angel, rather than a spirit guide.

Michael also attempted to answer a thousand and one other questions tumbling from Rain's mouth. His grandfather listened attentively, now and then relighting his cigar when he became so involved in the conversation that he forgot to draw on it.

Rain noticed at one point that the woman appeared a little put out at his directing all his questions to Michael. But, after all, he recalled, she had been the first angel he had seen. When he asked his next question he looked at Angela, to see if she wanted to answer it.

No, she responded eagerly. Human spirits don't become angels after their souls leave their bodies. The only angels were the ones who were created at the beginning. However, there were many other things for human spirits to do in their afterlife.

Rain wasn't too interested in that. He had years and years before he faced the prospect of dying. So he tried another question. "How can this be happening now," he asked, "and other things going on where Tess used to live? How can she be here, with us, when she isn't even born yet in our time?"

Twin shrugs of white-robed shoulders greeted his query. Silver Eagle waited patiently, but Rain saw his grandfather's brown eyes twinkling as he watched the angels shift uncomfortably on the pew.

"Uh . . ." Angela finally began, "I guess there are

some things that just can't be explained, Rain. That's where faith comes in."

"But I thought faith was what we were supposed to have while we're alive—for those things that happen, though we can't figure out why."

A few more long seconds crawled by, and suddenly Rain said, "I know. It's like you said, Michael. Tess came here because that's what was supposed to happen in her life. So it doesn't really matter now what's going on back there, because she's here with us. We needed her worse than they did back there, and what's happening now is what's supposed to happen in her life."

"Makes sense to me," Michael said, looking relieved. "How about you, Angie?"

"Huh?" Angela said, a frown creasing her face. "I guess so."

"What about flying?" Rain asked, satisfied with his own explanation as to Tess's presence in his life. "Will I be able to do that when I live with you?"

"Maybe even before," Michael replied.

Angela nudged him. "I don't think we should tell him about the future."

"Shoot, Angie, he's already aware of some of the things in the future. Remember all that stuff Tess brought in her backpack? And this is 1893. Why, old Bill Henson's had his patent on that steam-powered plane in England for over fifty years. And the Wright Brothers will make their flight in nine years here in the United States. Rain will have plenty of chances to fly during his life."

"Could I try it now?" he asked in a partially pleading, partially awestruck voice.

When Angela glanced at Michael he looked overhead, then shrugged and said, "I don't see why not. You want to take him, Angie?"

"I'd love to," she said. "If we can get up now."

Michael stood and held out his hand to Angela. She joined him and flexed her wings wide, reaching for Rain's hand when he scrambled to his feet, filled with excitement.

He hesitated, and a little of his exhilaration died as he drew his hand back.

"Uh . . . I . . ." He glanced at Silver Eagle. "Is it all right, Grandfather?"

Silver Eagle smiled tolerantly at him. "It is good that you remember to ask my consent, Rain Shadow. Go. It is something you will always remember, though you will not be able to speak of it to anyone else."

"Thank you!" He turned back to Angela. "Are you going to give me wings like yours?"

"No." Angela laughed. "Just take my hand."

A second later she spread her wings wide and lifted from the ground.

Both Silver Eagle and Michael heard Rain's gasp of excitement and awe, and Michael settled back onto the pew as Angela carried the little boy higher.

"How about you, Silver Eagle?" he asked. "You want to take a flight after Rain gets back?"

"It is for the young ones to do," Silver Eagle replied. "I have seen many things in my life—and there will be more to come before I join your world."

Michael conjured another cigar and held it out to Silver Eagle, but the Indian shook his head.

"Keep it for later, then," he said as he stuck the cigar in Silver Eagle's belt.

The shaman nodded his thanks, then said, "I wish to speak further of Tess with you. She is my family now, too—the mother of my grandchildren. I have fasted and sought dreams, but I cannot see what will happen, and I do not want Rain Shadow and Mountain Flower to cry again. You must tell me if Tess will stay with them or if she will go back to her own time."

"I can't do that," he said sadly, "because Angie and I don't know either. But Tess has made a commitment to Stone with their marriage. She doesn't want to leave now."

Silver Eagle nodded solemnly. "It is as I feared, but my love for my grandchildren made it necessary for me to talk with you. You speak the truth as you know it. Tess has joined herself to Man Who Walks With Right today, yet I have seen many men and women part after they have sworn to always be as one. In the white culture they call it divorce."

"I see what you're worried about," he responded. "Tess wouldn't even have to get a divorce—all she'd have to do is go back through the time warp. But that warp will close someday, because those things shift around. That's why Angie and I weren't aware of it being there at first."

"I do not see the purpose of these . . . warps," Silver Eagle said in a hesitant voice. "Why they should be."

"That's one thing only Mr. G knows," he said with a shrug. "And he's the only one who knows if things will work out for Tess and Stone."

"I would ask you to speak to me again if you learn what I need to know."

"I'll do that," he promised. "If Mr. G lets us know, we'll tell you. If He says it's all right, of course."

"Who is this Mr. G?"

"Aw, it's my name for Him. He's like your Great Spirit."

"He allows you to call Him this?"

Michael shrugged. "I guess so. He's never told me I couldn't, anyway."

Angela floated back to earth, placing a steadying hand on Rain's shoulders when he wobbled slightly. As soon as Rain got his balance, he cried, "Grandfather, it's wonderful! You go for a ride now." He ran over and tugged Silver Eagle to his feet.

"I do not think . . ."

Rain pulled him toward Angela, and Angela held out her hand, looking at Silver Eagle with a challenge on her face.

"Go on, Grandfather," Rain said when Silver Eagle hesitated. "You can see everything from up there. Angela told me about the things Michael mentioned—the airplanes. Someday they'll carry bunches of people through the skies."

"Rain, remember, we cannot tell others of what we have seen this evening. They may call us crazy."

"Angela and I talked about that, too, while we flew around," Rain answered. "It'll be our secret. But you need to go, so I'll have someone to talk with about it."

"Perhaps so." The shaman took Angela's hand. "So I can speak with Rain Shadow of this."

"Of course," Angela murmured.

Michael and Rain watched the shaman's face as his feet left the ground. His eyes grew wide and his mouth fell open. He chanced a quick glance at his grandson, then schooled his face into Indian stoicism, though he did grab Angela's upper arm with his free hand.

"Good morning, husband," Tess murmured, snuggling up to Stone and wrapping her arms around his waist.

"'Morning, wife." He dropped a kiss on her head, then lifted her onto his stomach. "I think I could get used to this real fast."

"You'd better. I think it's going to take me a little longer, though. You hog the blankets."

"Sure," he admitted. "Then you have to cuddle up to me for warmth."

"Oh, is that how it works?"

"Uh-huh."

"Pa?" a voice said outside the tepee. "You awake yet?"

"Rain, get away from there." That was Flower's voice. "Let them sleep."

Tess blew a curl away from her face. "Duty calls."

"Yeah, I suppose. It's funny, though: Neither one of those kids had any time to spend with me yesterday. Rain took off with Silver Eagle, and Flower was with you all day. Then they show up at the crack of dawn today."

She looked around the tepee. "It's awfully light in here for dawn."

Stone rolled her to his side and reached across her for his denims. Digging in the pocket, he pulled out a watch.

"Good lord, it's after nine o'clock. I've never slept this late in my life."

"Oh, no!" She sat up and grabbed the doeskin dress she had carefully folded by the bedroll the night before. "We'd better get dressed. Oh, I wish I had my backpack. I don't want to wear this out there."

"Tess, darlin'. What on earth's wrong with you?"

"The whole camp's probably been out there watching this tepee to see when we get up!" Heat flooded her face. "They probably think . . . I mean . . . that we're . . ."

"Well, we were until just before daybreak, weren't we?"

"Darn it, Stone . . ."

"Honey, how many times before today do you think people have been married in this camp? And it sure wouldn't have done my image any good in front of the other men if they'd seen you out there at daybreak."

"What's that supposed to mean?"

He grabbed her and pulled her back down beside him. "What do you think it means?" he growled. "They'd think I didn't know how to satisfy my woman—that she'd rather be slaving over a hot cooking pot than in here making love to me."

"I see. Well, we can't have your manhood in doubt now, can we?" She slid her body closer and ran a hand teasingly over his hips while she watched his face. "Especially since I know there's not a darned thing lacking in that department."

"Woman, you're gonna get yourself in trouble."

"Trouble, huh? That's a funny word for it. I always thought people were supposed to try and stay away from trouble." She ran her fingers along his waist and inched her index finger between their bodies. She wiggled her finger slightly. "Here, Trouble. Here, boy."

Stone groaned and flipped her onto her back, muffling her giggle with his mouth.

Chapter Thirty-one

Two days later, after spending one night on the trail, Tess and Stone rode into Clover Valley. The owner of the livery stable on the edge of town was drinking a cup of coffee as they rode up.

"Hey, Chisum," he called. "You're in town early."

"Howdy, Jake," Stone replied as he dismounted. "You got room here for these horses for a few hours? I've got a little business to take care of before we head home."

"Sure. You want 'em fed, or just put up?"

"Just put up," he said, remembering his financial condition. "I'll grain them when I get home." He unwrapped the lead rope, tied to the mare he planned to give to Jasper from his saddlehorn. "This one's just off the range and still sort of skittish. I'll put her in the corral myself."

After Stone led the mare into the corral beside the

stable he glanced at Tess, who still sat on Sateen. The gray gelding stood patiently at the end of its lead rope, behind the black mare.

"You gonna get down?" he asked.

"As soon as you help Lonesome down," Tess replied.

He stomped over and reached for the dog that was lying across the front of Tess's saddle. "This darned animal's perfectly capable of walking on its own," he growled. "You spoil him, and he won't be a bit of good around the ranch."

"He likes to ride."

Instead of setting Lonesome on the ground Stone held him for a moment, and the dog reached up to lick his face. He shifted him to one arm and stroked his head.

"Let's get another rule down right now, fella," he said. "You can ride with Tess if she wants you to, but from now on you sleep at the foot of the bed. I didn't appreciate waking up this morning and finding you curled up between me and my wife."

"Wife?" Jake said beside him. When Stone glanced at him Jake lifted an eyebrow. "I guess congratulations are in order, huh?"

Stone dodged another lick that Lonesome aimed at his face and set the dog down before he grasped Jake's hand. "Yep, my wife."

"Glad to see you ain't spoilin' her like the dog," Jake said in an aside. "Most women think we gotta help them on an' off the hosses, an' we all know they got two good legs to do it themselves."

Despite Jake's low voice, Tess caught his words. She clenched her teeth and glared down at the two men before she tossed her head and slid to the ground. Sometimes this women's lib stuff wasn't worth a darn, she realized as she dusted the legs of her jeans. Men who confused simple courtesy with their idea of a man spoiling a woman . . . and acting like it was just fine to spoil a dog . . .

She raised her face when she heard the stable man choke and start coughing. She watched Stone pound Jake on his back until the other man hacked up a wad of tobacco from his throat and spit it on the ground.

"Nope," Stone said as Jake stood there gaping at her. "Ain't a thing wrong with my wife's legs."

Chuckling, Stone slipped an arm around her waist and led her away from the stable. "Keep the dog here for me, too, Jake," he called over his shoulder.

"Look," Stone said to her in a stern voice after they were out of Jake's hearing, "I don't want you traipsing around town dressed in those tight denims. We'll stop at Sid's store first and get you another dress."

"Stone, I can pick out my own clothes. You've got other things to do."

"Yeah, I do, but I have to speak to Sid first."

Stone ignored Tess's questioning look and guided her up the steps to the board walkway, then on past a small café and stopped at the general store. He held the door open for her and scanned the inside of the store, glad to see they were the only customers. He hated the idea of asking Sid to wait a few more days for him to pay his account in front of any of the other townspeople.

"Go on over and look at the dresses while I talk to Sid."

Tess nodded and walked away, while he took a deep breath and headed for Sid. The storekeeper looked up at him with a wide grin on his face and shook his hand in welcome, grabbing it again a second later and pumping it harder after Stone explained that he and Tess were married.

"Uh . . ." Stone began. "We've been out at the Cherokee camp and Tess didn't bring a dress with her. She needs to get one before we . . ."

"'Course she does," Sid interrupted. "New bride needs a new dress. There's some in the storeroom I just got in and haven't put out yet. You go on and do whatever you need to do, Chisum, while I fetch out the dresses for your missus to look at. I know men don't like to hang around while their women try on clothes."

"Uh . . . my account . . ."

"Sure," Sid said with a wave of his hand as he started away from the counter. "I'll put the dress on it. See you later."

He stared after the storekeeper, frowning. The last time he had come, he'd sensed a little reserve on Sid's part when he licked his pencil point and added up Stone's purchases. Now he shrugged and turned from the counter as Sid emerged from the storeroom with an armload of dresses. Half the town probably owed Sid money, and Sid ought to know by now that he couldn't keep a business going around here without letting people charge until they could pay.

"Stone," Tess called before he could open the door, "where do you want me to meet you?"

"How about over at the café in about half an hour? Think you'll be done by then?"

"That'll be fine."

He went out the door and tipped his hat as two women came toward him down the walkway.

"Good morning, Mr. Chisum," one of the women trilled. "My husband was just over at the stable, and I hear the territory has lost another bachelor."

"Yes, ma'am," he replied. "Word sure gets around fast."

"Well, where is your lovely wife?" the other woman asked. "We can't wait to give her our best wishes. Perhaps the Ladies' Guild could host a small reception for you in a few days."

"Guess you'll have to discuss that with Tess," he said. "She's in the store, picking out a dress."

He glanced past the two women to see Rose Brown sitting on her horse in front of the hitching rail. He tipped his hat to her, but before he could call a greeting, Tillie Peterson emerged from the café and called to him.

"Good morning, Stone! And Rose. How are you, Edith and Fredwina?" she continued as she sped down the walkway toward them.

"Good morning, Tillie," Stone responded as he turned to her with an expectant grin on his face. He was well aware of what the first words out of either Edith or Fredwina's mouth would be and was eager to see Tillie's reaction.

Edith beat Fredwina to the punch. "Oh, Tillie," she said, "have you heard? Stone and Miss Foster are married. We must plan a party for them."

"How wonderful!" Tillie stepped up to him to plant a wet kiss on his cheek, and he smiled to himself in satisfaction. "I'm so glad my little talks with you have finally gotten through that thick skull of yours, Stone Chisum."

His smile altered into a wry grin and he tipped back his hat on his forehead. "Well, now, Tillie, I think maybe mine and Tess's feelings for each other might've had a little something to do with it, too."

"I should hope so," Tillie huffed. "Where is Tess? I want to hear all the details. I suppose you didn't invite us because it wasn't your funeral." Tillie giggled at the private joke between herself and Stone.

"We got married out at the Cherokee camp," he answered. "It was a lovely ceremony."

"And just as binding as if a minister had performed it," Tillie said, tapping him on the shoulder. "Don't you forget that."

"I wouldn't think of it, Tillie."

"Well, are you going to tell us where Tess is? I hope you haven't gone off and left her alone this early in your married life."

"Tess is in the store," he repeated. "I'm sure she'll be glad to see you. If you ladies would like to come over to the café with Tess in a little while, I'll buy you all a cup of coffee or tea."

"We'll do that." Tillie glanced up at Rose, who still sat on her horse. "Are you coming, Rose? We've got plans to make."

"I don't have time right now," Rose said in a tight voice. "You can let me know what you decide later."

"All right," Tillie agreed. She and the other two women hurried into the general store.

Stone stepped down into the street, and Rose hurriedly dismounted.

"Stone," she said, placing her hand on his arm. "Why did you do it?"

"What?" he asked in a puzzled voice. "You mean, why did I marry Tess?"

"Yes. I thought . . . you and I . . . you've always been there when I needed you."

"Don't worry," he said, patting her hand. "I'll still help you out when you need it. That's what neighbors are for, and Tess won't mind."

He pulled his arm free, and Rose abruptly turned her back on him, but not before he thought he caught a glimpse of tears in her eyes.

"Rose?"

She quickly turned back to face him, a brilliant smile on her face. "I wish you both the best. Would you mind helping me up on my horse? I just remembered I forgot to bring something with me, and now I have to ride all the way back out to the ranch to get it."

He nodded and cupped his hands. After Rose mounted she turned her mare and galloped out of town. He continued across the street, whistling a jaunty tune as he headed for the bank.

"So there, Michael," Angela said. "You read Rose's thoughts, too. She's been trying to get Stone in her bed for years. She even waited for him the other morning in her nightgown when she knew he was coming to check her sick calf, and pretending to be astonished that he'd arrived so early. You saw her fake a stumble and fall against him, and she was livid when Stone only steadied her and told her to go back in the house and get dressed. Do you still think Rose might have been a good wife for Stone if Tess had decided to go back to the future?"

"Not on your life." Michael shivered. "That woman could be dangerous. I can still hear what's she's thinking while she's riding toward her ranch, and it's even worse now. Did you know her father left her when she was fifteen, then her fiancé dropped her the day before their wedding? She even blames her husband for having the gall to up and die on her, though he'd already told her he was sick and tired of her shrewish temper and mood swings. Good grief, Angie. Now she's thinking that at least her husband had the decency to die, instead of leaving her, like he'd threatened to do. Don't you think she might be on the verge of a breakdown?"

"If you'd taken the trouble to look into her background as I did, Michael, you'd know she's always been like that. I never have figured out why, but it seems like some people are born bad. But Rose is just smart enough to keep something of a lid on her meanness and try to manipulate people into doing what she wants without giving herself away."

"What else did you find out about her?"

"Well, you're right. Her father left her and you heard her thinking about that. But the reason he left was because Rose's mother was just like her. He put up with them both all those years, then just couldn't take it anymore. Rose's mother helped Rose set her cap for a rich man's son back in New Orleans, where they lived. She figured she and Rose would both have an easy life if Rose married that young man."

"But he found out before the wedding what she was like, huh?"

"Uh-huh. He was engaged to another girl, but Rose seduced him, then told him she was pregnant. He . . . she . . . uh, this is a little embarrassing to say. Maybe you should just go back a few years in time and see for yourself."

"Oh; come on, Angie. We've talked about embarrassing things before."

Michael waited while she fidgeted with her fingers. Suddenly she saw him blush hotly and wave his wings to cool his face.

"You don't have to tell me," he said. "I read it in your mind. A stain all over the back of her dress, huh?"

"As she and the young man were leaving the hotel dining room the evening before their wedding," she confirmed. "Of course, her fiancé knew right away what had happened and that she'd lied to him about being pregnant."

"Then she married Mr. Brown a few months later. He moved to Texas, then up here to Oklahoma, after Rose's mother died. She set her sights on Stone after her husband died."

They couldn't see Rose any longer, unless they flew higher, but Michael continued to read her thoughts aloud.

"Rose blames her husband for not getting her pregnant," he continued.

"She's probably barren by design," Angela mused. "Think of what kind of mother she would make!"

"I agree. But she's built up this fantasy of her and Stone in her mind, Angie. Since they've got adjacent homesteads, Rose thinks that combining them would give her and Stone enough property to make a better living, rather than her having to scrape by. And she'd be someone more important than just the dressmaker in Clover Valley—be accepted because Stone's an important rancher, instead of only being tolerated for her dressmaking skills by women who don't know a needle from a thimble. She thinks because she's attracted to Stone he should feel the same way—that he's only being a gentleman by not making a pass at her."

"Michael, she's furious at Tess. And she hates Flower and Rain because they're half Indian. She figured she could talk Stone into sending them back to the reservation if he married her—she's even been behind the Ladies' Guild trying to force Stone into giving up his children. Oh, dear, Michael. She's wicked!"

Suddenly Angela glanced at the street below them. "Michael, look!" she cried. "Oh, dear, we've been standing here gossiping when we should have been watching what was going on. Oh, my word! Is he ever angry!"

"Uh-oh. We'd better get over there with Tess."

After leaving the bank Stone stormed across the street toward the general store. Ignoring the steps, he leapt to the walkway and shoved open the door. His fists clenched, he strode to the back of the store, where Sid was hanging women's dresses on a rod.

Stone glared, then shoved the dresses aside as though he'd find Tess cringing behind them.

"Can I help you, Stone?" Sid asked as he came out of the storeroom.

"Where the hell's my wife?" he snarled.

"Over at the café would be my guess," Sid said as he took a step back. "She changed clothes in the back room, then she and the other ladies left. Said they were supposed to meet you for a cup of tea."

"What the hell's the balance on my account, Sid?"

"Same as it was the last time you were here. Except for the dress for Miz Chisum and the new pump she wanted."

"New pump?"

"Well, yeah. She said you were gonna pipe water into the house. I'll have to order the pipe you'll need from Oklahoma City, though. It should be here in a few days."

"You don't seem to be too worried about my being able to pay my bill, Sid." His eyes narrowed. "Not like you were the last time I asked you to put stuff on my account."

"Hell, Stone, I figured you'd take care of it in full this time. You've got close to a thousand in the bank. I put it in there like Miz Chisum told me to do after the banker's wife paid me for that ring Miz Chisum left for me to sell."

Stone drew in a ragged breath and let it out slowly. A ring. Tess had sold a ring. A damned expensive ring, too. Probably a ring that bastard with the moldy money had given her. And she hadn't bothered to tell him—just had the money deposited in his bank account. If she thought he was going to touch one penny of that money . . .

"And you probably won't even need any money to pay those damned unfair taxes the legislature tried to sneak on the homesteaders," Sid continued. "I've heard that movement your wife started last week is already working to get them repealed. Shoot, Oklahoma's going to be a state one of these days. Those fools know we'll remember every damned one of their names when it comes time to vote."

"The movement Tess started," he repeated.

"Yeah. You must be pretty proud of her. You know, it's not every man who'll let his wife help out other people. Most of them want the little lady at home, to fetch and carry for them. I'll tell you, everyone around here's real grateful you let Miz Chisum get this thing started."

Stone turned away without another word and strode for the door.

"Uh . . . Chisum," Sid called after him. "Your account . . . ?"

"Talk to my wife about it!"

Chapter Thirty-two

"Excuse me, ladies," Stone gritted. "I'm afraid I'm going to have to postpone having that coffee with you. I need to speak to Tess."

Tess stared at Stone, sensing the barely held in check anger and realizing that he had called her Tess, instead of his wife, as he had seemed to make a point of doing since the ceremony at the Indian camp. He hadn't even removed his hat inside the café, but she could see the glint beneath his half-mast eyelids—a spark in the brown depths that boded the start of another one of their confrontations. What on earth had she done now? She hadn't even been with him the past half hour.

The other three women started to stand, but Stone waved them back to their seats.

"No, don't bother," he said. "We'll go outside. Here." He laid a coin on the table. "That will take care of your drinks, and maybe we can do this another time."

Against her will, Tess pushed back her chair. "I'll see you later, Tillie. It was nice to meet you, Edith and Fredwina."

"Don't forget the Ladies' Guild meeting next Thursday, Tess," Tillie said. "We'll finalize the plans for the reception Saturday evening then." She glanced up at Stone. "That is, if it's all right with your husband."

"I'm sure it will be fine," she replied. When Stone's lips tightened even further at her words she threw him a puzzled look. "We don't have any plans for Saturday evening, do we, Stone?"

"We'll discuss it," he shot back before he turned and strode out of the café.

"Oh, my," Fredwina tittered. "What have you done to upset him, my dear? I guess at the meeting on Thursday we'll have to let you in on some of our little secrets about how to get our own way with our men, yet let them think it's their own idea."

Embarrassed that the women had noticed Stone's attitude, Tess ducked her head and picked up the package holding her denims and shirt. Her embarrassment quickly shifted into resentment at Stone's high-handedness. She tucked the package under her arm and picked up her coffee cup, draining it and carefully placing it back in the saucer.

"I've enjoyed talking with you ladies," she said. "And I'm looking forward to joining your meetings. Tillie, I'm glad you told me how the Guild women helped Mandy Calder with the campaign against the taxes. Maybe we can find another cause to pursue as soon as this one's successful."

Tillie looked through the plate-glass window and

saw Stone pacing back and forth on the walkway. "Well, we can talk about it Thursday."

"There were a couple of things I thought we could be thinking about," Tess continued, refusing to acknowledge the fact that all three of the other women clearly thought she ought to be hurrying outside to kiss her husband's ass. "I think it's a mistake for the schools that have been set up for the Indian children to try to erase the children's heritage from their lives. After all, our country was founded by a melting pot of different cultures, not repression.

"And speaking of repression." She poured another dab of coffee from the pot on the table into her cup. "I think it's time women voted. I'm sure you're aware that even the male slaves were given the vote after the war."

"You know," Edith said as Tess sipped her coffee, "that's something that's been bothering me for a long time. We're smart enough to raise our children, teach them, and manage a household. But we're not smart enough to help choose the leaders of our country."

Edith tilted her head and giggled. "My husband doesn't know it, because I always pick up the mail, but I've been getting some of those pamphlets from other women's groups speaking out for us to get the vote. I'll bring them with me to the meeting."

"Can I come on home with you and look at them now?" Fredwina said eagerly. "Your husband's off with mine on that cattle-buying trip. We don't have to worry about them catching us."

"Of course," Edith said. "Let's go right now. Do you want to come, too, Tillie?"

"I surely do." Tillie rose to her feet and nudged

Tess with her elbow. "I think you've made your point by now, my dear. But would you like us to walk out with you?"

"I'll finish this last drop of coffee first," she said with a grin.

But as soon as the other women left, her smile deteriorated. She gave a deep sigh of resignation and set down her coffee cup. Her reluctant legs carried her toward the door, but as she reached for the doorknob, her shoulders stiffened.

"It's about damned time . . ."

"You embarrassed me in there," she interrupted. "I am not your chattel—I'm your wife."

"What the hell's that supposed to mean?"

"It means that if you think I'm going to drop whatever I'm doing every time you crook your little finger and beckon me, you've got another think coming!"

"You sure as hell made that clear, didn't you? I've been standing out here for ten minutes!"

"Tough. I was having a discussion with my friends, and I didn't appreciate you storming in there and acting like Genghis Khan! I'm sure Tillie and the other women were embarrassed, too."

"You want to talk about embarrassment?" Stone grabbed something out of his shirt pocket and thrust it under her nose. "This is your own damned bankbook. I transferred the money you put into my account into one of your own. I don't appreciate the whole town knowing my wife's paying my bills—especially when she's doing it with money she made selling jewelry given to her by another man!"

"Banking business is supposed to be private," she gasped.

"Then you admit it," he said through clenched teeth. "Your old lover gave you that ring. And the news didn't get around from the bank itself. You think Sid's gonna keep quiet about something like that? Or the banker's wife while she flashes that ring in the eyes of every woman in this town? And the other women, who tell their husbands?"

Stone shoved the bankbook at her again, but she clasped her hands behind her back. He glowered at her for another moment, then slipped the bankbook into the low-cut bodice of her dress.

"We're going home," he said angrily. "We can talk about this there, where we won't be making a scene that'll add fuel to this town's gossip mill."

He whirled and strode down the walkway, pausing after a few feet to glare back at her. "Come on!"

She nonchalantly picked out the bankbook from her bodice and placed it in her skirt pocket. "Just leave Sateen at the stable for me and I'll be home later. I've got a couple of more things to do."

"I suppose you want to check on your *campaign.*"

"That's one thing," she replied in a mild voice. And she was sure she could find a few more errands to keep her busy, at least long enough for his temper to cool before she returned to the ranch.

"Don't forget to pay your account with Sid!" he snarled before he turned away.

"Oh, boy," she breathed. "Oh, boy, oh, boy, oh, boy."

She stood rock-still, watching Stone as he arrived at the stable yard and tossed Jake a coin. He climbed through the gate and called his gelding to him, then threw the tack on and caught Jasper's mare and the gray gelding, tying both lead ropes to his saddlehorn before he led the horses outside the corral. Ignoring Lonesome, who pulled on the rope tied around his neck in an attempt to follow him, Stone mounted and reined his gelding around.

She waited to see what he would do. The road to his ranch led through town, but when he saw her still watching, he reined his gelding back past the stable.

Childish, she thought to herself. He'd rather ride out around town than pass by her. She resolutely shoved aside the additional thought that tried to crowd in about her rather immature actions in making Stone wait for her on the boardwalk.

Oh, no, not childish, her mind continued. That was a man's anger she had faced. Unjustified anger, she tried to tell herself. She hadn't purposely not told him about the money from the ring. She just hadn't thought real hard about whether she should tell him or not.

Not true.

"Oh, shut up," she murmured. "Okay. Maybe I was a little bit afraid of how he'd react. But I've been handling my own business for years—all my life. Anyway, he needn't think I'm going to ask his permission every time I want to do something on my own. That campaign against the taxes benefitted a lot more people than just him."

"That it did, my dear." Tess turned to see Mandy Calder behind her. "Or, at least it's looking like it will."

Mandy stepped up and took Tess's hands in her own. "I understand congratulations are in order, Mrs. Chisum. Or I guess the congratulations are supposed to go to your new husband, and my wishes for happiness to you—according to the manners book, anyway."

"Thank you," she said. "I think."

"Don't worry, Tess." Mandy laughed. "All our men have us talking to ourselves at one time or another. We women understand how it is with each other."

"Were you saying that the campaign against the taxes is doing well?" she asked to change the subject. "Tillie already mentioned that she and the Guild were involved."

"And our town's attorney, too," Mandy said. "Jack Pierce. Why don't we walk over and let him tell you about it?"

Mandy slipped her arm through Tess's and they stepped into the street.

"We decided that letter writing was too slow," Mandy explained as they crossed the street. "The money you gave us was put to good use. We started a telegram campaign, and the whole territory got word faster and joined in with us. The next land rush is scheduled for the middle of this month, and the taxes were supposed to go into effect the day before it. We wanted the entire thing settled before then."

"I wish I'd been here to do my part. But Stone was going out after some wild horses by himself. After what happened with that snakebite the last time I figured I should go with him."

"And I'll bet he didn't appreciate your concern one bit, did he?"

"No," she admitted dryly. "He also didn't appreciate the fact that I'd started this tax campaign without asking his *permission.*"

"Oh, dear." Mandy paused in front of the lawyer's office. "I see why you were standing there grumbling. I saw Stone ride out. I guessed you'd had a few words before he left."

"More than a few."

The office door opened, and the dapper little man who appeared drew back in surprise.

"Hello, ladies," he said. "Were you coming to see me?"

"No, Jack," Mandy said. "We were just taking a shortcut through your office to the alley in back."

"Help yourself," he replied with a grin.

His bantering tone made Tess like him immediately, and she held out her hand.

"I'm Tess Fos . . . Chisum, Mr. Pierce. I understand from Mandy that you've been assisting the Guild on the tax campaign."

"We elected him the head of it, Tess," Mandy informed her. "We thought we'd have more clout if we had a man as our committee leader. You know how it is."

"Yes," she admitted. "I'm afraid I do."

"Well, I didn't have much to do," Jack said deprecatingly. "Mandy explained the plan you laid out for her, and I just pointed them in the right direction. Your plan tied up everything neatly, Mrs. . . . uh . . . Chisum, did you say? I assume you and Stone must have just recently married."

"You're probably the last person to know that, Mr. Pierce, even though we only arrived in town an hour ago." She laughed. "And please, it's Tess. I'm still not quite used to my name change."

"Fine. And it's Jack to you. Come on in, ladies." He held the door for them. "I can do my errand later."

Tess immediately walked over to the few law books Jack had on a shelf, her eyes avidly searching the titles. The law library in her New York firm covered half of one floor in the tri-story suites of rooms the firm occupied. She slowly shook her head. Stone was probably right about one thing: The law was way too complicated. People governed themselves fairly well in this time period, though life was less complex. But then, if the laws were simplified, how would lawyers make a living?

Her last thought brought a rueful smile to her lips.

"Are you interested in the law, Tess?" Jack said beside her.

Tiring of the charade she had been living the last few weeks, she replied, "I'd better be, since I'm a lawyer."

Jack scratched his graying head. "I hadn't heard that women were being admitted to practice. I'm gonna have to start attending our yearly conventions back East again. Haven't been for the last few years."

"Women will be doing a lot of things men never thought they were smart enough to do over the next few generations," she answered. "You men had better start getting used to that."

"Guess I should have had an inkling that you had some sort of training," Jack mused. "Say, let's look at the folder I started for the committee, and let me show you how well everything's coming together."

Over the next few minutes Tess found her pride in herself growing by leaps and bounds. She'd never felt this sort of stirring even when she'd won an especially difficult decision in favor of a client company. Maybe that was it: She had always used her talents and sharp mind for the benefit of corporate conglomerations, telling herself she was saving jobs for their employees. Now her plan had directly benefitted a group of people who were part of her life.

And directly benefitted the man she loved—even if he wouldn't admit it yet.

"Stone should be pleased," she told Jack.

"Yes, the homesteaders who know about you being the one to start this drive are all grateful your man allowed you out of the kitchen long enough to help them out," he said. "Especially when he didn't have to worry himself."

She looked up from the file in astonishment. "He? You mean Stone? Stone didn't have to worry about paying these taxes?"

"Of course not," Jack said, frowning. "Why should he? His land came to him from the Cherokee, namely Silver Eagle—not under the Homestead Laws. I'll admit, I had to get the transfer approved through the Indian Bureau, but what with Stone raising those two Indian children, I didn't have a problem at all. Especially since Silver Eagle wanted the kids' names on the deed, too."

"Does Stone know this?"

"About the kids' names being on the deed? Sure; I gave him a copy of it."

"No. No, I mean about his land not being subject to these taxes."

"Well, that could change in the future," Jack admitted. "But to answer your question, I don't rightly recall ever talking about that very point with Stone. All he'd've had to do was come and ask me about it, though."

"Thank you, Jack." She rose and shook the lawyer's hand. "I have to get out to the ranch."

"Not before you answer a question for me, I hope," he said, refusing to relinquish her hand.

"Of course."

"I just want to find out if I'm going to have some competition around here."

"Why, Jack, lawyers have to keep things confidential."

She pulled her hand free and headed for the door. "See you Thursday, Mandy," she called.

As she opened the door, she glanced back and caught the woebegone look on the other attorney's face. She really liked him—she shouldn't leave him hanging, especially after all the help he had been.

"Jack," she said, with her hand on the door, "I don't see how I'd have time to properly practice law with all the other things I have to do."

Jack returned her wink, and she hurried out the door and headed for the stable.

Chapter Thirty-three

Tess's excitement abated in direct proportion to the number of miles closer to the ranch she rode. She kept recalling Stone's anger-flecked eyes and snarling voice. He probably wasn't going to be a bit happy when she turned out to be the one who gave him the good news about his taxes. It would be just one more thing she had taken it upon herself to investigate without his knowledge.

It wouldn't matter that Jack had volunteered the information inadvertently and she had immediately picked up on it. The news would be another blow to Stone's own macho concept of himself.

Kill the messenger.

Oh, good grief, where had that thought come from? People didn't do that any longer. But that didn't mean the urge to do exactly that didn't crop up in the receivers of the messages.

She pulled Sateen down to a slow walk when she caught sight of the ranch up ahead and felt Lonesome shift as he lifted his head. In the corral beside the barn she saw Stone's horse and the gray gelding, along with Jasper's mare.

Good. With the man Stone had hired to look after the ranch while they were gone still there, surely Stone wouldn't start another battle with her. Would he?

Her stomach dropped an inch or so when she saw Jasper lead another horse from the barn, then walk to the corral and throw a rope over the wild mare's head. A moment later Jasper passed her, leading the mare behind him. He tipped his hat and nodded as he rode by.

Gathering every remnant of courage she could dredge up, she rode into the ranch yard. Lonesome leapt down by himself this time and ran around the yard to get reacquainted with his domain while she dismounted and unsaddled Sateen, promising her a rubdown in a little while as she led her into the corral. After closing the gate she turned, her eyes searching for Stone.

Maybe he was in the barn.

Surely he would have come out when he heard her ride in, though.

He must be in the house.

She glanced at the back porch and could see that the door was closed. On such a warm day Stone wouldn't have closed the door so the air couldn't circulate.

Had he gone somewhere? She should've asked Jasper.

She trudged toward the cabin. Just as she lifted

her foot to step onto the porch step, the back door opened and she froze.

Stone walked onto the porch and stopped above her, slipping his fingers into his back pockets. "You trying to imitate Lonesome when he marks his territory with that pose?"

She set her foot down with a clump and raised her chin as she climbed the steps. "You surprised me. I didn't think anyone was here, since the door was closed in this heat."

Backing away when she reached the porch, Stone asked, "You get all your business in town taken care of?"

All right, so he was still mad. She blew out an exasperated breath. "Can we please talk for a minute without throwing darts at each other?"

"I'm not fixing to throw anything at you." He spread his fingers and looked down at his empty hands. "Oh, I guess you mean word darts. You'll have to excuse my lack of understanding. I'm not as up on the tricks of language as you are."

Groaning under her breath, she walked over and sat down in the rocking chair. Maybe she'd appease him a little if she took the lower point of contact. At least, all the management courses she had ever taken had taught that the taller person always appeared dominant.

That didn't work, because Stone sat down on the top step and leaned against a support post. Well, at least he hadn't stomped off and ignored her.

Before she could lose her courage she quickly explained to him what she had learned about the taxes. She interspersed her explanation—much to her own disgust—with assurances that Jack had offered the information in the course of their conversation.

His face remained unreadable. Indeed, he only glanced at her one brief time, mostly keeping his gaze trained on the ranch yard. Boy, she'd hate to play poker with him!

She finally quit talking and stubbornly refused to utter even one more word until he responded to her information. She plopped her feet against the floor as soon as she realized the rocking chair was swinging back and forth in rapid sweeps, in time to her agitated thoughts. When he continued to stare off into space—the only sign of movement his clenching and unclenching jaw—she started to rise.

"That's good," he finally said, and she eased back into the chair. "There's plenty of other things I can use that money from the horses for."

"I . . . uh . . . I bought a pump at the store."

"Sid told me."

"Oh, I forgot to go over and pay my bill. I'll ride in tomorrow and do that."

"I'm sure Sid will appreciate that." He rose to his feet. "I'm going out to check the cattle; then I've got chores to do. Don't wait supper for me. I'll fix something when I come in."

She gripped the rocking chair arms until her fingers ached as he walked away. As soon as he entered the barn, she rose and stomped into the house, slamming the door behind her.

That's good. There's plenty of other things I can use that money from the horses for.

Well, what the hell had she expected? She'd known he wouldn't be pleased at receiving the news from her. And at least she'd escaped another chastising, male chauvinist lecture about sticking her nose into men's business.

She picked up a tin coffee cup Stone had left on the table and hurled it at the dry sink. It clattered loudly, and the coffee dregs spewed over the wobbly seamed curtains.

"Shit!" she spat, then for some reason clamped her hand over her mouth, horrified at the expletive. She could almost hear Granny's admonishing voice. But Granny had been dead fifteen years.

Her training hadn't died with her grandmother, she realized, though she had allowed that portion of Granny's teachings to sort of slide into the back of her mind these last few years.

She counted to ten, then walked out of the kitchen. She would spend the afternoon moving her remaining clothing from Flower's room to hers and Stone's bedroom.

At the door to their bedroom, she stopped, and her anger began to evaporate when she saw her backpack, which had been tied on the gray gelding, inside the open closet door. He had even laid his nightshirt, the one she had been wearing, on the bedspread.

Her eyes flew back to the closet. Stone's clothes weren't there! She ran over and peered inside, as though her actions would make the clothing materialize. She saw her other two dresses hanging on the rod, looking lonely in their solitude.

She hurried out of the room and opened the door to Rain's bedroom. It now held two beds, one of them a cot she hadn't seen before. Stone's bedroll—familiar to her from the nights she had already spent on it—lay open on the cot.

"You bastard!" she muttered. "I've heard of women withholding sex from their husbands to get their way, but if you think you're going to pull that on me, you'd better think again!"

She ran out the back door just as Stone was riding across the ranch yard. She raced down the steps and came to a halt with her hands perched on her hips.

"You get your ass back here, Stone Chisum!"

He pulled on the reins and the gelding stopped. He sat for a second, then neck-reined the gelding around until he faced her.

"What do you want?" he called.

She lifted her long skirt and paced toward him. "I want to know what the hell's going on. Did you shut the door so Jasper wouldn't walk in and see you moving your clothes out of our bedroom?"

The gelding shied away a step, but Stone bunched the reins tighter and held them in place. "It's your bedroom now. Flower and Rain will expect you to sleep in it."

"With you!" she yelled. "What the heck are we supposed to say to Flower and Rain? Tell them I've got a fever or something?"

"Tell them whatever you want to. A good lawyer can always twist the facts around to his own benefit."

"To her client's benefit," she gritted. "And a good lawyer doesn't twist the facts—she just brings them out in the right order, so the truth becomes known."

"Then tell the kids the truth," he began.

"Maybe I will—if you'll tell me what it is first!" She swept at a curl that had worked loose from the ribbon holding back her hair, impeding her vision. Fighting the urge to jerk him off that darned horse, she buried her hands in her skirt, her fingers flexing convulsively. Damn it, why didn't he answer her, instead of gazing anywhere except at her face.

"Tell them we got married too quick," he said at last, his words filling her with pain. "Tell them we aren't really suited to each other, and we don't want to take a chance on your getting with child at this point. Tell them . . ."

He reined away the gelding. "Aw, hell. Like I said, tell them whatever you want."

She gulped back sobs as he galloped out of the yard. The pain she had felt after Robert's betrayal paled in comparison to the stabs of agony creeping into her heart now. How many times had she read the words "a broken heart"? How well that described what was happening to her right now. Her heart was breaking into a thousand pieces, each one a jagged, saw-edged lump that tore at her chest.

She whirled and ran into the cabin. She raced down the hallway and threw herself on Stone's bed, pounding out her pain on the pillow as her sobs echoed in the empty room.

The next day, Tess rode into Clover Valley, paid her general store account, and made arrangements for Sid to hire a man to bring the pump and pipe out to the ranch when the equipment arrived from Oklahoma City. And, in a still simmering fit of rebellion, she bought two dresses for Flower and a shirt and denims for Rain. Browsing around the store, she found a shelf of lotions and perfumes, adding a couple of bottles of each for herself. A bolt of yellow material that would be perfect for window curtains came next. At least making curtains would give her something to fill the time, which looked like it might hang heavy until Stone stopped acting like such an ass.

She started to toss the pair of men's slippers she had picked up back on the shelf, then sniffed in disapproval of her actions and carried them to the counter. They weren't a peace offering. She only hoped they would remind Stone of that evening in the kitchen, when she had sensed that maybe he'd begun to care a little for her.

When she ran into Jack Pierce and he invited her for a cup of coffee she learned that she had misinterpreted Jack's expression in his office. If she hadn't left so quickly, the attorney told her, he would have explained that they really needed another lawyer in town. Jack's wife was threatening dire harm if he didn't cut back his long hours. In fact, he could probably refer enough clients to her so Tess could have a profitable practice built up in no time.

After assuring him that she would think over his proposition, she rode back to the ranch, wondering how she could take a bar exam and get licensed to practice a hundred years before she even went to school. Anyway, it gave her something else to think about besides Stone's asinine idea of withholding lovemaking to bend her to his will.

She distributed her purchases in the various ranch bedrooms before she built a fire in the stove and carried in several pails of water. She took a long bath that evening in the kitchen, hoping every noise she heard would herald the door opening and Stone walking in. But the hours passed as she waited for him and, growing tired, she finally fell asleep.

The next morning the only sign of Stone's presence in the house was the dirty plate from the supper she had left for him the night before. Frustrated, she left the curtain material in her closet. She needed a lot more physical action than sewing to work out her anger. She weeded Flower's garden—denuding dozens of stems in the rows of blossoms and putting a bouquet in each room, saving the prettiest one for the kitchen table. She stripped the beds and did the laundry, cursing the lack of pumped-in water with every bucket she carried from the well to heat on the stove.

She returned to the garden and picked everything she found ripe, storing almost all of it in the root cellar until Flower returned to help her can. She fixed a salad, new potatoes and green beans, and fried ham for supper, then sat at the table and watched the salad wilt and grease congeal around the crispy ham slices and on top of the bowl of green beans and potatoes.

A petal dropped from a wild rose onto the table, and she laid her head down and wailed.

The next morning Tess stumbled to the sink and splashed water from the bucket into her swollen red eyes. After patting her face dry with a hand towel she turned and stared at the table. Stone's slippers and bolo tie sat there—mocking her attempt at reconciliation.

Her lower lip trembled and her face started to crumble. Just as suddenly, anger rose inside her.

Her rage grew more quickly than her tears fell, and she glared at the gifts she'd given Stone until she was sure they would go up in flames from the heated sparks she could almost feel shooting from her eyes. Holding back a scream of fury, she stomped over and grabbed everything.

A few seconds later she emerged from the little building with the half moon on the door, brushing her hands together, her lips tight. One slipper and the tie were gone, but the other slipper was tucked, toe out, under the wooden cover over one hole. She wanted no shadow of a doubt in Stone's mind about where her gifts had gone.

Her anger carried her back into the cabin and through her packing. Her heart wrenched when she tossed the picture she had taken of Stone on the cot in Rain's room just before she headed out the door, but she quickly stifled her pain. A clean break—wasn't that what she'd always heard was best? No reminders—except her memories, of course.

She left her bankbook in the tack room, where Stone would surely see it and realize she hadn't stolen the tack for Sateen. As she was riding out of the yard, she remembered that today was Thursday, and she had promised to be at the Ladies' Guild meeting.

Too bad. She wasn't about to face the sympathetic looks of Tillie and her friends when they saw her swollen eyes. And there was no sense getting involved in anything else here in this time period. History would handle the problems in its own time.

She whistled for Lonesome and headed for the spot on the hill, where she had arrived in 1893.

* * *

"Don't you dare say a word, Michael," Angela warned. "I'm perfectly aware that you've had doubts all along about them making it together. But right now I'm too upset to listen to any of your I told you sos."

"Angie, honey, I'm just as upset as you are. Dash nab it, can't Stone see what he's losing? He's being a stubborn jackass!"

"Michael, watch your language."

He shot her a disgusted look. "Well, what the blue blazes would you call him, then?"

Reluctantly, she nodded. "A jackass. Or maybe even something worse, but I wouldn't say it out loud."

"Same thing." Michael smirked. "I can read what you're thinking."

"Yes, and I'm getting a little tired of that. If we had time, I'd stop and show you that I can block off my thoughts from you. But it takes a few minutes to do that."

"I suppose that's one thing you've neglected to teach me so far, huh?"

"Michael, we don't have time to argue right now. We've got to stay with Tess."

"Yeah, we've been arguing enough the last few days. I still think you should've let me bring Stone back into the cabin while Tess was taking a bath. One look at her, all rosy and pink . . ."

"Will you hush? Everything's falling apart. Tess isn't thinking straight. She should be fighting for her marriage to Stone, instead of letting her anger get the best of her. She's going to try to go back through that time warp to New York in retaliation for Stone's actions the past few days."

"You know, Angie," he mused, "far be it from me to try to second guess Mr. G, but do you really think He's going to let Tess find that time warp and go back home?"

"I keep telling you—"

"I know. I know! We aren't allowed to know what's going to happen. But . . . uh-oh. Look over there."

"Where?" Her head swiveled and Michael pointed. "That's Rose Brown. What's she doing here? She was supposed to go to that meeting in Clover Valley today, too."

"She probably figured that's where Tess would be, and this would be a good time for her to sneak over here and see Stone. Look. She's spotted Tess. Now she's . . . Angie, listen to what she's thinking! She's going to sneak around the other way and ambush Tess!"

"I told you that woman was wicked! Michael, sneeze or something. Get rid of her!"

"Now, just wait a minute."

Michael took her arms and led her higher, until they could see out over the hilltops. She kept insisting that he explain his plans to her, but he carefully kept his mind blank.

While she had her eyes on him, tugging at his sleeve, Michael dived back down, a satisfied look on his face.

"That woman has her rifle out down there, Angie. We better concentrate on Tess now."

"Tess doesn't have a gun!" she gasped. "She'll be shot!"

Michael waved his arm. "She does now," he said in a grim voice. "She'll just think she didn't notice that the rifle was in the scabbard when she saddled Sateen."

"As careful as Tess is around guns, you think she wouldn't notice a thing like that?"

"You have a better idea?"

"Yes. Sneeze Rose out of here!"

"Now, now. This is my assignment, and I've got it all figured out."

Chapter Thirty-four

Tess swiped at a tear running down her cheek. A sense of *déjà vu* swept over her as she dismounted and walked to the exact spot where she had been sitting so many weeks ago. She'd been telling herself on that day, too, that she was damned well not going to cry anymore.

Then, though, she had hiked up and down the Adirondack Mountains at a too-fast pace, attempting, she realized now, to outrun her embarrassment at being duped by Robert as much as her imagined broken heart. But this time there was no doubt in her mind that her heart would never heal. A very large piece of it was lying beside Stone's picture on his cot.

Blast it, she could've at least brought it with her. Keeping a firm hold on Sateen's reins, she knelt and stroked Lonesome's head.

"What do you think, boy?" she asked in a forlorn

voice. "Should I go back and at least get the picture? There's sure as heck no chance of running into Stone. You can bet your tail he won't be back until well after dark."

Lonesome whined and licked her face, flicking his tongue back and swiping at his nose when he tasted the salt there. He dropped down and laid his head on his front paws, his tail sweeping up a cloud of dust from the trail as he continued to whimper.

"Please don't cry, Lonesome," she said with a sniff of despair. "Don't you see—I just can't take anymore. He won't even talk to me so we can try and work things out. And even then, I don't know if talking would accomplish anything. He hates me. He doesn't even want to touch me. Darn it, he doesn't even want to see me."

Sateen nudged her back, and she rose to fling her arms around the mare's neck. Burying her face, she struggled against the threatening sobs. When she at last lifted her head she saw the corner of a rifle butt sticking up from the scabbard on the other side of the saddle and frowned.

"I don't remember that gun being there when I saddled you, Sateen." She shrugged and turned away from the mare. "What the heck? There's enough money in that bank account to pay Stone for it, too."

She chewed her bottom lip for a moment or so as she debated whether to go back for Stone's picture. She regretted throwing his slipper and tie down the toilet hole, too, but there wasn't much she could do about that now. His picture, though, would have been a precious reminder—not the painful memory she had thought she was leaving behind in her childish pique.

Cut off your nose to spite your face.

She groaned under her breath as another one of Granny's old sayings crept into her mind. That adage didn't apply just to his picture, either—she was allowing her stubbornness to cut Stone right out of her life.

It just wouldn't work, though. No matter how much she loved him, she would never be able to kowtow to a chauvinistic male who thought she had to ask his permission every time she even wanted to go to the bathroom. She choked back a laugh that was more a sob of misery as she pictured herself raising one finger or two, as Granny had told her that students had to do in school in her day.

No, it wouldn't work. Stone had made it clear the last three days that he wouldn't compromise with her. It had to be his way or none.

So none it had to be. She couldn't bear any more of the anguish she had suffered these last few days. When she had looked in the mirror this morning her red-rimmed eyes had shocked her, and she had realized they would destroy each other—destroy the wonderful love they had found.

And, yes, she had lied to Lonesome. She knew Stone still loved her, but they were worlds apart. His teasing jibes about being boss at his ranch were no joke, and she could never tolerate being dominated by him.

She grabbed Sateen's reins again and led the mare forward a couple of feet. She clicked her fingers at Lonesome, and the dog rose and walked to her. Staring around her for a few seconds, she assured herself that indeed this was the exact spot where she had been sitting when she realized she wasn't on Saddleback Mountain any longer.

So, now what? Should she close her eyes and click her heels together three times while she murmured, "I want to go home"? Recalling that Dorothy had had Toto in her arms, she reached down and hefted up Lonesome.

Lordy, the dog had gained weight. She hoped whatever happened would happen quickly, before she dropped the dog. Feeling sort of silly, she closed her eyes. She couldn't force herself to say the words, though—probably because the last thing in the world she really wanted to do was go back home.

The dog grew heavier and heavier as the long minutes passed. Finally he started squirming to get down, and she peeped through her eyelashes. Nothing had happened yet. She was still in Oklahoma. With a sigh, she bent down to set Lonesome on the ground.

Something whined over her head that sounded like an angry bee. A split second later she heard the crack of a rifle. Acting on instinct alone, she dropped the dog and screamed at him to run, then whirled in a crouch and scrambled around Sateen.

Another bullet kicked up dirt in front of the mare as she jerked the rifle from the scabbard and whacked Sateen on the rump. The mare leapt forward, and she dived behind a boulder on the hillside, gripping the rifle in her hands.

"Michael, what are you going to do?" Angela grabbed his arm and shook it. "That woman's going to kill Tess!"

"Angie, Angie, behave yourself. I thought you enjoyed watching what was going on down there—just like the movies."

"This isn't a movie!"

"Well, just pretend it is, honey." He patted her hand on his arm and settled back to watch the show.

Tess lay on the ground, rocks biting into her stomach and her fear giving way to fury. What the hell was going on? Who the hell was shooting at her?

And, yes, she acknowledged to herself—she was being shot at. One bullet might have been a stray from a hunter's gun, but not that second one, which barely missed her horse.

The first one, too, had been an attempt to kill her—and it would've done just that if she hadn't leaned down with Lonesome. She was getting damned good and tired of her whole experience here in Oklahoma. She'd suffered a broken ankle, a broken heart, and now someone wanted her dead.

Well, she'd just see about that!

Snarling in anger, she inched forward, trying to see around the boulder. Suddenly Lonesome began barking wildly, and she jerked around to see him near her feet.

"I told you to run, dog!" She started to shift around to call him nearer the boulder, where he would be better protected. Though she was lying flat, she felt her body tilt, as if the ground were giving away beneath her right leg. Lonesome leapt forward and grabbed her jeans, just above her left ankle, whimpering and tugging.

For just a second she thought perhaps the dog was trying to warn her of a snake in the rocks. Another bullet hit the boulder sheltering her, sending chips flying, and she instinctively rolled toward the dog. At the same time, she craned her neck to look for the snake. Horrified, she watched her right leg reappear from the void into which it had fallen.

The time warp! She could see it now—a black void stretching back along the hillside. She'd almost fallen through it again! No wonder she hadn't found it a while ago, back here behind the boulder. Maybe her impetus during her first flight through the warp had carried her out onto the hillside where she'd found herself. That would explain how she'd missed seeing it before.

Another bullet spat into the hillside beside her, and she flinched. It would be easy to enter the time warp and escape, but she had no intention of running from whoever was attacking her. Whoever it was would pay for scaring the hell out of her!

She belly-crawled forward and looked around the boulder. On the opposite hillside, she caught a glimpse of blond hair as someone ducked back behind a rock.

A blonde. Tillie Peterson was blond, but that rock didn't look big enough to shelter her. And why would Tillie want her dead? Tess pulled the rifle to her shoulder and drew a bead on the rock. Her bullet kicked up splinters when it hit, and she heard a cry just before a figure scrambled out and ran behind a larger rock, beneath an overhang on the hillside.

Rose Brown! That vicious bitch! Rose had made no bones about the fact that she wanted Stone, and she still thought she could have him if she got rid of Tess. As clearly as though she were reading Rose's mind, she knew what the other woman's plan was.

Rose would leave her lying out there for Stone to find, then be right there to console him over his wife's death. Catching the glint of sun on a rifle barrel, Tess barely drew back before the next bullet hit.

And she'd console Rain and Flower, too, Tess realized as she jacked another bullet into the rifle chamber. Flower already had reservations about Rose, but she might overlook them in her grief over Tess. A red haze appeared in front of her eyes, and she blinked rapidly and breathed in a few slow gulps of air until it cleared.

Well, she'd just see about that, too!

She jackknifed her body until she could sneak a look out on the other side of the rock. Yes, that would work. She didn't really want to kill the other woman, but something told her that she could if she had to. If it meant her life or Rose's, somehow she'd find the courage to send a bullet into the other woman's chest. But first she'd try something else.

Remembering Stone's instructions, she carefully centered the little bead on the front of the rifle barrel into the slot at the rear again. Her finger slowly tightened on the trigger. She didn't even feel the kick of the rifle this time, and she whooped with joy when the bullet plowed into the overhang above Rose's hiding place.

At first the rocks only creaked, and when Rose jumped up Tess shot again. Rose screamed in horror as the overhang gave way and tumbled down the hillside.

Tess scrambled up and whistled for Sateen. The mare galloped up to her, and she swung one-handed into the saddle, keeping the rifle in her grip. For just a second she could have sworn she heard the sound of hands clapping, but she shook her head after she glanced up at the sky. She was alone out here—except for that bitch who had been shooting at her. With Lonesome at Sateen's heels, they made their way down the hillside.

Tess kept watch on the rockslide, allowing Sateen to find her own footing. She saw Rose's rifle at the bottom of the hill, well below the tangled heap of beige riding skirt and blond hair lying amid the rocks. It hadn't been that large of a slide, and unless Rose had broken her neck or been knocked unconscious, she was probably only stunned.

Rose started moving. Tess could hear the groans as Rose shook off small pebbles and tried to gain her feet. She stopped at the bottom of the hill and dismounted to pick up Rose's rifle, which she shoved into her own scabbard.

Stone pulled his gelding to a halt as soon as he topped the ridge opposite the hill where he had first seen Tess. Even the echoes of the gunshots that had drawn him away from his hunting had faded by now, and he stared down the hillside, trying to determine what the heck had been going on.

Obviously, there had been a rockslide, and somehow Rose Brown had been caught in it. What had she been doing out here? And Tess was standing at the foot of the slide, glaring up at Rose instead of trying to help the other woman. Tess held his extra rifle, which he had left in the tack room, trained on the blonde.

He started to urge the gelding forward, then pulled back on the reins when he heard Rose scream out a curse.

"You bitch!" Rose screeched. "Why the hell did you have to show up?" She stumbled a few feet down the hillside toward Tess. "He was mine. All I wanted was a little more time!"

"If you're talking about Stone," Tess yelled back, "he's got too much sense to marry a she-goat like you! And if you had even a smidgen of the brains God gave a goose, you'd know that!"

"He would've needed me soon!" Rose screamed. "He didn't have any money—everyone in town knew he was having trouble paying his bills! He had to have money to replace the things he lost in the fire at the line shack, too!"

"A fire that you set, didn't you, Rose?" She narrowed her eyes as she recalled the problems Stone had been having. "And you poisoned his waterhole, didn't you? I'll bet you were damned upset when only a few of his steers died!"

"There would've been more if those two idiots I hired had finished the job!" Rose glared down at her. "I told them to get all the waterholes, so Stone would have to come to me and run any cattle he had left on my land. But they skipped out with my money before they finished the job!"

Tess swallowed her horror as she gazed up at Rose's hate-filled face. "You could have killed one of the kids! Flower or Rain might've taken a drink from one of those waterholes!"

"So what?" the blonde snarled. "Then they'd have been out of the way, too. We wouldn't have had to ship them off to some school and pay to keep them there."

"You're insane!" Tess gasped. "You don't care how many people you have to kill to get to Stone, do you? If I hadn't ducked with Lonesome, you would've killed me with that first shot!"

"I meant to. Oh, how much I meant to! I can't believe I missed you, you stupid . . . strumpet! You must have a damned guardian angel watching you. I've never missed a shot in my life!"

A movement above Rose drew Tess's eyes away for an instant, and she saw Stone riding down the hillside toward them, his face contorted in fury.

Rose raced toward her, stopping short a bare two yards away when Tess aimed her rifle at Rose's chest. Rose clenched her fists and raised her arms as she stared wild-eyed at the gun.

"If you didn't have that gun, I'd kill you with my bare hands!" she spat.

After glancing briefly up to see Stone riding his horse around the slide before he could reach them, Tess looked back at Rose. She sure as hell didn't need a man's help to take care of this blond-headed witch!

"And I also don't need a *gun* to take care of a bitch like you," she said aloud as she tossed the gun aside and lunged for Rose.

She caught Rose around the waist and they went down in a heap, screaming invectives as they rolled over and over in the rocks and dirt. Though Tess was larger, Rose's insane fury lent her strength, and she landed a blow on Tess's chin, snapping her head back. Tess responded with a right hook that knocked Rose completely off her, then scrambled to her knees and lunged again.

She got a handful of hair this time and jerked it loose, but Rose kicked her in the stomach. Tess omphed and rolled aside, and when Rose stood up to take another flying leap at her, she caught the blonde in the belly with her feet; her well-muscled legs tossed Rose over her head.

They scrambled to their feet and Tess reached out and spun Rose around with a vicious slap. Rose screeched in fury, then bent down and grabbed a rock. It whizzed by Tess's head when she darted aside. Tess locked her hands together and swung them, connecting with the side of Rose's head.

Rose crumbled to the dirt, and Tess stood over her, panting in both anger and exertion. She started to bend down and grab Rose, but a handful of dirt hit her full in the face.

Coughing and sputtering, Tess dropped onto Rose's body. She wrapped her arms around the blonde's neck and buried her face on her shoulder, wiping her eyes back and forth to try to clear them, while Rose pounded on her back. Rose gave a lurch, and they spun over and over once again, landing with Tess on top.

Rose arched her nails at Tess's face. "I'll kill you!" she screamed as Tess, her eyes now clearer but still blurry, somehow caught her hands. "I'll kill you! I'll kill you!"

Tess gritted her teeth and held on as Rose began bucking wildly beneath her. Rose jerked a hand free, and Tess landed a blow on Rose's nose with her fist. Blood spurted and her stomach heaved when she saw Rose's nose tilted to one side. There was a front tooth missing when Rose opened her mouth to scream in agony.

With everything in her, Tess wanted to leap to her feet and run away from the horrible, blood-smeared, puffy countenance she had created. Somehow she controlled her nausea and grabbed the neck of Rose's blouse, then lifted her clenched fist in readiness to land another blow.

Tossing her head to swing her tangled hair out of her eyes, Tess gritted, "I want you to tell me right now that you'll get out of Oklahoma and never come back. If you don't, I'm going to keep beating you until you do say it. And if you say it and I find you still here tomorrow, I'll catch you out somewhere and start in on you again."

"Tess," Stone said as he stood over the two women, "let the sheriff take care of her."

"We don't have enough evidence to send her to jail." She ignored the urge to look at him. "If we did, I'd prosecute the bitch myself! And you just stay the hell out of this!"

Holding up his hands in surrender, Stone backed away.

"Answer me, damn it!" She clenched her fingers tighter in Rose's blouse. Her fist wobbled, but she forced herself to say, "Or do you want more of the same?"

"No. No, please," Rose moaned. "I'll go. I'll leave. Just don't turn me over to the sheriff or hit me again."

Tess got to her feet, wiping her hands on the legs of her jeans and trying to ignore the sticky feel of blood on her knuckles. She stood over Rose, gulping in air as she watched the other woman lift a tentative hand to her face.

"You'll remember what you've done every time you look in the mirror for the rest of your life,

Rose Brown," she spat. "And I'll tell you another thing: I'm going to have you watched for as long as you live. You'll either send me your address from wherever you are or I'll hire someone to find you and I'll track down those men you hired to poison the waterhole. If their testimony won't convict you, I'll hound you until there's not a place left on this earth where you'll be able to live in peace. If you ever even think about harming another person, I'll know. And I'll hang your hide on a mesquite tree so anyone passing by will remember what happens to a woman who tries to harm a child."

Sobbing in misery, Rose rolled to her side and struggled to her feet. She stood swaying for a moment, then glanced up the hill.

"My horse is up there," she whined in a piteous voice.

"Then I guess you better get moving," Tess said as she took a step toward the blood-smeared blonde.

"I'm going!" Rose wobbled a few steps before she looked at her. "My . . . my rifle."

"You're out of your mind if you think I'm going to give that gun back to you. Move!"

"But my ranch . . . it's mine."

"You should've thought of that when you started setting fires and poisoning waterholes. I don't suppose there's any legal way I can keep you from selling it, but you do it by mail. And you use any money you get to stay the hell away from Oklahoma territory and my two kids!"

Rose started climbing the hillside, and Tess kept her gaze on the blonde. At one point she marched over and picked up her rifle.

"If she's got another gun on her horse, she's going to get a surprise," she murmured.

Finally Rose disappeared over the top of the hill. A few seconds later there was the sound of a horse galloping away. Tess waited for at least a minute after the hoofbeats faded before she rounded on Stone.

"Now you!"

Chapter Thirty-five

"I'm sorry," Stone hurriedly said, raising his hands shoulder high. "I apologize. I've been acting like an ass, when I should've been proud of what you were doing. I was coming home today to tell you how sorry I was."

"Sure," Tess sneered. "You can say that now, after I've spent all this time feeling like you'd stopped caring for me. Do you have any idea what I've gone through the last few days?"

"Yeah," he said in a soft voice. "I've been going through it, too."

"I don't much give a damn! Do you hear that? I could care less how you've been feeling. I've spent three days in hell, and to top that off I've been shot at and ended up in a fight with a blond bimbo who thought she'd crawl into your bed as soon as I was dead. That same bed that you've been denying me because you think I'll get so lonely I'll crawl to you on my hands and knees and beg you to forgive me for something that I've got every right to do."

"I agree," he began, but Tess waved around the rifle and continued to yell.

"I pull my weight around that ranch. I cook your meals, wash your dirty clothes, and teach my kids. Do you know how many buckets of water it takes from that stupid well to wash a week's worth of laundry?"

He did, but he wasn't about to try to tell her that—not with the rifle wavering in front of his face.

"I counted them yesterday," she went on. "Twenty buckets of water. And I'll bet you that well's a hundred feet deep."

"A hundred and twenty-five," he whispered to himself.

"So if you think I'm going to tell Sid to cancel that pipe order, I'm not!"

"All right." He could feel his patience starting to slip. "But anything you buy with that damned money you've got had better be to make things easier on you and Flower. I don't want one penny of it spent on me."

"Fine," she agreed. "But I'm not going to come to you with my hat in my hand every time I want a few dollars to spend."

Suddenly Tess blinked and stared at the rifle, then glanced down at her finger.

"You either need to put down that gun or go ahead and shoot me," he said. "My arms are going to sleep."

She inched her finger away from the trigger guard and shifted the rifle into her arms. She tilted her head a little, studying his face.

"You can put your hands down now," she finally said.

He dropped his arms and took a step forward. Tess shook her head and backed away.

"We're not done talking yet," she insisted.

"Is that what we've been doing?" he asked. "I thought you were issuing ultimatums and I was agreeing with them."

"Was I?" she murmured. "Oh. Well, let's hear your side of it now."

"My side of it's just this: I love you. Whether you believe me or not, I've thought of you every second the past few days. I finally realized that part of the reason I fell in love with you was because I admired and respected you. If I try to change you, you won't be the Tess I fell in love with." He chuckled wryly. "Not that I'd have any success at trying to do that anyway."

"Yes, you will." She threw the rifle aside and ran into his arms. "I love you. All I need to know is that you love me, too, and we can work out anything. I promise we can."

He buried his face in her hair and held her tightly. "God, I've been so miserable," he whispered. "And I was so damned scared when I found you out here. Not just because of Rose, either."

She jerked away, her eyes starting to flash again. "What's that supposed to mean? It didn't bother you that that bitch was trying to kill me?"

"Damn it! Of course it did. But you were taking care of that without any help from me. What really scared the daylights out of me was you being out here—like you were trying to find your way back to where you'd come from. Like you'd finally gotten fed up and wanted to leave me for good."

"Oh."

"Is that it? 'Oh'?"

Tess shrugged, and stared at the ground. "Well, even though I found the time warp, I didn't really want to go." She raised her head and laid her hand on his chest. "Let's go home, Stone. I want to go home."

"In a minute," he whispered as he pulled her close and kissed her.

But it was a lot longer than a minute. Michael had plenty of time to savor the success of his plan and explain to Angela just how he'd accomplished it as they flew well away from the hillside, where Stone was making love to Tess.

"I put blanks in both their rifles," he told his angel partner. "I didn't want to be a part of either one of them getting killed or wounded. I knew Stone was just over the hill, and that the gunfire would bring him running. Not that Tess ended up needing him."

"It worked out beautifully," Angela admitted. "But what about that fight between Tess and Rose?"

"Hey, you can't blame that on me. That was all Tess's idea. She lost her temper and tore into Rose all on her own. Other than changing the bullets to blanks, all I did was help that slide out a little bit."

"I still can't believe Tess let that . . . that blond bimbo go."

"Angie," he said in mock horror. "Watch your language!"

She blushed prettily. "Well, I can't. Stone heard Rose's confession, too. Wouldn't that have been enough to put her behind bars?"

"Tess evidently didn't think so, and she's the lawyer. 'Course, Tess is thinking in terms of law back in 1994. But you've gotta remember that, even though she chose to go into corporate law, she had training in the criminal end of it in law school. And sometimes even their corporate clients end up breaking other laws—or their kids do, and they come to the first lawyer they can think of when they need one."

"Maybe she handled Rose the best way," Angela mused. "Can you imagine living the rest of your life looking over your shoulder—knowing someone's always out there watching you—waiting for her to show up at any minute?" Angela gave a delicate shiver.

He guffawed. "Yeah, and what about looking in the mirror every morning and seeing that missing tooth? There are no dentists back here who know how to put a missing tooth back in. Anyway, Rose swallowed it. I don't imagine she'll . . ."

"Oh, hush," Angela giggled. "You know," she continued when her giggles had subsided, "you've been doing so well on this assignment that you really don't need my tutoring any longer."

"So what's that supposed to mean?" he asked in a worried voice.

"I thought you understood. My job's just to teach you what you need to know about being a guardian angel, although I think I've learned a lot myself on this assignment. Anyway, when you're capable of carrying on alone, I'm supposed to go back and see who my next pupil is."

"You mean, leave me? Angie, honey, you can't do that!"

"But I . . ."

"Look, they can get hold of you if they need to, can't they?"

"Yes, but . . ."

"Don't you want to see what's going to happen with Tess and Stone? And don't they ever let angels work in pairs?"

"Of course I want to know if Tess stays here, but you can tell me later. And it's very rare for angels to work in pairs. I've only heard of one other case, and those two actually requested it."

"You can't go yet, Angie," he said suddenly. "I'm still not comfortable navigating my wings. You haven't taught me how to concentrate on my guardianship duties and still fly at the same time."

"Oh. If you're still uncomfortable doing that, then you're right. We'll have to take care of it, won't we?"

"Darn right we will." He grinned to himself. "We'll have to practice those freewheeling flights we've been doing some more. I'm sure that sooner or later I'll get the hang of it."

Or, he continued, forgetting to block his thoughts from Angela, *when we get a break here I'll see if Angie wants to go with me and talk to Mr. G. Shoot, we've got a good team going here. He might let us stay together.*

He glanced at Angela and saw a brilliant smile on her face, immediately realizing she'd read his mind. Her smile must mean she agreed with him.

"Well?" he asked.

"I think that's a wonderful idea." She sighed.

Chapter Thirty-six

Stone propped his head on his hand and watched Tess climb out of the creek bed. Water streamed down her shapely body as she paused to wring out her hair, and he eyed the tiny bathing suit she wore with appreciation. Who'd have ever thought a couple of scraps of material like that could tantalize him even more than her naked body? Dressmakers in the future sure knew what they were doing when it came to stirring up a man's fantasies.

The future. Damn it, if he could only stop thinking about finding Tess on that hillside—her admitting that she'd been searching for the time warp. He'd been stupid to waste even one minute separated from Tess, let alone almost three entire days. He should have been securing his relationship with her, loving her day in and night out, as he had been the days since her fight with Rose. Maybe then the thought of leaving him never would have crossed her mind.

Would she always feel she had that option when they disagreed, as they surely would from time to time? He couldn't live with that uncertainty—yet he couldn't bring himself to confront her, ask for her promise to never, ever go near that time warp again.

The kids were due home today, the Sunday two weeks after they had left. He should have felt a little guilty about neglecting his work the past few days since he and Tess had arrived home, but he couldn't find even a speck of remorse in his conscience. And he'd already decided to talk to Jasper about becoming a permanent hired hand.

As soon as he discussed it with Tess, of course. After all, she'd be the one who would have to do extra cooking for another mouth, and extra washing, which Jasper would expect to be part of his wages.

One thing he could do was order one of those wooden washing machines from Germany that he'd read about. Some of the money he'd got for those horses would buy that, especially since he didn't have to worry about the taxes. And who knew? Maybe someday someone would use this new electricity they claimed to have invented to make a few machines to lighten the workload for women. Harvesters, for both baling and threshing, and cotton gins were fairly common now, and a harvester was on his want list. He still couldn't quite figure out how that horseless carriage worked, though.

"Whoo hoo! Where is everybody?"

Lonesome jumped up barking and Tess let out a gasp.

"Stone, that's Tillie. What's she going to say when she sees me in this bikini? Oh, why didn't I bring my clothes with me?"

He tossed his shirt to her with a laugh and stood up. "Let's just hope I've got time to get my jeans on before she gets here. My underwear floated away while we were . . . busy."

"Busy getting into trouble." Tess giggled as she slipped into his shirt and worked on the buttons.

"Huh-uh," he said with a wicked grin. "Trouble was busy getting into . . ."

"Stone!" A blush stole over her cheeks. "Oh, no! Lonesome, come back here!"

Tess took off after the dog, expecting any second to hear a wild screech from Tillie. But when she ran out from the trees lining the creek bed she found Tillie standing with one hand on a slightly slimmer hip, shaking a finger at Lonesome.

"Now, we're going to come to terms, dog," Tillie said. "I'm going to be a frequent visitor here, and I'm not about to have to worry about repairing my skirts every time I go home. Do you hear me?"

Lonesome sat down on his haunches and lifted a paw.

"That's much better." Tillie shook the paw, then looked up at Tess.

"There you are. It's so hot, I thought maybe you'd be taking a swim when I found the house empty. I drove out to see why you weren't there for our meeting, and to tell you all the latest news."

"Let's go on back to the house . . ." she began.

Tillie glanced over Tess's shoulder and snickered. "Oh, my. Did I interrupt something?"

"Would it bother you if you had?" Stone asked as he walked up to them, wearing his jeans and a towel draped around his neck. "Remember, we're married now. We can't be part of all the juicy gossip in town any longer."

"Such a shame," Tillie replied with pursed lips. "I did so enjoy keeping you on your toes, Stone. But I guess I'll have to turn that job over to Tess now. She seems perfectly capable of handling it to me."

Stone threw back his head and laughed. "That she is, Tillie."

"Well, I did want to let you both know that I sponsored a change to the bylaws for our Guild. We're going to get involved in social issues, too, not just things that affect the town. After what you said, Tess, we decided to start a drive to integrate our school in Clover Valley—allow children of any race to attend, and get a teacher who can teach the different cultures to all the children."

"Tillie, that's wonderful," she said. "Your Guild will be well ahead of its time in doing something like that."

They started walking toward the house as Tillie explained, "Things will never get done if people don't start working on them. Uh . . . I wanted to talk to you about one other thing, too, Stone."

"What's that, Tillie?"

"Daddy's home. At my house, I mean."

"He's done his time, Tillie. I've no quarrel with him, as long as he doesn't pick one with me."

"Good," Tillie said.

"Besides, I think you might need him around to shuffle through your suitors if you keep losing weight the way it looks as if you've been doing."

"Can you tell already?" Tillie simpered.

"Sure can. Good thing I'm safely married now."

Tess swatted him on the arm. "And don't you forget it, either."

"I won't, I won't." Stone raised his hands in mock alarm. "I'm outnumbered here. I'll get on with my work and let you ladies gossip."

"Gossip!" Tess said. "Why is it that when men talk about each other, it's a discussion, but women gossip?" She shook a finger at him. "You'd better watch out, or your chauvinistic tongue will get you into more trouble."

"Not trouble. Oh, please, not trouble," he groaned. "Trouble's tired."

Tillie smiled and shook her head as they broke up in laughter. When Stone walked away Tillie and Tess started for the porch, and Tillie gave her a nudge and a teasing look.

"I don't guess you're going to need any of Fredwina's lessons, are you?"

"Not yet," she agreed as they climbed the steps. "Let me go get some clothes on, Tillie."

"Please don't bother." Tillie sat in the rocking chair, smiling. "I can only stay for a moment. I just wanted to make sure you hadn't changed your mind about joining our Guild."

Tess dropped down on the porch step and curled her legs beneath the hem of Stone's shirt. "No, I haven't. Something just . . . came up this week, and I couldn't attend."

"Rose Brown wasn't there either. It's the most amazing thing. I heard she'd moved without even a word to anyone. I drove by her place on my way out here, and she's gone, all right. The place is deserted."

Tillie tapped the floor and set the chair to rocking. "And you know what else is funny? Even though she didn't say a word to anyone, she left a note on the table saying she'd be in New Orleans. That's where she used to live, you know. Anyway, I've been thinking about maybe buying her place and building a newer house there. Daddy's so bored in town, and he could have a little garden—maybe raise some chickens or something."

"I'd like to have you for a neighbor," Tess said. "But I thought your father was more of a professional man."

"He took up gardening in prison," Tillie said without embarrassment. "He said he found out he had a green thumb, whatever that means. But he says he can grow beautiful flowers. I thought perhaps your Flower would sell him some seeds and bulbs."

My Flower, she thought to herself with a smile. Flower was her daughter now, and Rain her son. She couldn't wait for them to come home and be part of her family. She and Stone—and *Trouble*—would still have their nights.

"Uh . . . Tess, is something wrong?" Tillie asked. "You're not listening."

She shook herself back to reality. "No, Tillie. Everything's fine. As I said, it will be nice having a neighbor I like. I never really cared for Rose."

"I don't doubt that." Tillie giggled. "We all knew she had her eye on Stone. Maybe that's why she packed up and left—she knew with you in the picture Stone would never, ever give her a glance. Not that he ever did, but Rose couldn't see that—though I liked to tease Stone about her."

Tillie stopped the chair and stood up. "I really should be going. I'm due at Edith's for lunch. Would you do me a favor, though, Tess?"

"If I can."

"You know that Stone and I don't—well, to put it mildly—we don't quite see eye to eye about things. I'm afraid if I ask him, he'll turn me down flat."

She raised her eyebrows and waited for Tillie to continue.

"'Course I have to check with Jack first and see if he can find Rose," Tillie mused. "But Daddy's just not up to doing a lot more than his gardening, and it would be a shame for all the rest of that land not to be used."

"Are you trying to say that you want to lease the land you can't use if you buy Rose's ranch, Tillie?"

"Lease it with an option to buy whenever Stone can afford it," Tillie said. "Do you think Stone would be interested? Oh, probably not, coming from me. After all, I sure gave him a lot of problems, butting into his business. I know he's acting as if he might have forgiven me, but . . ."

"If he won't, I will, Tillie. Stone needs more land if he wants his ranch to grow. But I wouldn't lease or buy the land without discussing it with him first."

"He'll probably say no."

"You let me work on that. Okay, Tillie?"

Tillie returned Tess's wink and walked down the steps. "Don't forget next Thursday," she called as she headed for her buggy. "We're going to have weekly meetings for a while, instead of bimonthly. Just until we get a handle on the new direction we want the Guild to take. And we still have to plan that reception for you and Stone."

"I'll be there." Tess crossed to the rocking chair Tillie had vacated and sat down, keeping one eye on the barn in case Stone decided to take a break and join her. He'd spent a lot of time with her the last few days, but she knew he did have chores to do. She would try to tolerate his almost workaholic attitude as best she could. Maybe they could afford a hired hand.

She mentally bit her tongue when the thought flitted across her mind that they could most definitely afford to hire help if Stone would allow her to help pay for it, until the profits from the ranch were enough to afford the hand's wages. Tillie's idea was logical, also, and Tess had been fairly confident as she'd assured Tillie that she might buy the land herself. Yet she had felt compelled to add it would only be after a discussion with Stone.

They still had so many things to work out. She really wanted to talk to Jack Pierce about doing just some part-time legal work with him, but she would have to catch Stone in the right mood to discuss that. And she wanted all the discussions she and Stone shared from now on to be carried out in a mature manner. She was committed totally to him now, and she would never, ever childishly threaten him with going back through the time warp if she didn't get her own way.

As much as they had enjoyed the past few days since they had found each other again on the hillside, she sensed just a tiny reserve in Stone. Tonight, after the kids went to bed, she would have a heart-to-heart with him, and give him her solemn promise to always work things out between them.

She looked at the corral when a flicker of movement caught her eye. Sateen trotted out from behind the barn and over to the fence, nickering in Tess's direction. The mare obviously wanted to be exercised, as had become Tess's daily habit. But she wanted to wait until Stone could join her, and he was busy right now.

She frowned as she stared at the horse. Sateen's presence was the one thing for which she couldn't find a rational answer. She had accepted the fact that she had fallen into a time warp—one waiting to engulf her when she fell down the mountainside. But Sateen? How had the mare got here?

Another idea had been tugging at her mind, too, since she now knew exactly where the time warp was. What would it hurt for her to at least take the computer and diskettes back and leave them on Saddleback Mountain, with a note telling whoever found them to deliver them to the law firm? Someone would surely notice them on the hiking trail sooner or later. She had no idea how much time had passed back in her former life, but even if Robert's former company's attorneys had won a summary judgment, it could be appealed for up to thirty days afterward.

She continued to feel a stab of guilt now and then about having the necessary documentation with her to clear Robert, although she had absolutely no feelings left for her ex-fiancé. But she had no desire for revenge against him, either. She just hadn't been able to figure out how to approach Stone about her idea.

When she turned her gaze away from Sateen she saw three riders far down the road and recognized Rain's gray gelding. Silver Eagle was bringing the kids home. After glancing down at her bare legs she walked into the house to get dressed. The shaman had been shocked to find his granddaughter in pants; what would he say if he found Flower's mother prancing around half naked?

In deference to Silver Eagle she slipped on one of her dresses. Tess wished the weather would break. Back in the Adirondacks there were probably already signs of fall in the air, but she didn't really know whether Oklahoma's leaves changed each year. She did remember seeing weather reports of snow in the winter down here. And one of the firm's attorneys had come back from a spring seminar in Dallas raving about the beautiful wildflowers and dogwood he'd seen on a tour of the area. She'd bet spring would be gorgeous here.

When she stepped out on the porch again she saw Silver Eagle and the children dragging a bundle from the barn. A second later, she realized it was the tepee. At the Cherokee camp some families still lived in their tepees, although a few had already begun building permanent houses. She guessed the shaman must be planning to stay for a few days.

Rain and Flower caught sight of her and raced to the cabin, where Rain overcame his little-boy reluctance and hugged her tightly, along with Flower. They both began chattering at once, trying to fill her in on their visit to the Cherokee all in one breath.

"Whoa," she finally said. "You'll both have plenty of time to tell me everything you've done. Let me go say hello to your grandfather. And I'd like to learn how that tepee goes together, since I was busy in the cabin the last time it was put up."

She hugged them both again, one in each arm. "I'm really glad you're home, kids. I've missed you."

"Us, too," Flower said as she linked her arm with Tess's and walked out into the yard. "But the nicest thing was that we knew when we came home this time you'd be our real mother. With you and Pa married, I mean. Tess, you won't go away now, will you?"

"I'm going to be your mother forever," she reassured her. "You won't have to worry about that ever again."

Flower gave a deep, contented sigh, and Silver Eagle held out his hand as they approached. But Tess stepped up and kissed his weathered cheek. "Welcome to our home," she said. "I wanted to ask you if it's all right for me to call you Father now."

"You are the mother of my grandchildren," the shaman said with a smile. "I would be honored."

"I'm the one who's proud of it," she replied. "I hope you're planning to stay for a while."

"Only for two days. We have a saying among the Cherokee that fish and relatives smell after three days."

She laughed gaily. "I thought that was a white saying. Can I get you any bedding or . . ."

"Tess," Flower hastily put in. "Wait 'til you see what I made for you at the camp." She grabbed her arm and started to pull her away, but Silver Eagle shook his head at her.

"It is—how does your new mother say—okay, Flower," he said. "She has only been part of the Cherokee for a few weeks. You can teach her our customs."

"What's wrong?" Tess asked, frowning. "I did the wash—everything's clean."

Rain snickered, but cut it off when Silver Eagle gave him a stern look. "Uh . . . it's like this, Ma," he said, and her heart swelled at the term. "It's sort of rude to offer our sheets and stuff—like you think what Grandfather brought with him isn't clean."

"Oh. I'm sorry," she said, then added, "well, I hope it's not rude to offer chocolate cake. I made a huge one early this morning, and I'd hate to have to eat it all alone."

"Chocolate cake's fine," Rain assured her seriously, glancing around in surprise when they broke into laughter.

Chapter Thirty-seven

Where in the world was everyone? Tess asked herself when she realized how quiet the cabin was the next afternoon. And why was she sitting in here at the table, hemming the curtains she and Flower had cut out? She could just as well do that out on the porch, where it was a little cooler.

She gathered up another pair of curtains and carried them, with Flower's sewing box, out onto the porch. Well, there was Flower—watering her rose bushes with the umpteenth bucket of water from that well. She really wished Sid would get that pipe out here. How long did it take for orders from Oklahoma City to arrive, anyway? Probably quite a while by wagon, she realized, since no trains ran to Clover Valley.

Stone, of course, had ridden out to check on the cattle, but he should be back any minute. She'd heard Stone ask Rain to keep an eye on the mare in the barn, in case she showed signs of foaling early. Perhaps that's where Rain and Silver Eagle were—in the barn. She tossed the curtains on the rocking chair and set the sewing box on the seat.

"Flower," she called, "have you seen Rain?"

"He and Grandfather rode out a few minutes ago, Mother," Flower called back.

Tess allowed herself a smile of pleasure at Flower's new title for her, and a brief thought that she hoped she never took the meaning of the term for granted, before she said, "Do you know if he checked on the mare before he left?"

"Probably," Flower replied. "He's pretty responsible about doing whatever Pa asks him to."

He was, Tess agreed silently. She glanced at the curtains, but Sateen called to her from the corral. The poor mare; she hadn't exercised her yesterday—it had slipped her mind after the children had returned. And she hadn't had that heart-to-heart with Stone, either.

Once again the mare reminded her of the time warp and the computer diskettes. As hard as she tried to convince herself that Robert deserved whatever happened to him, she couldn't overcome her guilty feelings.

If she did take the computer and diskettes back, and if someone did find them, whatever hullabaloo her disappearance had caused would probably be stirred up again. Yet no one would ever find her back here in 1893. After seven years she would be declared dead and her estate settled. The only real asset she had was her life insurance policy. She hadn't changed the beneficiary on it, having planned to get around to it sometime before the wedding. Instead of Robert benefitting from it, as he would have as her husband, it would still go to set up a yearly scholarship for a deserving student at her hometown high school in West Virginia.

She quickly reentered the cabin and hurried to the bedroom, changing into her jeans. A few minutes later, as she strode to the barn, she relayed to Flower her plans to take Sateen for a run. Her daughter waved a hand to indicate that she understood and bent to pull out a weed from the roots of the rosebush she had just watered.

Good, Tess thought. *Flower didn't notice the leather case I'm carrying.* Propping it against a corral post, she hurried into the barn and returned with tack for Sateen. A short time later she mounted and rode out of the yard, the leather case in the hand that wasn't controlling the reins.

As she headed toward the hillside, a niggling thought came to her—perhaps she should have tried harder to discuss this with Stone—asked him to come with her. But he might not have agreed that this was the best thing to do. He didn't much care to discuss her former fiancé and his moldy money.

Sateen tossed her head and balked for a second when Tess urged her up the hillside.

"I know," she said. "You'd rather head out to the range and go for a full-tilt run. We will, before we go back to the corral."

The mare snorted, then obediently took the path up the hillside. The steep climb forced Tess to keep Sateen at a walk, and just before she rounded the same bend in the trail that had given her the first glimpse of Stone, she became aware of voices ahead of her. She pulled Sateen to a halt and listened quietly.

Rain and Silver Eagle's voices—so that's where they had gone. But she could swear she also heard a woman's voice. She cocked her head as another strange male voice reached her ears. Who else was up here on the hillside? She kneed Sateen forward, around the bend.

She pulled up the mare again and stared in astonishment. The two figures hovering in the air above Rain and Silver Eagle disappeared with a tiny poof, but the misty fluffiness where they had stood remained.

"Michael, the cloud!" Tess heard the woman's voice say, and the white cloud dissipated.

She blinked her eyes—rubbed at them—then closed her open mouth with a snap. She shook her head and stared at the place above Silver Eagle's head where she had seen—no, of course not. She looked higher, at the sky. All the other clouds were far above her.

Oh, shoot, what was she thinking? She drew her gaze back to the shaman and her son. Rain ducked his head and shuffled a foot in the dust, but Silver Eagle stared back at her with a thoughtful look on his face.

"What . . . ?" She cleared her throat with a croak. "What—or *who*—was that? Did you see . . . ? Were you talking to . . . ? Were those sp . . . sp . . . spirits?"

Angela whispered frantically to Michael, "What are we going to do? Oh, we're in trouble now. We weren't supposed to let her see us, and we forgot while we talked to Rain and Silver Eagle."

Michael cocked an ear upward. "I don't hear Mr. G yelling at us yet," he whispered back. "Maybe it's all right. Uh-oh. Look at Tess!"

Tess slid from her horse and marched toward Rain and Silver Eagle, carrying the leather computer case with her.

"They *were* spirits, weren't they?" she asked, astonished. "And I've heard those voices before—up on Saddleback before I fell, and outside the cabin one day. Who are they? They've got something to do with how I got here to Oklahoma, don't they? Or, if not me, then they sure as heck brought Sateen here! I can believe that *I* fell through that time warp, but Sateen had to have had some help!"

When Silver Eagle and Rain remained silent she stamped her foot and crossed her arms, holding the computer case against her chest. "Answer me, darn it! I demand to know what's going on here!"

"But you haven't fasted, Ma," Rain began in a tentative voice. "I mean, we didn't either this time, but we did the first time."

She gripped her arms tighter and glared at Silver Eagle. "Who were they?"

Silver Eagle glanced at Rain, and Rain looked overhead, then shrugged his shoulders at his grandfather. Tess could have sworn that Rain's actions indicated he had consulted with one of the figures, which could still be hovering over him, invisible to her.

"Rain!" she almost shouted.

"They *were* spirits," Silver Eagle finally said. "They say they are your guardian angels."

"My . . ." Her jaw fell again and locked open. Her arms dropped to her sides, and she slowly shook her head. "Ah . . ." She lifted a hand to pop her jaw closed so she could speak. "I don't believe you."

"It's rude to call Grandfather a liar, Ma," Rain said in a hurt voice. "'Sides, I saw them first and told him about Michael and Angela."

"Michael and Angela," she repeated. "Oh, my God. You're telling me the truth, aren't you?"

Rain sighed in exasperation. "'Course we are. Angela came with you that day on the hill, and Michael just after that. They've been here all the time, but I couldn't try to talk to them until after Grandfather and I fasted at the Cherokee camp. We knew they'd come with you—they never follow anyone else."

"I see," she murmured. "Or do I? Rain, I'd like you and Silver Eagle to leave me alone now. There are a couple of slices of cake left down at the cabin, in the kitchen."

When Rain hesitated Silver Eagle smiled and laid a hand on his grandson's shoulder, urging him toward their horses.

Rain mounted Smoky, and as soon as Silver Eagle settled in his pinto's saddle, they both reined their horses past Sateen and headed down the hillside without another word to her.

Suddenly she wished she'd asked them to stay. Despite the bright daylight it felt rather spooky here now. Maybe she should have asked the shaman to help her talk to the angels. But when she looked behind her Rain and Silver Eagle were already out of sight.

She turned back and took a deep breath.

"Uh . . . Michael. And Angela. I'd like to speak to you."

She stood quietly for a long moment, but nothing happened. Then she repeated her request in a firmer voice.

"What should we do, Michael?" Angela whispered.

"You got me," he replied. "Are there any rules for this?"

"I don't know. Rain and Silver Eagle saw us all along; but then, Silver Eagle's a shaman. I've never slipped up and let an assignment see me before, and ask to speak to me. Maybe we're supposed to use our own judgment."

"All we can do is try it and see what happens," he said. "If Mr. G doesn't want her to see us, we probably won't be able to appear to her."

"Look," Tess said, her voice taking on a slight edge, "I've already had a glimpse of you, so I know darn well you're there. You were up on Saddleback with me, weren't you? And you followed me here, didn't you? You kept me from being hurt when my horse threw me off out there after the wild stallion attacked, didn't you? You brought Sateen here, too."

Her voice rose another notch. "Didn't you? Now you get your little butts back on that cloud and come out here where I can see you!"

She gasped and backed up a step as the mistiness began materializing in the air again. Her hand flew to her throat, and she stared in astonishment at the two figures on the cloud. What an incongruous pair. They both had beautiful white wings folded on their backs, and the woman looked the most angelic, what with her white robe and pretty blond hair. The man was pudgy and balding, wearing a pair of flowing white pants.

Tess giggled and shook her head. How could she be afraid of these two?

"Hello. I guess you're Michael and Angela, huh?"

"Yep," Michael said. "And I guess you can see us. We weren't sure if you'd be able to."

"You let Rain and Silver Eagle see you."

"That's different," Angela said, but she didn't offer any further explanation.

"Well, if you can choose who you're visible to," Tess said, "make sure it's just me who can see you. I don't want anyone to come looking for me and see me talking to you two. They'll think I'm crazy."

Angela nodded and waved her hand. "Now," she said, "we'll answer some of your questions, Tess, but please remember that there may be some things we can't discuss with you—things we might not know."

"That's ridiculous," she said. "You're angels. You're supposed to know everything."

"Sorry," Michael said. "Only Mr. G knows *everything.* Angels aren't allowed to know things like the future, any more than you are."

"Who's Mr. G?" Tess asked.

Michael rolled his eyes skyward, and Tess uttered a short exclamation of understanding. Then she said, "But, anyway, it's not the future. It's 1893. It's the past."

"Sure, it is," Michael replied, "but it's also your future. Don't you see? You're still living your life, even though you're in the past, so your future's still ahead of you."

"That doesn't make a darned bit of sense!"

"Sure it does." Michael sat down and crossed his legs. "Now listen: You had a future in 1994, and you still have a future in 1893. See?"

She remained silent for a moment before she nodded her head. "As convoluted as your reasoning is, Michael, I understand now." She glanced at the boulder beside her. "Say, you two wouldn't be able to do me a big favor, would you?"

"We can't take the computer back for you, Tess," Michael said.

"Shoot," she grumbled. "And you can read my mind, too."

"Yep," he admitted.

"Well, why can't you take it back for me?"

"That would be considered meddling in human affairs," Michael explained. Angela looked down at him and opened her mouth to speak, but Michael nudged her in the leg with his elbow. "It *would* be, Angie. Tess's ex-boyfriend will just have to live with the consequences of his actions."

"Michael doesn't care much for your former fiancé," Angela explained. "We're really not supposed to judge people, but sometimes it's hard."

"After knowing Stone I can't imagine what I ever saw in Robert either," Tess murmured. She held out the computer case and stared at it. "I guess it's completely up to me, then."

Stone rode into the ranch yard, tired after his long day in the saddle, but eagerly gazing around for Tess. He noticed Flower on the back porch in one of the rocking chairs. He seldom saw his daughter idle, but now she sat gazing toward the hillside, where he'd first found Tess.

Tess. Every time he even thought her name, it brought him a warm glow—at the ranch, anyway. At times, riding the range alone when Rain was spending time with his grandfather, those crazy doubts surfaced.

What did he really have to offer her? Hell, that ring she'd sold in town had brought her a thousand dollars. It would be years before the ranch showed that much profit on a steady basis. Yet he believed her when she said she loved him—knew in his heart the wild passion they shared wasn't faked on her part. Sometimes he saw a frustrated look on her face, though. He'd think she was going to talk to him about whatever was bothering her, but something always intruded. At times one of the kids needed her—other times he had to attend to his stock.

The worst times were when she mentioned some work-saving device it would be nice to have on the ranch. That man in her past—or her future, whatever the hell it was—probably would've instantly complied with any request she made—dug in his pocket and pulled out a handful of money—told her to buy whatever her little heart desired.

Rain and Silver Eagle emerged from the barn. At first they didn't notice Stone sitting there on his gelding. They both glanced up at the hillside, and Stone followed their gaze.

Damn! That was Tess's mare up there! And Tess. Even from this distance he recognized her slim figure.

"What's she doing up there?" he snarled at Silver Eagle.

The shaman deliberately avoided Stone's eyes and turned his back. Stone knew immediately that the Indian's actions indicated that he didn't wish to talk—perhaps feeling he might have to lie. He'd seen other Indians use the same tactic at times. His heart began to hammer in his chest, and he glared at Rain.

"Do you know why she's up there, Rain?"

"Pa, please . . ."

"Answer me!" he demanded.

Flower flew from the porch and ran toward his horse. "Pa!" she called. "Tess took something from her backpack with her. I don't know what it was, but I saw it in her pack the day she was taking our pictures. She had it in her hand when she went out to saddle Sateen. I'm worried, Pa. Rain and Grandfather were up there, but they left Tess alone. And that's where she came to be with us—and where she could go away from us."

"She told us to leave," Rain said. "She wanted to talk to them alone."

"Who?" Stone asked.

His son dropped his head, and Silver Eagle laid a hand on Rain's shoulder. "You must ask Tess, not us," he said. "It is not for us to say."

He glared at them for a second, then dug his heels into his gelding's sides and slapped his reins against the horse's rump. The gelding leapt into an almost immediate gallop. Usually he didn't abuse his horses, but his frantically beating heart overruled his senses. He slapped the reins once on the other side of the gelding, then leaned down on its neck, yelling at it for more speed.

He reached the hillside in record time and urged the horse up the steep slope. Rocks clattered beneath the horse's hooves as it surged up the hill, falling over the side of the trail. He never let up on bellowing at the horse for even more speed, despite the danger to both him and his mount. One slip would mean they both would plunge off the trail to their possible deaths.

As skilled a rider as he was, twice he almost lost his seat when the gelding negotiated an extremely narrow portion of the trail. But at last the horse rounded the bend, and Stone pulled it to a plunging halt at the place where he'd seen Tess a few minutes earlier.

Sateen threw up her head, neighing in fright. Stone ignored her.

"Tess!" he shouted. "Tess, where are you? Answer me, Tess!"

Sateen nickered at him again, but otherwise only silence met his ears.

"Tess!" he yelled again as he jumped from the saddle.

Gritting his teeth, he forced himself to look at the ground. He saw the tracks of several horses, intermingled with both small and larger moccasin prints, which obviously belonged to Rain and Silver Eagle. Disregarding those, he found Tess's footprints—the distinctive waffle pattern of those shoes she called Reeboks.

Dropping his horse's reins, he studied the footprints. She'd stood in one place for a while, then walked toward the big boulder beside the trail. He followed the footprints around the boulder. On the other side the footprints continued, and he walked onward. Suddenly the ground disappeared in front of him and he froze.

A black abyss split the hillside. Instantly he understood it was the time warp. Her footprints ended there.

Hoping against hope, he bent down and picked up a small rock. He tossed it into the abyss and listened for several long moments but never heard the rock hit bottom.

"Tess?" he whispered in a tortured voice. "Tess?" louder.

"Tess!" he shouted. "Oh, God, Tess, come back. I love you!"

A sob broke from his chest. She couldn't be gone. His stomach heaved and his shoulders shook. He couldn't make it without her.

But she wasn't there. She'd disappeared, just as Rain had said she'd appeared on the hillside. And she'd gone willingly. He saw no signs of shuffling in her footsteps—no drag marks indicating someone had forced her. She'd gone back to that damned bastard with all the money.

Stabs of agony tore through his chest, and he doubled his arms across his stomach. His head bowed and he sank to the ground.

If only he could talk to her one more time. She could use every penny of her money to buy whatever she needed to lighten her workload at the ranch. He'd work his fingers to the bone to give her anything she wanted.

He stared again at the abyss. It stretched endlessly—but it did end somewhere. He knew exactly where—it ended at the point of Tess's former life.

He could follow her, but what would he find on the other side? She might laugh in his face. Or, knowing Tess, she would probably try to explain in that voice that would haunt him for the rest of his life why she had left. And Flower and Rain needed him. They'd be devastated when they realized Tess was gone for good.

He swiped at his cheek, then stared down in surprise at the moisture on the back of his hand. A small whimper left his throat—then a larger one. He choked until he almost strangled, but at last the sobs of agony broke free.

A long ten minutes later he forced himself to his feet. Still half-blinded by tears, he stumbled around the boulder and grabbed Sateen's reins before he staggered toward his horse. His children had to be told. He laid his head against the gelding's neck. How could he tell them?

Chapter Thirty-eight

Tess yawned and opened her eyes. What was she doing sleeping on the ground? Had she and Stone just made love?

Suddenly she sat up, staring around her. She was on a ledge, and beyond her stretched mountains she recognized. A cool breeze caressed her cheeks, and a falcon floated on a wind draft nearby, its wing tips adjusting to spiral in a wide sweep.

"Oh," she whispered, recalling she'd stepped into the time warp. "I'm back on Saddleback Mountain." Her eyes quickly found the computer nearby, and she reached for it.

"Okay," she murmured. "Now what?"

She stood up. The ledge was wide enough to hold her safely, but there was no way she could climb back up to the trail on her own. A rock cliff extended above her, its face offering not even a hint of a handhold. All right. She had guardian angels, didn't she?

"Michael! Angela!" she called. "I need you!"

"Miss Foster?"

She looked above her to see a male face peering down at her. "Are you Tess?"

"Yes," she answered. "Help me up. Please."

"Sure."

The man disappeared for a second, then reappeared, tossing down a rope to her. She stuck the handle of the computer case between her teeth and clamped down. Seizing the rope, she pulled herself upward, hand over hand. As she neared the top of her climb, the man holding the other end of the rope dropped it and grabbed her beneath her arms, heaving her onto the trail. Now that she could see the rest of him, Tess realized he wore the uniform of a park ranger.

"I'm Dane, and this is Phil. We've been looking for you all day, Miss Foster," the ranger said. "Freddy reported that you never checked in on Mt. Marcy last night."

"Today's Sunday?" she asked in astonishment. "August 1? 1994?"

"Uh . . . yes. Look, why don't you let us take you down to the first-aid station so they can check you out." Dane glanced toward the other ranger. "If you don't feel like walking, Phil and I can carry you."

"I don't need any first aid," she said in a determined voice. "Here." She thrust the computer into the ranger's hands. "There's an address inside the case. Please deliver it to them. It's very important."

"Okay. Fine," Dane said. "But how long have you

been down on that ledge? Phil and I've been over this trail twice already today. We didn't notice you down there."

She smiled mysteriously at him. "You'd never believe me if I told you."

Dane glanced at her feet. "Miss Foster, you're not allowed on the trails in tennis shoes. You're supposed to be wearing hiking boots. Didn't Freddy tell you that before he let you on the trail?"

"My boots are in Oklahoma," she answered giddily. "And my name's Mrs. Chisum, not Miss Foster." She waved the hand with Stone's ring under Dane's nose.

"Uh . . . right." The ranger reached for her arm. "Let's just go down to the first-aid station and let them know you're all right. There are a bunch of reporters hanging around. They're causing a big stir about us allowing you to hike up here when the trails had been declared unsafe due to the rains."

She jerked her arm free. "Well, you'll just have to explain to them that I'm okay. I've got to get back to Oklahoma."

She started to move, but Phil blocked her path to the edge of the trail.

"Now look here . . ." she began.

Phil lunged toward her, and she barely managed to avoid him. She ducked Dane's extended arm and backed toward the other side of the trail. She could only go so far, though. The mountain rose behind her, and she'd have to clamber through the rocks and underbrush to escape.

"Miss Foster . . . Chisum," Dane soothed, "you're obviously suffering from exposure. You've spent the night up here in the cold. We'll get you treated."

"Get the hell away from me," she snarled. She reached down and grabbed a dead limb, backing up against a huge pine.

"She's out of her mind with shock," Phil said.

"I am *not* insane!" she screamed. "And I'm not hurt. You two just go on about your business and forget you've seen me. I'm not going to be here when you get back."

"Now, Miss Foster," Phil said, "this *is* our business. We're responsible for finding you."

She threatened them with the limb as she tried to edge back toward the cliff face. At least she managed to get out onto the trail again, away from the huge pine above her. Now she could see up through the treetops to the sky.

"Michael! Angela!" she shouted. "Get your butts here to help me!"

Phil moved, and she shook the limb at him. "I swear, I'll cold cock you with this if you come any closer!" she warned.

"Miss Foster . . ."

"The name's Mrs. Chisum! And I'm going home to my husband! And my kids and my dog and my horse! Michael! Angela!"

"Go get her," Phil instructed Dane.

"Me? You're the senior ranger here."

"Yeah, and you're in training to learn how to do things. Now go get that woman so we can take her down for treatment."

"Huh-uh. Not me."

Phil blew out a breath and inched forward. Tess swung the limb as though batting at a ball, then clenched it in front of her.

"Michael! Angela!" She threw her head back, her

lungs straining as she took a deep breath to yell again.

The cloud materialized above her, and she glared at the two angels. "Get me out of here!"

"You have to decide to do it, Tess," Michael said. "We can't help you."

"Then keep them away from me!" she demanded.

Phil lunged for her again. His feet flew out from beneath him, and he sat down with a thud. Dane stared in surprise at the banana peel on the trail.

Taking advantage of the opportunity, Tess dropped the limb and ran. Without a pause she leaped off the side of the mountain.

Stone sat at the kitchen table, staring at Tess's picture. It was a little crumpled by now—and finger-spotted. Still, the picture had caught her very essence—green eyes smiling teasingly at him, and that glorious hair sunlit by the rays from the window.

His children had finally gone to bed. Rain had tried for hours to reassure him that Tess would come back, never once seeming to waver in his belief. He had further angered Stone with his nonchalance over Tess's disappearance, saying something about Michael and Angela taking care of it. Stone even seemed to recall his son admitting that he wasn't allowed to talk about those two spirits—Michael and Angela, he'd called them again—but Rain felt awful about Stone's being so upset.

"Oh, for the faith of children," Stone whispered, shaking his head. He hadn't bothered to question his son about Michael and Angela. His pain was much too fresh to discuss anything with anyone.

He almost felt as though Tess had died, and it would take time for him to heal enough even to speak her name again.

The door opened, and his head jerked around. But it was only Silver Eagle. The shaman crossed to the stove and poured a cup of coffee, then lifted an eyebrow in question as he gestured the pot at Stone.

"Yeah, go ahead and pour me a cup," he said. "I won't get to sleep tonight anyway."

Silver Eagle carried over the coffee and filled Stone's cup.

"Sit down," Stone offered.

Silver Eagle shook his head and moved back to the stove, where he set down the coffeepot again. "Do you wish to talk?"

"I don't know." He shifted to straddle the table bench and sipped his coffee. "She lied to me. She'd been letting me believe she'd decided to stay with me. And she broke a promise she once made. She told me that if she ever decided to leave, she wouldn't go without saying good-bye."

Silver Eagle shrugged. "Maybe it was not the time for a good-bye."

"Look, I've told you before that I want Flower and Rain to keep their Indian beliefs, but I'm sick and tired of your riddles. I've no objection to my son seeking his vision in two years . . ."

Stone bit off his words in shock as Tess flew through the doorway, landing with a crash and a flurry of flailing limbs. She screeched and jumped up, rubbing her behind.

"Thanks a lot for the ride down the hill, Michael!" she yelled. "Next time I'll remember how clumsy you are." Then she flung herself at Stone, kissing him wildly and ignoring the coffee cup, which clattered across the floor, spilling the contents.

"I'm back! Oh, darling," she murmured between kisses, "I'm back."

As Silver Eagle slipped through the door, Stone finally managed to stand and grabbed Tess, pushing her away.

"Where the goddamned hell have you been?" he snarled. "Do you have any idea what I've been going through?"

Tess gaped at him, her mouth falling open in astonishment. "Uh . . . I had to take it back, Stone. Let me explain. . . ."

"Yeah," he snapped. "You do that! Explain to me why you just *had* to go back and see your old lover one more time!"

"I didn't go back to see him, Stone. I never laid eyes on him, and I had no intentions of seeing him. It was something I had to do."

"And it had nothing to do with him, huh?"

"Well, sort of. But . . ."

He dropped his hands from her and clenched them into fists at his sides. He wanted to strangle her. He wanted to sweep her up and carry her into their bedroom and make wild, passionate love to her, hear the throaty cries of fulfillment he could bring from her.

"I came back to you, Stone," she whispered. "I really never left—I only went on an errand."

He grabbed her and pulled her down onto the bench with him, burying his hands in her hair to hold her still. He kissed her, nuzzled her neck, kissed her again. She was real—not a figment of his overheated imagination. She gazed up at him with a hint of tears in her eyes, and he kissed them away before he claimed her mouth again.

Suddenly she pushed at him. "Wait, darling," she insisted when he tried to kiss her again. "I have to talk to . . ."

"If you tell me you're going to talk to someone named Michael and Angela," he groaned, "I'll . . ."

"But I am. Didn't Silver Eagle and Rain tell you about them?" Tess shoved free and stood up as he reluctantly nodded his head and rose from the bench.

"Well, anyway, Rain mentioned them," he admitted, "but I really wasn't in the mood to hear about a couple of crazy spirits who've supposedly been following you around. I thought you'd gone for good!"

"Shoot, Stone, I told you I'd made my decision to stay here with you."

Her nonchalant tone fired his ire again, and he took a menacing step toward her, forcing her to back away from him. "Then why the hell did you go on your *errand* without telling me?"

"Uh-oh," she murmured. "Stone, please. I'll always discuss things with you from now on. Really, I will."

"Sure you will," he muttered, still glaring at her.

"Uh . . . Michael. Angela," she said in a squeaky voice. "Help."

"Tess . . ." His words froze in his throat when a soft poof sounded and a cloud appeared. On the cloud stood two small figures, one male and one definitely female. He groped behind him until he found the table and sat down with a thump.

"Hello, Stone," the female said. "I'm Angela, and this is Michael."

Stone nodded his head stupidly, unable to utter a sound. He tore his eyes away from the cloud and stared at Tess, shaking his head in disbelief.

"Michael and Angela are my guardian angels," Tess explained in a relieved voice. "It's their job to take care of me. Rain says they've been with me all along."

"All along," he repeated.

"Uh-huh. They kept me from getting hurt when my horse threw me when we went after the wild mares. And I guess they protected me from Rose's bullets."

"Well, that was Michael," the female who had told him her name was Angela explained. "It's really him who's your guardian angel, Tess. I'm just here as sort of an . . . adviser."

Tess started speaking again, and Stone felt dizzy as he jerked his gaze back to her.

"Well, I want to thank both of you for what you've done," Tess said. "You brought me here to find Stone and the kids, kept me from making a big mistake with . . . uh . . . that other guy."

Michael puffed out his chest, but Angela gave him a stern look. "Pride, Michael."

Michael sighed and sat down, motioning for Angela to join him. "You're giving me a little too much credit, Tess," he said shaking his head. "You made your own decision in New York, and I just changed the bullets in the rifles to blanks so neither you nor Rose would get killed. You did the rest yourself."

"Whatever," Tess said, negligently waving her hand. "We never finished our discussion up on the hill."

"I know what you want me to tell you, Tess," Michael said.

Tess said in an aside to Stone, "They can read my mind."

Michael chuckled, then said, "You want to know how your life will be with Stone. But as I said, even Angela and I don't know the future. I can tell you one thing, though."

"What?" Tess asked eagerly.

"You've heard the saying that marriages are made in heaven, haven't you?"

Tess nodded, and Michael continued, "Mr. G made marriage a sacred sacrament. However, as humans, you both have free wills, so it's completely up to you both what sort of married life you'll have. But if you treat your love as a sacred gift, and honor and respect each other—why, think what a wonderful life you can have together!"

"Oh, Michael." Angela sighed. "That's so . . . profound."

"*I* thought so," Michael said with a tiny smirk of satisfaction.

"That's good enough for me," Tess said. "How about you, Stone?"

"Huh?" He snapped closed his mouth. "Uh . . . yeah, I guess so. Say, are you two going to be around all the time from now on? I mean . . . *all* the time?"

Angela giggled and shook her head. "We like to practice flying at night. Sometimes we even go in the daytime. Michael still has a problem from time to time with his wings."

"Don't I know it," Tess said, rubbing her rear.

"Tess," Michael said softly, "we've appeared for you this time, and even let Stone see us. But this will have to be the last time. We aren't really supposed to show ourselves, and I've been afraid of getting reprimanded for the past few minutes."

"From Mr. G?" Tess asked.

"Who's Mr. G?" Stone interrupted. Tess rolled her eyes upward, and Stone drew in a gasp of breath. "G . . . God?" he asked, awe-stricken.

Tess nodded, then looked back at Michael. "You're leaving then? But please, tell me one more thing before you go. You both seem so perfect together, but I've never heard of a *pair* of guardian angels. You aren't going to have to separate, are you? You did say that you were only an adviser to Michael, Angela."

"We're going to talk to Mr. G about that," Michael replied. "I'm going to try to convince him that I need Angie around for at least another millennium to help me over my clumsy flying. It will probably take at least that long, since I wasn't able to master it in the past millennium."

"I've just met you, but I'll miss you," Tess said tenderly. "Could we . . . could we at least hug before you go?"

The two angels looked at each other, then nodded. Tess held out her arms, and Michael and Angela hopped to the floor, growing before Stone's eyes until they were almost the same height as Tess. The three of them spent a half-minute hugging, and Tess kissed each of their cheeks.

Somehow Stone managed to get to his feet and shake Michael's hand. He lifted up Angela and pulled her close for a second before he landed a kiss beside her ear.

"Will Rain and Silver Eagle still be able to see you both?" he asked as he carefully lowered Angela to the floor.

"You'll have to ask them," Michael said with a wink.

A soft wind sighed through the kitchen, and Stone

blinked. When he opened his eyes the kitchen was empty except for him and Tess.

He grabbed her and whirled her around. After he pulled her close and kissed her soundly he shoved her away and whacked her on the rear.

"Go put on that pretty dress you wore to the social," he ordered. "And tell Silver Eagle and the kids to come on."

"Is that an order?" Tess asked with a slight frown, rubbing her behind.

"Sorry," Stone said with an unconcerned grin. "*Please* go put on your pretty dress. I'll tell the others to get ready."

"What for? I thought you'd rather be alone with me this evening."

"I would, but we're going into Clover Valley and get married again first. We'll wake up the minister if we have to. I don't want any doubt in heaven's mind that we're well and truly married."

"I love you, Stone," she whispered.

"I love you, too, darlin'. Now and for all time."

TRANA MAE SIMMONS

A mysterious horseman has Jessica's ranch hands convinced they are seeing spirits, but the sable-haired beauty isn't afraid of ghosts. She vows to find the buried payroll of gold she is searching for, and unmask the sexy master of disguises who seems determined to see her fail. But when solving the mystery leads to a night of unbelievable ecstasy, Jessica has to decide if discovering the cold truth is worth shattering the passionate fantasy.

_3472-2 $4.50 US/$5.50 CAN

LEISURE BOOKS
ATTN: Order Department
276 5th Avenue, New York, NY 10001

Please add $1.50 for shipping and handling for the first book and $.35 for each book thereafter. PA., N.Y.S. and N.Y.C. residents, please add appropriate sales tax. No cash, stamps, or C.O.D.s. All orders shipped within 6 weeks via postal service book rate. Canadian orders require $2.00 extra postage and must be paid in U.S. dollars through a U.S. banking facility.

Name____

Address____

City ______________________________ State______ Zip______

I have enclosed $______in payment for the checked book(s).

Payment must accompany all orders. ☐ Please send a free catalog.

Passionate Historical Romance by Love Spell's Leading Ladies of Love.

Bittersweet Promises by Trana Mae Simmons. Cody Garret's life turns head over heels when a robbery throws Shanna Van Alstyne into his arms. With a spirit as fiery as the blazing sun, Shanna is the most thrilling woman ever to set foot in Liberty, Missouri. Though it will take the patience of a saint to melt her touch-me-not facade, Cody will use his devilish charm to besiege Shanna's hesitant heart—and a wild seduction to claim her heavenly love.

_51934-8 $4.99 US/$5.99 CAN

Hunters of the Ice Age: Yesterday's Dawn by Theresa Scott. Named for the beast sacred to his people, Mamut has proven his strength and courage time and again. But when it comes to subduing one helpless captive female, he finds himself at a distinct disadvantage. Never has he realized the power of beguiling green eyes, soft curves, and berry-red lips to weaken a man's resolve. He has claimed he will make the stolen woman his slave, but he soon learns he will never enjoy her alluring body unless he can first win her elusive heart.

_51920-8 $4.99 US/$5.99 CAN

Gilded Splendor by Elizabeth Parker. Bound for the London stage, sheltered Amanda Prescott has no idea that fate has already cast her as a rakehell's true love. Visiting Pinewood House to honor her father's last request, she succumbs to Patrick Winter's burning desire. Amid a glittering milieu of wealth and glamour, Amanda and Patrick make all their fantasies a passionate reality.

_51914-3 $4.99 US/$5.99 CAN

Dorchester Publishing Co., Inc.
65 Commerce Road
Stamford, CT 06902

Please add $1.75 for shipping and handling for the first book and $.50 for each book thereafter. NY, NYC, PA and CT residents, please add appropriate sales tax. No cash, stamps, or C.O.D.s. All orders shipped within 6 weeks via postal service book rate. Canadian orders require $2.00 extra postage and must be paid in U.S. dollars through a U.S. banking facility.

Name____

Address______________________________________

City ______________________ State______ Zip______

I have enclosed $______in payment for the checked book(s).

Payment must accompany all orders. ☐ Please send a free catalog.

Timeswept passion...timeless love.

Forever by Amy Elizabeth Saunders. Laurel Behrman is used to putting up with daily hard knocks. But her accidental death is too much, especially when her bumbling guardian angels send her back to Earth—two hundred years before she was born. Trapped in the body of a Colonial woman, Laurel arrives just in time to save a drowning American patriot with the kiss of life—and to rouse a passion she thought long dead.
_51936-4 $4.99 US/$5.99 CAN

Interlude in Time by Rita Clay Estrada. When Parris Harrison goes for a swim in the wild and turbulent surf off Cape May, she washes ashore in the arms of the most gorgeous hunk she has ever seen. But Thomas Elder is not only devastatingly sexy, he is also certifiably insane—dressed in outlandish clothes straight out of a ganster movie, he insists the date is 1929! Horrified to discover that Thomas is absolutely correct, Parris sets about surviving in a dangerous era—and creating her own intimate interlude in time.
_51940-2 $4.99 US/$5.99 CAN

Dorchester Publishing Co., Inc.
65 Commerce Road
Stamford, CT 06902

Please add $1.75 for shipping and handling for the first book and $.50 for each book thereafter. NY, NYC, PA and CT residents, please add appropriate sales tax. No cash, stamps, or C.O.D.s. All orders shipped within 6 weeks via postal service book rate. Canadian orders require $2.00 extra postage and must be paid in U.S. dollars through a U.S. banking facility.

Name____
Address____
City ______________________ State______ Zip______
I have enclosed $______in payment for the checked book(s).
Payment must accompany all orders.☐ Please send a free catalog.

A Time to Love Again by Flora Speer. When India Baldwin goes to work one Saturday to update her computer skills, she has no idea she will end up backdating herself! But one slip on the keyboard and the lovely young widow is transported back to the time of Charlemagne. Before she knows it, India finds herself merrily munching on boar and quaffing ale, holding her own during a dangerous journey, and yearning for the nights when a warrior's masterful touch leaves her wondering if she ever wants to return to her own time.

_51900-3 $4.99 US/$5.99 CAN

Time Remembered by Elizabeth Crane. Among the ruins of an antebellum mansion, young architect Jody Farnell discovers the diary of a man from another century and a voodoo doll whose ancient spell whisks her back one hundred years to his time. Micah Deveroux yearns for someone he can love above all others, and he thinks he has found that woman until Jody mysteriously appears in his own bedroom. Enchanted by Jody, betrothed to another, Micah fears he has lost his one chance at happiness—unless the same black magic that has brought Jody into his life can work its charms again.

_51904-6 $4.99 US/$5.99 CAN

Dorchester Publishing Co., Inc.
65 Commerce Road
Stamford, CT 06902

Please add $1.75 for shipping and handling for the first book and $.50 for each book thereafter. NY, NYC, PA and CT residents, please add appropriate sales tax. No cash, stamps, or C.O.D.s. All orders shipped within 6 weeks via postal service book rate. Canadian orders require $2.00 extra postage and must be paid in U.S. dollars through a U.S. banking facility.

Name ______________________________
Address ______________________________
City ____________________ State ______ Zip ______
I have enclosed $______ in payment for the checked book(s).
Payment must accompany all orders. ☐ Please send a free catalog.

Timeswept passion...timeless love

A LOVE BEYOND TIME

FLORA SPEER

When he is accidentally thrust back to the eighth century by a computer genius's time-travel program, Mike Bailey falls from the sky and lands near Charlemagne's camp. Knocked senseless by the crash, he can't remember his name, address, or occupation, but no shock can make his body forget how to respond when he awakens to the sight of an enchanting angel on earth.

Headstrong and innocent, Danise is already eighteen and almost considered an old maid by the Frankish nobles who court her. Yet the stubborn beauty would prefer to spend the rest of her life cloistered in a nunnery rather than marry for any reason besides love. Unexpectedly mesmerized by the stranger she discovers unconscious in the forest, Danise is quickly arroused by an all-consuming passion—and a desire that will conquer time itself.

_51948-8 $4.99 US/$5.99 CAN

LOVE SPELL
ATTN: Order Department
276 5th Avenue, New York, NY 10001

Please add $1.50 for shipping and handling for the first book and $.35 for each book thereafter. PA., N.Y.S. and N.Y.C. residents, please add appropriate sales tax. No cash, stamps, or C.O.D.s. All orders shipped within 6 weeks via postal service book rate. Canadian orders require $2.00 extra postage and must be paid in U.S. dollars through a U.S. banking facility.

Name ____
Address ____
City ______________________ State ______ Zip ______
I have enclosed $______ in payment for the checked book(s).
Payment must accompany all orders. ☐ Please send a free catalog.

TIME'S HEALING HEART

MARTI JONES

No man has ever swept Madeline St. Thomas off her feet, and after she buries herself in her career, she loses hope of finding one. But when a freak accident propels her to the Old South, Maddie is rescued by a stranger with the face of an angel and the body of an Adonis—a stranger whose burning touch and smoldering kisses awaken forgotten longings in her heart.

Devon Crowe has had enough of women. His dead wife betrayed him, his fiancee despises him, and Maddie drives him to distraction with her claims of coming from another era. But the more Devon tries to convince himself that Maddie is aptly named, the more he believes her preposterous story. And when she makes him a proposal no lady would make, he doesn't know whether he should wrap her in a straitjacket—or lose himself in desires that promise to last forever.

_51954-2 $4.99 US/$5.99 CAN

LOVE SPELL
ATTN: Order Department
276 5th Avenue, New York, NY 10001

Please add $1.50 for shipping and handling for the first book and $.35 for each book thereafter. PA., N.Y.S. and N.Y.C. residents, please add appropriate sales tax. No cash, stamps, or C.O.D.s. All orders shipped within 6 weeks via postal service book rate. Canadian orders require $2.00 extra postage and must be paid in U.S. dollars through a U.S. banking facility.

Name ______________________________

Address ______________________________

City ____________________ State ______ Zip ______

I have enclosed $______ in payment for the checked book(s).

Payment must accompany all orders. ☐ Please send a free catalog.

Time of the Rose by Bonita Clifton. The dread of all his enemies and the desire of all the ladies, young Colton Chase can outdraw any gunslinger and outlast any woman. But even he doesn't stand a chance against the spunky beauty who's tracked him through time. Soon, Colt is ready to hang up his six-shooters, throw away his spurs, and surrender his heart to the most tempting spitfire anywhere in time.
_51922-4 $4.99 US/$5.99 CAN

Tears of Fire by Nelle McFather. Swept into the tumultuous life and times of her ancestor, Fable relives a night of sweet ecstasy with Andre Devereux, never guessing their love has the power to cross the ages. Caught between swirling visions of a distant desire and a troubled reality filled with betrayal, Fable seeks the answers that will set her free—answers that can only be found in the tender embrace of two men who live a century apart.
_51932-1 $4.99 US/$5.99 CAN

Dorchester Publishing Co., Inc.
65 Commerce Road
Stamford, CT 06902

Please add $1.75 for shipping and handling for the first book and $.50 for each book thereafter. NY, NYC, PA and CT residents, please add appropriate sales tax. No cash, stamps, or C.O.D.s. All orders shipped within 6 weeks via postal service book rate. Canadian orders require $2.00 extra postage and must be paid in U.S. dollars through a U.S. banking facility.

Name ______________________________
Address ______________________________
City ____________________ State ______ Zip ______
I have enclosed $______ in payment for the checked book(s).
Payment must accompany all orders. ☐ Please send a free catalog.

NELLIE McFATHER

Bestselling Author of *Tears of Fire*

Legend says that the moonstone will bring love and good fortune to whoever possesses it. Just one touch of the magic stone sweeps Annabel Poe back through the years to an ancient English castle. Caught in a world of poets and highwaymen, lovers and thieves, Annabel is drawn relentlessly to a virile nobleman whose secrets threaten untold peril—while his touch promises undreamed ecstasy.

_51964-X $4.99 US/$5.99 CAN

Dorchester Publishing Co., Inc.
65 Commerce Road
Stamford, CT 06902

Please add $1.75 for shipping and handling for the first book and $.50 for each book thereafter. NY, NYC, PA and CT residents, please add appropriate sales tax. No cash, stamps, or C.O.D.s. All orders shipped within 6 weeks via postal service book rate. Canadian orders require $2.00 extra postage and must be paid in U.S. dollars through a U.S. banking facility.

Name____
Address_____________________________________
City ____________________________ State______ Zip______
I have enclosed $______in payment for the checked book(s).
Payment must accompany all orders. ☐ Please send a free catalog.

Three captivating stories of love in another time, another place.

MADELINE BAKER

"Heart of the Hunter"

A Lakota warrior must defy the boundaries of life itself to claim the spirited beauty he has sought through time.

ANNE AVERY

"Dream Seeker"

On faraway planets, a pilot and a dreamer learn that passion can bridge the heavens, no matter how vast the distance from one heart to another.

KATHLEEN MORGAN

"The Last Gatekeeper"

To save her world, a dazzling temptress must use her powers of enchantment to open a stellar portal—and the heart of a virile but reluctant warrior.

__51974-7 *Enchanted Crossings* (three unforgettable love stories in one volume) $4.99 US/ $5.99 CAN

LEISURE BOOKS
ATTN: Order Department
276 5th Avenue, New York, NY 10001

Please add $1.50 for shipping and handling for the first book and $.35 for each book thereafter. PA., N.Y.S. and N.Y.C. residents, please add appropriate sales tax. No cash, stamps, or C.O.D.s. All orders shipped within 6 weeks via postal service book rate. Canadian orders require $2.00 extra postage and must be paid in U.S. dollars through a U.S. banking facility.

Name______________________________________
Address____________________________________
City ______________________ State______ Zip______
I have enclosed $______in payment for the checked book(s).
Payment must accompany all orders.☐ Please send a free catalog.

THE MAGIC OF ROMANCE PAST, PRESENT, AND FUTURE....

Every month, Love Spell will publish one book in each of four categories:

1) *Timeswept Romance*—Modern-day heroines travel to the past to find the men who fulfill their hearts' desires.

2) *Futuristic Romance*—Love on distant worlds where passion is the lifeblood of every man and woman.

3) *Historical Romance*—Full of desire, adventure and intrigue, these stories will thrill readers everywhere.

4) *Contemporary Romance*—With novels by Lori Copeland, Heather Graham, and Jayne Ann Krentz, Love Spell's line of contemporary romance is first-rate.

Exploding with soaring passion and fiery sensuality, Love Spell romances are destined to take you to dazzling new heights of ecstasy.

SEND FOR A FREE CATALOGUE TODAY!

Love Spell
Attn: Order Department
276 5th Avenue, New York, NY 10001